"SECRETS, TREACHERY, BLACKMAIL, AND UNEXPECTED LIAISONS ... THE REVENGE IS DELICIOUS."—*Publishers Weekly*

The emotional landscape of Laura Andros's heart was already strewn with mines of tragedy when she met incredibly rich and attractive Roger Ambler. How wonderful that he wooed her with such glittering symbols of endearment, and such honorable intentions. But soon Laura realized she was at the mercy of a master manipulator ... and she had to escape.

But when a very different kind of man brought joy into her life, Roger came back, burning with revenge, terrifying her with his fierce need for control, cunningly plotting his endgame....

LAURA

A Literary Guild and a Doubleday Book Club selection

LAURA

Hilary Norman

A SIGNET BOOK

SIGNET
Published by the Penguin Group
Penguin Books USA Inc., 375 Hudson Street
New York, New York 10014, U.S.A.
Penguin Books Ltd, 27 Wrights Lane,
London W8 5TZ, England
Penguin Books Australia Ltd, Ringwood,
Victoria, Australia
Penguin Books Canada Ltd, 10 Alcorn Avenue,
Toronto, Ontario, Canada M4V 3B2
Penguin Books (N.Z.) Ltd, 182–190 Wairau Road,
Auckland 10, New Zealand

Penguin Books Ltd, Registered Offices:
Harmondsworth, Middlesex, England

Published by Signet, an imprint of Dutton Signet,
a division of Penguin Books USA Inc.
Previously published in a Dutton edition.

First Signet Printing, November, 1995
10 9 8 7 6 5 4 3 2 1

PUBLISHER'S NOTE
This is a work of fiction. Names, characters, places, and incidents either are the prod-
ucts of the author's imagination or are used fictitiously, and any resemblance to actual
persons, living or dead, events, or locales is entirely coincidental.

For Ella Grünwald and Gertrud Stock

ACKNOWLEDGMENTS

As always, a number of kind people have given me valuable assistance during the research and writing of this novel. I owe special thanks to the following (in alphabetical order):

Koula Antoniou; Howard Barmad, who never fails me, and for whose generosity and patience I am endlessly grateful; Carolyn Caughey; P.C. Paul Cotton, Hampstead Police; M. Jacques Dubost, Casino de Monte-Carlo; Sara Fisher; John Hawkins; Jonathan Kern; Elaine Koster; Audrey LaFehr; Brian M. Levy; Herta Norman; Helen Rose; Anne and Nicholas Shulman; Richard Spencer; Dr. Jonathan Tarlow; Michael Thomas.

There is a point at which running away is no longer possible, and no longer worthwhile. When escape has, in itself, become pointless.

It isn't just a matter of guilt, or of trying to come to terms with that guilt. It's not just a question of fear, or of striving harder to conquer that fear. And there's no longer anyone else to blame, and there isn't a single person left on earth who can help you. No matter how much they want to, or how deeply they love you.

Because there is no refuge. Not when the terror from which you have been trying to flee for so many years is inside yourself. No matter where you go, no matter what you do, or who you try to become.

No escape.

PART ONE

CHAPTER 1

Laura loved being naked. In the mornings, while she made up her face for work, or in the evenings as she got ready to go out, she sat naked at the small pine table she'd found in a flea market near Earls Court Road, and which she'd placed at her bedroom window, and smoothed on her foundation, pale beige with just a touch of warmth, stroked a little shadow onto her eyelids, twisted her mascara wand over her lashes, and brushed her dark, almost black hair into its sleek jaw-length bob. And only then, after she had dabbed a little perfume behind her ears and onto her wrists, did she rise and slowly make her way over to the full-length mirror on the back of the bedroom door, where she stood, for just a moment, checking herself over, before slipping on her satin briefs and deciding what to wear.

Laura's pleasure in nudity had little to do with sex, but it had everything to do with freedom. She had been in her rented flat in Finborough Road for more than half a year now, and except for the coldest days in winter, she maintained her deliberately gentle, lazy routine with the sash window at least a little open, loving the breeze, warm or cool, touching her skin, joining her, she liked to think, with the day outside, with the rest of the world. She had spent so many years severed from that world, with something always dividing her from it. Glass, bricks, steel, concrete, mostly just other people.

She wore satin panties and brassieres whenever possible. She would have preferred silk, but all she could afford were Marks & Spencer's silky-to-the-touch polyesters. If she had the money, she thought she would wear nothing but silk or pure cotton next to her skin. There were few feelings better than those first moments after a warm bath, when you were dry and snug and fragrant, and if you could slip straight into silk, she imagined, you could probably retain that feeling all day long. Laura wasn't especially vain. She liked the way that she looked, knew that she was striking, that she was fortunate in her face and her body and her hair; but if she made a conscious point of taking those moments to study herself in the mirror morning and evening, it was only because she knew that she was free to do so, that she had the time, and that no one would rebuke her or mock her for it. Laura never looked at her reflection for long. She regarded her naked body, shapely, slender, full-breasted and slim-waisted, studied her face to check over her makeup, looked directly at her eyes, sharp and green and clear. But she never really looked into those eyes.

Laura forgot sometimes that Gus was in the flat. It was only two rooms, plus their tiny bathroom and kitchen, but Gus, more than anyone, knew the value of personal space, and their living relationship, just three months old, suited them both to perfection. They had each other, had the companionableness and solace of their friendship, but they had the privacy they both so urgently needed, too.

Gus was Laura's best friend. Her only true friend. Through most of the worst years of her life Gus had been her life support, her salvation, and when she'd thought that they might never meet again, Laura had felt, not for the first time, that she wanted to die. But then Gus had reappeared, so painfully briefly, just for long enough to save her again, to pick her up and set her back on her feet, and then she had vanished again, until just over twelve weeks before; and when Laura had realized that this time Gus was going to stay, that she was going to be her friend for life, Laura had known at last, really known, that she might, after all, stand a chance.

* * *

"You're still in recovery," Gus had told her, that day in June, after Laura had shown her around the flat, every inch of every wardrobe, every neatly folded and ironed tea towel, every polished and antiseptic surface in the kitchen. "In denial. All this perfection."

Laura had smiled. "You sound like Fisher."

"It's nice, though," Gus had said, in her rough, grudging voice. "We can eat off the floor."

"You'll stay then?" Laura had wanted her to, desperately, but had been afraid to hassle her. Gus despised pressure. "For dinner?"

"Dinner, is it now?"

"Tea, then." Laura was apologetic. "I meant tea."

"It was dinner when you first got to Kane. Got you your first slapping, remember?"

"I know. I'm sorry."

Gus's cool, gray eyes had gentled then, and her expression had grown warm. "You don't have to be sorry, kid. Not with me. Not ever."

Gus had stayed for dinner and had never left. They'd gone together to fetch her things from the squat she'd been living in, and Laura had wanted to give her the bedroom so that Gus could sleep in a bed for once, but Gus had taken one look at the sofa that Laura had found on Portobello Road, and had staked her claim.

"Got a telly?"

"Not yet."

"I'll get us one cheap."

"Clean?"

"Course not," Gus had said.

"I'd rather wait till we can afford one." Laura's voice was even, though her stomach churned with her fear of hurting Gus's feelings. Of driving her away. "If you don't mind."

"It's your place," Gus said. "Your rules."

"Our place now."

"We'll wait then." Gus shrugged her square shoulders. "It might be fun, going straight."

"Do you mean that?" Laura asked.

"Try anything once," Gus said.

* * *

It hadn't always been that way between them. On that day when Gus agreed to move into Laura's flat, the only thing that Laura was really afraid of was losing her again. The first time Laura Andros had ever laid eyes on Augusta Pietrowski, she had been scared to death of everything about her. As scared as she had been of most of her contemporaries in those days. And at the very beginning, at least, Gus had exploited that fear, had used it to her own ends, as most of them did.

It was different now. Now it was the summer of 1982, and they were both starting over, both absorbed in the business of leaving the past behind, of shedding old skins and deciding exactly what their new selves were to be. That was one advantage of bad times, perhaps; there was little or nothing about them that you had to worry about holding onto. Everything was now. Now was the one-bedroom flat near Fulham Road and not a million miles from the heart of Chelsea. Now was Laura's job with the agency—a real job, at last, not just temping, going from one place to the next. Now was Gus looking through the situations vacant columns in the newspapers—Gus truly, genuinely looking for a legitimate way to help pay the rent. Now was the two of them on Saturday evenings going for a drink or to the cinema, or getting a takeaway, and almost always taking a stroll along King's Road or sometimes even Knightsbridge and Beauchamp Place, gazing into the store windows at the clothes, at strange Miyake and Comme des Garçons' oriental styles, at Montana and Mugler and Ralph Lauren and even at Valentino; Laura and Gus had come to an understanding that window shopping was the only kind they were allowed, since going anywhere *near* a store during opening hours— especially for Gus—spelled danger.

They got along so wonderfully well, the two best friends. Even after Ned came onto the scene, even when Laura first invited him to supper at the flat. She was anxious, at first, about Gus's feelings, in case she felt left out, or worse, much worse, got into old bad habits again, but she ought to have known better, for Gus was better than that, stronger and braver than that.

"You would say if you ever minded him being here, wouldn't you, Gus?" Laura asked her one Sunday, when Ned had gone home after lunch.

"Sure I would."

"I mean he's not important to me—I mean he *is,* I suppose, a little—but not the way you are." Laura paused, her eyes bright with intensity. "You know."

"I know." Gus smiled. "You worry too much."

"It's because he says he loves me but I know I don't love him," Laura said. "I like him a lot, but I don't love him. It makes me feel guilty."

"Everything does, kid."

They both fell silent in the lazy Sunday afternoon stillness, neither really noticing the television from the downstairs flat, or the constant noise of London traffic outside.

"Do you think I'll ever change?" Laura asked, after a while. "Stop feeling so guilty about everything, I mean."

"Hard to say." Gus shrugged. "Maybe not."

Laura sighed. "I wish I were more like you."

"You're nuts."

"At least you don't have a guilt complex."

"That's because I never really thought what happened was my fault," Gus said. "You did. You still do."

Laura said nothing.

"Time to put it behind you. Things are good now."

"I know they are."

"Then try to forget." Gus paused. "Let yourself off the hook, kid."

The past flooded back into Laura's mind, as fresh and clear as it always was.

"I can't," she said.

CHAPTER 2

<hr>

She was a happy child. It was hard to imagine a happier early childhood, even though both her parents had been killed when she was less than four years old.

"Such a tragedy," almost everyone had said at the double funeral. "Poor little orphan. Childhood over before it's even begun."

"She'll have forgotten them by the time she's six," one man had dissented, and at least twenty pairs of eyes had turned on him accusingly.

He was, of course, perfectly correct. Had it not been for her grandfather, Laura Andros would probably not have remembered the slightest thing about either her mother or father, and as it was, she went on after their deaths to have what she later recognized as the eight most uncomplicated, purely happy years of her life. And when those eight good years were at an end, when she might have welcomed with all her heart those sympathetic friends of her parents', they were, inevitably, nowhere to be found.

In the early summer of 1966, when Olivia and Anthony Andros, Laura's English mother and Greek-born, British-educated stockbroker father, both perished in the wreckage of the light plane carrying them from London to Le Touquet, Laura, their only child, was just three weeks away from her fourth birthday. So far as she was aware, one moment her parents were cuddling her, explaining that they were leaving for a week's holiday, and the next they were disappearing in a black taxi, spitting gravel, out of the oval-shaped drive of their Berkshire house and out of sight, never to return.

Within a fortnight, services over and arrangements completed, Laura had been taken by her grandfather, Theophanis Andros, from that abruptly altered and unhappy house, to his home in Greece. She had met her *pappous,* her grandfather—a big round-shouldered man with silver threads in his shiny black hair—a number of times when he had come to stay with them in England, but Laura had never seen Chryssos, his villa just outside the little town of Souvala on the island of Aegina in the Saronic Gulf.

While most of the bad memories of those few weeks—including the confusion of leaving home, the turbulent flight to Athens and their noisy, hectic arrival at Hellenikon airport—all vanished in time into the merciful oblivion of early experience, Laura never quite forgot her first glimpse of the house that was to become her second home. The white stone villa, named Chryssos, or "golden," for its ocher-tiled roof that glimmered pale yellow under the hammer of the midday sun and glowed a warmer, more reddish gold at sunset, stood high on rocks overlooking the sea, its gardens shielded by sparse pine woods, with a path leading down steeply to its own small private beach. Laura had felt so perplexed and desolate for the two weeks since the disappearance of her parents, yet the instant she had laid eyes on the tranquil beauty of Chryssos, she had felt somehow consoled.

Inside, too, the villa had brought relief and comfort. Ideally constructed for its position and the island's climate, almost every part of the house was cool in summer and warm in winter. The floors were stone, some pale marble, though comfortably shabby, but all the bedrooms had rugs, some old Persian, some locally handmade, and although the villa's central heating system tended toward unreliability, there were large stone fireplaces in many of the rooms. Each window had heavy wooden shutters which were regularly closed during that first summer by Madame Demonides, the housekeeper, to protect the interior from the ravages of the sun, but Theo Andros, always a believer in the power of light, would stride around the villa throwing the shutters open again, so that Laura, his beloved little granddaughter, should find no dark, gloomy corners in his home.

"You will like it, you think, *moraki mou,* little one?" Theo asked her anxiously on the afternoon of her arrival as Maria Demonides, black-clad, black-haired and black-eyed, but with smooth olive skin and a welcoming, kind face, brought them tea in his wildflower garden, from the edge of which one could see the sea.

"Yes, thank you, Pappous."

Laura looked down toward a plump tabby cat washing itself near their wooden table, and then smiled back up at her grandfather, and Theo looked into her slanting eyes and knew, with an enormous sense of relief, that she meant what she said. He had adored this little raven-haired, pale-skinned, green-eyed child of his son's from the first instant he had seen her almost four years earlier in her crib in England, but in the past two weeks, while he had dealt with all the formalities of burying her parents, the child had seemed so terrifyingly small and vulnerable to him, intensifying the burden of knowledge that he would, from now on, be responsible for her.

Adam Demonides, Maria's six-year-old son, did more than anyone to see to it that Laura felt settled as swiftly as possible. Tall for his age, with gleaming curly hair, eyes black as olives, a crooked nose and an engaging grin, he had lived on the top floor of Chryssos all his life. Until Adam's fourth year, Dimitrios Demonides, his father, had lived there, too, but then Dimitrios, a handsome, well-muscled gardener and caretaker, had made a fool of himself with a girl from Kipseli half his age, and Maria had thrown him out, refusing to take him back. Adam attended school these days, studying hard, aware, even at the tender age of six, that his success was important to his mother, but at home, too, in the villa, Adam did all he could to help out. Theophanis Andros had assured Maria that her job was secure, but the position that his mother now held alone had originally been intended for a married couple, and, strong as she was, there were some things, Adam felt, that only a man could do.

Adam and Laura were friends from the first, the older boy treating the orphaned child with tenderness and care in the early days, but as time passed, he came to realize that the little girl, with her dark hair and white, English skin, her pretty oval face with its determined, pointed chin and her green cat's eyes, was clearly a survivor. Before long, Laura hardly missed her old home at all, so enchanted was she by her new surroundings. She loved the villa itself, but, except when winter came—and even then only on the coldest, dullest days—the house was little more than a shelter, a comfortable, secure shield from darkness or winter rain, while her real world was now outdoors. The beach, with its pale sand and cool rocks, was an endless joy to her, as were the two mongrel dogs and three tabby cats who lived in or around Chryssos, all the animals playful and gentle, yet all living free and easy lives, with no regulated feeding times or collars to restrict them. And then there were the wild birds and flowers and, especially, the pine forest that shielded the villa, mystically lovely when shafts of sunlight penetrated their soft green darkness, or when the *meltemi*, the strong, northwesterly summer wind, blew through the trees, almost bringing them, Laura felt, to life.

They were, in many ways, removed from the real world on Aegina. As mainlaud Greece lurched from disruption into turmoil, as King Constantine failed in his attempts to overthrow the military regime that had toppled him, and fled with the rest of the royal family to Rome; and as the junta censored the press, prohibited free political activities and banned the miniskirt and *rembetika*, the earthy folk music beloved of Greek bohemians, life in Chryssos continued on its own, gentle way. Neither Theo nor Maria Demonides especially liked the mainlaud, and when Laura was taken, just once, by ferry to Piraeus and then into Athens for a few hours' shopping, she was so relieved to escape the noise and heat and claustrophobia of the city that she never argued with Adam again when he told her that everything worth having in the world was there, with them, on the island.

In the early autumn of 1968, not long after Laura's sixth birthday, Theo Andros retained the services of a tutor. Jonathan Evelyn Payne was an Englishman who had lived in Athens for twenty years, thriving on the chaotic political times and writing detective stories earnestly, adequately and with limited success, and who was therefore happy for an opportunity to enhance his income.

Offered an alternative source of education for her son, Maria Demonides decreed that Adam must continue to attend school, but she was nevertheless grateful for the chance for him to share extra lessons in the afternoons in English language and literature with Laura.

"Why can't I go to school with Adam, Pappous?" Laura asked her grandfather, mortified at the prospect of being treated differently. "Why can't I be with all the other children?"

"That time will come, little one, one day," Theo told her. "But in the meantime, I owe it to your mother and father to give you the education they would have wanted for you."

"But if I lived in England I would go to a real school, wouldn't I?"

"To a real English school, of course—which is why I have found Mr. Payne to teach you here on Aegina."

"But I'm not really English anymore, am I?" Laura said. "I'm almost Greek, like you, Pappous."

Theo took her hand gravely. "You are just the same as you were when you were born, little one. One half of you like your mother, the other like your father, though he, of course, became almost an Englishman."

"But if Daddy became English," Laura reasoned, "why can't I become Greek?"

"Because that was not what your parents wanted for you."

Laura, knowing from experience that her grandfather, when determined, was not to be swayed, moved on to the future. "But I will go to a real school some day, Pappous, won't I?"

"Of course you will, *moraki mou,*" Theo said, and still he

held onto her hand, his grip warm and strong, but his face had grown sad.

Theophanis Andros had, in his day, been a successful and moderately wealthy man. He had lived on Aegina much of his life, had owned a substantial pistachio farm and a small fleet of fishing boats, but in recent years, after the death of Christina, his wife, he had lost interest in business and had turned, increasingly, to gambling, for which he had always had a weakness. Frequently, until his granddaughter's arrival and the oppressive decrees of the junta, Theo had gone to the mainlaud to play roulette and chemin de fer in Athens, often not returning to the island until the next day, and his liking for roulette had grown so fervent that he had purchased and installed his own wheel, concealed in a specially built table in the library at the villa. Acquaintances of a similar persuasion still dropped by as often as was decent, and at least one night a week, after Laura and Adam were safely asleep in their beds, Chryssos was also the setting for drunken games of poker. Madame Demonides disapproved strongly, and grumbled quietly on the mornings when she had to clean and air the smoky, ouzo-scented library, keeping the door locked so that the children should not learn of her employer's weakness; but always fearing for her security, and aware that he was, on the whole, a good and decent man, she never voiced her complaints too loudly. It might have been better if she had, since Theo Andros was also for the most part, as so many addicted gamblers were, a loser.

In the space of one year, he lost his car, an old Mercedes, three times, winning it back twice until the third occasion, when it disappeared forever from his garage. He also lost a small motorboat, his gold Rolex wristwatch, his oldest but favorite silk suit, and considerable sums of money. There were certain things that Theo would not, under any circumstances, gamble with: his wedding ring or any of the numerous ornaments that his late wife had brought into their home; the gold and silver frames that held photographs of Christina and himself, or of Antonis and Olivia, his son and daughter-in-law, and, of course, of Laura; and while he did not, on the whole, consider money itself of paramount importance, he could vow with confidence that he would never lay a finger on the savings he had set aside to fund his future plans for Laura's education.

As the generals of Greece's ruling junta tumbled from power to be replaced by a democratic government, and as the Greek people used their renewed freedom to vote for an end, forever, of the monarchy, Laura Andros was blissfully unaware that her time of tranquil joy would soon be at an end.

Her grandfather, certain until recent weeks that she would be thrilled by the news he was now ready to present to her, found himself waiting until the last week of February 1975, to tell Laura, suddenly unsure, after all, of how she would react.

He came into the big, airy room on the second floor of the villa that had been used as a schoolroom for the past six and a half years, just as Jonathan Payne and Laura were putting away their books on Elizabethan history. It was a gloomy late winter's day, and the lights were switched on, illuminating Laura's most recent paintings on the walls, most of them of himself, Adam and Maria Demonides, and of Achilles, Laura's favorite mongrel dog.

"*Yasas, Pappous.*" Laura looked up and smiled.

Theo never ceased to be warmed by that smile, such an open, clear smile. She was perhaps not destined to be a classic beauty—she was too much of a combination of her father and mother for that—but there was so much strength in her features, and yet there was roundness, feminine softness, too. Olivia's eyes and pale skin, Antonis's hair, nose and chin—just that touch of Grecian forcefulness, but sitting perfectly in a gentle, female frame. She was so happy. It was always evident, that happiness, like a lovely spring flower with its face up to the sun. Laura had rooted here, on Aegina, and Theo wondered now, not for the first time, whether it was perhaps an unkind, even cruel act that he planned.

"Laura's doing very well, *kirie*," Payne said, rising from his chair. A thin, courteous man, he had grown to love his sessions with this young girl who liked learning well enough, but who openly confessed to preferring to sail or to

swim or just to be outside with Adam and the animals.
Payne knew what was coming soon, knew that his time with
Laura was drawing to a close, and though he recognized that
Theo Andros was almost certainly making the right decision
for the girl's future, the knowledge nevertheless depressed
him.

"I need to speak with Laura alone, Mr. Payne," Theo said,
quietly. "If you have finished, of course."

"We have." Payne turned to his pupil. "Don't forget your
essay, Laura. Drake's defeat of the Armada, no less than
three pages—and not in your largest writing, if you please."

"Yes, sir."

The tutor smiled at her grandfather. "And since it's still
raining, I suppose we may even hope it may be written without too much sacrifice." He picked up his battered leather
attaché case and walked toward the door. "French grammar
tomorrow morning, Laura."

"Oui, Monsieur," Laura said.

"Adio, Mr. Payne," Theo said. The door closed, and he sat
down on the tutor's chair and gestured for Laura to be seated
again too. "I have news for you, little one."

"What sort of news?"

"Important news, I believe."

Laura waited, interested but calm.

"In six weeks' time," Theo said, slowly, "you will be going to school."

For a moment, Laura did not speak, and then hot pleasure
flooded her eyes and flushed her cheeks. "To *dimotiko*—to
real school?" she asked. "With Adam?"

"To real school, yes," Theo said. "But not with Adam."

A tiny frown etched itself between Laura's fine dark eyebrows. "Where then?"

"In England," he said. "You are to go to school in England.
Osborne College is its name, in the county of Wiltshire."

Laura sat very still, and her cheeks lost their glow.

"No," she said.

"Hear me out, little one," Theo went on. "Osborne College is a fine school, with many acres of beautiful land.
They will teach you what you need, to be an English lady,
to prepare you for—"

"No," Laura said again, more emphatically. She picked up an exercise book and a plastic zip-case of pens and pencils, and stood up.

"It's what your parents would have wanted," Theo said.

"How do you know?"

"I know."

"Did they tell you?" she asked, defiantly.

"They told me of their hopes for you, of their dreams."

Laura clutched the book to her chest and raised her chin, Antonis's pointed, determined chin. "Did they know then, when I was just a baby, that they would be killed, and that you would bring me to Aegina?"

"Of course not, but—"

"Then they didn't know how happy I would be here," she reasoned. "If they knew how much I love it, they wouldn't want you to send me away."

Her grandfather shook his head. "I'm not sending you away, little one. I would like to keep you here with me forever."

"Then let me stay." Laura's voice quivered.

"You will be here during every holiday," Theo said, "and school is not forever—and besides, you may find that you love it there more than here. Your father was very happy in England—it was the right decision to send him there."

"I'm not my father."

"But you're very like him, in many ways." An old image of his son, smiling into a camera lens with his university friends, all of them so confident, so alive and intelligent, came back to Theo, hardening his determination. "It may be difficult at first, Laura, but you will grow used to it."

"Never." She put the book and pencil case back down on her desk. "I won't grow used to it because I won't go."

"You must go," he said gently but firmly. "It's time. If we wait any longer, it will be too late."

"Let it be."

Theo stood up and walked toward her, tried to put his arms about her, but she stepped aside, evading him. "You must consider this for a while, little one. It's a shock, I know, but when you take a little time to think, you will understand that it is for the best."

"The best is here," Laura said, stubbornly. "With you and

Adam and Maria and Mr. Payne. You always said he is a good teacher—I learn all I need from him."

"No," her grandfather said. "He cannot know everything you need."

"More than you, anyway," Laura cried, and abruptly, as the first tears sprang into her eyes, she ran from the room.

Adam found her on the beach an hour later, huddled on a sea-smoothed rock, her arms wrapped around her knees, her long hair flying in the cold wind.

"You'll freeze to death."

"I hope so." Laura's eyes, narrowed and fierce, stared out over the winter-gray waters of the Saronic Gulf.

"Come inside," Adam said. "It's raining."

She shook her head, liking the chill damp on her face.

"Move over, then."

He sat down beside her, and she felt the comfort of his warm, familiar body, and her throat ached with tears that she was suddenly too proud to shed.

"Do you know?" she asked.

Adam nodded.

"How long have you known?"

"Just now. When I came home. Your grandfather told me."

"Did he ask you to talk to me?"

"Sure."

She could not look at him. "Do you want me to go?"

"Don't be crazy."

Her face turned a little way toward him, enough to see his eyes. "You mean that?"

"What do you think?"

"I think Pappous has gone mad," Laura said.

Adam shook his head. "I don't think so."

"Why should he want to send me away now, when he never even let me go to school here before? It doesn't make sense."

"He says it's what your parents wanted."

"My parents are dead," Laura said flatly. "I don't even re-member them, not really. They're just photographs and my grandfather's stories."

"He remembers them. Perhaps he's right."

"Traitor." Laura stood up and scrambled off the rock.

"I'm not." Adam came after her, close to where the waves surged over the sand. "I don't want you to go, not to England or anywhere else. You're my best friend in the world—you're like my own sister, you know that."

"Then why say he's right?"

"Only about your parents, that's all I meant. Probably they did want you to be a young English lady. It's what your mother was, wasn't it?"

"I don't care what she was." Laura turned to face him, and her eyes were imploring. "Adam, you have to help me change his mind. This is my home. I'm not English anymore—maybe I'm not exactly Greek like you are, but I'm *me,* and I don't want to be changed by people who don't care about me in some horrible place I don't know."

"No one could ever change you, Laura." Adam put one arm around her shoulders. "You'll always stay the same wherever you go, just as I will."

"But no one's going to try to change you, are they? You'll always stay here, on Aegina, in your home."

"I don't think so." He shook his head. "My mother will need money when she's older. That's why she wants me to work hard at school—that's why I try to succeed." He shrugged. "Probably I'll go to Athens, maybe to the university, maybe even farther away."

"But you want to be a fisherman," Laura said, shocked.

"I know enough to know that I can't just do what I want. There isn't enough money in fishing." Adam shrugged again. "Anyhow, we're not talking about me, we're talking about you, your education. England could be very exciting, it might even be wonderful, who knows?"

"I'd hate it."

"Maybe not. Not when you got used to it." He smiled down at her. "You just hate change, *moraki mou.*"

She scowled. "Don't call me that—it's what he calls me."

"But you're my little Laura too, you always will be."

"If I let him send me away, we won't see each other anymore."

"Sure we will, in all the holidays."

"It's not the same."

* * *

Laura kept up her battle against Osborne College for more than a month. In the third week after her grandfather had broken the news to her, she determined that, since nothing else had changed his mind, more drastic measures were called for.

"I'm going on a hunger strike," she told Adam, on their early morning walk in the woods with the dogs. "I shan't eat anything until he agrees to let me stay."

"That's just foolish."

"It's the only way. I've tried everything else."

"But if you don't eat, you'll be ill."

"If I don't eat anything at all, I'll starve to death, and then he'll be sorry."

"Not as sorry as you," Adam told her, bluntly. "Anyway, they wouldn't let you die, they'd force you to eat."

"They couldn't."

"Sure they could, and it would be terrible for you."

"Not so terrible as going to Osborne College."

"Want to bet?"

She kept it up for four days, then found herself, against her will, in the kitchen with her head in the refrigerator, staring at the leftover bowl of *stiffado* that Maria had left there. Oh, God, she was so hungry she couldn't stand anymore, and besides, her grandfather had shown that he didn't care, and that nothing, even her slow starvation, was going to change his mind.

If I'm beaten, she thought, gazing at the stew, imagining the wonderful flavor of the meat and onions and garlic, *I may as well eat before I tell him that he's won.*

In spite of her defeat, it was the most delicious meal she had ever eaten. "I'm going to England," she told Theo coldly later that evening. "You'll be rid of me soon."

"Is that really what you believe? That I want to be rid of you?"

"What else should I believe? You kept me here for eight years because you owed it to my parents, and now you can be free again."

"For what would I like to be free, do you imagine? For loneliness?"

Laura shrugged. "Don't ask me."

Theo's craggy face was drawn and unhappy. "Little one, I

wish you could understand that I am truly doing this for your
sake. There's no real future for you here. Aegina's a wonderful
place for a child or an old man like me, but you need—"

"Please don't tell me again what I need," Laura said, still
cold, though she longed, more than anything, to run into his
arms, to forgive him and to be held by him. "I've given in.
I will go to England, to this Osborne College, and I'll let
them change me into what you want."

"I don't want you to change at all," Theo said.

Laura looked into his sad eyes, and her voice grew gentler.
"But I will," she said.

On Laura's last full day on Aegina, she and Adam rose long
before dawn and took their bicycles south, leaving them as
close as possible to the temple of Aphaia, and climbing the
rest of the way on foot. On its wooded mountaintop more
than six hundred feet above the sea, the ruined temple was
famous as the most exquisite vantage point on the island,
and as the sun rose that April morning, Laura and Adam
gazed down at the pale rose sea, and for the longest time,
neither of them was able to speak.

"I'll never forget this morning," Laura said at last. "Not
as long as I live."

"Nor will I," Adam said, putting his arm around her
shoulders, for it was cold up there, with the wind nipping at
their cheeks and making their eyes tingle.

Laura turned away from the view, and looked at him, at
his black olive eyes, and his crooked nose and his high
cheekbones. "I'm going to remember you, too, just like this,
the way you are right now." She reached out and took his
hand. "My brother," she said, and the tears she had vowed
not to shed were perilously close. "You'll always be that,
won't you, no matter what happens?"

"Forever." Adam swallowed hard. "And you'll always be
my little sister, my little Laura." He forced a smile. "But
you'll be back in the summer, and it will be the same as it's
always been."

"Better, because we'll have missed each other."

"It couldn't be better," Adam said.

"No," she said.

* * *

They did all the best things, that day, that they had ever done. They lazed on the beach and swam in the too-cold crystal water, they played tennis on the bumpy red clay court that belonged to one of the other villas closest to Chryssos, and they took the dogs into the pine forest and sniffed the newness and purity of the fresh spring grasses, and listened to the birds and the eager barking of the dogs. And in the late afternoon, they took a boat out, and Adam rowed, while Laura lay back and stared up at the sky, so blue that day, so sweetly, cruelly perfect, and they fished for a while, and spoke in low, gentle voices, and all the time, Laura felt a dull, painful hollow in the pit of her stomach, and was aware that this was only the beginning of what real loss felt like.

"Don't be too unkind to him," Adam said to her, when they had been out on the water for almost two hours. "It's painful for him, too, having you leave. Perhaps even worse than for you."

"Do you really think so?" Laura asked.

"I'm certain of it. He had to make the decision. You only had to accept it. And now he feels even guiltier because you're making the journey without him."

Theo had lately been unwell, and an attack of pleurisy had forced him to listen to his doctor's advice that a trip to damp, springtime England was the worst thing for him.

"I'm not afraid to go alone," Laura lied. "But I wish I really understood him. It makes no sense to me, even now. Less than ever now that I really have to go. Why cause pain, when it could be avoided so easily? When we could all go on as we are."

"We couldn't," Adam answered simply. "Not forever."

"But why not? Because of my parents? Because I had an ambitious father who didn't want to live his life on an island?" She shook her head again. "I've thought and thought, and still it makes no sense. He denies my own right to choose what I want, where I live."

"He feels he's giving you a greater choice."

"That's what he says, I know, and I believe that he thinks he's right. And maybe the day might have come when I wanted to go somewhere else, to see what I've missed, but at least that would have been what *I* wanted, not someone else." She sighed softly. "Too late now. Tomorrow I'll be gone. Laura Andros will be gone."

"She won't have gone," Adam said. "She'll just be traveling, that's all."

Laura shook her head. "I don't believe that."

She and her grandfather talked that night, really talking for the first time in weeks. Now that Laura had agreed to go, now that her suitcases—handsome pale beige leather suitcases that had been Christina's—were packed and all the arrangements were finalized, she knew with certainty that she did not want to leave Aegina with a bitter taste. That she was finished hurting Theo Andros who had, after all, never done anything but love and cherish her.

"I would like to feel," he said to her, as they sat together on the veranda after dinner, "that you understand."

It was too cool for sitting outside, but by the time the warmth of May and June arrived Laura would be far away, and at least they would both be able to think back to this last evening, with the soft sounds of the cicadas and the waves, and the rustling of the pine trees.

"I think I do," Laura said. "Now."

"But you still can't agree."

"No." She paused. "But I know you truly believe this is right for me, and I've made up my mind to try my hardest."

"To be happy," Theo said. "I know you will try to work—you've always been a good child—but it's your happiness that is important to me." He gave a heavy sigh, leaning back in his cane chair. "I'm so afraid, you know, *moraki mou,* of being wrong. And if I am"—he sat forward again, and his eyes were intent—"if I am, Laura, you must promise me that you will tell me. If you are truly unhappy—"

"I won't be."

"But if you are, if, after a time, you are still homesick, or if someone is unkind to you, you must tell me, and then you will come home again."

"I'll be all right, Pappous." Suddenly, after the weeks of hating him, Laura found herself wanting, needing to reassure her grandfather. Suddenly, it was so transparently plain that he did love her, that he did believe that this English school was what she needed—and maybe, if he believed it so strongly, he might even be right.

"How do you feel, little one?" Theo reached for her hand and held it. "Tell me."

"Afraid," she said. "A little excited, too, but mostly afraid." She paused. "And sad, to be leaving Chryssos. Adam, Maria—the animals. You. Most of all, you."

They went inside, for it was getting too cold to sit and talk, and there were things that he wanted to say to her, important things that she needed to know if she was going to be living alone, without family.

"I loved Antonis very much," he said, when they were sitting in the living room, where a fire burned in the hearth, its glow turning the white marble floor to dusky pink. "But in some ways I think I adored your mother almost more than my own son." He turned his head toward one of his many photographs of Olivia. "She was the sweetest person I ever met, until you came to me. She was gentle and kind, but you are stronger than she was. You have your father's strength and obstinacy."

Laura smiled. "Do I?"

"I think so."

"I wish I remembered them better. Sometimes I think I don't really remember them at all, that it's just your memories and the pictures."

Her grandfather rose from his armchair and came and sat beside her on one of the big, silk-covered settees, kept clean by Maria Demonides but growing shabby nonetheless with time and living.

"It's you we have to think of now, Laura. You as yourself, not their daughter, nor my granddaughter."

"I know," she said softly.

"I don't know how it will be at this school. I have read what they sent me, and I have spoken to the teachers and to parents of other girls who have studied there, but I can't know how it will really be." He paused. "It will be, I imagine, like any community. Like Souvala, a small town—like Athens, even. Some people friendly and warm and caring, some unkind and dishonest. Like life."

"Not here," Laura said.

"Exactly." Theo paused again. "Am I forgiven sufficiently to give you a little advice?"

Laura smiled, and this time it was she who took his hand and squeezed it. "Please," she said.

Theo nodded. "Stay as gentle and kind as you are, but keep your strength. Be honest and straightforward, and true to yourself and what you believe in. Give way when you have to, but never let others trample on you."

Laura sat very still, saying nothing, just listening.

"If God is good, you will always be surrounded by love and kindness, but even so, little one, there may be some who are unkind, or jealous, and who may try to hurt you. If they do, it's always wisest to try to walk away—but if that's not possible, then you may have to stay and fight."

"You make it sound frightening, Pappous."

"That's not my intention. Osborne College is a fine school, little one, with great teachers. If I didn't believe you would be safe there, I wouldn't dream of sending you."

"Then why talk of—?"

He stopped her. "Because in the same way that Aegina and Chryssos are not all of life, neither is Osborne College. Because I'm growing old, and who knows for certain if I will have another chance to tell you the things I want to?"

"Of course you will," Laura said urgently. "I'll be back in just a few months."

"That's right," Theo said. "You will."

"And if I need help, I can write to you, or telephone."

"Night or day."

"But I won't need help, Pappous," she said quickly, still possessed by that wish to reassure him, perhaps to eradicate the guilt she knew he was feeling over sending her away, the guilt that she had made him feel. "It will be wonderful there, new and exciting and wonderful."

Theo squeezed her hand. "I hope so," he said.

CHAPTER 3

Though it was, in truth, a nineteenth-century Gothic-Revivalist manor house, it looked to Laura like a castle or a fortress, built of gray, wintry stone, with four round towers and turrets, and though there was neither a moat nor drawbridge, her initial approach, in the small, empty green bus that had been sent to meet her, sent chills up and down her spine.

"Impressive, eh, miss?"

It took a moment for Laura to realize that the driver had spoken. He was a friendly man, had been courteous and helpful when he had collected her, with her suitcases, at Salisbury station, yet in spite of that she felt as if she were about to be shut away, helpless and friendless, in a dark, medieval prison.

"It doesn't look like a school," she ventured.

" 'Tis though."

The bus rumbled on along the straight, narrow road that led toward the arched entrance. Laura gripped the edge of her seat as they passed into a short tunnel that plunged her, for a few seconds, into blackness, and then they were out again, into the gray English day, and the bus was coming to a halt in a large, round, cobbled courtyard, and two women were standing there, waiting, Laura knew, for her.

Her knees shook as she climbed down from the bus. One

of the women, dressed in a tweed suit, stepped forward, her right hand extended.

"Welcome to Osborne College, Laura." Her voice was low and even, her eyes were blue and clear, and her skin, lightly powdered, was very fine. "I'm Mrs. Helen Williamson, your principal, and this"—she indicated her companion—"is Miss Thorpe, who will be your housemistress."

"How do you do?" Laura shook their hands. The principal's grip was firm and warm, the other woman's strong but cold, though not nearly so icy as Laura's own hand.

"So what do you think?" Miss Thorpe asked, heartily. A foot taller than the headmistress, she wore a beige wool twinset over a plain brown skirt; her pepper-and-salt hair was parted neatly in the middle of her head and fastened back off her thin face with two tortoiseshell clips.

"Think?"

"Of Osborne." Miss Thorpe smiled, and her teeth were large and white, like horses' teeth. "Magnificent, isn't it?"

"Yes." Laura looked up at the stone castle, and suppressed a shudder. "It's very big." For the first time in her life, she was conscious of her accented English. She had never noticed it with Jonathan Payne.

"It must be terribly different," Helen Williamson said, gently, "from what you have grown used to."

"Yes," Laura said again, helplessly. A picture of Chryssos sprang into her mind, and she longed, with all her might, to be there. "It is different."

"All that sunshine." Mrs. Williamson's smile was a little wistful. "And, of course, the sea."

"No sea anywhere near here," Miss Thorpe said briskly. "We're quite landlocked here in Wiltshire. Though we do have our fair share of ruins."

Laura's face felt frozen. She experienced a desperate urge to turn and run back down that straight, flat road, but she quelled it and stood very still.

"Why don't we go inside?" the headmistress suggested.

Laura looked back at the bus.

"Your things will be taken to your dormitory," Miss Thorpe told her. "You'll find them there, safe and sound, after Mrs. Williamson has given you a cup of tea and you've taken a tour of the school."

The tea was too milky for her taste, the scone floury and heavy, but the headmistress's private drawing room was tranquil and book-lined, overlooking a small garden. From her straight-backed armchair, Laura saw a lovely tree, its slender, leafy branches all bowed over, almost brushing the soft green lawn.

"My favorite weeping willow," Mrs. Williamson said, and Laura remembered a tree of that name in one of the books Jonathan Payne had given her to read, and felt a rush of gratitude to her tutor.

She remained too nervous to swallow her scone, too afraid of dropping her cup and saucer to take more than a few sips of tea, but her twenty minutes with Helen Williamson were a gentle, encouraging interlude, made less formal when a scratching at the door was followed by the entrance of a short-legged, barrel-shaped dog with a pointed, foxlike head and erect ears.

"This is Henry." Mrs. Williamson patted his head fondly and stroked his back. "Have you ever seen a Welsh corgi before, Laura?"

Laura admitted she had not, but felt emboldened enough to speak of their two dogs and cats on Aegina, and once Henry planted himself at her feet, gazing longingly up at her plate, and the headmistress gave her permission to drop a small piece of buttered scone onto her carpet, Laura felt sufficiently comforted to believe that life at Osborne College might not, after all, be entirely as terrifying as she had feared.

Those feelings of tentative confidence vanished without trace when Miss Thorpe returned to take her on her promised tour of the school. It was difficult to absorb. What looked on the outside like an awe-inspiring castle was, within, a feat of drabness. The walls were all plain plaster painted an ugly shade of green or grayish cream, and the ceilings were so high that the fluorescent striplights far above failed to properly illuminate the endless corridors. Doors, for the most part, were closed, but those rooms into which Laura was allowed to peep were all equally cold and damp and deserted.

"No classes first day back," Miss Thorpe explained briskly. "Girls all busy with their unpacking and gossip. It's especially quiet now, of course, because you've arrived earlier than most."

The classrooms Laura saw were much as she had imagined; rows of wooden desks, each with their own drawer and inkwell, hard-looking chairs with faded, fraying green leather seats, and a blackboard taking up most of one wall. In one room she saw a large globe and maps pinned to notice boards; in another long wooden tables, stacked with glass beakers, test tubes and Bunsen burners.

"Our chemistry lab," Miss Thorpe told Laura. "Did your tutor teach you any chemistry?"

Laura shook her head. Jonathan Payne had gone to some trouble to try to prepare her for what she might find in an average British school, and she had read a series of novels about a girls' boarding school in Switzerland which Mr. Payne had said was a rather idealized account of school life, but still, he had told her, certain things were fundamental and immutable.

Like most boarding schools Osborne College, Laura learned, was divided for practical purposes into four separate "houses," though in Osborne's case these were located in the four towers that Laura had seen from the bus.

"Banbury and Alderley Towers," Miss Thorpe told Laura, "Jacob and Coombe. You're to be in Alderley, my house." She smiled heartily. "Far be it from me to encourage bias, but it is, of course, the best house."

"I'm looking forward to seeing it," Laura said, longing to sit down again.

"And so you shall, just as soon as we've finished our little tour."

As they left the building by the back entrance Laura's spirits rose again, for here, at last, was what her grandfather had spoken of, what the brochures of the school had hailed as "one of the most charming locations in the country." The day was still gray, yet the green of the surrounding land was soft and rich, and it was hard to tell where the gardens and playing fields of Osborne ended and the Wiltshire countryside began. They walked past a string of tennis courts, past an outdoor swimming pool, empty and leaf-filled, and through a series of vegetable gardens, and for much of the time Miss Thorpe kept up a commentary of such enthusiasm that Laura began to feel quite buoyed up.

"We set great store by sporting achievements at Osborne," she told Laura. "I don't suppose you've ever played lacrosse, or netball, but we'll soon get you started. What about hockey?"

"Not yet," Laura said humbly, inadequacy returning. "I played tennis and swam—"

"Good, good, that'll be a strong beginning for you this summer. What about riding? The girls are encouraged to use the stables about a mile away, if time allows, but never without hard hat and jodphurs, of course." Miss Thorpe eyed Laura. "Have you come equipped?"

"I'm afraid not."

"Not to worry, dear."

Out of the corner of her left eye, Laura saw a blur of movement, and turning a little she saw two girls, one golden blond, the other chestnut-haired, coming toward them.

"Have you ridden?" Miss Thorpe asked.

Laura turned back to the teacher. "Excuse me?"

"Did you say you had ridden?"

"Not really," Laura said.

"Either you have or have not. Always be precise, dear."

Laura took a breath. "I have ridden, a few times," she said, "but never a horse."

"What have you ridden?"

"Ena moularin." She thought. "A mule."

"Good grief!" a voice said derisively.

Laura turned around. The blond girl's hair was long, wavy and gleaming, her eyes blue as a china doll's and alight with amusement.

"Hello, Lucia. Nothing funny about riding a mule, actually," Miss Thorpe said briskly. "Rather harder, in fact, than a horse."

"Is this the new girl, Miss Thorpe?" The blonde now spoke with respect.

"Indeed she is." The teacher stood legs slightly apart, feet firmly planted. "Laura Andros, here are two of your fellow pupils, Lucia Lindberg and Priscilla Carling. Not only are you all in Alderley Tower, but you'll be sharing the same dormitory." Her smile was warm. "Welcome back, girls. Have you been sent to find us?"

"Yes, Miss Thorpe." The second girl, less glamorous than the blonde, had long, very straight, chestnut-colored hair and a husky, attractive voice. "Mrs. Williamson asked us to show Laura to the dorm."

"Very well," Miss Thorpe said, and turned to face Laura. "I can leave you then, in the capable hands of these two young ladies."

"Yes, Miss Thorpe." Laura's stomach turned over.

"Now, Lucia, Priscilla, you're to take care of Laura. Remember how tiresome it is to be new, especially in the middle of the school year."

"Of course, Miss Thorpe."

The housemistress flashed Laura a last horsy smile. "See you all later then," she said, and was gone, striding back toward the college.

"Well, then," Lucia Lindberg said.

"Well, then," Priscilla Carling echoed.

And Laura's bad times began.

The dormitory, on the third floor of Alderley Tower, was horseshoe-shaped with five narrow windows. Seven beds fanned inward from the walls, each with its own bedside table and locker, though the wardrobes containing most of the girls' clothes and personal belongings were one floor down, together with the bathroom and showers.

It was customary, Lucia told Laura, for all the girls to unpack in the dormitory and to pile their belongings onto their beds for all to see before they were put away. It was important, she said, for the communal spirit of the house, for their morale. Nothing must be concealed, no secrets kept, everything out in the open.

Laura's bed was in the center of the horseshoe, the only

bed in the dormitory without even a scrap of window. She had unpacked Christina's suitcases, and now all her belongings—from the regulation navy blue knickers that had been mailed to Aegina, together with the rest of her school uniform, from Harrods, to the two jars of home-grown pistachio nuts and *baklava*, packed for her by Maria Demonides—lay on the green candlewick bedspread.

"Where are the rest of your undies?" Lucia asked, tossing aside the knickers.

"That's all there is," Laura said. "What more do I need?"

"It's hardly a question of need, is it, Cilla?"

Priscilla picked up a pair of tiny lacy briefs from her own bed. "Speak for yourself. I couldn't bear having to wear those hideous things all the time—they're so scratchy, too."

With a clattering of shoes and a banging of doors, another girl rushed into the dormitory, breathless from the spiral staircase.

"*Freddy!*" Priscilla shrieked, and she and Lucia fell on the newcomer.

"Who's this?" the girl called Freddy asked. Her shoulder-length hair was very dark, almost as black as Laura's, and her eyes were a rich dark brown.

"The new girl," Priscilla answered.

"The Greek," Lucia said. "Laura Andreakis."

"Andros," Laura corrected.

"Andreakis, Andrex, whatever," Lucia said, airily, and the others laughed hysterically as Freddy produced a roll of Andrex toilet paper from the trunk by her bed.

"My name is Fernanda Garcia," she said, gravely, in a low, accentless voice. She gave Laura her hand to shake. "Freddy for short."

"I'm pleased to meet you," Laura said.

"She's *plizd* to meet you." Lucia giggled.

"Don't be horrid, Lucia," Freddy rebuked. "She can't help being Greek."

"I'm only half Greek," Laura pointed out.

"Which half?" Priscilla asked.

Another girl, with very short red hair, arrived in the dormitory.

"Gerry, thank God!" Lucia ran to embrace her. "I thought you might have been expelled."

"No such luck," the girl said, cheerfully. "How was your Easter?"

"Brilliant."

"Mine was grim. Family all the way." She looked at Laura. "Who's that?"

"Let me introduce you." Freddy took Laura's hand and drew her over to the red-haired, freckle-faced girl. "Geraldine Parkinson, Laura Andrex."

Laura flushed. "Andros," she corrected.

"Lovely name," the newcomer said. "But I prefer Andrex."

"That's it then," Lucia decreed. "Like it or lump it."

"Everyone has to have a nickname," Freddy explained. "We never call Geraldine anything but Gerry, and only Miss Thorpe calls me Fernanda. Even Willy calls me Freddy."

"What do they call you?" Laura asked Lucia.

The blonde, easily the prettiest of them all, drew herself up to her full five feet. "No one shortens my name."

"For obvious reasons," Gerry said.

Laura looked blank.

"Well, we could hardly call her Loo, could we?"

"Maybe she doesn't know what a loo is," Freddy suggested.

"It's all Greek to her," Lucia said.

For the first week, it was little more than teasing, good-natured enough from most of them, with a touch more malice from Lucia. In a place as large and confusing as Osborne, populated by scores of utter strangers, Laura was almost grateful to have anyone to talk to, even if none of them had as yet ever said a nice word to her, at least out of earshot of Miss Thorpe. It was only when they were openly insulting about her Greek background, or worse, when they were nasty about her grandfather or Adam, that Laura attempted to fight back, but whenever she retaliated in any way, Lucia Lindberg saw to it that some kind of punishment came her way.

"Do all your people have greasy hair?" Lucia asked one

morning before assembly, glancing at one of the photographs of Theophanis Andros on Laura's bedside table.

"My grandfather does not have greasy hair," Laura said hotly.

Lucia prodded the photograph. "What's that then?"

"It's glossy in the light," Laura said. "Give it back, please."

"Pliz," Lucia mocked.

"I said give it *back*!" Laura snatched the photograph, and a corner of the brass frame scratched Lucia's palm.

"You've cut me!"

"It's just a scratch."

"How dare you answer me back." Lucia was enraged, nursing her hand. "I'll probably get blood poisoning! Get me some Dettol from the bathroom."

"We'll be late for assembly."

"And whose fault will that be? I'll only have to explain that you attacked me, and then you'll be for it. Now get the Dettol, you little Greek cow, or I'll report you."

When Laura got back to the dormitory with the bottle of antiseptic, she found the photograph of her grandfather torn into shreds on her bed.

"No more than you deserve," Lucia said, righteously, dabbing her scratch. "And don't even think of telling tales, or you'll get worse."

Things grew worse in the second week, when Laura woke out of a restless sleep to find her sheets and nightdress damp. Getting quietly out of bed, she knocked a book to the floor. A light was switched on.

"That's *disgusting*." Anna de Vere, a girl who had scarcely spoken to Laura since her arrival, was staring at her nightdress with distaste.

Laura looked down, saw blood and gasped. For a moment she thought she must be hemorrhaging, that she was going to *die*—and then, suddenly, she understood.

"What's going on?" Gerry, two beds away, sat up grouchily.

"The new girl's bleeding all over the dorm."

"What's she done to herself?"

"Nothing, it's just her curse."

Laura still stood by her bed, mortified, hardly daring to move, feeling the fresh menstrual blood trickling down between her thighs.

"Well, do something, for heaven's sake," Gerry said, and lay down again.

At the other end of the horseshoe, first Priscilla and then Lucia woke up.

"What's all the fuss?" Lucia asked, sleepily.

"I think Andrex is having a period," Priscilla explained, looking interested.

Freddy, too, had woken up. "Haven't you got anything?"

"No," Laura whispered, her face scarlet with embarrassment.

"Anyone got a spare ST?" Priscilla inquired loudly.

Lucia sat up and opened her locker. "For God's sake, give her one of these." She hurled a small package roughly in Laura's direction; it bounced off a wall and landed on the floor.

Trying to keep her knees together, Laura picked it up and stared at the printing on the label.

"Anyone would think she's never seen a Tampax before," Lucia drawled. "Need some help putting it in, Andrex, dear?"

"Thank you, no," Laura said, hating her.

With a flash of pity, Freddy got out of bed. "Come on, let's go to the bathroom. I'll get a towel to cover the sheet."

"Has she got more than one nightie?" Lucia called.

"Put a sock in it, Lucia," Freddy said.

It was a night Laura would never forget. Once Freddy, having given her the briefest of instructions, had gone back to bed, she found that she was still so rigid with humiliation and anger that it was impossible to insert the tampon. Not daring to return to the dormitory she sat weeping for more than half an hour on the edge of the lavatory seat, until at last, gritting her teeth and refusing to be beaten, she tried again and, with a final sob of triumph, succeeded. Upstairs, the dormitory was silent and pitch dark, and it took several minutes of panic and fumbling before she found her bed again and lay, sleepless, until dawn.

Next morning, in the bathroom, standing in one of the shower stalls, she heard Lucia talking to Priscilla.

"I'm surprised, really, Willy taking in someone like that."

"Maybe she thought it would be good for our education."

"Mixing with Greek peasants, you mean?"

"I thought her father was something in the City."

"God, Cilla, you're so trusting. Her people are obviously trash."

In the shower, Laura turned her hot face up to the cool water, and felt it flow down her cheeks, mixing with her tears. She thought of her gentle grandfather, and her beloved Adam, and Maria and Jonathan Payne and Chryssos, and she missed them so much she thought she would die. She detested all these girls, except perhaps Freddy who had finally come to her aid last night, but Lucia, with her blue doll's eyes and pink rosebud mouth, was the cruelest, the worst of them.

"Di misso," she said into the water. "I hate her."

The emotion shocked her a little. She had never hated anyone before.

CHAPTER 4

It grew worse. Laura tried to focus on the few good things in her new, bleak world, especially on the learning, which became more important to her as the rest of life became increasingly miserable. Jonathan Payne had prepared her well for most subjects; having had her tutor's sole attention stood her in good stead when it came to English literature, French and Latin, geography and history, though chemistry, with all its inherent, unpleasant odors and seemingly lethal experiments, left her bewildered, and mathematics, especially algebra, perplexed and bored her. She got on well with the teachers, received regular letters from her grandfather and from Adam, wrote frequently back to them, becoming adept at the fiction with which she carefully filled her letters.

My best friend, she wrote to Theo Andros, *is called Fernanda, though we call her Freddy. All the girls are kind and friendly, and in exchange for their helpfulness, I am teaching some of them to speak Greek.* Freddy had, in fact, avoided her for days following that hideous night, but Laura knew that Lucia had ragged her friend for being kind to her, and she almost—though only almost—understood.

Her success in the classroom and the praise she received from the teachers, made life in the dormitory even more nightmarish. Laura came into Alderley Tower one afternoon after receiving high marks on an English grammar test, to find that her locker had been ransacked, and the pages of her

Greek–English dictionary scribbled on and so torn as to render the book scarcely usable. Having won a singles tennis match the previous week and going to change into her whites one morning, she found that her skirt had been smeared with chocolate, and going to her wardrobe for her spare skirt, she discovered that that one, too, had been soiled. On the day after she had been singled out by Mademoiselle Lupine for the excellence of her French translation, she woke to find that the prep she'd finished the previous evening for that day's French class had been cut up with scissors.

She put up with it all, knowing that reporting the incidents would only make matters worse, and hoping against hope that turning the other cheek with some dignity might make them stop. It did not. It was common knowledge in their dormitory that Laura hated the cold, so she was scarcely surprised when her blanket vanished from her bed one evening; and when, on the day of their class outing to Stonehenge, all her navy blue regulation pullovers disappeared, Laura braced herself and strode ahead of the others across icy, windswept Salisbury Plain, refusing to allow them to see her shivering. It was only when, in the fifth week of term, she took Adam's latest letter out of her bedside locker to reread it and found that someone had spilled ink over both sheets of paper, that Laura knew she had had enough.

She went to Miss Thorpe's study.

"That is a shame," the housemistress sympathized, handing her back the ruined letter. "But accidents do happen."

"It wasn't an accident, Miss Thorpe."

"Of course it was, dear."

"But I didn't do it. Someone else did."

"That doesn't mean it was not an accident."

Laura stood her ground. "The letter was fine when I put it into my locker."

"What exactly are you suggesting, Laura?" The sympathy left Miss Thorpe's face. "That another girl stole the letter from your locker and deliberately vandalized it?" Her mouth pursed in disapproval. "Are you accusing anyone in particular? Have you any proof?"

"No, Miss Thorpe."

The housemistress's tone grew even frostier. "Then I suggest you forget all about it as quickly as possible." She paused. "You know, Laura, you might be wise to learn from this. You should realize that there are few things your fellow pupils will despise more thoroughly than a telltale." She unbent a little. "I'm sorry that your letter has been spoiled, but you had, after all, already read it, hadn't you?"

Laura's cheeks were hot, but she said nothing more.

"So may I take it this will be the end of the matter?"

"Yes, Miss Thorpe."

"Good girl."

From that day on, the gang of her tormentors emerged from anonymity and became more brutal. Lucia Lindberg, as Laura had known, was their ringleader, and Priscilla, Gerry, Freddy, and a girl from another dormitory in Alderley Tower named Abigail Butcher, all followed Lucia's lead with unquestioning devotion.

With the weather growing warmer, life at Osborne was led increasingly outdoors, in the playing fields, on the tennis courts and in the open-air swimming pool, bracingly unheated. When Laura had to play tennis with any of Lucia's gang, a ball would, now and again, strike her hard on her body, once even on the back of her head. When she played hockey she came off the field covered with bruises she knew perfectly well might have been avoided. And then once, as she was riding her bicycle to the riding stables, she was struck on the right shoulder by a stone.

She confronted Lucia that evening in the bathroom.

"I could have been seriously hurt today."

"I have no idea what you're talking about."

"Of course you know." Her shoulder painful, Laura was angry. "Are you crazy or something?"

"Are you *crezzy*?" Lucia mocked.

"I'll go to Mrs. Williamson next time."

"Like you went to Thorpe after the letter? That didn't get you very far, did it?" Lucia strolled toward the door. "I'd be careful who you accuse, little Miss Andrex, and who you threaten."

* * *

Two days later, while Miss Oliver, the swimming coach, was looking the other way, Laura, practicing backstroke at the deep end of the pool, felt her feet being grabbed by a pair of strong hands. Dragged underwater, choking and struggling, she flailed around desperately with her arms, lungs bursting, heart racing, her panic overwhelming, until the hands released her feet. Her head free of the water, Laura gasped for breath, coughing and spitting, clutching at the rail on the poolside, several seconds passing before her burning eyes were clear enough for her to look around.

Abigail, Priscilla and Freddy were all at the shallow end, laughing together. Gerry was on the low board, preparing to dive. Lucia was nowhere to be seen.

Three nights after that, Laura lay down in bed to find that her pillow had been smeared with raspberry jam.

"For God's sake!" She jumped out of bed again. "I'm getting sick of this!" Furiously, she stomped out of the dormitory down to the bathroom.

Staring at her reflection in the mirror, at her white face and angry eyes, Laura didn't hear them until it was too late.

"You need a hairwash."

She turned. They were all there, Lucia, Priscilla and Gerry and Abigail Butcher from the dormitory upstairs, with Freddy standing guard at the door. Laura saw that she'd fallen into a trap, that this was an ambush.

"Get out," she said.

Lucia smiled. "I'd think you'd be glad of a little help with that sticky hair. Don't you think she needs a hand, Cilla?"

"Absolutely."

"Freddy?"

Freddy looked a little uncomfortable. "Do you think this is such a great idea, Lucia?"

Lucia turned cold blue eyes on her. "Yes, I do."

"Come on, Freddy," Gerry encouraged. "It's just a bit of fun."

"Not fun at all, actually," Lucia said.

Except for the trauma in the swimming pool, it was the

first time that Laura had felt cold, harsh fear. Four against one, with no chance of help.

"This isn't funny." She fought to keep her voice calm.

"Didn't you hear?" Lucia said. "It isn't meant to be funny."

They were on her then, and it was as if they'd rehearsed it, for their moves seemed orchestrated, perfectly organized, with Priscilla clamping a bony hand over her mouth to stop her screaming, and with Gerry, the strongest, and Abigail both grabbing her around the middle, pinioning her arms as they maneuvered her toward one of the lavatories. Laura struggled madly, tried to shriek through Priscilla's fingers, fought to kick at anyone, any part of them she could reach, but then Lucia had her by the ankles, and she was hanging upside down, blood rushing to her head, and outrage roared through her, almost blotting out the fear—but when Priscilla's hand released her mouth there was no time to scream before her head was in the bowl, her face in the cold, disgusting water, her forehead banging against the hard ceramic—and then she heard the noise of the chain being pulled, and the flushing water poured in over her, and again she was choking, unable to breathe, and she thought she would vomit or faint. And then they let go of her legs, and for an instant she was terrified that she would fall farther, that her face, her nose, would strike the bottom, perhaps be broken. But instead, she sprawled on the floor like a dropped rag doll, and she heard them retreating, heard their soft, cowardly footsteps treading away, heard the door open and close again.

She did vomit then, retching over and over again, and sobbing and sobbing, her hands, clenched fists, pounding the sides of the lavatory bowl. *"Tous misso olous!"* she cried softly between the bouts of retching. "I hate them all." And when it was over, she slumped against the wall, and was very still.

"Are you all right?"

She heard the voice, and looked up in disbelief. Freddy stood in the doorway.

"I thought you might need some help." Freddy's face was pale and guilty.

"You're not serious." Laura's voice was rasping, her throat sore.

In one hand, Freddy held a bath towel. With the other she reached down to try to help Laura to her feet.

"Don't touch me."

"But you need—"

"Don't *touch* me," Laura snarled, and Freddy stepped back quickly. "Just get out and leave me alone."

"I only wanted to—"

"Get out of here right now," Laura said, and the violence in her voice was startling, even to her own ears. "Get out, or I'll kill you."

Freddy backed toward the door.

"I'm sorry," she said. "It went too far."

"Get *out!*"

The door closed. And after a few moments, when Laura knew that she was, finally, alone, the sobbing, harsh and racking and bitter, came back.

Lucia threatened her the next day, in the gymnasium. Laura was standing in line, waiting for her turn to vault over the leather horse.

"I hope you're not thinking of blabbing about last night."

Laura said nothing, kept her back to her.

"You're not the first to get a ducking, but you'll get a lot worse if you go to Thorpe or Willy."

Laura felt sick, and her knees trembled, but still she kept silent.

"I'd advise you not to ignore me, Andrex."

The girl in front of Laura took off toward the horse, and sprang neatly over, ankles together and well clear, landing perfectly.

"Come on, Laura!" Miss McLean, whistle hanging between her breasts, stood solidly between her and the horse.

"Go on then, Andrex," Lucia hissed in her ear.

Laura fell before she reached the horse, her knees buckling. Miss McLean was at her side instantly, helping her up.

"All right?" She checked Laura over, saw no injuries. "Jolly good."

Behind them, Lucia, one of the few girls who could look glamorous in a divided skirt and gym shoes, began her run.

"Whoops," Miss McLean said, whisking Laura out of harm's way.

Lucia made a perfect vault.

"Well done, Lucia," Miss McLean said.

Laura wished she had broken her neck.

Two days later, while Laura was on duty in the vegetable gardens, one of the allotted school jobs she really enjoyed, she heard a dull thud. Looking up from her digging, she saw four of them, the whole gang except Freddy, standing shoulder to shoulder.

"That was careless, Cilla." Lucia regarded the fallen clay pot on the ground at their feet, seedlings and compost spilled.

"Andrex can clean it up," Priscilla said.

Lucia raised her hand. She was holding a trowel, brandishing it like a weapon. "You didn't seem to be listening, the other day in the gym," she said. "So we thought you might need another reminder."

Laura stared at her. "Why don't you leave me alone?"

"That wouldn't be very nice," Priscilla said.

"What have I done to you?"

"You sneaked to Thorpe, for one thing," Lucia said.

"Only after you did all those things to me." The fear was high in her chest, in her throat. She felt her heart beginning to race.

"You failed the test," Abigail said.

"What test?" Laura's voice trembled.

"That's just it," Lucia said. "You're too stupid, too foreign to understand. You thought you could just come to Osborne and be accepted. As if you were one of us, as if you thought you could be as good as us."

"As good as *you*?" Laura's anger bolstered her. "You're the worst, the most disgusting people I ever met—you're no better than thugs."

The punch in her stomach was such a shock, and so painful, that it was a few seconds before she saw that it was Abigail who had delivered it. Through watering eyes, Laura saw her looking at Lucia, at her leader, seeking praise, seeking encouragement.

"Shall I hit her again?" Abigail asked.

Laura, still doubled over, backed away.

"Someone might come," Gerry warned.

"Not today, Abby," Lucia said.

"She hurt my hand." Abigail flexed her fingers gingerly. "Another time."

"If you touch me again," Laura said through chattering teeth, "I swear I'll go to Mrs. Williamson."

"If you do that, you'll have an accident." Lucia's smile was cold and unafraid. "A really awful accident."

Laura was at the stables when she saw it. She was alone, in the tack room. It lay on an overturned wooden box. A knife, the kind that folded back into its handle, like a penknife but bigger. She picked it up and folded out the blade. It was a little rusty, but sharp. Laura did not stop to think. She had never stolen anything in her life, but it was what she needed, more than anything. She had no friends, no one to protect her. This would be her protector.

She slipped it into the pocket of her jodphurs, felt it hard against her right thigh, thought that someone would notice the bulge. But they did not. She rode that afternoon with pleasure and confidence, made taller by the horse's height and by the awareness of the knife.

She would keep it on her at all times. In her pocket or, if that was not possible, taped to her leg, and at night she would sleep with it under her pillow, and she would carry it with her into the shower. They would be inseparable, and the next time that Lucia or her cronies tried to lay a finger on her, she would let them see it, and they would know that she had, at last, found a friend.

Mrs. Williamson stopped her in the corridor one morning after assembly.

"Are you all right, Laura?"

"Yes, thank you, Mrs. Williamson."

"You're looking rather pale. You're sure everything's all right?"

Laura looked up at the headmistress's kind, calm face, and she thought for just a few seconds that she might tell her everything, but then she remembered what would happen if she did. After all, it was just her word against theirs, and even if Mrs. Williamson did believe her, she could hardly expel all five of them. And so long as even one of Lucia's friends remained at Osborne, Laura knew that she would never be safe.

"Are you feeling unwell, Laura, dear?"

Mrs. Williamson's voice jolted her.

"No, Mrs. Williamson."

Many years of experience had taught the principal not to accept denials at face value. "Come and see me later, Laura."

Laura was dismayed. "But there's nothing wrong—"

"Four o'clock in my study."

With a rustle of her black cloak, she was gone.

Laura knew that one of them would see her. She went to the study as close to four o'clock as possible without being late, so that she would not have to sit outside, but as luck would have it, Mrs. Williamson looked around the door at one minute past the hour to let Laura know she was running behind schedule, and so Laura would have to wait just a little longer.

Priscilla Carling walked by, three minutes later, carrying a pile of books. Seeing Laura sitting on the wooden bench, she stopped and stared at her. Laura felt as if she were looking right through her, and she knew that it was only a matter of time before Lucia, too, knew.

Hardly aware that she was doing so, Laura laid her right hand on her leg, over her cotton dress. She had strapped the knife to her thigh, unwilling to risk the possibility of it falling out of her pocket in front of the principal. Feeling it there, safe and solid, she looked back at Priscilla.

I dare you, she thought.

The door to her right opened. Priscilla walked on.

Laura had made up her mind. With only a few days to go before half term, when she was due to fly home for one week's holiday, she felt she was hanging on by her fingertips. Nothing had happened since Priscilla had seen her outside Mrs. Williamson's study; nothing, at least, except for any number of cool, penetrating stares from Lucia Lindberg's doll eyes. Laura still hugged her secret weapon close, still drew on its strength, but fear was a strong master. Nothing had happened, no one had cornered her or threatened her, and none of Lucia's gang had even spoken a word to her, yet still the fear blossomed and grew. She reasoned with herself: they hadn't dared touch her after she had seen the headmistress, for anything that happened to her now might be laid at their door. But then again, Laura realized, the more days that passed without any of them being summoned to Mrs. Williamson's study, the more confident they could be that Laura had not, after all, reported them. Which meant that she was still at their mercy.

So she had made up her mind. She would keep silent until she had been driven out of the school grounds, until after she had been carried by the Olympic Airways jet away from England, until after she found herself snug in her grandfather's embrace at Hellenikon airport. Until she had been reunited with Adam and Maria and the animals, and was safe at home in Chryssos. And then she would talk, would tell her grandfather everything, all about Lucia and Priscilla and Abigail and Gerry and Freddy, and he wouldn't let her come back to Osborne College, wouldn't let her leave Aegina again, and then it would all be over, and she would be safe. Truly safe.

Only a few days to go, but the fear never left her. In the classrooms at least, under the teachers' gaze, she knew they could not physically harm her, yet still she sat rigid and unable to concentrate. In the building itself, and outside, on the playing fields, in the gardens, on the tennis courts, she moved tensely, constantly wary of sudden attack. She never went to the cloakroom or to the bathroom unless another girl, not one of Lucia's own, was going too, and at night, in the dormitory, she lay sleepless, watching shapes in the dark and listening, for the rustling of sheets, for the padding of bare feet, for the sound of her tormentors' breathing anywhere near her.

Nothing happened.

* * *

They went, en masse, on the day trip. The whole junior school, in a noisy, excitable gaggle of buses, discipline relaxed a little as a concession to the fact that they would be breaking up the next morning. They were to travel northwest to visit the Westbury White Horse—one of seven ancient horses cut into the Wiltshire chalk downs—where they would walk and picnic before moving on to see two more horses at Cherhill and Pewsey; and then they would return to Osborne for supper and packing and the special evening assembly to which they were traditionally summoned before every full or half-term holiday.

The prized seats were in the rear of the buses, the full-width seat at the very back and those directly in front, all well away from supervising eyes and with the added benefits of the big rear window and a good view of everyone else in the bus. In one of the Alderley Tower buses, Lucia had taken up two spaces, a two-pound box of Milk Tray and a small pile of magazines beside her—*Honey* and *Screenplay,* with a few illicit articles from *Cosmopolitan* tucked between their pages—and her faithful acolytes surrounding her. Laura sat right at the front, Anna de Vere, neither friend nor foe, beside her.

Anna spoke to her little, craning her head to chat to Susan Frost, a girl from Abigail Butcher's dormitory. Anna and Susan had hoped to sit together, but Miss McLean had seen Laura sitting alone and had, with her PE briskness, made Anna move forward into what she considered the best row in the bus.

"Have you seen any of the white horses before?" Laura asked Anna.

"No," Anna said, bored.

"I saw one from the train, at the beginning of term."

"I don't travel by train," Anna said. "The chauffeur drives me."

"The one at Westbury's very old, you know."

"Who cares?"

Laura gave up, and gazed out of the window at the English countryside, content because Lucia was too far away to torment her, at least until they arrived at their destination. In any case, she decided, she might as well make the most of the lovely landscape since by the following evening she would have left it all behind, she hoped, forever.

Miss Thorpe, who had traveled in the other Alderley bus, lectured them at the start of their walk near Bratton. "No one is to go off on their own," she said, her voice booming. "It's easier than you realize to get lost in unfamiliar territory, and for goodness' sake, treat the escarpment with respect and keep away from the edge." She paused. "Blazers are to be worn, not to be used as blankets. When you have finished your picnic, make sure that you pack up all your rubbish."

"Remember the country code," Miss McLean interjected.

"Exactly," Miss Thorpe echoed. "And most important, remember that you are representatives of Osborne College. Any unruly behavior reflects on your school—"

"And on our parents," Lucia Lindberg finished for her.

"Well said, Lucia." Miss Thorpe flashed her teeth. "Now come along, girls. Best feet forward, and let's enjoy ourselves."

In the beginning it was easy for Laura to stay close to the main body of girls, to try to make herself invisible, just one of the crowd. Lucia and the other four, the monstrous sisterhood, walked together chattering idly, giggling from time to time. None of them ever seemed even to glance in her direction, yet Laura couldn't rid herself of the sensation that they knew precisely where she was and what she was doing, even thinking, every step of the way.

As the large group began to break up into smaller clusters, Laura attached herself to Anna de Vere and Susan Frost who had themselves joined up with three girls from Banbury Tower.

"Who's this?" One of the other girls looked at Laura.

"No one," Anna said.

"I'm Laura Andros." Normally Laura would have taken the snub and melted away, but she wanted, more than anything, to cling to this safe group.

"Why don't you go and join your pals?" Anna said, not too unkindly.

Laura gritted her teeth, hating herself. "I'd rather stay with you."

"Well, we're very sorry," one of the Banbury girls told her briskly, "but we want to talk, so you can't."

"Buzz off," another girl said.

They walked on. Laura stood still, alone. She did not dare to turn around. The sense that she was being watched, that they were there, behind her, was very acute.

"Now then, what's this?"

The voice made her jump. Miss Thorpe was red-cheeked from fresh air and walking. "All alone? That won't do."

Laura stared at her. Suddenly the housemistress seemed her savior. She would stay with her, walk with her, hang on her every word if she had to.

"Don't gawp, Laura. Run along and catch up with the others—you don't want to spend your day with me, do you?"

"I don't mind, Miss Thorpe." No prospect had ever seemed sweeter.

"Nonsense."

"Really, I'd like to stay with you."

Miss Thorpe bared her big teeth briefly. "Don't be silly, dear. Ah," she said, looking back, "here come the others—now you'll be all right. Hello, girls—here's a lost lamb for your flock, all right?"

"Fine, Miss Thorpe," Priscilla said.

"Of course, Miss Thorpe," Lucia said. "We'll look after her."

"Good show," Miss Thorpe said, and patted Laura's arm. "Off you go then, dear, and try to have fun."

Laura could hardly believe it. The Wiltshire hills were thronged with Osborne girls in their navy blazers and pink dresses, and yet the fates had been cruel enough to deliver her straight into the open arms of her enemies. It was a nightmare.

"How splendid," Lucia said.

"Lucia's been hoping for a word with you," Abigail said.

Freddy kept silent, and Gerry laughed.

"Why can't you leave me alone?" Laura asked Lucia, her hatred undisguised.

"Because Miss Thorpe asked us to look after you." Lucia looked at the others. "You all heard her, didn't you?"

"Sure did," Priscilla said.

"Didn't you hear Miss Thorpe, Laura?" Abigail asked.

"Maybe she didn't understand," Lucia said.

"Her English isn't that bad," Priscilla grinned.

"No," Lucia agreed, "it *izzent*."

Laura began to walk away. They walked with her, two on either side of her, one behind her. She walked faster, her eyes on the turf, refusing to look at them. The sound of their lace-up shoes tramping on the ground echoed in her ears, vibrated through her. They walked on and on, and Laura had no sense of where they were going, and it did not seem to matter.

"She's trying to pretend we're not here," Abigail said.

"Rather rude, don't you think, Lucia?" Priscilla asked.

"Maybe all Greeks are rude," Lucia said.

Laura stopped. She remembered, suddenly, her grandfather's words on her last evening on the island. *There may be some who may try to hurt you,* he had told her. *It's wisest to walk away, but if that's not possible, you may have to stay and fight.*

She took a breath. "For your information," she said, her voice loud and clear, "the Greek people were already going to the theater when you barbarians were still painting your faces with woad."

Lucia stood very still, staring at her.

Laura knew that it was madness. Her legs trembled and her heart pounded, but it was as if all the weeks of fear and misery and cowardice had rolled up suddenly into an internal ball of bravado.

"We invented democracy," she said, Jonathan Payne's teachings flowing back into her mind. "We gave you the seeds of the Renaissance when you were just ignorant savages."

None of them spoke. Laura felt their shock, their outrage.

"How dare you?" Lucia's voice was hushed. Her face was pale except for two small red spots of anger high on both cheeks, and her blue eyes glittered. "How *dare* you?"

Slowly, smoothly, silently, Gerry and Freddy, Abigail and

Priscilla moved, surrounding Laura. The fiery ball of courage disintegrated. Laura licked her dry lips.

"You made me," she said, quietly.

Lucia raised a golden eyebrow. "We made you?"

"If you would just leave me in *peace*—"

"She wants us to leave her in piss," Gerry mocked.

"Don't be crude, Gerry," Abigail said, "or little Miss Andrex will have some more to say about us."

"It isn't funny, Abby," Lucia said, tightly.

"I know."

Lucia stepped one pace closer to Laura. "It wasn't funny either, you going to see Willy."

Laura swallowed. "That had nothing to do with you."

"I'm sure."

"It's the truth."

"I saw you," Priscilla said. "Waiting to go into Willy's study. I knew why you were there, and you knew I knew."

Laura shook her head. "She asked to see me. I didn't want to."

"And what did you talk about?" Lucia asked.

"Nothing."

"You don't honestly expect us to believe that," Freddy said.

"It's true." Laura looked at their faces, all of them coming closer, surrounding her, and began to panic. "Mrs. Williamson saw me that morning and thought something was wrong with me, and I said there wasn't, but she didn't believe me, and she told me to come to her study, so I had to, but that was all." She could hardly breathe. "I didn't tell her anything," she said urgently. "I could have, but I didn't."

Lucia looked around. "Do you believe her?"

"No," Abigail said.

"Cilla?"

"Of course not."

"I don't know," Freddy said. "I mean, surely if she had told Willy, we'd have been called in, wouldn't we?"

"Not if Willy didn't believe her story," Gerry said.

"There wasn't any story," Laura said, panic mounting. "She kept asking me what was troubling me, and I just said everything was fine."

Lucia's doll eyes were colder than ever. "We don't believe you."

"No," Priscilla echoed.

"So I think we're going to have to punish you, don't you agree, girls?"

"Absolutely," Abigail agreed.

"Now, or later?" Lucia asked.

"We can't let her get away," Gerry said. "She'll only blab again."

"I *won't*!"

"Shut up," Lucia said.

Freddy looked worried. "We can't do anything out in the open."

"There's no one close enough to see," Priscilla said. "Don't be wet, Freddy."

"I just don't think it's worth getting ourselves into a jam, that's all."

"We won't," Priscilla assured her.

"But I didn't *tell*!" Laura heard the terror in her own voice. "Please, just let me go and you'll be rid of me—I'm going home, and I'm never coming back again, so you won't have to worry about me telling anyone."

"You have to be punished," Lucia said. "All the more reason, if you're leaving, to do it now."

Until that instant, Laura had not registered exactly where they were standing. She'd seen only their faces, looming at her, hadn't realized that the rest of the girls had vanished, had all gone ahead, passed them by, had craned their heads to see what they could of the great white horse beneath them, and had moved on, thinking of their picnic lunches.

She had felt alone when they had trapped her in the bathroom in Alderley Tower, and when Abigail had punched her in the vegetable garden and Lucia had threatened her.

I'll go to Mrs. Williamson, she'd said then in terror.

If you do that, Lucia had answered, *you'll have an accident.*

Laura stared past Lucia now, through the gap between her left arm and Priscilla's right, and she saw that they were almost at the edge of the escarpment. A cement works lay below in the valley, an ugly blot with a tall white chimney blowing smoke, but above and beyond, softly rolling into haze, the counties of Wiltshire, Somerset and Avon spread up into the horizon, softest greens rising into the gentle English spring blue.

She looked back at their faces. All unsmiling except Priscilla, whose lips turned up a little at the corners. She might almost be a cat, waiting to be fed, quietly anticipating. Abigail looked hard and uncompromising. Freddy's eyes would not meet hers.

And then there was Lucia.

The doll eyes blinked, just once.

"Right, girls," Lucia said, and suddenly her voice and face were filled with excitement. "Let's do it."

It happened in slow motion. Laura saw them move, almost but not quite together, for this had not been preplanned and they were watching Lucia, taking her lead. And Laura knew that this was it, knew that they were going to take her, to grasp her by the arms and cover her mouth, and that they were going to throw her over the edge—

Her hand moved swiftly, down to the hem of her dress, pushing it up, feeling for the knife, and it was there, as she had known, strapped securely—too securely, for the sticky tape held it too tightly for an instant, fighting her—but then she had it, and while they were still moving, their arms coming for her, she was unfolding the blade—and it was easy, easy, for hadn't she practiced, in the privacy of the lavatory, over and over again?

"My God, she's got a knife!"

Laura heard Priscilla's shocked voice, heard Gerry's gasp, but she was focused now, hadn't known it was possible to be so entirely, perfectly concentrated on anything or on anyone as she was now, at this moment, on Lucia Lindberg—on her face, on her mouth, a little open, on those eyes that she hated so much, so *much*.

"Get it," Abigail hissed.

Priscilla made a dive for her, and Laura ducked and swung with her right hand, and Priscilla jumped clear. "You're mad!" she shrieked, but her eyes were frightened, and Laura experienced a tiny triumph—and then Gerry, tougher, sturdier than the others, had her from behind, one strong arm around her, holding her left arm and gripping her about the chest.

"Grab her, Lucia!" Abigail shouted, keeping watch.

Lucia's eyes were narrowing, and her face was very white, and her mouth closed, lips clamped tightly now with anger, and Laura saw her coming closer, felt her force even before she touched her, and the knife was clenched in her right hand, and she knew that nothing, no one would make her let it go—

"Give it to me." Lucia stared into her eyes. "Give it to me, you little cow." She held out her hand. "Hold her, Gerry—get her over to the edge."

Laura felt the strong girl's grip tightening, felt herself being propelled forward, and she began to scream then, to scream as loudly and wildly as she could—

And then Lucia came at her, charged at her, and Laura felt all the terror and all the injustice and rage surging through her, and she brought her right arm forward, and at the instant when Lucia's body struck the knife, the impact jarred right through her, jolting her elbow, startling, shocking her. And she tried to drop the knife then, let go of it, but it did not fall to the ground, just stayed where it was, stuck into the left side of Lucia's stomach, and for one more moment there was no blood—it looked like a fake rubber knife from a child's magic set. But then, suddenly, with terrible, horrifying force, the blood surged, and Laura tore her eyes from the knife up to Lucia's face, and she saw the hated eyes widening, glazing—and then Lucia was toppling, backward, and Laura realized that the other girls were all screaming, Priscilla and Abigail, and Gerry and Freddy, screaming and screaming their horror and terror, as their beloved Lucia, their leader, fell over the edge of the escarpment and disappeared from sight.

They stopped screaming.

"You've killed her," Gerry said, and her voice was strange and thick.

"My God, Laura, I think you really have," Freddy said, looking awestruck.

"She's killed Lucia." Priscilla's voice rose shrilly.

Laura stared at them, unseeing.

"I didn't tell," she whispered. "I didn't."

She felt a rush of air, gradually heard the movement and the voices, saw out of the corner of her right eye the surge of blue and pink as the girls came running, heard the sounds of excitement and confusion, and of hysterical weeping and of adult voices, teachers' voices, giving orders, sending for help, demanding answers to questions.

No one came near her. No one touched her or spoke to her.

Laura stepped closer to the edge and looked down. Lucia's fall had been halted by trees some way below the belly of the horse. She lay on her stomach, one arm sprawled out, the other folded beneath her, hidden. Her golden hair shone in the sunlight. She did not move. Laura knew that she was dead.

And the mass of blue blazers and pink dresses backed away again, shepherded to safety by Miss Thorpe and Miss McLean. Away from the edge, away from danger, from Laura.

Away from the murderess.

CHAPTER 5

Augusta Pietrowski's childhood had ended on her ninth birthday. It had never been much, as childhood went, but on the day Augusta turned nine, her mother, Alice, received a letter from the hospital confirming that she had breast cancer. Alice had not intended her daughter to know, but right in the middle of the special birthday tea Alice had prepared for Augusta and three of her friends from school, Pavel Pietrowski had come home early.

They had thought they were safe that afternoon. It was a Friday, and Pavel always spent Friday afternoons at the bookies, blowing all the money he'd been paid for his window cleaning job—all that was left, that was, after he'd been to the Crown and Sceptre. Alice had stopped expecting to see any of Pavel's money years before. She held down three jobs, one as a cleaner at a factory near Bristol Bridge, one as a waitress in a Fishponds café and the third, her favorite, as a cloakroom attendant at the Empress restaurant near the Theatre Royal. She could only work the lunch shift there, because she didn't dare leave Augusta with Pavel in the evenings, but even in the middle of the day the people were so glamorous, their clothes so beautiful and their scents, that just being close to them lifted her spirits, made having to leave the elegant heart of Bristol and go home to Eastville and her drunken, endlessly disappointing husband a little more bearable.

On Augusta's ninth birthday, Alice had prepared so meticulously, trying, as she had done every day since she had first noticed it, to forget the lump, to forget the biopsy, to forget Pavel. She cleaned their small basement flat until the surfaces gleamed with her polishing, and she pinned her hair up into a French pleat, her favorite hairstyle, and she and Augusta worked for a long time straightening her daughter's wildly curling hair with a dryer. She had saved for weeks to buy a present, and to be able to pay for a cake and ice cream and party hats—it would have been cheaper and nicer to have baked the birthday cake herself, but Pavel might have asked questions, tried to spoil it, maybe even put a stop to it.

At least on a Friday afternoon, Alice had calculated, with Pavel safely ensconced in the betting shop for better or worse, she could be reasonably sure that the children would be gone before he got home. But whether the cash had run out more quickly than usual, or whether he had simply spent every last penny on beer, Pavel arrived on that particular Friday afternoon at two minutes past four o'clock, just after the girls had sat down at the table.

"What's this?"

Alice saw how drunk he was. There were three stages to Pavel's drunkenness: the first, belligerent; the second, enraged; the third and easiest by far to cope with, falling down. This afternoon, he was at stage two. His thinning fair hair was disheveled and his blue eyes were red and bleary. Alice, her heart sinking, placed herself between him and the table.

"It's just a little party, Pavel, for Augusta's birthday."

"Get them out." His speech, heavily accented, was very slurred. The children stared.

"They've only just started their tea. They won't be long."

"I want them out now."

"I didn't expect you so early." Alice tried to take his arm, gently, to divert him from the children, but he shook her off. "Usually you stay out later on a Friday."

"What does that mean?"

"Nothing," she said, carefully. "Just what I said."

The red eyes narrowed into nasty slits. "What do you usually do on Fridays then?"

"Nothing special."

"Maybe you got a boyfriend."

The girls at the table shifted uncomfortably. Augusta stared miserably down at the red foil cracker by her plate. She hated her father. She could not recall a time when she had not hated him.

"Keep your voice down, Pavel, please."

"You telling me what to do, whore?"

"I'm not a whore," Alice said quietly. "You're drunk, and there are young girls present."

"Present?" Pavel sneered. "Can't just say *here* like anyone else."

"Dad, please," Augusta said.

Pavel did not even look at her. "What you want?"

"Can't we just finish our tea?" Augusta's voice, like her mother's, was gentle West Country.

"Where it all come from, that's what I want to know?" His voice grew louder. "All the fancy food cost money—money I work for."

"I paid for it, Pavel," Alice said, her wide gray eyes calm. "I earned every penny."

"What's yours is mine, I thought."

"Augusta is your daughter, too."

"Maybe."

Alice said nothing, just moved closer to the table, stood behind Augusta's chair. It had been a mistake thinking they could have something as normal as a birthday party in this place. She wished the children could go now, before he got worse, but she couldn't just turn them out into the street, when their parents might not even be home yet.

"How many time I have to say it?" His face was growing redder, his nose most of all. His nose was like a warning indicator of the level of his rage—the more fiery it grew, the greater the force of the explosion when it came. "I want these children out from my table, *now*!"

His fist thumped the wall, and the children jumped. One stood up.

"I want to go," she said.

The two others followed her lead. Augusta sat still, too ashamed to speak.

"You didn't have coats or jackets, did you, girls?" Alice asked. It was a hot day. She remembered that she had bought three sets of marker pens in brightly colored plastic holders as going-home presents, but she wasn't sure if she dared to find them now. She went to the front door and opened it. "I'm very sorry. Be careful getting home, won't you."

"We will," one of them said. "Thank you for having us." None of them ever called her Mrs. Pietrowski because they couldn't pronounce it.

"Thank you for coming," Alice said.

She shut the door behind them. She couldn't worry about them getting home safely. More than likely, they were far better off out there on the bright, sunny street than here, with Pavel.

Augusta still sat at the table, saying nothing. Her father walked over to the sideboard, swaying. He picked up the envelope from behind the electric clock. Alice turned from the door and saw him.

"That's mine, Pavel."

"What they want?"

"Nothing much. It's not important." She went over to him and held out her hand. "Please give it to me."

"If it's not important, why you want it?"

"I just want to put it away, that's all."

He opened the envelope and took out the letter. Augusta watched Alice put one hand out to the wall, to support herself. Her mother's face was very white. It was only one page, but he read for a long time.

"Malignant," he said.

"Not now, Pavel," Alice said, softly. "We can talk about it later."

"You got cancer?"

Alice did not speak.

Pavel put the letter back on the sideboard and looked at his wife, at her face first, and then down at her chest. "They going to cut it off?"

"Maybe," Alice whispered.

"Which one is it?"

Alice put up her right hand and touched her left breast. "This one." She watched his face.

"You were pretty once," Pavel said. "Not anymore."

"Thank you." Alice flushed.

"Now you going to be grotesque."

At last, Augusta stood up. "Mum's very pretty," she said.

"Shut up," Pavel said. He looked up from Alice's breasts to her face. "You going to die?"

"No!" Augusta ran to her mother's side.

"I don't know," Alice said

"When they going to cut it off?"

"I don't know," she said again. "They may not."

"Your boyfriend won't want to look at you anymore."

"I don't have a boyfriend."

"Your Friday man." Pavel grinned. His teeth were bad, and his breath smelled. Augusta couldn't bear it when her father came near her.

"Is that all you have to say to me?" Alice asked, her voice still soft.

The grin disappeared. "What you want me to say? How sorry I am? How I will miss you when you die?"

"Mum isn't going to die!"

"I told you shut up!" The nose became redder. "Clear the table."

Augusta stayed close to her mother.

"You do what I *tell* you."

"Not if you're going to be so mean to Mum."

Pavel hit Augusta on the side of her head. She staggered a little, but did not fall. Alice put both her arms around her.

"You're a swine," she said. "I wish to God I'd never married you."

"You want I teach you, too?" He stepped threateningly closer. "You want I kill you, before the cancer?"

Augusta buried her face in her mother's blouse. She'd heard it all before, the threats and the sound of blows raining down on her mother, the slaps against her cheeks, the punches to her eyes, to her ears, to her body. She longed to run away, but she couldn't leave her mother now, and Alice was just standing there, very still, as if she was rooted to the ground and could not run.

"You strike me now, Pavel Pietrowski," she heard her mother say, "and at least I'll know, when I'm dead and gone,

that you'll never be joining me, that you'll be burning in hell
for all eternity."

Augusta heard the bellow, felt her hair fan out with the
speed of his arm, swinging over her head. She heard the
punch, felt her mother stumble, held onto her, heard and felt
the first sobs beginning to rise, and still she held on, thinking that he would not kill them both, not together. And then
she heard the door, opening, closing. And she opened her
eyes.

That was all it had taken, really, to end her childhood. He'd
done worse, much worse, to both of them, especially to Alice. But somehow, it was the combination of things that afternoon that had destroyed it for Augusta—the ruining of her
birthday and the humiliation before her friends; the news of
her mother's cancer; her father's savage inhumanity. She had
known, there and then, while she and Alice still clutched
each other, still reeling from his last blow, that it would
never get better. And it had not.

Alice's surgery had been radical, followed by weeks of ra-
diotherapy, with side effects that had depressed and drained
her, making life at home with Pavel even more difficult. Augusta had begun taking off from school early during that
time, and when Alice discovered a second lump and when
the long, last period of her terminal illness had begun, Augusta became a regular truant. She had to help her mother,
there was never a shred of doubt in her mind about that, and
she had to protect her against Pavel as well as she could.

The easiest way to provide that help and protection was
by stealing. With Alice no longer able to work, there was
hardly any money, and Pavel never considered that he might
try increasing his own workload. If there was no food on the
table when he chose to come home from the pub, he was not
above hitting his wife, even when he could see how ill she
was, how pitifully thin she had become. Her sickness disgusted him. He told her she was a hideous bag of bones, he
told her that she smelled, he told her that he looked forward
to the day when she would be dead and gone. If Augusta had
hated him in the past, there were no words to describe what
she felt about him now. He deserved to be killed, but it

never occurred to her to try to kill him because she realized that then they would lock her up, and her mother would be irrevocably lost. And so instead she did all that she could, by stealing.

It was just pilfering in the beginning. Food, mainly, the easiest items to lift from supermarket shelves, the odd apple or plum from barrows, chocolate bars from Woolworth's or corner shops—Alice had always loved chocolate, and even now it seemed to raise her spirits a little. Making her mother feel just that little bit better was the most important thing in Augusta's life, and so she stole magazines for escapism, and books—though after a time even paperback books were too heavy for her mother to lift—and even perfume. The only thieving she despised herself for was when she stole for her father, but as long as Alice had earned money, she had always bought cigarettes and beer for Pavel. It was insanity, in a way, to go and out and risk arrest just to provide him with the very thing that made him even more bestial, but Augusta felt she had no choice. It was either that, or taking the chance of him beating her mother or herself. She could cope with the odd black eye, but it would distress Alice terribly, and Alice already suffered enough.

In the beginning, Alice did not realize that Augusta stole. She told her mother that she was delivering newspapers in the mornings and that she had a Saturday job, and that was how she managed, but after a while, Alice began to understand what her daughter was doing. At first, she pretended not to know, horribly aware that everything Augusta did was for her, but toward the end, as she grew weaker and the pain grew worse, she tried to speak to her.

"It's too dangerous," she said, and her voice was little more than a whisper. "It isn't worth you wrecking your whole life."

"I won't wreck it," Augusta murmured soothingly. "I'm always very careful, Mum."

"But one of these days they'll realize, and they'll wait for you," Alice fretted. "I couldn't bear it if they punished you—they wouldn't understand that you only do it for me."

"I always go to different places, Mum—nothing's going to happen."

Alice felt for Augusta's hand. "You have to stop it now, my darling. It doesn't matter to me anymore what he thinks, what he does. He can't hurt me anymore."

"Because I won't let him."

"It'll be better when I'm gone."

"Don't talk like that, Mum."

Alice squeezed her hand more tightly. "It's all right, my love. I want to talk about it—we need to be honest. And I really think it's just me he hates so much. When the time comes, and you're all he has left, it will be better for both of you."

"It could never be better for me without you, Mum." Augusta held back her tears, knowing they would cause her mother extra pain, but the loathing for her father was like a red-hot poker in her chest.

"You'll see," Alice whispered. "He may surprise you."

He surprised her, all right. Two nights after Alice died, the evening before her funeral. He had gone to the pub at six o'clock, and at about eight, Augusta had gone to her room, ready to switch out her light as soon as she heard the front door. He'd come back shortly after ten, and she had turned off the lamp and pulled the covers up, prepared to feign sleep in case he looked in, as he sometimes did.

She heard her door open and lay perfectly still, her eyes closed.

"Gussie," she heard him whisper. He only called her that when his mood was abnormally good. She did not move.

He came closer. She thought perhaps he might have removed his shoes because his tread was so silent, but she could smell the stench of him, the beery, nauseating smell she knew so well.

"Gussie, let me in," he whispered. "I need you, little one."

The horror of it sent her brain reeling. It was an agony of self-control not to jump up and scream her disgust at him, but she just lay still and prayed to a God that she did not believe in to send him away.

"I'm so alone, Gussie." She thought he must be kneeling

beside her, for suddenly his voice and his stinking breath were on the same level as her face, and she thought she would gag with revulsion.

And then he touched her. Not the clenched or open violent hand that she had grown almost accustomed to over the years, but a softer, gentler hand that reached for the sheet that covered her and drew it back a little, that began to unbutton her pajama top.

Augusta lay still for one more second, and then she opened her eyes.

"If you ever, ever touch me again," she said, and her voice in the darkness was very loud and clear, "I swear to you I will kill you."

The hand went away. Augusta sat up and switched on the light.

Pavel was kneeling beside the bed, and he was naked. He looked, she thought, old and ugly and ridiculous. She stared down at him, at his hideous, erect penis. She had never seen a man naked before, except for some pictures in a magazine. It was the most revolting thing she had ever seen.

"If I didn't mind being sent to prison," she said, and her voice shook just a little, "I would kill you tonight." She took a deep breath. "Even if you were to beat me now, it would not be long until you fell asleep, and then I would do it. For my mother."

"I'm not going to beat you, Gussie," he said, and she had never heard him sound that way. He sounded humble. It was a strange, unfamiliar sound, and she remembered what her mother had said about him hating only her.

"Get out of my room, Pavel," she said, for she knew that she would never call him her father again. "And get some sleep. I'll wake you in time in the morning." She paused. "It's my mother's funeral tomorrow, in case you've forgotten."

"I haven't forgotten."

"Then get out."

Augusta paid for the funeral herself, for Pavel had no savings at all, and Alice, having had no vanity or expectations, had set nothing aside for the purpose. Augusta, knowing that the time was near, had broken her first shop window just five days before her mother's death, stealing a suitcase full of radios, cassette players and hair dryers. It had been her first experience of trying to find a fence, and she had been well and truly cheated, but together with what she had struggled to put away over the months it had been enough, at least, for a simple but dignified service.

She left home that evening. Pavel had gone straight to the pub after the funeral, had slept some of it off during the afternoon, and had then gone back again. Augusta was prepared. She had stolen a rucksack two weeks earlier, and a Thermos flask, and now she took the few clothes that she would need, all the photographs of herself and Alice that she could find in the house, and her mother's favorite gray chiffon scarf, the one that had matched her lovely eyes, and she filled the flask with hot Heinz vegetable soup and took every single crumb of food that was left in the fridge, so that he would have nothing that night, and nothing the next morning.

She left him a note, propped up on the kitchen table, that said: *She said you would go to hell. I hope it's soon.* She took one more look around, remembered all the times that Alice had protected her and cherished her and done her best for her. And then she went.

She was on the street most of the time, around crowds in the daytime, sleeping in doorways, keeping well covered up, partly for warmth, partly so that no one would see how young she was. She slept little, always on the alert, determined not to be picked up and taken back. It was hard, it was cold and wet and frightening most of the time, but it was worth it to be free of him. She knew she might be safer leaving the area, maybe heading to London, but she had lived in Bristol all her life, and her mother had always told her that the devil she knew was better than the unknown. She spent some time around Avonmouth Docks, pinching things, getting to know people. There were regulars, faces she grew to trust, who liked seeing her, seemed to like taking care of her because she was so young; and there were those who might look okay, but who were like weasels inside, who wanted to use her, who reminded her of Pavel, but she was fast as well as small, and if there were men she might not have outrun on a straight road, she could twist and turn and get into nooks and crannies that grown men couldn't even attempt.

She learned a lot, more than she'd ever learned at school. She moved in, for a while, with a group of older girls, living in a squat. Three of them were ex-borstal and harder than anyone Augusta had ever met, but the others weren't bad at all. They didn't ask a lot of questions about where she was from, they knew about life, and about fathers from hell. They seemed to enjoy having her around, treated her like a mascot. They taught her basics, like how to break into cigarette machines and the things not to steal, or at least not to sell, and she earned her keep by going with them on jobs and either standing watch, or distracting potential victims while they picked their pockets or snatched their bags, or sometimes crawling into tiny windows that they couldn't manage and then letting the others in to houses or flats or shops. She didn't much like taking from homes, especially when they reminded her of Alice, and how much she would have hated this, but she knew she was in no position to be choosy. She was lucky to be off the street, lucky to have the big girls to look after her. It didn't last, of course. The first time they all had to move, they took her along to their new place, but not long after they were kicked out again, and this time they all agreed that Augusta was too much of a liability.

The police picked her up for the first time almost six months after she'd left Pavel. She wouldn't talk at all, wouldn't even tell them her name, and they took her to a children's home, and it wasn't bad at all having a bed again, and a bath, and hot meals and lessons; but one rainy evening, when she was feeling really snug and happy not to be outside, she forgot about being careful, and once they had her name, it was just a matter of time before they found him.

He was sober when he came to get her from the home. For a moment, she wasn't even sure it was him, because he looked so clean and tidy in a dark suit, and his nose was hardly pink, and when he came close to her, he didn't even smell of beer.

"Hello, Gussie," he said, and his eyes were quite emotional.

"Say hello to your father," one of the women nudged her, but she didn't say a single word.

"I been worried sick about you," he said, and he tried to put an arm around her, but she pushed him away and he didn't try again. "You come home with me now, where you belong."

"You're a lucky girl," the woman told her.

He pretended to be glad that she was home, but she didn't believe him. She knew he'd reported her missing to the police, but she guessed he hadn't bothered too much after that. Still, she supposed it was probably better for him, having her there to cook and clean for him, and for the first three weeks after she got home he saw that she went to school, and even came to fetch her in the afternoons, and when he went to the Crown and Sceptre in the evenings, he locked her into her bedroom, and she didn't really mind, because at least he was out of the flat.

When the novelty wore off and he stopped watching her all the time, she realized that she could go again if she wanted to, but she thought she'd stay this time, at least until she'd made some sort of plan. All sorts of mad schemes passed through her mind, even going to the docks and stowing away on a ship, but she'd seen enough to know that she was too young to get away with anything for long. It wasn't too bad now. She'd repeated her threat once, soon after he'd brought her home, told him that she'd kill him if he ever tried to touch her again, and she could see that he believed her. He still hit her when he was either very drunk, or if he hadn't had enough money to get drunk enough, but she was used to that. If her hatred had not been quite so deep, if she hadn't been so determined to stay loyal to Alice, she might almost have been glad to be back with the devil she knew. But it was only a matter of time before she had her plan properly worked out, and then she'd be off again and there'd be no stopping her.

* * *

He surprised her for the second time in her life, fifteen months after he'd got her back, and it was a better kind of surprise than the time he'd tried to sleep with her. It was a Friday afternoon. He'd gone to the pub at lunchtime, then on to the bookies for an afternoon's betting, and he'd won twice. They told her later that he'd gone back to the Crown and Sceptre to celebrate, and that he'd been in such a rare good mood that he even ordered a round for some of the other regulars. He hadn't got around to paying, though, because he'd dropped dead in the middle of picking up the first pints off the bar, and the others had had to pay for their own drinks after all.

This time, the children's home drove Augusta nuts. They were so soft there, so *wet*. Almost from the beginning, she wanted to get away. She was twelve that summer, one month after she got there, but she felt so much older than all the other girls, so much more experienced. She had expected that not having to steal anymore would be a relief, but she found herself longing to carry on. She could hardly remember the early days, during her mother's illness, when she'd felt so guilty and scared whenever she'd steeled herself to pinch some fruit or some sausages or a magazine. Once she'd moved into the squat with the girls, crime had started giving her a buzz—she hadn't noticed it at the time, but now that she was deprived of it, she missed it badly.

She began with cigarettes. Some of the teachers smoked, and Augusta would sneak into the staff room and steal packs from their handbags or even pick their lockers. They caught her, and punished her, but that wasn't such a big deal compared with the things the borstal girls had described to her; some of the beatings they'd had had made even Pavel Pietrowski's bashings seem like child's play. She started taking money and other things she fancied: lipsticks, sunglasses, books, whatever caught her eye. They were allowed to go to the library once a week, and she couldn't use the lipsticks or the other things, but that wasn't really the point anymore. She was daring them to catch her at it. She wasn't sure why.

* * *

She was caught for shoplifting three times before the police took action. She used to climb out of her window at the home in the afternoons, after lessons were over, slide down a drainpipe and go to the local shopping center. She was pretty good at it by now, but they nabbed her in a record shop, in a newsagent's, and finally in a chemist's, where an assistant caught her stuffing perfume testers into her pockets. Maybe if she hadn't sworn at the girl, she wouldn't have called the police, and maybe if she hadn't thumped her and tried to get away, they wouldn't have pressed charges and taken her to the police station and put her in a cell until she cooled off. She was scared then, but she felt as if some kind of a demon had got inside her, and she almost liked the fear and so she went on making a nuisance of herself. She kicked a tray of food against the wall, and refused to clean it up. She yelled and cursed and banged on the door of her cell, and then later, when they came to let her out, she bit one of the officers on the hand.

The juvenile court put her into the care of the local authority, who moved her to a community home near Bath. Kane House was a tougher proposition altogether, though Augusta admitted later on that it wouldn't have been too bad a place if it hadn't been for the inmates. The staff were tough but fair, doing their best to get the kids to learn from their mistakes, but many of the kids, in for crimes ranging from theft to drug-pushing and assault, had other ideas.

They slept in dormitories, long, narrow rooms with hard, narrow beds, damp, thin blankets and pillows like boulders, but it wasn't the discomfort that bothered Augusta, it was the fact that every night after lights out, half the girls in the room got out of their own beds and into someone else's. She didn't give a fig what they all got up to, except that their noises kept her awake when she wanted to be dead to the world, but she was blowed if anyone was going to try to slide between her sheets, such as they were.

She'd thought she was hard before, but she realized then that she wasn't nearly hard enough. This was a new life altogether; it might not be the front line that the borstal girls had described, but she suspected she was nearing the outskirts of the battleground. She woke up one night to find one of the girls—it was too dark even to see who it was—getting on top of her. The punch she delivered was simply a reflex action, but it helped bring home her message.

"Anyone tries to fuck me again," she said, loudly enough for the whole dormitory to hear, "will get their sodding arm broken."

She never let anyone call her Augusta again. She cut her awful wiry hair very short, dyed it bright scarlet with some stuff she stole on one of the days she escaped from the home to go on a spree, and she became Gus, the hard case. Of course, there were others there who were harder, and the fights they had were almost legendary. Gus didn't enjoy the punch-ups and wrestling bouts, but they were necessary; she had to give better than she got. A girl broke her nose, but before they came to take her to the hospital, Gus smashed the other girl's front teeth—her nose could be fixed, but the other girl would never get her real teeth back again, which made Gus the winner. Being as near to the top as possible had nothing to do with ego in that place; it had everything to do with survival.

She knew there was something different about the new girl the first time she saw her in the playground. For starters, there was her fear. Gus had seen a lot of frightened kids in her time—even in the children's home, the youngest and weakest had been nervy, and in this place God only knew there was good reason to get scared. But this girl wasn't just terrified of the place, nor even of the people around her. She looked to Gus as though she was seriously petrified of her own shadow.

She stood in a corner, in the shade of one of the high stone walls that surrounded the playground. Her dress hung on her, making her look scrawny, and her face was very white and drawn. As Gus came closer, she saw that she was quite a pretty little thing with long, almost black hair and green, wide eyes, with just a touch of slant to them. She'd have to be careful in her dorm, Gus thought right away, or some of the others would be in like Flynn—though maybe she mightn't mind, maybe that might be the comfort she needed.

"New girl, right?"

The girl flinched.

"I'm not going to bite," Gus said.

"I'm sorry," the girl said.

"You've got an accent." Gus's own gentle West Country burr had deliberately been hardened through necessity.

"Yes," the girl said.

"Well, tell me then."

"What?"

"What is it? The accent?"

The girl shifted uneasily from one foot to the other.

"Greek," she said.

"Greek?" Gus was surprised. "You don't look Greek."

"Half," the girl said.

"Like me."

The girl's eyes widened. "You're Greek too?"

"Course not. I'm half Polish." Gus saw the fleeting flicker of hope vanish. "You got a name?"

"Laura."

"I'm Gus." She noted the surprise, somewhere behind the green eyes. "You think that's a weird name?"

"No." The fear grew stronger.

"Good."

And Gus turned her back.

She realized, with a little jolt, that she'd almost forgotten, for a few moments, that she was Gus, the hard case. There was something about this one that had made her feel quite gentle, almost protective. She hadn't felt that way about anyone since Alice. She'd better watch herself. You couldn't afford to go soft, not in a place like this.

She waited until she was at the far end of the concrete playground before half turning for another look. She could see her out of the corner of her eye, still in the same spot, close to the wall as she could get, as if she hoped she might blend right in, perhaps even disappear through it. Gus wondered what her story was. She'd get it out of her, later, and maybe, just maybe, she might give her a couple of tips about toughening up. You couldn't tell, but the kid might even get to be useful. That was the name of the game for Gus now—if she saw something she needed, or just fancied, she pinched it.

Christ, the kid looked scared.

CHAPTER 6

In the beginning, Laura talked to Gus because she was afraid not to. She had never met anyone like her before. She was less than a year older than Laura, but she might have been eighteen, or any age at all. Thirteen going on a hundred, Gus said once, in that dry way she had.

Gus was taller than Laura, thin as a rake with bony, square shoulders. Her hair, cut raggedly short because she would never let anyone else touch it, was very curly, almost frizzy, and, apart from its brown roots, bright scarlet. Her gray eyes were the only soft thing about her, though most of the time her aggressive expression sharpened them, too, to steel.

There were plenty of girls at Kane House Community Home who seemed more approachable than Gus, and certainly less daunting, but Laura sensed from the start that they weren't really interested in her. For reasons Laura could not comprehend, Gus was very interested. And if Gus ordered her to talk about herself and what she'd done to bring her to Kane House, Laura knew that she had no alternative but to obey. She was like a rabbit with a snake. Gus just had to fix her with one of her iron stares, and Laura was hypnotized into responding.

"Have you noticed the way most of them steer clear of you?" Gus asked Laura one day in the canteen. It was

braised liver and onions with dark Bisto gravy for lunch—
the whole house smelled of onions.

"Yes," Laura said.

"Do you know why?"

"They don't like me." Laura was accustomed to rejection.

"Like has nothing to do with it. They don't like anyone."

"Then why?"

"Respect," Gus said. She watched Laura's face. "It's true.
Partly because you're the only killer here." She saw the pale
cheeks flush. "But mostly because I let you spend time with
me."

"Why do you?" Laura asked softly.

Gus shrugged. "You're different. I don't mean special,
just different. You're not a user, like the rest of us—not yet
anyway." Her thin lips twisted in a small ironic smile. "And
I reckon you might come in useful one day."

"How?"

"Don't know yet."

In many ways, Laura's life at Kane House was much more
bearable than it had been at Osborne College. The girls were
infinitely more dangerous than Lucia's gang had ever
been—Laura understood that now, too late—but there was
an honesty about their violence, even—not that it made
much sense—about their dishonesty. No one at Kane pretended to be better than anyone else. Harder, certainly, more
wily, less vulnerable—they pretended to be all those things.
But they were all just kids, down on their luck. Most of
them had probably never had any luck in the first place.

Not like Laura. She'd had over eight years of luck. She'd
had Aegina, and Chryssos. She'd had her grandfather and
Adam and Maria and the animals, and Jonathan Payne, and
a life, a world that she'd loved. And freedom. She'd had her
share of luck.

And she had lost it.

It was too easy just calling it a nightmare. You couldn't call
the rest of your life a nightmare. It was just life, just the way
things went, the way things had of changing. At first, after
Lucia died, she had felt so enveloped by the nightmare, by

the terrifying blackness of it, that her old life, those eight good years, had seemed more dreamlike than the present.

She heard a girl at Kane saying one day that one could forget pain, that the brain blocked out the memory of really bad pain, but Laura didn't believe that. Nothing was ever going to stop her remembering the way it had been after Lucia had died. After she had killed Lucia.

It had been questions, mostly, in the beginning.

"Why did you do it, Laura? Do you know why you did it?"

"They were going throw me over the edge."

"Lucia was going to do that to you?"

"They all were."

"But you attacked Lucia, not the others."

"She was their leader. I didn't mean to kill her."

"But you stabbed her with a knife."

"Yes. No."

"No, you didn't stab her?"

"She was coming *at* me."

"And?"

"And she—she went into the knife."

"Try to stop crying, Laura. We're nearly finished now."

"I'm sorry."

"The other girls say that you deliberately stabbed Lucia, that they saw you swing your right arm into her. Aren't they telling the truth?"

"They were all round me—they wanted to push me *over*—"

"They all deny that, Laura."

"They're lying."

"And do you deny that you stabbed Lucia with the knife?"

"No. No, but I didn't mean to *do* it!"

"Just answer yes or no, please. Did you stab Lucia Lindberg?"

"Yes."

They all asked the same questions. Over and over and over again. Different people, men and women, in and out of uniform, most of them kind. But she knew that none of them understood, not even the woman who said she was going to

represent her in court. Even Laura did not really understand
what had happened. What she had done. What Lucia had
done to her. Her tormentor was dead, she knew that was
true, had known it when she had first looked over the edge
of the escarpment and seen her lying so still. She had
wished, more than once, that Lucia would die, and yet she
thought that she had not really wanted that; she had just
wanted to be allowed to leave Osborne and never come
back, never have to see any of them again.

They had driven her away that day, in the back of a car, to the
police station in Trowbridge. A solicitor had been called, and
the police surgeon, and they had taken away her clothes
and she had been examined for evidence of cuts or bruises,
and Laura, almost too shocked to speak, had told them what
she was able, and then they had charged her with murder, and
fingerprinted her and put her into a detention room, and for the
first time she had begun to cry. She wanted her *pappous*—she
sat huddled in a corner of the cell-like room and shut her eyes
and tried to imagine him coming into the police station and
making them let her out and taking her back with him to Aegina, but he never came.

   She had appeared in Juvenile Court and had been remanded into the care of the local authority until the time of
her trial in the Crown Court, and they had placed her in a
children's home near Melksham. The men and women in
charge of her had been kind, and there had been no bars on
the windows, but Laura felt that she was in prison, and could
not bear it.

   Helen Williamson came to visit her in the first week. She
looked so familiar in her tweed suit, with her gray hair so
neat and her blue eyes so concerned, so sympathetic, that
Laura burst into tears and Mrs. Williamson held her for a
few moments before they sat down on hard, straight-backed
chairs to talk.

   "Why didn't you tell me how bad things were, Laura?"
Mrs. Williamson asked.

   "I couldn't."

   "I asked you what was wrong with you—I knew something was the matter, but you wouldn't talk. Were you so afraid?"

"They said they would punish me if I told."

"Who said that?"

"She did."

"You mean Lucia?"

"She said I'd have an accident if I told."

Mrs. Williamson shook her head, and looked sad.

"I didn't mean to kill her."

"No. I'm sure you didn't."

The silence hung heavily for a moment.

"Where's my grandfather?" Laura asked the question that preyed most on her mind, and which no one else had answered. "Why hasn't he come for me?"

The headmistress took her hand, very gently. "I'm sorry to tell you your grandfather has been taken ill."

"Ill?" Laura felt terror clutch at her.

"He's had a heart attack. He's in hospital, in Athens."

Laura looked into Mrs. Williamson's eyes. "Will he get better?" she asked softly.

"I'm afraid I don't know. I'm told that he's very poorly, but stable. Do you understand what that means?"

"Yes." Laura understood. It meant that Pappous was not going to come for her. It meant she might never see him again.

"Are you all right, Laura? Are they treating you well?"

"Yes, thank you." Mrs. Williamson started to take her hand away, but Laura held onto her, for just another minute. "I didn't mean to do it," she said again, urgently. "Do you believe me?" More than anything, she needed someone to believe in her.

The headmistress's blue eyes were very bright.

"Of course I do."

When the case had come to Bristol Crown Court, Laura's defense lawyer, black-robed and wigged, claimed that she had wielded the knife in self-defense, that Laura had been carrying the weapon because she was terrified, not because she had wanted to harm Lucia Lindberg. That Lucia had collided with the knife blade, and that the police pathologist's report confirmed that had Lucia not fallen down the steep hill—thereby embedding the knife more deeply into her abdomen—she might, in fact, have survived the stabbing, and that this was, therefore, a case of manslaughter. The prosecution, however, claimed that since there was no question that Lucia would not have fallen had she not been stabbed, Laura was guilty of murder, having acted, by concealing the knife on her person, with malice aforethought.

The other girls in Lucia's gang denied Laura's story. They admitted they had teased her a little, in the way that all new girls were teased, that they had played a few tricks on her, and they all regretted that now, deeply, but no one had ever dreamed of hurting her in any way. Called as witnesses for the prosecution, Freddy told the court that Laura had once threatened to kill her, and Gerry said that Laura had acted nervily since her arrival at Osborne; and Priscilla agreed that Laura was highly strung and paranoid about Lucia, that she tended to blame others for her own carelessness, citing as an example the time that Laura had accidentally spilled ink over one of her letters and had claimed that someone else had done it deliberately. Abigail Butcher said that none of them understood why Laura had pulled the knife, or why she had even been carrying the knife, and they had all simply been horsing around together in a friendly way when it had happened, when Laura had pulled the knife and stabbed Lucia. Abigail and the other girls began to weep, and Laura, desolate, looked at the jury box and saw that the eyes of some of the women were moist, too.

The trial had been one long, hideous dream. Laura had alternated between bouts of panic when she was scarcely able to catch her breath, and complete numbness, during which she felt oddly detached, almost as if she were floating above the courtroom.

Although Helen Williamson, a prosecution witness, testified that in spite of what had happened, Laura was, in her opinion, a gentle and honest child, Miss Thorpe told the court that Laura had had problems fitting in with her contemporaries. It was often quite difficult to join a new school in the middle of a year, she said, with friendships already forged, cliques formed. It was easy for an insecure new-comer to feel like an outsider, although in the vast majority of such cases, the new girls settled down in due course.

"I have never experienced such a tragedy in all my years of teaching," Miss Thorpe told the prosecution.

"How would you describe the personality of the accused girl?"

"Nervy. Highly strung—perhaps even hysterical."

"You were also well-acquainted with the victim. How would you describe her?"

Miss Thorpe's eyes filled abruptly with tears, and her lips drew tightly for a moment over her big, horsy teeth. "Lucia was very vivacious," she answered, when she could steady herself. "A high-spirited, lovely girl—a little sharp-tongued, perhaps, sometimes, but that was to be expected of a natural leader."

Cross-examining Laura, the prosecutor asked her why she thought that Lucia and her friends had done the things to her that she claimed.

"Because I was different."

"In what way do you believe you were different, Laura?"

"I'm not English. I'm half Greek."

"And you believe that this was the reason that they—to use your word—tormented you?"

"I think so."

"But isn't it true that a number of girls in your class came from non-British backgrounds? One girl from Singapore, one from South Africa. In your dormitory in Alderley Tower, there was Fernanda Garcia—and even the victim, Miss Lindberg, had a non-British grandfather. Is that not true?"

"I don't know." Laura's voice trembled. "I suppose so."

"Were any of these girls treated differently?"

"No."

"Then why do you feel they singled you out because of your nationality?"

"I don't know."

* * *

Great emphasis was placed on the knife with which she had stabbed Lucia.

"Where did you get the knife, Laura?"

"At the stables."

"Did someone give it to you?"

"No. I was in the tack room, and I saw it on a box."

"And you took it?"

"Yes."

"Did you ask anyone if you could take it?"

"No."

"You stole the knife? Please answer the question. Did you steal the knife?"

"Yes."

"Why did you steal it?"

"To defend myself."

"Against what or whom?"

"Against them."

"Tell us who you mean, please."

"Their names?"

"Yes, please."

She gave their names.

"Why did you feel you had to defend yourself against these girls?"

"Because of the things they did to me."

"Tell us what they did."

She told them.

"Did you tell anyone about these incidents, Laura? Did you report them to one of your teachers?"

"I told Miss Thorpe about my letter."

"Miss Thorpe has told us about that. You claimed that you found a letter in your dormitory locker with ink spilled on it. You couldn't tell Miss Thorpe who had done it, and Priscilla Carling has testified that she believes you spilled the ink yourself."

"That's not true."

"Was that letter one of the reasons you went out to steal a knife?"

"No, of course not. I told you about the other things they did. And then they said—Lucia said—I would have an accident if I went to Mrs. Williamson."

"Why didn't you tell Mrs. Williamson about those things, Laura? We know that she invited you into her study because she was concerned about you and wanted to help. Why didn't you tell her? You must have known that she could have stopped anyone hurting you."

"I wasn't sure she would believe me."

"Why wouldn't she, if you were telling the truth?"

"Because they—the others—would have said I was lying. And I couldn't prove anything."

"Why did you steal the knife, Laura, instead of going to your headmistress and telling her that you were afraid of the other girls?"

"I *told* you why." Laura was weeping.

"Just a moment longer, and I'll be finished. All right? Good. You told us that you stole the knife to defend yourself. So you did intend to use it when you stole it."

"Only to frighten them."

"You must have known that a pocketknife of that kind was an extremely dangerous weapon. You have told the court that you carried the knife with you for more than a week before you used it. What were you waiting for?"

"For them to threaten me again."

"And then what did you plan to do with the knife? To kill Lucia?"

"No! I didn't mean to hurt her—I never wanted to kill her. I just wanted them to leave me alone."

In his summing up, the prosecution lawyer told the jury that there was no doubt that Laura Andros had committed the most dreadful crime. She could not, and did not, suggest that it was an accident. She had had every opportunity to tell any one of her teachers at Osborne College about her fears, and her headmistress had actually invited her to confide in her, but she had chosen not to do so.

"Laura Andros stole the knife, intending to use it," he said, "and she did indeed use it to kill Lucia Lindberg, a brilliant and beautiful young girl."

Except for Helen Williamson and the psychiatrist called by the defense to testify that he felt Laura had—whether re-alistically or not—believed herself in danger from the victim, there was no one to speak up for Laura or to support her version of events. When the red-robed judge addressed the jury, he advised them that it was clear that Laura had killed Lucia Lindberg, though it seemed probable that she had acted under some sort of internal duress.

"If you are not satisfied that this was a case of murder," he told the jurors, "but if you feel that this was a case of unlawful killing, you may find the defendant guilty of manslaughter." The judge paused. "It is up to you."

They found her guilty of manslaughter. Passing sentence, the judge told Laura that even if it had not been her intention to kill Lucia, she had stolen a lethal weapon, and she had used it, causing the death of a thirteen-year-old girl.

"You are too young to go to prison, and I am therefore placing you in the care of the local authority. You will remain in their care until you are no longer a juvenile, and it will be entirely up to the authority to decide how best to deal with you."

Laura had not realized until just before the end of the trial that the man and woman sitting near the back of the courtroom were Lucia's parents. She had noticed them before. They had sat very straight throughout, and sometimes the man had held the woman's hand. Laura had never really thought about Lucia having a mother or father. She had not imagined anyone really loving her tormentor. But suddenly she had heard the sound of the woman weeping, and when she looked back, Laura saw that she was golden haired, just like Lucia, and she saw that her husband's face, too, was wet with tears, and she knew then who they were.

It was also only really then that the full understanding of what she had done had come home to Laura. She had taken a life. She had done the very worst thing in the world. She had broken the fifth Commandment. She had stolen much more than a knife. She had stolen a future. Not just Lucia's but also her parents' future as a mother and father.

The moment had come back to her then. The exact instant that the knife in her hand had gone into Lucia. Into her stomach. She remembered the awful, ugly, terrifying sensation—the softness of Lucia's body and the paradoxical jarring in her elbow, the shock when the blood had suddenly come flowing, spurting. She saw all over again Lucia falling backward, Lucia disappearing over the edge. She heard the screaming. She saw Lucia's body, halted by the trees beneath the belly of the White Horse.

She knew then that no matter how or why it had come about, whether it was called manslaughter or murder, they were right to have convicted her. She had caused a death. She was a killer. And the guilt had begun in earnest.

When they broke the news to her two days later that Theophanis Andros had passed away, Laura knew that she had killed her grandfather, too, for although no one had been savage enough to suggest it to her, she was certain that the news of what she had done had brought on his heart attack.

And the guilt had magnified. The real guilt, deep and dark and sickening and devouring. And endless.

Gus was a good listener. She never said much, never openly sympathized, never gave advice about feelings. Feelings were your own affair, and there was hardly ever anything anyone else could say to change them.

"One thing I will say. You've got to toughen up in here. It's one thing them knowing what you did to get put in Kane, but that's not going to last if they think you're just a wimp."

"I don't want any trouble," Laura said. "I've had enough trouble."

"You think keeping quiet's going to save you from that?" Gus shook her scarlet head. "That's only going to get you into deeper shit. The way I see it, you've got two choices. Either you play it noisy and rough—learn to swear like the rest of us, learn to fight. Or you can keep quiet, if you like, but they've got to think you're silent and mean, a bit of a hard case, like me."

"I don't want to fight."

"Okay, I can go for that. But you've got to stop looking so soft."

"How do I do that?"

Gus thought about it. "You're still scared, right? You need to try to turn that into something else."

"What do you mean?"

"The shrink told me that's what I needed to do."

"Dr. Fisher?"

"Sure. He wanted me to turn my anger into something else."

"What?" Laura asked, intrigued.

Gus shrugged. "Search me. Into something useful, he said, only he meant schoolwork, or one of those dozy crafts they're always trying to ram down our throats." She smiled. "Only he doesn't understand what places like Kane are really about, that the most useful thing you can have in here is anger."

"I don't have anything to be angry about," Laura said.

"You're kidding me." Gus looked stunned. "After those bitches put you in here."

"They didn't put me in here," Laura said. "I did that."

"Oh, sure, we all know you stuck a knife in Lucrezia." Ever since Gus had heard about the poisonous Borgia family in a history lesson, she'd referred to Lucia that way. Laura hated it, mostly because it made her want to smile, and that only increased her guilt. "And we all know she bloody deserved what she got."

"Don't."

"That's even worse for you, you know, kid. Guilt's a damned sight worse than being scared. It'll poison the rest of your life, if you're not careful—and you're still here, even if bloody Lucrezia isn't."

Time passed more swiftly than Laura had expected, weeks into months, months into years. It wasn't a bad place, better, in many ways, she felt, than Osborne had been, though there, of course, she had spent the short time she'd had in misery and fear. There was fear at Kane House, too, certainly, and it was usually fear of violence, but it wasn't the never-ending, humiliating brand that Laura had experienced at the boarding school. At Kane, a fight could erupt from one second to the next, and they could be lethal fights with no holds barred, when you either joined in or cowered in a corner. But when the battles were over, a kind of peace came over the place, as if everyone accepted that there had to be a boiling over from time to time, and it did more good than harm, and after all a few bloody noses and even the occasional busted bone were a damned sight less dangerous than a broken mind.

Laura didn't know how she would have survived if it hadn't been for Gus. And the letters from Adam. He'd been so distraught and angry with her at first for not having told him what was happening to her at Osborne—if she'd only trusted him, he wrote, he would have found a way to take her home. But then the hot anger had abated, and he'd begun to do his best to conceal his sorrow, and his letters painted pictures for her of their old world as he tried to convince Laura that one day it could all be hers again.

"My grandfather's house has been sold," Laura told Gus. "But Adam and Maria are still there, thank goodness—he says they're going to keep looking after it for the new owners."

"Shame it couldn't have been kept for you," Gus said. "Still, the cash'll come in useful when you get out of here."

Their world at Kane was, in its own gritty way, just as unreal as Osborne and Aegina had been, a closed society in which the inmates were totally provided for. Since Kane was a community home and not a prison, there were no bars on the windows, and determined escapees got out regularly, for it wasn't all that hard to wriggle out through the small high window in the upstairs cloakroom and shinny down the drainpipe, or to get away when they were taken out on excursions. The day trips were mostly designed to enable the young offenders to visit the type of factories and other places of work where it was hoped they might, on release, find jobs. The crafts they were taught at school were all practical, from typing to plumbing. False hopes were not encouraged. No one had ever heard of a film star or brain surgeon or prime minister coming out of Kane House.

"You could be a model," Gus told Laura one day, after they'd emerged from another dreary typing lesson. Gus was sixteen now, and Laura, fifteen, and while Gus had retained her reed-thinness, Laura had developed perky breasts and a waist. "When are you going to let me cut your hair?"

"So it can look like yours?" Laura laughed. Ever since punk had gone public, Gus had discovered herself. She supposed she'd been naturally punk for years, but once the magazines and TV had started filling up with the hard, shocking-to-some, images of boys and girls with electrocuted hairstyles, bizarre makeup and rings through their noses, Gus had flung herself into the fashion as wholeheartedly as Kane would allow.

"No way," Gus said seriously. "Punk isn't your style— you're a classic—and I don't mean one of those po-faced deb types." She regarded Laura at length. "You should have a bob. With a fringe. You've got the kind of hair that could really swing, not like my rat's nest."

"Could you do that for me?"

"Maybe." Gus shook her head. "No, I suppose not. You need a really good hairdresser for a style like that."

"Like Vidal Sassoon, you mean?"

"Sassoon's not really in anymore—Daniel Galvin would do you a lovely bob."

While Laura had rediscovered the joys of reading novels, and loved few things more than escaping into anything from Thomas Hardy to Sidney Sheldon, Gus was an avid magazine reader. She didn't so much browse through them or even read them as rake them with her eyes.

"You should try this book," Laura told her one night before lights out. "It's really sexy, you'd like it." She passed over her library copy of *Scruples*.

"Why would I want to read about sex?" Gus asked. "It's hard enough avoiding it in this sodding place."

"It's full of your kind of language, for a start," Laura said.

Gus looked at the first page. "I think I read something about this. No, it's not for me." She tossed it back. "D'you think about it much then?"

"What?"

"Sex. You never join in when the others are banging on about it."

"Nor do you," Laura said.

"It's different for me." So far as Gus was concerned, Pavel Pietrowski was the first and last man who was ever going to lay a finger on her. "You're made for it, I reckon."

"Do you really?" The lights went out. Laura put down the book and felt her cheeks grow warm in the dark. "Why do you say that?"

"You've got a great body, for a start."

Someone whistled and another girl made a lewd, grunting sound.

"I'd like to see your bod, Andros," a voice said from the far end.

"Wouldn't need books if you had the real thing, love," another voice said.

Gus sat up in bed. "Anyone lays a finger on her, they'll get more than one broken arm."

"Gus wants Laura for herself," someone jeered.

"What's she waiting for then—Christmas?"

Laura sat up, too. "Why don't you all piss off?"

"*Pees* off," one of the girls mocked.

Laura lay back again, and smiled. It was funny, really, that she could smile about it. It was the same kind of teasing that Lucia and her cronies had put her through, yet it never wounded or humiliated her the way it had when they'd done it. She wasn't sure if it was because these girls were fundamentally less cruel, in spite of what some of them were, or if it was because she'd grown up a bit since she'd come here. If only she'd learned how to take it at Osborne, she might have been free now, she might have been back on Aegina, might have left school out of choice. And Lucia might not have been dead.

It never really left her, the knowledge of what she'd done. Not for long.

CHAPTER 7

For all that she'd had to grow accustomed to the violence that was a part of life at Kane House, deep down Laura never ceased to be appalled by it. She'd had to learn to hide her feelings, to confront the periodic uproar and unpleasantness, but still, whenever she was faced with a fight at close quarters, when she saw the wildness in the eyes of the combatants, the weird kind of bluntness, almost blindness as they scratched and slapped and punched and kicked—and worse, when she heard the sounds of it, the panting, the thuds of fists landing on flesh and bone, she still felt sick and afraid. Laura knew that what really terrified her was the possibility that one day she might lose control again. Fighting seemed a release to many of the other inmates, but Laura could not afford to fight. She couldn't trust herself to lash out, couldn't be quite certain that she might not pick up something, anything—a chair, a glass, even a heavy book in the library. Anything could be a weapon, you didn't need to have a knife.

The worst times for her were when Gus fought. She knew that she had to, knew it was part of being Gus the hard case, part of keeping her status with the others. But seeing her that way, witnessing that almost savage capacity to strike out with purpose, wounded Laura because she knew that it wasn't an untamed kind of wildness, but a learned brutality, a skill that Gus had taught herself over the years, knowing that it would stand her in better stead in this world than any amount of office or homemaking skills.

While Gus remained Laura's defender in the physical sense, as time went on Laura became increasingly protective of Gus in other, more subtle ways. The other girl lived strictly in the present, never allowing herself to think of a future outside Kane. Survival was now, Gus insisted. If you fell into the trap of day-dreaming about all the great things that might happen to you later, you only woke up to find you'd stepped in shit or fallen down some black hole. Laura encouraged Gus in scarcely perceptible ways to broaden her horizons. She got Gus to cut her hair the way she'd talked about, and it wasn't too bad, and she said that Gus ought to think about going into hairdressing when she got out.

"You must be joking," Gus said. "Me having to listen to women's gossip all day and having to be polite? I'd end up strangling the customers."

"I bet you'd be great," Laura told her. "You could go straight to one of those posh London places, you could be an apprentice, and then you'd end up in one of your magazines."

"Get real, kid," Gus said.

"I mean it."

"I know." Gus smiled.

It was Laura, too, who tried to talk Gus out of her regular escape bids. Gus didn't want to leave Kane House permanently—she knew when she was well off—but every now and again she felt she just had to get out for a few hours to stop the awful restlessness that started like an itch and grew until it was everywhere, in her body and limbs and in her brain, stifling her, driving her wild.

"If you just stayed put for a while," Laura pointed out to her, "they'd let you go out anyway."

"Sure," Gus sneered, "I'm just dying to go to some old museum and pretend to look at crappy pictures while they breathe down our necks until it's time to drag us back."

"It's better than being in here all the time, and at least you wouldn't get punished for it."

In the second week of December that year, Laura and Gus were taken, with eight other girls, to see the Christmas lights in Bath. Outside Woolworth's, Gus drew Laura a little to one side.

"I'm going to split," she said, her mouth close against her ear.

"You can't," Laura whispered.

"Sure I can."

"But why?"

"I need to get away, be by myself." Gus paused. "You can come, if you like."

Laura looked shocked. "I couldn't."

"Want to?"

"No."

"Okay." Gus shrugged. "See you later. Cover for me."

"Wait." Laura grabbed her arm. "Please, Gus. They'll take away all your privileges—it's crazy."

"I'll make out I got separated by accident, got lost. They can't prove different." She looked hard at Laura. "Just for an hour, that's all. If you came too, we could look out for each other."

If Adam had been like a brother to Laura, then Gus was now her sister. She looked into the thin, determined face, at the narrowed gray eyes.

"Okay," she said.

Laura knew it was a mistake from the beginning, but she never dreamed how terrible a mistake. Gus had the devil in her that afternoon—once they had freed themselves from the others, once the cold winter air and bright lights had sparked off Gus's old, remembered needs and pleasures, Laura could not stop her. Except for the knife in the stables at Osborne, Laura had never stolen anything in her life, but that afternoon she stood by, transfixed with horror, while Gus pinched a bag of sweets, a black eyebrow pencil with which she swiftly painted her eyes and lips, and a paperback novel.

"For you," she said, and gave it to Laura.

"I don't want it."

"Suit yourself." Gus dropped it into the gutter. "Come on."

"Are we going back?" Laura asked.

"No way."

Laura had a bad feeling. "Where are we going?"

"I want to show you something."

Every time Laura tried to insist they went back, Gus told her to go, that she wasn't stopping her, but that *she* couldn't go back, not yet. Before Laura quite realized what was happening, they were walking along the A4 heading out of town, and Gus was jerking her thumb in the air and looking expectantly at passing drivers.

"What are you *doing*?"

"Hitching. Haven't you ever hitched?"

"No, and I don't want to now."

"Then go back."

"And let you do this alone?"

They got a ride all the way into Bristol with a lorry driver who'd only stopped for them because he liked the look of Laura, but after Gus planted herself between them, he gave up all hope and turned the radio up high, and Gus sang along with almost every number in her raucous voice until he dropped them off near the docks.

"Do you know what we've done?" Laura demanded. She was angry and scared. "God knows what they'll do to us when they catch us."

"They won't have to catch us," Gus assured her. "We'll be back by ten."

"What have we come here for then?"

"I want to show you where I used to live, if you're interested."

"Of course I am, but—"

"Come on then."

It was strange looking at the house where their flat had been. Gus didn't know, after all, why she'd wanted to come. She'd been unhappy in Fishponds Road for as long as she could remember.

"Christ, I hated him."

"Your father?"

"Course my father."

"But you loved your mum."

Gus nodded, silent for a moment. She stared at the ugly,

dark terraced house, at the steps that had led down to their home. Alice had tried so hard to brighten those rooms, but Pavel could have made the sunniest room seem dark, she supposed.

"I want to go to the cemetery," she said, suddenly.

"Now?"

"Well, I don't think they'll let us pop back tomorrow."

"But it's dark," Laura said.

"So?"

Laura saw the locked gates with relief. Gus insisted on following the high brick wall for several hundred yards, looking for a place to climb over or break in, but finally she gave up.

"Shit," she said, then shrugged. "I haven't got any flowers anyway."

A car, with headlights dipped, came slowly down the road toward them and stopped.

"Police," Laura said, aghast, and grabbed Gus's arm.

"No, it isn't."

The driver leaned over and opened the passenger window.

"Hello, girls."

"Piss off," Gus said.

"That's not very friendly," the man said.

"I said piss off."

"Daft cunt." He spat into the gutter, and drove away.

"What did he want?" Laura asked.

"What do you think?" Gus shook her head. "You still don't know much, do you, kid?" She'd always called Laura that, even though they were almost the same age. "He wanted to fuck us."

"You're joking."

"It was you he wanted," Gus said.

"Don't be crazy."

"They're always going to be after you."

"Why?"

"Because you're great looking."

"Thank you," Laura said. "I think you're great looking too."

Gus snorted derisively.

"I'm serious."

"I don't want to be good looking," Gus said. "I don't want men to want me."

"But you're not—" Laura stopped.

"I'm not a dyke, no. I don't think I'm anything, really."

A string of cars passed them, before another one slowed down to a crawl.

"Here we go again," Gus said.

"Just ignore him," Laura said.

"Dirty old pig."

"Let's keep walking." Laura felt the fear again, wished she could be as brave as Gus, but she knew she never would be. All she wanted was to keep out of trouble, not to make waves, not even a ripple if she could help it, so that she could get out of Kane, maybe next year, and go back to Greece.

The driver stopped the car. It was big, old and American, with a long front seat that stretched from door to door. He poked his head out of the window.

"Want a lift, girls?"

"Original," Gus said.

"You look like you could use a little help," he said.

"You look like a filthy old pervert," Gus said.

"Don't, Gus," Laura whispered. "Let's go."

The car followed them, stopped again, and the door opened.

"He's getting *out*," Laura said, panicking.

Gus stopped and turned to face him. "Why don't you fuck off and leave us alone?"

The man smiled. In the yellow sodium-vapor lamplight, his face was eerie, the smile leering. "You don't mean that, do you? I'll bet your little friend doesn't, anyway."

"I said fuck off," Gus repeated.

"Can't she speak?"

"Go away," Laura said. "Please go away."

"That's better," the man said. "Not so crude as your friend." He looked Laura up and down.

"I'm warning you." Gus bent down and picked something up.

"Gus, be careful." Laura saw that it was a lump of concrete, the broken-off corner of a paving stone. Her bad feeling magnified. "Gus, for God's sake let's run."

"I like a bit of rough," the man said. "Work as a team, do you?" He reached out for Laura's right arm, and she shrank away, clutching at Gus and trying to push her on up the street, but Gus stood her ground.

"Don't you dare touch her."

He laughed. "Who's going to stop me?"

"I'm warning you."

"Gus, for God's *sake*!"

He was drunk. They could both smell the whisky on his breath. He put out his hand again, and touched Laura's coat, just over her left breast—

"Bastard!" Gus hit him with the stone, struck him on the shoulder and he gave a yelp, more of surprise than pain.

"You bitch!"

He made a grab for the stone, but missed. Gus hit him again, grazed the side of his face, and he bellowed.

Laura saw the police car first. In another world, in her old life, she would have been relieved, would have known they were coming to help. But this wasn't the old world, and she knew better now.

Because Gus was now seventeen, the juvenile court was able to order that she be removed to a borstal a hundred miles away from Kane House. After the police station in Bristol, where they shared the same cell, clinging together and crying, even Gus, they took Laura back to Kane alone, because the man had let her off the hook, had laid the blame entirely on Gus's square, bony shoulders. She'd flagged him down, he told them, and he'd stopped to try to help, and then she'd hit him with the stone. They knew it wasn't going to make any difference to Gus if the police knew the man had been cruising. It was still assault, and Gus was done for whatever they said.

"Do you think they'll let you come back to Kane?" Laura asked, before they were separated.

"Not a chance, kid. I'll get borstal for sure." Gus scrubbed at her eyes. "I've really screwed up this time."

"I'll write to you." Laura was weeping openly. "Will you write back?"

"No promises," Gus said. "Got to keep your wits about you in borstal. No time for writing letters."

"I love you," Laura said.

"Don't be soft," Gus said, but her eyes were still wet. "You be careful without me: Remember I made you come— I've told them you didn't want to."

"But I did."

"Only to look after me." Gus managed one of her wry smiles. "Always told you I was a hard case. Bloody stupid, too."

Laura hadn't really minded the unremitting bleakness, the drabness of Kane House, so long as Gus had been there. It was a bit like starting out all over again, learning a different set of ropes. Gus was no longer there to protect her, and the other inmates had long since realized that although Laura might be in there for manslaughter, on her own she was nothing they couldn't handle.

Outwardly, she tried to keep up appearances, to keep up the bravado that Gus had taught her was so necessary, but inwardly she knew that she'd crawled back into the old bleak small space inside herself. She did what she had to do, what was expected of her and a little more. She studied as hard as she could, careful not to incur the sneers of her fellows. She trod a fine, practical line, balancing on the fence between offenders and authority. She was neither hostile nor gratuitously friendly, was deferential when she had to be, stood up for herself when that was the right thing to do. It was no good trying to be two-faced in an institution like Kane House, for the streetwise young women were too sharp to be duped, and yet you had to know when to tell lies like the devil. Sometimes, Laura hardly knew who or what she was anymore. She had ceased to wonder how it might have been if her grandfather had not sent her to Osborne, or if she had confided in Helen Williamson, or if she hadn't seen that knife. Gus had taught her that looking back was pointless and dangerous. The only time Gus had given way to the past was when they'd gone off to Bristol. Laura blamed herself sometimes for not having stopped her, somehow, but realistically she knew Gus had been unstoppable, and anyway, Laura had enough guilt stored up inside herself for a lifetime.

She wrote frequent letters to Gus, as well as to Adam.

When we both get out, we mustn't lose touch. If you like, we could get a place together. Maybe I'll go home to the island—you'd love it there, I think. It's the freest place in the world. For God's sake be careful, Gus, won't you? Don't let them get you down and don't do anything too crazy.

I hate it here without you, but I try to pretend you're still here, telling me how to act. I know you never really needed me, but just in case, if you ever do, I'll always be there for you.

Gus seldom wrote back, and when she did, the letters never filled more than one side of paper, but Laura treasured them. She became so intent on waiting for Gus's sporadic letters that a number of weeks passed before she noticed that Adam's letters from Aegina had stopped. She went on writing to him, scolding him first for his laziness, then, growing more troubled, begging him to let her know that all was well with him and Maria; but then one of her own letters was sent back to her marked: *Return to sender. No forwarding address.* It was another terrible blow, but Laura found she was growing almost inured to sorrow, and there was nothing to be done except to wait and to hope that Adam would get in touch.

In February of 1980, Helen Williamson came to visit Laura. She was waiting in the visitors' room when Laura came in. They had not seen one another since the trial, and Laura thought she looked older but otherwise unchanged.

"You look very well, Laura." They sat on vinyl chairs, a Formica-topped table between them.

"Thank you."

"You're a young woman now."

Laura said nothing.

Mrs. Williamson had always been direct, and that, too, had not altered. "The reason I have never visited you before," she said, in the pleasant, soothing voice that Laura had always liked, "was because I was asked not to by Osborne's board of governors."

"I understand," Laura said.

"I wanted to," Mrs. Williamson went on, "very much. But the board considered that it might cause offense to some people."

"To Lucia's parents," Laura said.

"Yes."

They were both silent for a few moments.

"I tried to write to them once," Laura said, her voice strained, "but it was too difficult. I couldn't explain without . . ."

"Without saying bad things about Lucia," Mrs. Williamson finished. "I think you were right not to do that."

"It's a strange feeling, knowing there are people out there who must hate me more than anyone else in the world."

"I think they believed that you didn't mean it to happen."

"That can't stop them hating me," Laura said.

Mrs. Williamson leaned forward. "You'll be leaving Kane House quite soon, Laura. Time to move forward, to stop punishing yourself. You were not the only person to blame for what happened."

"I know that."

"I hold myself responsible."

"You? Why should you?"

"I should have been aware of what was happening in my own school. I was very remiss. I offered my resignation to the board, but they would not accept it."

"I'm glad," Laura said, feeling real warmth for the teacher. "It wasn't your fault I didn't tell you."

"I can't agree," Mrs. Williamson said. "But thank you anyway."

Laura put her hands on the table. "Why have you come to see me now?"

"To talk to you about your future. And to give you certain information."

Laura felt a knot of excitement in her stomach. "About Adam?"

Mrs. Williamson looked puzzled. "Adam?"

"Adam Demonides. He was—is my best friend, on Aegina." Laura shook her head. "It doesn't matter. I thought you might have news about him."

"You've lost touch with him?"

"Yes."

"I'm sorry. No, the information I have for you is in connection with your grandfather's estate. I talked it over with the Authority, and they agreed that I might as well be the one to have this chat with you."

"Is it about Chryssos?"

"Your grandfather's villa? In a way, yes. You do know it was sold after his death?"

"Yes."

Mrs. Williamson hesitated briefly. "I'm afraid there's no easy way to tell you this, Laura. The villa had to be sold so that certain debts could be paid—that's quite usual, of course, with death duties and so forth. Unfortunately, in this case, the debts were considerable." She paused. "Were you aware that your grandfather was a gambling man?"

"A gambler?" Laura shook her head. "He made jokes, sometimes, about betting with his friends."

"I'm afraid it was rather more than that."

"Did he lose so much then?"

"I'm sorry to say he lost almost everything. I gather, from his lawyer, that he was trying to arrange some kind of trust for you when he fell ill, but it was too late."

Laura remembered Gus comforting her when she'd heard that Chryssos had been sold, telling her that the cash would come in useful when she got out of Kane. Now there wouldn't be any cash.

"Is there nothing left at all?" Laura asked. "I was hoping to go back to Greece."

"There's a little over three thousand pounds. Of course you could afford to go back if you wished to." Mrs. Williamson looked closely at her. "I can see why you might want to go, Laura. This country hasn't been very kind to you, has it?" She paused again. "But you do have some roots here, and I gather you've done quite well in your examinations, so if you did choose to stay, you'd probably be able to find a job."

"And if I go back to Aegina, it won't be the same anymore." The sadness was like a pain. "I did want to try and find Adam."

"That's something I might be able to help you with. I'm sure your grandfather's lawyer could at least try to trace your friend."

"Could I afford a lawyer?"

"You won't have to worry about that."

"But how else—?" Laura looked up. "I couldn't let you pay for me."

"I told you that I feel responsible," Mrs. Williamson said. "You can't change the way I feel." She smiled. "Please let me do this small thing to help you."

"I don't know what to say."

"Say nothing." She paused. "If you were to decide not to go back to Greece, where do you think you might like to settle? In this area?"

"No." Her own decisiveness surprised Laura. "London," she said. "I'd like to go to London and be a secretary."

Mrs. Williamson thought for a moment. "For some girls leaving a place like this, London might be a dangerous city to go to, but you're much luckier than most, Laura. Three thousand pounds isn't much, but if you look after it carefully, it should stand you in good stead." An idea struck her. "How would you like to come with me to London, for just one day? I think I could persuade the Authority, and you could get an impression of the city—we could even visit some employment agencies together. It might be quite useful."

"Wouldn't the Osborne governors mind?"

Mrs. Williamson smiled. "They don't have to know everything I do in my spare time. You won't be writing to tell them, will you?"

Laura smiled back at her, and there was almost a spark of excitement in her green eyes. "No," she said. "I won't."

She had always thought Athens the noisiest place on earth, but London was almost as bad. The clamor aside, however, she had never imagined that two cities could be so different from each other—Athens, white-hot and aggressive, and London, gray and venerable. It was a showery late spring day, and it was almost like having a light switched on and off; when the clouds merged and the rain began to fall, the streets became dull and those people without umbrellas walked with their heads tucked down, but then when the sun came out again everything seemed quite brilliant and gaudy, and the pedestrians smiled more and Laura found herself longing, like a child, to jump onto one of the red double-decker buses.

This was not a day for being a tourist, though. Time was short, and Laura realized that having Mrs. Williamson by her side was the best reference she was ever likely to obtain. They visited three different employment agencies, two in the West End, and one in the City. Laura was desperately nervous at her first interview, failing to get down in shorthand every word of the letter dictated to her, but after a cup of coffee in a café in New Bond Street, she pulled herself together, suddenly keenly aware that her performance this afternoon could have a vital effect on the rest of her life.

"What happened to you in there?" Mrs. Williamson asked as they emerged from the second agency into the sunshine. "You were almost a different person, Laura, much more confident."

"Do you think they liked me?" Laura asked anxiously.

"I'm certain they did." The headmistress smiled. "Will you share your secret?"

Laura looked up, her eyes grave. "I made myself think about the trial," she said. "About the judge, and the lawyers, and all the terrible questions. I thought that if I got through that, then I could cope with a shorthand and typing test."

They began to walk along Wigmore Street, toward Portman Square.

"I'm beginning to think you may adapt to being away from Kane House relatively easily," Mrs. Williamson said. "You have natural style, Laura, are you aware of that?"

"That's what Gus said."

"Gus?"

"A friend at Kane. She's not there anymore."

"Ah, yes, I've heard about her—Augusta, is that right? The consensus of opinion is that she was a bad influence on you."

"Opinion's wrong. Gus saved me. I wouldn't have got through without her."

"I think you would."

Laura shook her head vehemently. "No, I wouldn't. Gus is a wonderful person. She had a terrible life before Kane—she's the bravest person I've ever met. It wasn't her fault what happened. It wasn't right sending her to borstal."

"She attacked a man."

"She was protecting me. She didn't even really hurt him."

"Why did you both run away that day?"

"We weren't running away—we were going to go back that evening. Gus needed to get away. She really had to. It doesn't make her a bad person."

"Do you hear from her?"

"Sometimes. She doesn't write much." Laura stopped walking. "I'm going to try to help her when she gets out, if she'll let me. She's very proud—she may not."

"You're a loyal girl, Laura," Mrs. Williamson said. "It can sometimes be misplaced, but I've always admired loyalty. I'm sorry about Gus, but you'll make friends in your new life, too."

Before they left London, they visited a hostel to which Mrs. Williamson had been recommended. It was away from the center, to the north of town in Belsize Park. Laura liked the district at first glance; it was filled with lovely shops and restaurants and cafés, its pace more leisurely than in the heart of the city.

"It would be wonderful to live here," she said just before they entered the hostel in a broad, leafy side road off the main street.

"Don't get too excited," Mrs. Williamson cautioned. "If we could get you into this hostel, and if the Authority approve, it could only be a starting-off point for you. Like all attractive areas, it's expensive—I doubt whether you could afford to find a room to rent around here. The hostel's cheap and safe and they're quite selective about who they admit, but they never let anyone stay for more than three months."

"Why should they let me come? Surely with my record—"

"In the first instance, they've been asked to consider you favorably, and in the second, I think they're going to like you." She paused. "Come on, let's go inside."

Laura started up the stone steps ahead of the teacher, then stopped at the top and turned around. "Why are you doing so much for me, Mrs. Williamson? I know what you said, but I still don't understand."

Mrs. Williamson joined her on the top step. "Your grandfather placed you into my care at Osborne College, Laura. He loved you very much, and yet he was prepared to send you away because he believed that you would have a far better future if you had a fine English education. And I failed him—I failed you both."

"But it wasn't your fault," Laura said again.

"I failed Lucia, too, of course, and her family. But there isn't anything I can do to make it up to them, and I have to live with that knowledge."

"So you're helping me."

"I hope so."

Laura had not experienced such a rush of warmth for anyone since Gus. She wanted to reach out, wanted to hug the older woman, but knew it would be improper.

"I'll try not to let you down," she said.

"I don't doubt that."

PART TWO

CHAPTER 8

Roger Jefferson Ambler liked to think of himself as a mogul. He was a newspaperman, but journalism wasn't in his blood; he owned three radio stations, but broadcasting was not bread, water and air to him; he owned a publishing company, but he never read books for pleasure; he ran a corporation employing, indirectly, thousands of people, he owned property in cities across America, and he owned companies that manufactured machinery, fabrics, shoes and refrigerators, but he didn't really *care* about any of them.

"I know myself too well," he once told Tom Bailey confidentially while they were dining in the Jockey Club in Washington, D.C. "I inherited most of my wealth from my father, the way you did from your grandmother, and I don't kid myself that I'm a genius. I don't give a shit about trying to become a great newspaper baron, and I care even less if Zero publishes a Pulitzer winner. I'm in it to make money and to make things happen."

"You don't need any more money," Bailey said.

"Sure I do. I get high on money. Stocks, shares, bonds, bullion, Swiss francs—music to my ears."

"You're a Philistine, Roger."

"I'm a collector," Ambler said simply. "I collect companies and cash. If the companies go on making profits, I hold onto them, if they don't, I dump them."

"People, too," Bailey commented.

"Sure."

"When are you going to dump me, I wonder?"

"It wouldn't be any fun dumping you, Tom. It wouldn't matter to you." Ambler smiled. "Anyway, you're my resident genius, and I need you a whole lot more than you need me."

"No, you don't."

Ambler shrugged. "Maybe not. But I like you anyway."

They'd both inherited family wealth, but that aside, Roger Ambler and Thomas Bailey were as dissimilar as two white American males could be. Ambler was blond and stocky, with blue eyes, sharp, pointed features and a clear, precise voice. Bailey was tall, dark and lanky, with brown, humorous eyes and a deep, gentle voice. Ambler was a city man, a self-confessed vulgarian, capable of disguising that or any other streak in his character with a brilliant actor's talent. Bailey was a man of simpler needs with a respect for his fellows and a passion for the newspaper business. Ambler had not worn a suit, shirt or a pair of shoes that had not been made to measure for him since he was eighteen; he paused for a shoeshine each morning of his working life—and he worked every day of every week—and he had a girl come into his office or hotel suite at least once weekly to give him a manicure. The same three suits had hung in Bailey's wardrobe for the last fifteen years; if he could get away with it, he wore his preferred corduroy trousers, checked cotton shirt and battered cowboy boots, and he only got his hair cut regularly because it fell over his forehead and got in his eyes if he forgot.

Tom Bailey had been married once, to his childhood sweetheart, Julie, who'd died of bone cancer when she was just twenty-eight. Roger Ambler had had, to date, two wives: Suzy, a stunning blond heiress with whom marriage just hadn't worked out, and Patricia, a statuesque Harvard MBA businesswoman who'd tried, as he put it, to cut off his balls. Neither of the marriages had lasted a year, and neither of his wives had borne Ambler a child, a fact he genuinely regretted, but on the other hand, as he consoled himself, he could find himself a loving, maternally minded woman anytime he chose, and so long as she was young enough, there was all the time in the world for him to have kids.

Ambler's father, Arnold, would have liked to have passed on his name to his firstborn son in the dynastic manner that he had always admired and hungered after, but alas, he had always detested the name of Arnold, and since his parents had not bestowed a middle name on him that he might have juggled with, he had to make do with giving his boy a good, solid-citizen, safe name. His wife, born Mary Jefferson, thought that adding her maiden name to their scrap of an infant's burden was a touch pretentious, but her husband insisted.

"It isn't pretentious, honey," he had told her soon after Roger's birth in 1942 in the hospital in Paramus, New Jersey. "What it adds is distinction, that's all. Arnold Ambler suits a businessman well enough—or maybe a dentist or an accountant—but a man named Roger Jefferson Ambler can be anything he chooses to be."

"So long as you don't kid yourself our son's going to be president."

Arnold had stared at the tiny, scrawny, hairless baby, at his little fists already flailing in wordless demand. "Can't be sure, Mary, not about anything. Except that he's going to want things—I mean really *want* them."

Mary had smiled. "Right now, I think he wants his mother."

"Better accommodate him then, honey." On cue, Roger Jefferson Ambler opened his mouth and began to cry. "I don't think he's going to be the kind to take no for an answer."

The birth of their son had motivated Arnold Ambler to change into a higher gear. Until then, he had been a successful local businessman, the proprietor of a shoe manufacturing company, expanding into machinery by buying the firm that made the equipment that Ambler Shoes used, somewhat ashamed of having been found physically unfit to fight for his country; but after Roger came into the world, a new kind of ambition seemed born in his father, too. Suddenly, at the age of thirty-one, Arnold wanted to make his mark, to do something of which his son could be proud.

"Who wants to inherit shoes?" he said to Mary.

"You make beautiful shoes."

"And they pay our bills," Arnold agreed, "but they're hardly exciting or glamorous, are they? I need more."

"What kind of more?"

"I'm not sure, not yet. But I'll know it when I see it."

He took a year to find it. It was called the *Cullen Recorder,* a small, ailing, New Jersey tabloid newspaper about to hit rock-bottom. Until he overheard one of the *Recorder*'s reporters gossiping with a friend in a diner on Route 4 between Paramus and Cullen, Arnold had almost entirely forgotten that one of his boyhood fantasies had revolved around running a newspaper. He and his best friend, Norman Durrant, had gotten hold of one of those little printing sets and a pair of green plastic eyeshades that newspapermen wore in the movies, and for several months they'd written up stories and general tittle-tattle about their neighbors in a one-page newsletter they'd titled *How Now.*

Arnold had hardly seen Norman for more than ten years, but knowing that his old friend had been honorably discharged from the army, he'd gone straight over to the pay phone in the diner, got his number from the operator, and called him. Norman's wife had told Arnold that Norman was at work, but he left his number, and later that evening, Durrant had called back.

"Remember *How Now?*" Arnold believed in coming directly to the point.

"Sure."

"Want to do it again?"

"Do what again?"

"Run a paper with me—or rather buy it with me."

"I'm an optometrist, Arnold."

"So you're the right man to take care of our readers' eyesight."

"What are you *talking* about?"

Arnold heard the sound of the baby's crying upstairs, heard Mary's footsteps on the staircase, heading to take care of his needs. That was all he wanted to do, look after Roger's future needs, and he knew, he just *knew*, that this was the right place to start.

"I'm talking about turning fantasies into fact, Norman. You want to hear more, or not?"

Norman, still a boy at heart, wanted to hear more. They marched into the first-floor office of the *Recorder* together, met with the proprietor, took the grand tour of the printing room, gazed with barely disguised adoration at the ancient printing press, watched and listened like goggle-eyed kids as the only employee present took down and typed up the latest hot news about the flooded basement of a bakery in the suburbs, and made an offer that the proprietor felt he couldn't refuse. The fact that he considered it a grade A miracle that anyone should make any kind of offer at all for this shambles of a paper, he kept to himself. In any case, both Ambler and Durrant knew what they were doing. Neither of them was callow or foolish; they could afford the money, they could stand the loss if they failed, and neither of them had any intention of giving up shoes or eyes. But even if they did fail, they were going to have the time of their lives doing so.

It was only a beginning. When the *Recorder* levered itself off the ground, Arnold found himself a radio station in Connecticut that he wanted to buy; he had always had a soft spot for radio that television had never replaced. Maybe Roger could expand into television when he took over the business—or maybe he'd go for book publishing. There was honor in books, Arnold felt. He and Norman had launched an annual short story competition in the Cullen paper, and the staff had been bowled over by the weight of the response. Aspiring writers from all over New Jersey had heard about the competition, and the grand prize—a weekend for two at the Algonquin Hotel in New York City—and Arnold had got a major buzz reading the twenty short-listed stories. Sure, there'd been some dross, but there'd been three that had really touched him.

"You know what I'd like to do, Mary?" he'd asked his wife.

"What, dear?" She watched little, golden-haired Roger—

so much more like her, physically, than like his father. At the moment, he was up on his feet on the far side of the living room, toddling around in almost perfect safety since Arnold had taped padding on all the sharp edges in the house, but she could never afford to take her eyes off him for a moment.

"I'd really like to try publishing these three writers."

"You have published them, Arnold."

"Only in the *Recorder.*"

"Where else did you have in mind?"

"I want them to try writing whole books," Arnold said.

"And then what?"

"If they're as good as their stories, I'd like to publish them." He shrugged. "You know, print them, bind them, advertise them and sell them."

"You have no experience," Mary said, and held out her arms to Roger. "Come to Mommy, sweetheart."

"It's all common sense, honey."

"How much profit do you expect to make out of this?" she asked.

"A big fat zero, to begin with, anyway," he said.

By the time Roger Jefferson Ambler was given Zero Publishing as a twenty-second birthday gift, its offices were housed in a brownstone building on Eleventh Street just off Fifth Avenue in New York City. He knew that Zero—a name which was anathema to him—and the old New Jersey paper were the apples of his father's eye, but Roger was already a sharper businessman than Arnold had ever been, and what concerned him far more than sentiment were balance sheets.

"If you'd wanted me to be more like you, Dad," he told Arnold one day when they were arguing over whether or not to close down the *Recorder* for keeps, "you shouldn't have sent me to business school."

"Surely Harvard, of all places, must have taught you that profit alone isn't everything, son," Arnold said. The day that he and Mary had traveled with Roger to Cambridge had been one of the proudest of his life.

"I know that, Dad," Roger said.

"I'm glad to hear it."

"But it sure as hell comes in useful."

"I wish you wouldn't blaspheme, son."

"I'm sorry, Dad."

Roger had a great affection for his father and respected his achievements so far as they went, but he knew that Arnold Ambler had always been a limited man. Ideals were his stumbling block; they represented borders that a decent, old-fashioned type like his father was reluctant to cross. Roger believed that borders were there to *be* crossed, to be smashed down if necessary. Arnold Ambler loved his businesses—he honestly loved them. Roger knew that love and commerce were two separate entities that ought never to be mixed. He loved his parents and younger sister, Rona, but he felt not a grain of emotion for even the Ambler Corporation's oldest companies. Shoes, machinery, newspapers, books; they were just leather and vinyl and steel and oil and paper, and the men and women who worked for those companies only did it because they were paid good money to do so. Roger never doubted for an instant that every one of them—even someone like Sidney Morris, the general manager of Ambler Shoes, who'd never worked for anyone but Arnold in his entire life—would walk away if someone else named the right price.

"Everyone has their price," he told his mother, during one of the many arguments that had started after he'd left Harvard and joined the business.

"You father doesn't," Mary said.

"Sure he does."

Mary smiled. "Your father has never allowed anyone to buy him off unless it was what he really wanted."

"I didn't say the price had to be money, Mom. Everyone needs or wants something badly enough at some time to give up something else, even if that thing is really important to them."

Mary Ambler read the writing on the wall long before her husband did. She had always understood their children better than Arnold had. Rona, three years younger than her brother, was pretty much like Roger both physically and emotionally. She was all female, strong in her femininity, a

little fluffy, perhaps, for Mary's liking on the outside, but
with a strand or two of steel within. Rona had grown up with
all the comforts and security that the ever-growing Ambler
Corporation and her indulgent father had been able to provide, and Rona had always loved it. Three years after Roger
had gone to Harvard, Rona had gone to the Sorbonne in
Paris, partly to learn to speak French with a flawless accent,
partly to enjoy herself, but mostly because she had decided
to expunge every trace of New Jersey and to immerse herself in Parisian style. From her chic little apartment in the
rue de Furstenberg, Rona had waged a tactful but tough-
minded campaign to try to persuade her parents to move out
of Paramus. It wasn't that she had any intention of moving
back in with them when she returned to the United States,
but once she had a satisfactory job and apartment in Manhattan, she wanted a family home commensurate with her image to go back to for holidays and long weekends. By the
time Rona got back, Arnold had sold the old house, and he
and Mary had moved into a beautiful new home in Green-
wich, Connecticut. It was a little large for their lifestyle or
needs, but it was much closer to the Ambler Corporation's
head office in White Plains, and there was a far greater like-
lihood of both Rona and Roger spending time there as adults
than there ever could have been in Paramus. Arnold was not
a fool—he knew that his daughter had manipulated him, but
he also knew that he had willingly allowed her to. He'd always done everything in life for Mary and their children;
that was what made him tick, what he lived for.

Mary understood Roger, too. Arnold had predicted the
most forceful aspect of his son's character shortly after his
birth more accurately than perhaps he'd realized. "He's going to want things," Arnold had prophesied, and Mary had
observed with something like fascination as the baby had
grown from a demanding child into a high-achieving teen-
ager and then into a commanding young man. Roger had
certainly screamed his way through infancy, having had no
other means to express his desires, but once he'd grasped
speech, he'd abandoned tantrums for the greater power of
persuasion. From his earliest school days, he'd made friends
easily but selectively, liking to surround himself with win-

ners. That continued through college and into his early
working years; Roger was as absorbent as blotting paper,
drawing skills, intelligence and talent from those around him
and then moving forward, ready and eager for more. Mary
didn't think he was actually devious—or maybe she just
hoped that he wasn't, for she could hardly bear to contemplate disliking her own child for such a trait—but he was un-
doubtedly a most skillful manipulator.

Roger had always expected his father to retire while he was
still young and to hand over the reins completely to his son,
but as Arnold neared his sixtieth year, he clearly had no intention of stopping work.

"The business keeps me young," he said. "Keeps me
frisky. You don't want your old man going to seed, do you?"

"Of course not, Dad," Roger hastened to assure him. "I
just think you deserve some time to enjoy yourself with
Mom."

"Men like me die when they retire," Arnold told him.
"They make all kinds of plans for playing golf and taking
cruises with their wives, and then their widows end up doing
all those things alone."

Although in most material matters, Roger had always
been able to twist his father around his little finger, he was
aware that in this particular area he could not hope to change
his mind, and even as his own star continued to rise, as Arnold willingly handed over increasingly large slabs of the
Ambler Corporation into his control, Roger still knew that
there was no possibility of a full takeover. He recognized
that Arnold had created and built up a substantial business
empire that for many men would have been more than
enough, but in Roger's eyes his father was yesterday's man,
while he was tomorrow's. He wanted—he needed—
complete control, and he knew that he would have it in good
time, but he was growing impatient.

The diagnosis of Mary Ambler's terminal cancer in 1970
devastated her husband and children, but Roger was honest
enough to admit that even upon first learning the news a
small, icy sliver of his brain had homed in on the fact that

had seemed suddenly inevitable. Arnold adored his wife, and would never allow her to be cared for by strangers. No illness of his own, unless utterly incapacitating, could have persuaded him to retire, but Mary's needs, and his desire to spend as much time with her as possible while he could, blew all other concerns out of his mind.

"You're at the helm now, son," he told Roger, tears in his eyes.

"I wish I wasn't," Roger lied, though the emotional choking up he felt was real enough. It was a powerful, galvanizing moment for him; so many conflicting strings tugging at his soul. The sorrow of watching his mother starting to fade and of observing his father's anguish; the soaring sense of release and liberty as the old man handed him his destiny on a plate; and the honest-to-God shame he felt at his own hypocrisy.

"You'll be fine, son," Arnold said, clasping his hand. "You'll be better than fine. This was always meant for you, you know that."

"And Rona."

"Your sister has the same faith in you that your mother and I have. You may be partners in the business, but you'll always be the boss."

"I respect Rona's judgment," Roger said, and this, too, was true, for he and his sister had already come to an understanding that so long as her stock in the Ambler Corporation remained valuable enough to keep her in ever-increasing luxury, she would not interfere with her brother's decision-making processes.

"Don't fly too high, son." Arnold looked at his son's sharp blue eyes and his keen, pointed nose and determined mouth. "I know the sky's the limit, and I was never a plodder, but it's good to plot an ambitious altitude and then make damned sure you can cruise safely. You're carrying a lot of people with you now, Roger—they're all going to be depending on you."

"'And I'll take care of them, Dad." Roger smiled inwardly at his father's clichés, looked tenderly at the worn face, at the wrinkles that seemed to be deepening, at the white hair, starting to recede just a little now, but still pretty thick, thank the Lord, for Roger was a vain man and keen to avoid both baldness and the absurdity of toupees. "You just take care of Mom from now on. Take that cruise while she can still enjoy it, and don't worry about the business."

"I won't need to worry, son," Arnold said. "I trust you."

Roger was twenty-nine when Mary died, and thirty when he married Suzy Aldrich, a woman who appeared to embody his highest expectations—gorgeous to look at, with exquisite taste and reeking of old money. Suzy's family had known the marriage wouldn't last, despite Suzy's assurances that even though the Ambler Corporation had its roots in the shoe business, Roger's Harvard education hadn't been wasted. But Ivy League or not, Roger Ambler was still a "wanter," and Suzy's kind simply didn't lust after money, at least not as openly as Roger did. He was thirty-one when they divorced, and thirty-two when his father, too, passed away, after a massive heart attack.

When he and Rona stood by their parents' Connecticut graveside, they held hands and wept unashamedly because it felt right, the way everything in their lives now felt. They had both loved their mother and father, and were filled with nothing other than gratitude to Arnold for having left his estate in such perfect order. Rona was twenty-nine, and having saved Zero Publishing from the company graveyard by deciding that she wanted to become one of the most stylish and beautiful young executives in the book business, she was ready to start the far more crucial, and somewhat overdue, business of husband-hunting.

"We'll be okay, sis," Roger told her, when the last of the mourners had paid their respects and were filing away from the grave.

"I know we will."

"Do you want to keep the house?"

"I don't think so, do you?"

"I thought East Hampton might be more us, sis. Or maybe Sag Harbor."

"Oh, yes. Definitely East Hampton." Rona turned her face, waterproof mascara unsmudged, up to his. "I'm dreading sorting out their things. Daddy kept all Mom's clothes,

you know—he couldn't bear to part with anything, not a
handkerchief, not a lipstick."

"We'll do it together."

"I love you, Roger."

"And I love you, sis."

Rona's unswerving faith in Roger was well founded.
Whereas Arnold had loved to build, to take on fresh chal-
lenges, add on new companies and then sit back to watch
them flourish—to "take the time to smell the roses," as he
had often said—Roger was an unsentimental gardener, digging over the Ambler soil thoroughly, pruning and weeding
regularly, everything necessary to promote the most vigorous growth achievable. Having agreed with Rona that the
publishing company could survive, he insisted that any dead
wood be cut out, which included dropping the options of the
three writers who had been Arnold Ambler's protégés at the
very beginning. The Cullen paper was sold, in spite of pleas
from Norman Durrant, Arnold's old friend and partner in the
newspaper, but two more radio stations were added to the
original Connecticut music station that Arnold had bought in
1946; and when one of the scouts whom Roger had out
scouring the country for new projects came back to White
Plains with news of a pop music magazine on the brink of
oblivion, Roger authorized him to make a bid, and *Rock Star
Magazine* was born just three months later.

The next half-decade were years of phenomenal expansion
and adventure for Ambler. He moved successfully into computers, dipped a toe into oil and swiftly withdrew it again,
took over two more failing magazines and then, thirty-five
years after his father had bought the *Cullen Recorder,* he
made his own move into newspaper journalism, smoothly
and quietly buying up shares and manipulating the owning
family and stockholders of the *Boston Courier,* one of the
city's smaller evening papers, into his corner. A second
foray, with similar tactics, dropped the *Chicago Courier,* a
weekly broadsheet newspaper, into his lap, and from that en-
terprise sprang his first encounters with Tom Bailey, the paper's editor. Bailey came from an old Midwest newspaper
family, lived and breathed journalism and had become noted

in some of the more conservative enclaves of the industry as "Cowboy Bailey," mostly for his penchant for wearing his battered boots to every kind of meeting and lunch, even in the Ivy League clubs.

Bailey liked Ambler's approach, admired his honesty and willingness to let those who knew more than him get on with the job. Ambler, in turn, thought Thomas Bailey the most fascinating man he'd come across in the newspaper business. They were opposites in almost every way, yet they became friends. Ambler's detractors accused him of being a lightweight, arrogant man, a "jack of all trades and master of none" because his empire straddled such a vast array of businesses, but Bailey was one of those who defended him, reminding those stuffed shirts who criticized Ambler that he, at least, could admire a man who set such great store by drawing from the expertise of others and learning from their experiences.

There was never any danger of even the slightest of Ambler's companies suffering from neglect because Roger knew better than to spread himself too thinly. He was a workaholic who understood his limitations. He employed experts and consultants of the highest caliber in every field, sharing profits fairly and squarely when he had to, but he never relinquished overall control or power to anyone. Every Wednesday of every week of every year—even at Christmas—whether he was in the office in White Plains, Manhattan or San Francisco, or in a hotel suite anywhere else in the world, Roger received and read the reports that were telexed and, as time progressed, faxed in from the largest and smallest of the Ambler companies wherever they might be. He did not care to think of himself as a ruthless man, but if one of these compulsory reports failed to materialize on time, he noted its absence and demanded an explanation; nothing short of death or some equal calamity was acceptable, and no more than one warning was ever given before the employee responsible for the failure was axed.

While Rona had found herself, at last, a perfect husband in Nelson Howarth, the heir to the Howarth Publishing empire, and had wasted no time at all before giving birth to their

twin daughters, Anna and Susan, their proud uncle had come
to grief in a second marriage. When Roger had met Patricia
Field, he had truly believed that he had found a kindred
spirit—the only woman aside from his sister, he told Rona,
who had ever really understood him. He was, alas, entirely
right, for his bride understood him all too well. Patricia, who
was three inches taller than Roger, yet still insisted on wearing high heels everywhere except in bed, and who was the
managing director and powerhouse behind a burgeoning cos-
metic house, realized more rapidly than Roger that marriage
to a man even more passionately dedicated to work than she
was, was doomed, after all, to failure. One of Patricia's
greatest talents was speedy decision making and appropriate
measure taking; six months after their wedding, she set aside
thirty minutes of her hectic schedule for a meeting in her office with Roger, offered him her sincere and profuse apologies for taking up so much of his time, and filed for divorce
immediately.

"I guess I'm not destined for marriage," Roger said to
Rona.

"Only because you've married for the wrong reasons,"
Rona told him, gently. "They've both been deals for you,
darling—more mergers than real marriages."

"Mergers can succeed brilliantly," he defended, "in and
out of business. Take you and Nelson."

"Roger, I was crazy about Nelson when we got married."

"Honestly?" His surprise was genuine. "I always thought
you made your choice and elected to fall in love."

"I could have married at least five other men if I'd been
willing to settle for just suitability," Rona said. "Why do you
think I waited till I was thirty-two? I had my pick, you
know."

Roger smiled fondly at her. "You're telling me I should
wait for love."

"Love, and romance—and passion. Think of Mom and
Daddy—they were still wild about each other after thirty
years."

"I'm not like Dad."

"Maybe not, but you deserve the real thing—the whole
thing." Rona paused. "It's funny, you picking Suzy and

Patricia—such hard women, and so completely the opposite to Mom. Let's face it, darling, you're the manipulator, the great controller, and yet you married two real bitches."

Roger smiled again. "So now it's love, romance, passion and control—you're sure that's all?"

"And don't settle for anything less."

Roger had always listened to Rona. She was the only woman alive who had his best interests at heart, the only female who honestly loved him. At thirty-seven, he became an eligible bachelor again, playing the field as he had never done in his twenties, always prudent and selective in choosing his partners, whether it was for one night or for one month, but it was seldom for longer. He'd wasted time and energy, not to mention money, on marriage, and although the business had never suffered, he wasn't about to risk making any further errors of judgment.

By 1980, the Ambler Corporation had spread its tentacles into Europe via a chain of employment agencies that Roger had bought into in the States and had then expanded into France, Germany, Switzerland, and Britain. Other American and Canadian companies had plowed that particular furrow before him, some failing, one or two to great success, and as always, Roger was glad to climb onto their backs, learning from their mistakes and triumphs. There was never any shame in following, he had always believed, so long as you had that extra something to offer that would make you stand out. The agencies gave him a reason to spend time in England, to gradually, subtly, bring himself into the consciousness of people of influence. One of Roger's prime goals for this new decade was to get a foothold in the British newspaper industry, an ambition first sparked in him by conversations with Tom Bailey who had, since his own teenage years, nurtured an idealistic dream of producing a unique style of newspaper in the United Kingdom. Cowboy Bailey was too much of a dreamer, and Roger harbored no false hopes of a dramatic personal entry into Fleet Street, but he liked the notion of trying to sidle in from the provinces, where the funds he was dangling as bait had already been snapped up by a cash-starved Midlands newspaper group that had invested heavily in new printing technology and was now finding paying for it heavy going.

He was visiting the Oxford Street branch of the Ambler Agencies in the spring of 1983, when he first saw her. There were branch offices that he had never even seen, since he trusted Hal Deacon, his UK controller, to keep him as fully briefed in his weekly reports as every other segment of the Ambler empire always had; but the agency between Selfridges and Oxford Circus was their premier London office personnel branch, doubling as UK headquarters.

Every Ambler Agency in the United States and Europe was decorated and furnished as identically as was practical. In 1983, the agency colors were muted inky blue and off-white, and the offices were designed to give as spacious and airy a feel as possible. Roger had toyed, in the early days, with ordering uniforms for the men and women who manned what he called the shop front, but then he'd realized that an employment counselor needed to be a perfect example both to potential employees and clients. A uniform was merely a means of disguising individuality, and Ambler personnel in this image-conscious area were taken on as much for their personal style as their skills. If a counselor didn't know how to dress, they didn't belong in one of his agencies.

Striding in through the electronically operated double doors, leaving the Oxford Street hurly-burly behind him, Roger felt a sense of satisfaction. He'd flown into Heathrow in an uncertain mood, but here, at least, the agency was purring nicely with activity—he and Deacon agreed that a crazed, hyperactive buzz was undesirable and off-putting to nervous newcomers; all but one of the chairs in the waiting area were taken, the desks in the section where new applicants filled in their application forms were all in use, the electronic clatter from the testing booths was satisfactorily muffled, and the counselors to left and right all the way to the back were interviewing. The agency felt comfortable; the temperature was at sixty-five degrees, the air was fresh and unpolluted thanks to their new no-smoking regulations, and the atmosphere was energetic yet calm.

Beth Barker, the branch manager, and Ludovic Harris, the

area controller, were poised and waiting for Ambler, coffee freshly brewed and reports ready for his inspection.

"How are we doing, Ludo?"

"Nicely, sir. Apart from Moorgate, I'm quietly confident."

"Let's look at Moorgate first." Roger smiled at the branch manager. "We'll be a while yet, Beth. Perhaps you could join us a little later?"

He watched her leave the room, pleased, as always, with her appearance and demeanor, saw her bend, for a moment, over one counselor's desk, then move on, heading toward the staircase, going back to her own office. Someone stopped her again, a young woman in a cream suit and black blouse. Roger meant to look away, to attend to the Moorgate folder that Ludo had placed before him, but he could not.

She had black hair, cut in a jaw-length bob with bangs, hair that swung cleanly as she moved, and her face was pale and somehow dramatic. Roger wanted to get up and leave the room, to take a closer look at her, but he stayed in his chair and forced himself to return to the matter at hand.

"Okay, let's get to work," he said, and the brusqueness in his own voice acted on him as he knew it invariably did on those who worked for him. "Do we close Moorgate down, or is it worth saving?"

The meeting went on for two hours, and Roger became as absorbed as he always did in the facts, figures, triumphs, disasters and regular plateaus that were the common denominators in all his businesses. They worked through lunch, eating a sandwich—or what passed for a sandwich in England—and drinking more coffee, and at half-past two, when they emerged, the agency was quieter, as they all tended to be at that time of day.

Roger spotted her immediately, sitting at a desk near the back.

"New girl?" he asked Beth Barker.

"She's been with us for six months, sir."

"Name?"

"Laura Andros." Beth glanced toward her.

"Doing well?"

"Very."

* * *

She stayed on his mind all day. Roger attended meetings, went to a cocktail party at Condé Nast, to dinner at Mr. Chow with Nelson Howarth, his brother-in-law, who happened to be in London too, and after a restless night's sleep in his suite at the Ritz he was driven to Birmingham for a day of meetings with his editorial staff at the British *Courier* group, in which he now held controlling shares. By nightfall, back in London again, she was still in his thoughts, somewhere near the back, but niggling at him nonetheless, like a tickling finger.

He walked back into the Oxford Street office at a quarter past eight the next morning, aware that Beth Barker was always at her desk by then. She looked startled to see him again; Ambler never visited more than once a trip.

"The new counselor, Miss Andros."

"Yes, sir?"

"I'd like to see her personnel file."

"Right away."

It was unusual, but not unprecedented, for individual employees to catch his eye, for better or worse. Beth knew that Roger had once stalked into their Liverpool office in a bad mood and sacked a girl on the spot for chewing gum and slouching over her desk. Alarm bells rang in her head as she retrieved the file Ambler had requested; she was aware of Laura Andros's background.

If anything in the folder caused him concern, Roger did not show it. He scanned the details swiftly but thoroughly and handed it back to Beth.

"So you're pleased with her progress?"

"Perfectly."

"I'd like to see her. Is she here yet?"

"She may be. Laura usually gets in early."

He waited in the boardroom for less than two minutes. She wore a navy blue blazer with gold buttons over a cream skirt, and high-heeled plain pumps. The fabrics and leather were inexpensive, yet she presented a stylish overall image. Her legs, Roger noted, were excellent. She was a little breathless and there was a tiny hint of flush on the pale cheeks, but otherwise she was quite composed.

"Miss Barker said you wanted to see me, sir."

She had an interesting voice, Roger thought. Low and clear, with a touch of the Greek he might have expected from her name, but mixed with something else he couldn't immediately identify.

"I make a point of meeting new employees whenever possible, Miss Andros. No cause for concern." He did not invite her to sit.

She looked into his face, her eyes watchful. They were green and slightly slanted, and her makeup gave them the dramatic effect he had noticed two days earlier.

"I'm very pleased to meet you, Mr. Ambler."

Roger smiled up at her, aware that his smile suited him well, made his features less sharp.

"Are you happy here, Miss Andros?"

"Very happy, sir, thank you."

"Satisfied with your progress so far?"

"I think so—from my point of view, at least."

"From ours, too, I'm glad to say."

"Thank you," she said again.

The encounter was awkward and formal, exactly as he had intended. He knew that it would leave her feeling uncertain and uncomfortable, and that, too, was intentional.

On his flight to San Francisco, he replayed the brief meeting, brought her back to his mind's eye. Observation was a special knack of his. He often reflected that he would make a splendid witness to a crime, because of his ability to return, mentally, to a scene or to a specific individual. There was something about Laura Andros, however, that eluded him. He recalled the superficial details well enough: the chain-store blazer, quite well chosen but lacking chic or individuality, the shoes that were what he thought of as airline stewardess's shoes. He remembered the hair, rather well cut, as if the girl, living on her inevitably tight budget in overpriced London, had sensed that if there was one thing worth spending on, it was a good hairdresser—and he remembered the face. A fine face, oval and well-structured with a pointy chin and wide, curving mouth. And those eyes, the focal point, those dramatic cat's eyes.

All so young, the lips and the pale, soft skin, and the clear green eyes and the unlined neck. Intelligent, too, apprehensive in his presence but handling it well enough; no overplaying, just watching, listening and waiting, and giving nothing away. Elusive little kitten.

Leaning comfortably back in his first-class seat, his feet raised in the soft slipperettes the airline provided, Roger sipped his champagne and allotted another sixty seconds to her. Her personnel file had been incomplete, with more gaps than information. Beth Barker had known that before she handed it to him, Roger had seen that in her expression, but he had chosen to ignore the gaps, at least at that moment. Laura Andros might be no more fascinating than her façade, but he was sufficiently intrigued to wish to know more. Before the end of the week, he would know everything.

He was back in New York when it came. All that he wanted to know about her. His secretary handed him the envelope when he arrived in his office on Friday morning. Roger was fond of his office. The Ambler Corporation had moved into the black glass and steel skyscraper on the Avenue of the Americas a year before, and he had known when he'd first surveyed the space that his suite would be on the northeast corner of the thirty-second floor, giving him a view up Sixth Avenue straight into Central Park.

He did not open the envelope, but slipped it into his briefcase. The day was fully allocated: a late breakfast with Tom Bailey, then out to White Plains, back for a telephone conference with the editor of the *Boston Courier,* and meetings on the hour until the cocktails he'd promised Rona he'd get to at the Museum of Modern Art, where Zero was launching a new book on Monet, and after that he was dining at home, discreetly, with the editor of the British *Daily Post.*

Roger finally got around to opening the envelope in bed just after midnight. He was bored with his Central Park South apartment—the park view was still wonderful, of course, but the building was too old-fashioned, too stuffy, and the fact that the residents tended to put up with maintenance problems that they would never dream of tolerating at any of the plush hotels they surely stayed at, drove him crazy. Still, he consoled himself, his apartment in Trump Tower would be ready for him before Christmas, and just thinking about it gave him a kick of pride. He had a place in San Francisco, now, and he hoped, ultimately, to take an apartment in Paris, but Trump Tower was the power address he'd dreamed of since Donald Trump had announced it, and it was hard, even for him, to imagine wanting more.

The report on Laura Andros blew him away. For a while, as he sat up in bed with the folder open on his crisp white sheets, he experienced cold anger, for there was no way on earth that she should ever have been employed in any part of the Ambler Corporation, let alone in such a sensitive, people-handling area. But along with the anger came unprecedented excitement. He understood now why he had been drawn to her, why she had intrigued him. He had thought, at first, that it had simply been her youthful appeal, the possibility that here was a kid in her first flush who might just be talented enough for singling out; if you seized them young, Roger had learned over the years, and trained and groomed them, you sometimes found yourself with company expertise and loyalty that could seldom be achieved otherwise.

But there was much more to this attraction than business, he saw that now. She *was* young, and she did need grooming. She was good at her job, and she had a certain natural style. She had, without trying, captured his attention in a way that no woman had for years. Roger knew now that as well as being beautiful and bright, she was a survivor. But none of those things were what had drawn him so compellingly to her.

Laura Andros had done something that no one else he knew had done. She looked so innocent, spoke so calmly, appeared so normal. But she had killed. The report listed manslaughter, mentioned self-defense, but this girl had *killed.* She was a murderess.

And when Roger Jefferson Ambler paused to think about that, he got the biggest hard-on he had ever experienced in his life.

CHAPTER 9

In the early days after her release, Laura had found freedom daunting. The good things, of course, had far outweighed the bad. Stepping out unaccompanied into the real world, blending with guiltless, normal people, being one of the crowd. Standing outside on a starry night gazing up into the sky, hours after the inmates at Kane House had been locked up and told to sleep. Opening her bedroom window at will, keeping it open because she wanted to. Discovering Hampstead Heath and Kenwood and Regent's Park, tossing bread to the ducks and Canada geese, wandering through the zoo; riding on the top deck of a London bus, trying to remember not to stare at the free men and women around her. At Kane, if you stared at someone, they swore at you or even punched you.

For every pleasure there was a price to be paid. Sometimes, it was simply money—Laura had never had to think about money before—but other times it was having to make her own decisions. Being responsible for herself. For the first three months, while they let her stay at the hostel, it wasn't too hard; there was always someone to give her a little free advice when she needed it. Laura thought of the hostel as a kind of umbilical cord linking her to Kane and Mrs. Williamson, and oh, how she needed that cord, needed all the help she could get with the ordinary, commonplace things that the others out there in the streets took in their stride. Laura had never paid a bill in her life, never had a bank account or a checkbook. She had never cooked for herself, never shopped for groceries, never traveled on the tube.

Never had a job.

"Don't be too nervous," Beth Barker, the trim, red-haired counselor at her employment agency told her before her first day's work. "I won't tell you not to be nervous at all, because you're bound to be."

"I'm too terrified to be nervous," Laura said.

"There's really no need. Your skills are good, you're very presentable, and they won't ask you to do anything you're not able to."

"Do they know about me?"

The counselor understood what she meant. "They know all they need to. You can put it out of your mind now, Laura. All they want from you is a fair day's work for a fair day's pay. You'll be fine, believe me."

Laura tried to believe her, but it wasn't easy. Beth Barker had been assigned to interview and test her when Laura and Mrs. Williamson had first visited the employment agency near Oxford Circus. They'd chosen the Ambler Agency mostly because Beth had been so warm and natural with Laura, putting her at her ease, and when it had come to job seeking, Laura knew that Beth had consulted with her colleagues in at least two other Ambler branches before finding her her first position. Laura was very grateful, but the gratitude only added to her general burden of anxiety, and she fulfilled her own worst expectations.

"I expect you tried too hard," Beth said, when the company asked her to find a replacement for Laura. "It happens quite often. You load yourself with too much pressure, so you're bound to make mistakes."

"No one has *ever* made more mistakes than I did today." Laura was on the verge of tears. "I got lost on the way, I spilled coffee on my boss's desk and I ruined so many sheets of paper that I had to bring them home in a plastic bag in case anyone saw them in my wastepaper basket."

"Only one bag?" Beth smiled. "On my first day, I filled three."

Beth Barker did what she could to help. She respected Helen Williamson and liked and trusted Laura. So far as Beth was concerned, the young woman had paid her dues, but directives from above made it clear that nondisclosure of any criminal record was tantamount to perjury in the eyes of the Ambler management. Many of the substantial companies in which Laura might have started quietly and built up her confidence would not consider anyone with a history of violence, and most of the jobs Beth felt she could confidently send Laura to were mundane and lacking in prospects, so in the end she was forced to throw in the towel and send Laura to one of their branches specializing in temporary employment.

For eighteen months, Laura went from job to job, never knowing from week to week, sometimes from day to day, where she would be working next. It suited some people, but Laura hated the uncertainty and the insecurity. There was never any chance of making friends, and though she wrote regularly to Gus, making a point of repeating her new address in each letter, Gus never wrote back. She found a room in Paddington, off Praed Street. It was damp and dismal; there were cockroaches and, at night, Laura could hear scratching that she felt sure had to be mice, but she couldn't bear to put down poison or traps, had done all the killing she was ever going to do.

By February of 1982, she had seldom been lower. She had caught the flu in January and still felt under par; the room was cold and damper than ever; she had no appetite, and the last employers she'd been sent to had turned her out after a few hours because she was coughing so badly.

And then Gus came.

She turned up just before ten o'clock one night. Laura heard the knock at her door and sat very still. No one ever came to visit her. There was no one.

"Bloody hell."

She heard the voice, rough and familiar and beloved.

"Gus?" She got up and went to the door, hardly able to believe it.

"Open the sodding door, for Christ's sake."

Laura's hands were trembling. Gus looked strange, some- how, that was the first thing that went through her mind, but then the thought was gone, shoved aside by happiness.

"You look like shit," Gus said.

"I know."

"You ill?"

"I was. I'm better now."

"Don't look it."

Laura wanted to embrace her, but didn't dare touch her. Gus had never been one for hugs, except for that last night before they'd been separated, when they'd shared the cell at the police station in Bristol.

"Want some soup?" she asked, softly.

"That all you've got?"

Laura nodded.

"It'll do."

Gus told her that she'd been out for a while. Laura wanted to ask her why she hadn't come sooner, but she didn't dare. They weren't at Kane anymore; this was a new world, with new orders, new rules, but Laura sensed that Gus had been somewhere much farther away. It was nothing to do with her external appearance—her hair was frizzed out and dyed as black as the makeup around her eyes, and she looked gener- ally much the same; she'd always been thin and bony, any- way. This came from within. It was like looking at someone who'd been ill—really ill, dying maybe—and when they came back they were different somehow, altered.

Laura heated the canned vegetable soup on the two ring stove, while Gus sat in the single armchair. It was ancient, battered brown leather, horsehair stuffing protruding from long slits as if someone had once deliberately cut it, the way they did in movies when they were looking for cash or hid- den drugs. The whole room looked like that, old and abused and sordid.

"Was it really bad?" Laura asked, carefully.

"Yes," Gus said. "I don't want to talk about it."

"If you change your mind, I'm—"

"I won't. It's finished."

"Okay," Laura said.

Gus smiled for the first time then. A swift, thin, sad smile that went straight to Laura's heart.

"It's good to see you, kid," she said. "Even if you do look like shit."

Laura hardly dared to ask.

"Will you stay?"

"For a bit."

It was almost a week before Gus said anything at all about her time in borstal, and then it was just one simple statement. They were out shopping in Praed Street, were standing outside the greengrocer's when Gus suddenly stopped.

"I was scared the whole time. Every day, every night." The knuckles of her hands, holding the brown paper bag of apples, were white. "It made Kane look like a bloody picnic. Vicious bastards everywhere, inmates and screws."

"Gus—" Laura stood facing her, feeling sick.

"That's all there is." Gus's thin face was very white. "I'm all right now. I really am. I got through it—a lot of them don't. But I'm a survivor, like you."

That was it. She never said another word about their time apart, and Laura knew better than to ask. It was enough that she was there, with her. Another human being. Someone who cared.

Gus put her own past away, and set about getting Laura into shape. She saw to it that she ate properly, brought her a new blanket, and Laura knew she must have pinched it, but she didn't say anything, though she couldn't imagine how anyone could shoplift something that size, and she was terrified that Gus would get caught. If she did, it wouldn't be borstal, it would be prison, probably Holloway, and that might be the end of her, and she knew she ought to challenge her about it, but she didn't dare and was still too weak, and anyway, Gus was back, Gus was in charge.

"You've got to look after yourself, kid."

"I do. I will."

"I won't always be here. And Christ knows, I can hardly look after myself, never mind you."

"You're stronger than I am, Gus."

"That's just crap."

"You're Gus, the hard case, remember?"

"Not anymore."

Two weeks after Gus had come back, Laura received a letter from Adam Demonides. He was in Athens, working as a clerk in an office. The new owners of Chryssos had sacked Maria in 1979, and soon after that, while working as a bricklayer in the city, Adam had fallen from a wall and been badly injured. By the time he had been released from hospital, Laura had left Kane, and neither her letters to Aegina nor his to the community home had been sent on.

> *I was so afraid I would never find you again, but thanks to your kind teacher, I have your address at last. I want to know everything, moraki mou, all the good things and the bad.*
>
> *When will we meet again? I would come to you, but I have no money, and your Helen Williamson has told me that life is not as easy for you as you deserve. Write to me soon, little sister, and tell me everything.*

All her joys came together, tumbling like blessings onto Laura's head. She had Gus again, and Adam, and now Beth Barker contacted her to let her know that she had been promoted to branch manager at the employment agency, and to say that she wanted to see Laura with a view to a permanent job.

"She wants me to be a counselor," Laura told Gus. "She thinks I could do it—interview people for jobs and try to place them with clients."

"She's probably right."

"Of course she isn't. I'm not qualified."

"She must think you are."

"I couldn't—I'm not even any good at *being* interviewed."

"I'd forget that word if I were you," Gus said. "Interview's a cold word. How did this Beth talk to you when she was your counselor? What was it all about?"

Laura thought about it. "She tried to find out what I could do. What I was good at." She shrugged. "And then she tried to find the right job to suit me."

"So basically she just talked to you. Got to know a bit about you."

"And she filled out some forms."

"So big deal. You can write. You're great at talking to people mostly because you're a good listener."

Laura was still dubious. "The women there all seemed so efficient, so tough."

Gus smiled. "How long d'you think most of them would have lasted in Kane House? Talk about the school of hard knocks—you started at the top, kid. Anything else has to be child's play."

Beth Barker agreed with Gus. The agency business was competitive and stressful and frustrating, but Beth felt that she'd never met anyone better qualified than Laura for the work.

"Survival's the name of the game here, and that's you in a nutshell. You're a survivor, and to top it you look good, you learn fast and you've been temping for eighteen months, so you must have picked up a lot of useful tips about clients."

"The clients are the employers, is that right?" Laura asked. "And the ones who're looking for work are the applicants?"

"That's it. And your job is to put them together. Placements. As many as you can, week in, week out. You've got to learn how to read people better than they read themselves. Sometimes they come in off the street and tell you what they want to do, and it's your job to judge if they're right, and if they're wrong, it's your job to convince them what they should be looking for."

"And then to find it for them?"

"That's right." Beth smiled. "What do you think?"

Laura looked around the manager's office. "No more having to call in to find out where I'm going to be next morn-

ing, or if I'm going to be working at all." She paused. "No
more nasty shocks when I get there."

"I can promise you the odd shock all right, and plenty of
tension, too," Beth said. "There are few industries as competitive as employment, Laura. You'll be joining a great
bunch, but when you start work every morning, you go into
a kind of battle—we're all on the same team, but everyone
wants to make more placements than everyone else, for the
money and to get ahead. And not everyone can take it."

"But you think I can?"

"If I didn't think so, you wouldn't be here."

Laura was silent for a moment.

"What about my record? Won't it matter to the management here?"

"You've proved yourself to me," Beth said. "I'll help you
with your application form. You won't tell any lies, but you
don't have to put down every last detail of everything that's
ever happened to you." She paused. "And if and when you
do start work here, you don't have to tell your colleagues too
much about yourself either. I'm not saying you shouldn't
trust people, but working relationships are different from
other friendships—it's better not to tell anyone anything
they could use against you."

"Ammunition," Laura said.

"Especially if you do well. The higher you go, the more
jealous some people get. Even if they like you."

"Are they jealous of you now?"

"Certainly. I like to think we get along pretty well, but
popularity and success don't really go together."

Laura was afraid to go shopping with Gus for the new
clothes she needed for work. Every time she tentatively
brought up the subject of Gus's future, of the jobs that she
might be suited to, her friend shut up like an oyster. It was
apparent that Gus hadn't yet made up her mind what was going to happen next, that she was not yet ready to try for nor-
mality. Laura was scared of putting temptation in her path in
case old habits prevailed over common sense.

"What are they going to pay you?" Gus wanted to know.

"Six thousand a year, plus commission. I get ten percent of the fee for every placement I make."

"You're talking like one of them already." Gus smiled at her. "Now we find you somewhere to live."

"What's wrong with here?"

"What's right with it? Listen to me, kid, you're on the move now. Things are coming right for you, and about bloody time. This is the moment to jack in all the bad stuff—shove it in the fireplace and strike a match. And that includes this dump. If you're going to do a hard day's work, you need a good night's sleep and somewhere to relax when you get home."

"Think I can afford it?"

"Damn right you can."

Gus spent three days flat hunting with Laura, made herself respectable enough to go to the bank with her and stuck to her like glue until her new lease—on a flat in Finborough Road near Earls Court—was signed.

"You'll be okay now, kid," she said to her that evening, watching Laura pack her few belongings into boxes.

"I love the flat, don't you?" Laura was ecstatic.

"I think it's great."

"We'll have to get one of those sofa things that folds out into a bed. You can have the bedroom."

"The bedroom's all yours, kid."

Laura smiled. "We'll talk about it when we get there."

But in the morning, Gus was gone. She had left a note. *I'm not ready for this yet. You are, but not me. Maybe soon, but not yet. Don't worry about me, kid. I'll be fine. And you'll be the best counselor ever.*

Laura wept bitter tears, of anger as well as loss. She felt betrayed, felt that Gus was cruel to have come back and let her believe it was all going to be all right from then on, only to vanish again. But the anger soon disappeared, melted under the storm of grief. And then, when she'd cried enough, she dried her eyes and got on with moving into her new flat. It was what Gus wanted her to do—what *she* wanted to do. And Gus would come back again, she was certain of that. Certain enough to be going on with.

* * *

By the time Gus did come to the flat in Finborough Road, Laura had been there for three months, had settled into its bright, airy cleanness, had grown used to her job, to the bus journey there and back, to working as part of a team with the other young women at the Ambler Agency, had even grown accustomed to the daily shock of the Oxford Street crowds.

Nothing could have prepared her for the shock of seeing the scars on Gus's wrists. Gus showed them to her deliberately, the first evening, rolled up the sleeves of her sweatshirt and held out her hands, palms up.

"You'd only get to see them by accident otherwise."

Laura stared at the two scars, thin and red and ugly. Pain pierced her, hot and sickening.

"They'll fade a bit, I expect, in time."

Laura looked up into Gus's face.

"For God's sake, why?"

Gus dropped her hands to her sides. "Things got to me. Don't really know why. Funny, in a way. All those years when it was really rough, and then it was being free that tipped the balance."

Laura said nothing, just waited.

"Listen, kid"—Gus looked into Laura's eyes, right into them, gray on green—"it's not going to happen again. I swear it." She paused. "If I didn't believe that, I'd never have come here. I wouldn't do that to you."

"Why—?" Laura swallowed. "Why didn't it—?"

"Why didn't I die?" Gus's smile was gentle. "It wasn't because I changed my mind, not then, anyway. I was in a squat, and I thought I'd locked the door, but apparently I hadn't."

"Maybe that was deliberate."

Gus smiled again. "Maybe."

She stayed for dinner, and this time there was a refrigerator full of food, and then she and Laura went together to Gus's squat to fetch her few things, and Laura saw the look of contempt that one of the men there gave them both; her because her clothes marked her as the enemy, Gus because she was deserting.

"I want you to have the bedroom," Laura said to Gus when they got back to the flat.

"No way."

"It makes sense." Laura tried to convince her. "I'll be getting up early in the mornings, and I won't have to disturb you."

"Yes, you will, your clothes'll be in the wardrobe." Gus sat down on the sofa. "Anyway, I like this room better. Is this the sofa bed you were going to buy?"

Laura shook her head. "I couldn't find one cheap enough. But we can go and get one together."

"No need. This is fine." She patted the blue cushions, then stood up again. "Nice and comfy. Pretty, too."

"But you ought to have a bed."

"I've been kipping on floors for the last three months."

"Even more reason—"

"Forget it," Gus said.

For once, Laura ventured a hug. She put her arms around Gus, just a gentle circle, no pressure, no threat.

"You won't ever do that again, will you?" she asked, very softly. "I couldn't stand that. Not that."

"I told you," Gus said.

"Cross your heart?"

Gus stepped back.

"I want to live, kid," she said.

Ned Archer was Laura's first boyfriend. Twenty-six years old, with limitless energy, very short, almost crew-cut brown hair and all-round good looks, he owned the snack bar in Duke Street where she often went for a quick sandwich and espresso. He had come to London from Kent, where his family had run a small market garden, after dropping out of school inadequately qualified for his parents' aspirations on his behalf.

"Oxford," he told Laura. "At the very least. And then, ideally, medicine, preferably a surgeon. I don't mind slicing roast beef or ham, but there I draw the line."

What Ned had wanted to do was to photograph fashion models, to get down on his knees and snap away from floor level at Jean Shrimpton—Ned had always liked living in the past. But instead he'd ended up buttering mountains of bread and mashing hard-boiled eggs, and when his boss had got fed up with getting up at the crack of dawn for the early-morning rush Ned had gone to his family, cap in hand, and had bought the business. At least this way, he told his friends, he got to see and chat with some of the prettiest girls in the world on a daily basis, and what Ned might have lacked in application at school or in talent as a photographer, he made up for with his gift for chatting up women.

The first time he handed Laura a crusty cheese roll to take away, Ned asked her out on a date, but Laura, taken by surprise, grew flustered and escaped. Ned persisted, with every sandwich, every salad, every cup of coffee, a gentle, amiable persistence that finally won her over. They went out to dinner a number of times, went to the cinema—never to the theater, Ned hated the theater—went boating on the Serpentine. Ned's flat was in Charlotte Street, surrounded by Greek restaurants, and he took Laura to Anemos, where diners smashed plates and danced on the tables, and he listened, fascinated, to the stories of her childhood on Aegina, and forced himself not to dig too insistently when the happy tales ended and Laura closed up, sealing the rest of her past from him.

"Do you think I should tell him?" she asked Gus one evening, at home.

"What for?"

Gus was at the stove, stirring her latest creation—something with aubergines, she'd told Laura, unwilling to be drawn further. Gus had never dreamed that she might love cooking, until she'd had this little kitchen. Laura always found it an incongruous sight; Gus with her frizzed out, crazy hair, scarlet again now, an apron tied around her waist, but Gus thought it might have something to do with cooking reminding her of Alice. She felt closer to her mother again, after all those years, when she was peeling or chopping or bending over something aromatic in the oven.

"I don't know," Laura said. "Ned's so sweet, so funny—I feel dishonest, keeping something so important from him."

"If you tell him, it'll probably screw things up." Gus

turned around to scrutinize her. "You don't love him, do you?"

"No, but I like him."

"So why get your knickers in a twist?" Gus shrugged. "If I were you, I'd lock it away and throw away the key."

"I'll never be able to do that."

"You'd be better off if you could, kid."

It was good having Ned in her life. Laura had missed all those normal teenage years of first stirring interest in boys, first arousal, first kisses, necking in the back rows of cinemas. Now, so far as she could tell from magazines and the gossiping of the women in the office, it seemed to be all or nothing. If you let a man near you, let him kiss you, let alone touch you, that was it, next step the bedroom, and Laura sometimes felt as if she were creeping along in the dark, unsure what was expected of her.

"You don't have to do a bloody thing you don't want to," Gus told her. "If you don't want him touching you, don't let him. If that's all he's interested in, sod him."

But Ned Archer was patience personified. Ned was in love. He took photographs of Laura every chance he had, framed them and put them up in his flat and in the snack bar. He sang "Tell Laura I Love Her" every morning while he made bacon sandwiches and scrambled eggs; he put up with Gus's glowering looks when he went to Finborough Road—he even brought Gus flowers, anything to try and get on her good side. He told Laura that he'd decided he needed a secretary to help him keep his business in order, just so that she could be sure of one extra placement. He began to serve taramasalata and moussaka, though he drew the line at kabobs, which he loathed, but then he discovered that Laura's tastes were more English than Greek, and he reverted to shepherd's pie and chips.

Laura was thriving on work. Within three months of joining the agency, she had equaled the star counselor's placements record for four successive weeks. Beth had been right to warn her that the job could be frustrating. It was maddening to spend time and energy with an applicant, to channel your own enthusiasm into her, to find her the perfect client match, and then to have her fail even to show up at an interview. But Laura learned that those failures were just part of the routine, and that if you were going to make the grade as an Ambler counselor, you had to learn, too, to suppress disappointment and irritation and to get on with the job. When she did succeed in placing an applicant with the right employer, especially when she knew she'd managed to turn someone's life around, it brought her a warm glow of satisfaction that had nothing to do with the commission the placement would bring her. For the first time in her life, she felt worthwhile.

Gus, too, was working. Since coming to live at Finborough Road, she had tried, and given up on a number of jobs.

"Let's face it, kid," she'd said to Laura. "What am I trained for? I know six different ways to break into a house, I'm a dab hand at picking pockets and I know a few odds and ends about U-bends." She'd taken a brief plumbing course at borstal, but hadn't really fancied learning the ins and outs of a lavatory cistern.

"You'd be a wonderful counselor," Laura said.

"You are joking—look at me. Not exactly the corporate image, am I?"

"But your experiences, your toughness—"

"Think they'd let me beat the clients into taking my applicants?"

"You know you could do it, if you wanted to," Laura said.

"It's not really me, though, is it?"

"You could try hairdressing. It was you who told me to have my hair cut this way, and you were right." Shortly after joining Ambler Laura had blown a large chunk of her salary on a visit to John Frieda, and she had to admit that the new style did suit her well, accentuating her pointed chin and slender neck as well as dramatizing her eyes.

"I wouldn't mind, if they'd let me get on with it, but I'd have to spend ages washing hair and sweeping up." Gus thought. "If things had gone differently I think I might have gone into fashion, been a designer, maybe."

"You could still try. Apply for college, maybe."

"Don't be daft." Gus shook her head. "You've got to recognize your limitations."

"What about food?" Laura suggested. "You're such a wonderful cook."

"Years of training," Gus dismissed again. "Washing up, scrubbing floors, being a sodding dogsbody. I like cooking because I'm doing it for us, because I don't have to do it."

They'd found the perfect solution together, one weekend, browsing in Berwick Street market. Gus had always adored the jostle and sound of markets, and in the old days they'd presented much the easiest prey for her accomplished thieving fingers, but suddenly she saw their potential in another light.

"Wait a minute." She stopped dead, and grasped Laura's jacket sleeve.

"What's wrong?" Laura asked.

"Nothing's wrong. Everything's right." Her thin face was illuminated with sudden excitement. "This is perfect for me, don't you see? It's fucking *perfect*."

"You mean a stall?"

"Just listen to it." Gus closed her eyes for a moment, tilted her head, absorbing the noise of the sales patter, the intermittent squeals of pleasure as people struck a bargain, the clink of money changing hands. "This is me, kid. I could go legit somewhere like this. It's outside, it's free—no one shoving me around, no airs and graces."

"What would you sell?"

"Clothes. Wild, gorgeous clothes—and jewelry, maybe." She still gripped Laura's arm. "What do you think?"

"Where would you set up? Here?"

"Wherever I can. I'm sure there's loads of competition for good spots."

"Camden Lock's wonderful," Laura suggested.

"Or Portobello Road, or Petticoat Lane, or—who the hell cares, so long as I can do it." Gus let go of Laura. "So tell me what you think? Am I crazy or what?"

"Not crazy," Laura said. "Definitely not crazy." She couldn't remember ever seeing Gus's gray eyes so alight with joy. "So where do we start? What do we have to do?"

"Go round all the markets, seeing what's what."

"Market research," Laura quipped.

"Will you come with me, kid? I need someone sane, to keep my feet on the ground."

They had not realized how many markets there were around the capital, some open just one day each week, others on the weekends only, some every day, rain or shine. After the first excitement, they came down to earth a little, chatting to stallholders—many of whom had waited months, even years, to secure their pitches—and watching to see how tough it was to make a sale. There were some who clearly made good money just because they sold quality merchandise more cheaply than in shops, there were rip-off artists so gifted at selling that they could move junk no one else could hope to shift, and then there were abject failures.

Gus spent two days at Roman Road market before approaching a stallholder she'd been watching closely for hours at a time. He was selling coats, jackets and knitwear, and Gus had never seen anyone move so smoothly and sell so much.

"If I guarantee never to open up in three miles of you, will you show me the ropes, give me a few tips?" she asked him.

He hardly glanced at her. "Why should I?"

"Because you're the best I've seen," Gus said, simply. "And if I'm going to learn, I want to be taught by the best. I'll help out, do whatever you tell me."

"Free?"

"Free for two weeks. After that, if you've sold more because of me, we talk again."

He looked at her properly for the first time. "What if you get in the way?"

"You chuck me out."

His profits rose, and Gus stayed with him for five months, draining him of all his knowledge, until she was granted her own stall at Camden Lock, and from then on her life was transformed by work, just as Laura's had been. Her old talents qualified Gus to steal both suppliers and customers from other stalls in such an accomplished way that her competitors hardly realized what she was doing; she was a nat-

ural at putting deals together, at selecting the most easily
movable stock, and almost no one got away with pinching
stuff from Gus's stall. She developed eyes in the back of her
head and the voice that delivered her sales patter was loud
and clear, just on the edge of raucousness yet with a
strangely melodious quality that drew customers as effectively as the brilliant colors of her hand-knits and Indian
silks.

The day that Roger Ambler came, in person, into Laura's
life, was the most jolting she had experienced in a long
while. Their meeting, all three minutes of it, was almost a
nonevent, yet all Laura's instincts told her that it was cru-
cially important to her.

She had never seen anyone like Ambler before. Since
coming to London—and especially since her work had begun to take her out of the agency and into clients' offices—
Laura had met men and women of varying degrees of
elegance, wealth and influence, and with every rising level
of status she encountered she had almost subconsciously
raised her own performance and working image. Roger Ambler, however, was unlike any of the clients she'd met.
Roger Ambler was in an entirely different league.

"What did you think of our leader?" Beth asked her, later
that day.

"He's very—impressive."

"Isn't he just?"

"I've never seen anyone quite like him," Laura said.

"That's money you were looking at," Beth said. "And
power."

"I still don't know why he wanted to see me. I was scared
he was going to fire me."

"Hardly." Beth grinned. "I think he took a fancy to you."

"Really?" Laura was startled.

"You certainly caught his eye. He asked about you yesterday when he was in, then came back this morning and asked
for your personnel file. He does that sometimes with employees who are new to him. I don't know how he even
spots new people—he's hardly ever here."

"So he doesn't come to London often?" Laura asked.

"I'm sure he does, but he rarely comes in to the agency." Beth paused. "Handsome, isn't he?"

"Yes." Laura nodded, remembering the hawkish, sharp features, the golden hair, the clear blue eyes, the clipped, crisp voice. "Very."

Beth smiled again. "Do you know, you're the first girl I know who's ever met him who hasn't asked if he's married."

"I didn't think about it. Is he?"

"Not at the moment."

For the rest of that week, Ambler preyed a little on Laura's mind. Hearing that he'd looked at her file had troubled her. She had visions of him finding out about her past and ordering Beth to get rid of her. Beth was right; it was power, more than anything, that she'd felt emanating from him. Laura wished, in a way, that he had not noticed her. Judging from what she'd heard about his business empire, she was the merest fleck on his landscape. One flick of his finger, and she'd be history. Just the thought of that made her very uneasy.

Ten days after Ambler's visits to Oxford Street, Hal Deacon, the UK controller, walked into the office and told Beth Barker that she was being transferred to the troubled Moorgate branch. The move was couched in flattering words to make it seem as if Beth was the only person who could pull the other branch back up into profit, but Beth knew that any transfer away from the premier London branch was a demotion.

"Why would they do that?" Laura asked, when Beth came and told her. "It seems crazy—you're a wonderful manager."

"You should be able to answer that yourself soon," Beth said, her tone strangely cool.

"What do you mean?"

"Hal Deacon wants to see you right away. In my office."

"Me?" Laura felt her stomach lurch. "What have I done?"

"All the right things, apparently."

Deacon was a six foot tall Texan, slender and smooth. He turned charm on and off the way most people handled light switches. When Laura walked into Beth's office, he was wreathed in smiles, his right hand outstretched.

"Congratulations," he said.

"I'm sorry?" Laura was confused.

"I gather Beth didn't tell you the good news."

"You mean her transfer to Moorgate." Laura took a breath. "If you don't mind my saying, I think we all wish she were staying here."

"I think the new branch manager will be every bit as effective."

"I hope so."

Deacon glanced around the office. "You'll have to let me know if you need anything done to this room. It was redecorated a year ago, but if there's something specific you feel would make you more comfortable—"

"Me?" Laura stared at him.

The Texan smiled again. "I'd like you to take over as branch manager next Monday. If you agree with the promotion, that is."

Laura was stunned. This was why Beth had been so strange. This was why Roger Ambler had wanted to meet her, had looked at her file.

"Do you accept the offer, Miss Andros?"

"I"—she pulled herself together—"I'm sorry if I seem startled, sir. I wasn't expecting anything like this. I haven't been with the agency very long."

"Long enough," Deacon said, in his slow, almost lazy drawl. "We tend to observe our counselors pretty closely. It's usually apparent right from the outset when a new employee has management potential. You've made a strong impression, Laura—okay for me to call you that?"

"Of course." Laura knew that her usually pale cheeks were hot with excitement. "It's just—what about Beth? She's been wonderful to me, and she's such a good manager."

"May I give you a little advice, Laura?"

"Please do."

"Never argue with a promotion."

The attitudes of Laura's colleagues changed overnight. To her face, they were perfectly friendly, offering her congratulations, expressing their enthusiasm for her promotion, promising their support. But in the few days that Beth was still on the premises, it was evident to Laura that they felt she was usurping Beth's rightful role as their leader, and it was just as clear that at least two of them thought that if Beth had to go, they ought to have been chosen over her. Anne Lockhart, a svelte blonde who'd been the branch star before Laura's arrival, and Patsy Jones, another high achiever, had been aiming for promotion for more than a year. Now Laura felt their eyes were daggers whenever she turned her back on them; she hadn't felt such dislike since she'd first arrived in the horseshoe-shaped dormitory in Alderley Tower.

"It scares me a bit," she confided in Gus, on the Sunday night before she was due to assume Beth's mantle. They were sharing a bottle of rosé in the living room, the television they'd bought together a couple of months ago switched on, its volume low.

"Why?"

"It takes me back, I suppose. Bad associations."

"Don't be daft. This isn't bloody public school—and even if it was, you're top dog now, remember? It's a whole other ball game. They can't touch you, it's you who can harm them."

"I don't want to harm anyone." Laura's voice was soft and tense.

Gus's eyes grew gentle. "Come on, kid, put it away. Back in its box. You were trapped in that school with those little shits. You're free now. You're a grown woman, and you're on top."

"I do try not to think about it, Gus."

"I know. It's not easy forgetting, is it?"

"You, too?"

"It's different for me. I've told you. I've never felt guilty about any of it. You still do."

"I'll never forget what she looked like." Laura's eyes narrowed, grew darker with pain. "I still dream about her, lying there." She shook her head, trying to clear it. "I don't think about it all the time anymore, truly. It's just that some things bring it back."

"You mustn't let them. Especially not something good

like this. This is promotion, kid, not the guillotine. This is people believing in you, giving you a proper chance, and about sodding time too."

Laura brightened. "You're right, as usual." She sipped some more wine. "And think of the extra money. We could maybe take a holiday one of these days, think of that."

"You could go to Greece, see your Adam."

"I hadn't even thought of that." Her eyes became suddenly brilliant. "Gus, this really is wonderful, isn't it? Would you come with me? Not that I could even *think* of going for months and months, not if I want to hold on to this job."

"And I couldn't leave my stall unless I find someone I really trust to take care of things for me."

"Listen to us both," Laura said, laughing. "Two responsible, work-oriented members of society, can you believe it?"

"Sounds a bit dodgy to me," Gus said. "They certainly wouldn't believe it at Kane." She picked up her glass. "A toast."

"Let me pour some more." Laura got the bottle from the fridge. "To you," she said.

"You can toast me anytime. This is special, a one-off."

"Go on."

Gus raised her glass.

"Up theirs," she said.

CHAPTER 10

On the day before Christmas Eve, 1985, Roger Ambler, in the king-sized bed of his suite at the Drake Hotel in Chicago, had what he had decided would be not only his last fuck of the year, but his last, period, until the moment finally came when he either won, or irrevocably lost, his battle for Laura Andros.

The woman in his bed was exquisite. Five feet, five inches of purpose-built sex. Beige silk skin, long blond hair, gorgeous breasts, legs created for spreading, and a magnificent ass. Every red-blooded American male's wet dream, and Roger's Christmas gift to himself.

"Whatever you want," she told him. "Anyhow, any way, anywhere."

He had told her a little about his quest, not too much, just enough to engage her sympathy and intrigue. Tonight, he was entirely hers. Tomorrow, he would fly back to New York for a family holiday with Rona, Nelson and his nieces, and directly after Christmas he would put the next stage of his campaign into action. In a way, he supposed, he was playing a new kind of game, and the self-imposed celibacy would be part of it, like a gambler throwing everything onto the table.

During the period of Laura's branch managership in 1983, Roger had taken her out to lunch twice, once with Janice

Shenk, the London area manager, once with five other branch managers. He had seen her on only two other occasions, once at a branch managers' seminar at the Hilton in Park Lane, and once in her office. On each occasion, he had noted every tiny thing about her, how she looked, what she wore, the way she performed, but he was confident that no one present could have observed the intensity of his interest. He wanted no gossip about favoritism in the ranks, no rumors that Laura Andros had caught the boss's eye.

Roger had, as a matter of record, never had an affair with any employee in any of his companies, had long ago concluded that screwing the help was counterproductive—after all, the world was crowded with great-looking, bright, available women. But he was nevertheless well aware that on the few occasions when he had personally spotted talent among female staff and directed that rewards or promotion be given, spiteful company tongues had begun to wag. Roger had wanted Laura's rise to be smoothly orchestrated; she was handling the branch manager's position more than competently, and he saw no reason why the further elevation he had planned for her should be regarded as anything other than appropriate.

He had told Hal Deacon to activate the second promotion in the spring of 1984. Janice Shenk was pregnant and not planning to return after the birth of her child, and Roger was aware that every branch manager in London had been sitting up straighter, power-dressing like crazy and motivating their counselors to within an inch of overload. He was also aware that Laura did not expect to be chosen.

"Move Andros upstairs starting next Monday." Roger telephoned Deacon from his suite at the Baur au Lac in Zurich. "Give her my congratulations and tell her we'll meet on Tuesday. Breakfast at the Ritz, seven-thirty sharp."

"It's going to shake them up a bit, sir." It was Deacon's way of expressing his lingering doubts, but they both knew it would be the last time he raised them. Once the boss made a final decision, no one, not even Hal Deacon, spoke against it, whatever they thought.

"She'll be good for the company, Hal."

"I'm sure she will, sir," Deacon said, and that was that.

* * *

With Laura installed in her key position, Roger was now able to see her on his London trips without raising eyebrows. During the first six months, he took her to dinner twice, once to Rules with Hal Deacon, once to Shogun, alone. He noted, with satisfaction, how naturally and smoothly she had achieved a sharpening of her appearance; no more chain-store chic, Laura had moved on to the lower echelons of quality labels and even her makeup had improved. He supposed her growing poise was old family background emerging, breaking through in spite of everything she had endured. She had a long, long way to go, but when Roger considered that she was only twenty-two—just two years more than he was her senior—her sheer potential lit real sparks inside him.

He had never built a person before. He had, of course, shaped and groomed companies and employees, but he had never taken any woman and set about creating her in the image he had chosen for her. He had spoken to no one about what he was doing, not even Rona, whom he told most things—and in the beginning, he hadn't even been certain what he *was* doing. Usually, he believed in compartmentalizing his life: business, fun, serious relationships and family. This, though, was different. His perception of Laura Andros overlapped all such borders, like hot lava stealthily overflowing. He saw her as an employee, of course, as a commodity; he recognized her as a young woman who attracted him sexually as no other woman had ever done. But there was more besides, less easily definable. Just more.

He knew she was still seeing Ned Archer, but Roger was fairly certain that if there had ever been any heat in the relationship, it was cooling. Archer was young, good-looking and from good stock, probably an entertaining enough escort, but he was still a lightweight, the kind of Englishman who would probably expect his chosen woman to fall, in time, into his inadequate arms, forsaking all others, including her career. If Roger had harbored any fears that the snack bar owner might sweep Laura away, he would have acted promptly, but as it was, all he'd had to do was to see that Laura was simply too busy to spend much time with Archer.

Laura had never known it was possible to work so hard. While she'd managed the Oxford Street branch, she had worked out ways of maintaining a balance between business and a personal life, but since becoming area manager it had become impossible to do that. Hal Deacon had told her, without actually bad-mouthing her predecessor, that it was all too easy to turn the heavily financially oriented work into an excuse for sitting behind a desk every day. An effective area manager needed to be much more than an accountant and administrator; she needed to be out and about at all her branches, getting her staff accustomed to the fact that she was a hands-on manager, not a remote paper-shuffler, that she would walk into branches regularly, sometimes without warning. All that meant dealing with paperwork after closing time, often late into the evenings and during weekends.

"I never see you anymore," Ned complained on one of their rare evenings together.

"It can't be helped," Laura told him. "I hate it too."

"No, you don't, you love it."

"I love the work, yes, but I wish I had more free time."

"To spend with me?"

"Of course."

"And Gus."

"Sure."

"I wonder, sometimes, which of us is more important to you."

"Don't be silly, Ned."

"Which is it then?"

"I didn't know it was a competition."

"There's my answer."

Laura could not argue. She was never in the slightest doubt as to who was more important to her. Ned was a lovely man, fun to be with and caring, but he was just a boyfriend. Gus was family. The way Adam had been.

She had made her way to Greece, at last, in August the previous year, while she was still managing Oxford Street. She had gone alone, in the end, because Gus had said she couldn't risk leaving the stall for more than a couple of days, and anyway, she had her eye on a second site, which meant she had to look for someone to run it. But Laura was sure that Gus was just being sensitive, felt that she and Adam needed to be alone. And she would probably have been right, if things had gone as planned, but as it was, Laura had no sooner arrived in Athens, suffocated by the blazing, long-forgotten heat, than she had been called back to London by Hal Deacon because five out of her ten counselors had been laid low by a flu bug.

She and Adam had had just one evening. They had met in a taverna on Likavitos Hill, overlooking the city, and for the first few minutes, they had been wordless, just staring at each other, trying to take in the wealth of changes.

"You're very handsome," Laura said, and at twenty-three, Adam was just as she had imagined he would look, tall and lean, with his wonderful black olive eyes and the slightly crooked nose that she had always loved.

"And you're even more beautiful than I thought you would be," Adam said. "My little sister."

For another moment, he stared at her, taking her in, and then he took her in his arms, and they both stayed like that, not wanting to move, remembering the last time they had embraced, before all the terrible things had happened to Laura.

They had talked ceaselessly after that, eating little, too excited, too oppressed by the weight of the summer heat. They spoke of Aegina, of Theo Andros, of Chryssos.

"I wanted to go to the island," Laura said, "but now there isn't time."

"Perhaps it's for the best. It wouldn't be the same anymore."

They paused for a moment, then remembered how little time they had.

"How is Maria?" Laura asked.

"Older. Working too hard. When I told her you were coming, she was so happy she wept."

"I wish I could have seen her, too."

"She only has Sundays off. Next time."

Adam spoke very briefly about his job. "Not at all what I'd hoped for—fool's work, fetching and carrying, filing papers in a stuffy office." He shrugged. "But without university—I didn't even finish school."

"You must miss the sea," Laura said softly, remembering how he had loved it. "Was there nothing else you could do?"

Adam shook his head. "Since the accident, my back is too weak for fishing or sailing." He smiled. "Don't look so anxious—I'm quite fine for most things—I don't even limp, do I?"

"But you can't do what you want to." Suddenly, Laura wanted to cry.

"And you," Adam said. "What happened to you is a thousand times more terrible. Ten thousand times." He reached for her hand across the table. "I wanted so much to come to you."

"I know you did."

He looked right into her eyes. "Can you talk about it? Can you bear to?"

"No," Laura said. "I don't think I can. Maybe if I could stay longer—if we could just be together the way it used to be."

"But nothing is as it used to be, little one, is it?"

When she got back to London, Gus was outraged.

"You shouldn't have come back."

"I had no choice."

"You could have told them to sod off."

Laura smiled. "I suppose I could, but I don't think Hal would have been impressed."

"Seems fishy to me."

"Nothing fishy about flu."

"Surely someone could have kept things going, at least for a few days."

"That's what comes of being indispensable. You should know, Gus the entrepreneur. Have you found anyone yet to run the new stall?"

"Give us a chance—you've only been gone one day."

"You'll do it."

Gus grinned. "Damned right I will."

* * *

When Laura was promoted to area manager, it felt to her as if she had been plucked out of the level in which she had felt so much at home, the workers' level, and deposited on another plane. In her early days as a counselor, the job had been a challenge, the competitiveness between her and the others had been vigorous but never, to her at least, threatening, and being branch manager had felt more or less an extension of that work. This new job, however, was an entirely different kettle of fish. She had not sought it out, had never dreamed of winning it, but now that she had it she was surprised by the intensity of her urge to hold on to it.

The fact that Roger Ambler now seemed to be taking a personal interest in her career both excited and alarmed her. The girl who had survived life in Kane House had learned to do so by keeping a low profile, by trying not to get noticed. The Laura Andros who was now effectively being paid a high salary to control ten branches in the capital, was permanently on display, and the only two people to whom she reported were Hal Deacon and, when he elected to get involved, Ambler himself.

Increasingly, as she entered her second year as area manager, he was on the scene. She was aware that he was visiting London more often because of his newspaper involvements and other industries, but he often found time to call her when he was in town and to set up a meeting, usually after-hours. He took her to dinner, sometimes in restaurants, sometimes to his favorite nightclub, Annabel's. Laura had felt out of her depth the first time she had met him there. They were simply there for drinks, so her clothes presented no major crisis, but it was enough of an exposure to the most famous nightclub in the country to show her how lacking her wardrobe still was.

Not only her wardrobe, of course. Since first seizing her opportunity to tune in to the heart of the capital, Laura had begun habitually observing the women, young and old, independent, feisty or calm, who briskly walked its more lavish streets, who stepped elegantly and effortlessly out of taxis, who shopped and lunched, who went to the theater and to concerts and to auctions at Sotheby's, who were a part of this new world she found herself in. Laura understood the value of a composed, chic outward appearance, had still not rid herself of the sense that whatever natural style she might have developed if the bad years had not intervened, had been scrubbed off, leaving her raw and vulnerable. Things were better now, of course, immeasurably so, but she liked coming to places like Annabel's or the Ritz, where Ambler invariably stayed, partly so that she could study her contemporaries.

Ambler generally kicked off with a compliment, Laura noticed, and the evening in December, 1985, when he asked her to meet him at the club was no exception. She had made time to go back to the flat to change, and she was wearing the new black velvet pants suit she had blown half a month's salary on at Harvey Nichols. She'd put it on over a cream satin blouse to begin with, but Gus had agreed with her that with its pencil-slim lines, it looked far more stunning tightly buttoned with nothing beneath the jacket.

"You look very lovely," Ambler said, as she joined him at his corner table near the log-burning fireplace in the bar. A bottle of Dom Pérignon and two champagne flutes stood waiting to be opened, and Ambler signaled a waiter to pour.

"Are we celebrating?" Laura asked, settling herself comfortably. It was an easy room to feel relaxed in, more like an elegantly cozy drawing room than a bar.

"I am."

Ambler offered no further information, and Laura knew better than to pry. They drank some champagne, and enjoyed a moment of quiet, the first either of them had had all day.

"I'm doing my pre-Christmas checks, Laura," Ambler said. He'd been using her first name since her promotion, though she stuck firmly to formality as she knew she was expected to. "Doing the rounds, you might say. At this time of year, I like to make sure my staff are happy. That way, I feel I've earned my own holiday."

"I can't believe you're ever really on holiday, sir," Laura said.

"I know how to enjoy myself," Ambler countered.

"I'm sure."

"Well then," Ambler said, "are you happy?"

"I think the honest answer is I am if you are, Mr. Ambler." Laura paused. "I love my work. The company excites me—as does my job, though it also scares me a little sometimes."

"In what sense?"

"The sense that I may not perform well in a particular situation, that I may let the agency down, or myself."

Ambler smiled. "That's just diligence, and ambition. Have you often let yourself down? In business, I mean."

Laura felt the hint of a flush. "Not often, no, sir."

"Then I'm happy," he said, watching her steadily.

Laura didn't know what to make of Ambler. When agency business was on the agenda, he was the coolest, toughest human being she'd ever encountered, but when business was over he was more than affable. He made his interest in her progress apparent, both to her face and in front of Hal Deacon, which sometimes gave her a sense of security that she knew was unwise, if not exactly false. Men like Ambler could drop you as quickly as they plucked you from obscurity, and she tried never to forget it.

"I'm surprised he's never made a pass at you," Gus commented one Sunday, when Laura was visiting the market at Camden Lock. "Here, take this sweater—it's a great match for your eyes."

"It's gorgeous." Laura held the green sweater at arm's length. "Let me pay for it."

"Don't start. You know you're still paying the lion's share in the flat. Just take it, please, and don't make a big deal."

Laura took it. "What made you say that? About Ambler making a pass."

"He obviously fancies you."

"Of course he doesn't."

"Why so sure?" Gus asked.

"Because we're in different leagues, different worlds. I'm small fry."

"Men like that have been known to gobble up small fry, especially when it looks like you."

Laura smiled. "You've always told me that men would be

falling over themselves to have me, but if they do, I never
notice. Except Ned."

"Poor Ned," Gus said.

"You don't like Ned."

"Not much. But he knows he's beaten, and I feel sorry for
him."

Laura stood back for a few minutes, while Gus sold a
hand-knitted jacket to an American tourist.

"Think I should finish with Ned?"

"Not if you're still having a good time with him."

"I'm not really. It's always there, between us, the fact that
I won't sleep with him—not that he even tries that much
anymore."

"Would you sleep with Ambler, if he asked?" Gus asked.

"No, of course not." Laura stopped. "Even if I wanted to,
it would be crazy. But since he isn't going to ask, it's irrelevant."

"Maybe."

Gus was right in a way, even if Laura wasn't prepared to
admit it to herself. That was the thing about Roger Ambler
that she couldn't quite fathom. He was, without question, the
most attractive man she had ever laid eyes on, always so
marvelously dressed, the slick golden hair, the piercing eyes,
but she tried never to think of him in any way other than as
her employer, as a brilliant and powerful man who could
only regard her as another worker ant in one of his colonies.
And yet once in a while, during a managerial meeting, or
while they were having one of their less formal dinners or
lunches, she noticed those sharp blue eyes watching her,
moving over her—not in an overtly sexual manner, never
that, but with some odd kind of intimacy nonetheless. Those
moments were swiftly over, but Laura never entirely forgot
them.

Timing, Roger had always believed, was almost everything.
In business, he had made timing and preparation his watch-
words and had perfected their art. He saw no reason to believe that his campaign for Laura Andros should be
otherwise conducted than a planned takeover of a small
company by a powerful corporation. He might, of course,

have swept her up in a matter of weeks, could have enjoyed her and then either dropped her or tucked her away in a safe, organized place, but that had never been what he wanted from her.

As the months had passed, he had come to understand precisely what it was that he did want from Laura. He had thought, in the beginning, that it might simply be sex, that the knowledge of what she had done in her lurid past had triggered some base instinct in him, previously repressed. That was, he was still certain, perfectly true. That was the element that had led him to embark on his curious game of self-inflicted celibacy, the notion that storing up his desire, his sexuality, would make the moment of conquest, when it came, all the more intense, all the more remarkable. But it was not, after all, just sex. Laura Andros was a complex young woman. She had proven herself to be a gifted counselor and a competent, hard-working executive, a genuine asset to Ambler Agencies. Her family background was intriguing; the ambitious, successful, British-educated Greek father, the English, well-born mother, the risk-taking grandfather who had gambled everything away. Roger supposed that he saw in her a young woman who, had her life progressed to plan, might have become a much more obviously eligible match for a man in his position; and yet he knew, too, that it was the very disaster that had intervened in Laura's life, that darkest of deeds and the deprived, demimonde existence she must have led for several of her most formative years, that set her apart.

He could have simply had her. But he wanted more.

On May 1, 1986, Laura was called out of her Thursday morning counselors' progress meeting to take an urgent call from Ambler in Monaco.

"I want files on all your managers, Laura, plus up-to-date performance figures on every branch, and I want them by tonight. Can you do that?"

"Of course, sir." Laura's mind went into overdrive, wondering what kind of a shake-up this might herald. "Will you be coming into the office, or shall I come to the Ritz?" If their meeting was confidential, he would not want to see her in a restaurant or public place.

"I'm at the Hôtel de Paris in Monte Carlo—I'd like you to fly over. If you can't make the Air France flight at three, British Airways flies to Nice at seven o'clock."

Laura fought to maintain the composure in her voice.

"I'll need to pack some things."

"You may be away a few days—any problems with that?"

Excitement surged in her.

"No problems at all."

Gus helped her to pack, checked the Nice weather in the newspaper.

"Seventy degrees and sunny," she said. "You might need a bikini."

"Not for work," Laura said. She looked into her wardrobe. "The cream suit might do, I suppose—I wish I had a sundress."

"What about this?" Gus pulled out a polka-dot cotton dress.

"That old thing? It's hardly the Hôtel de Paris."

"Get you," Gus mocked.

"You know what I mean."

"Course I do." Gus smirked. "Don't suppose you'll need many clothes anyway."

"Think he'll send me straight back?"

"You know that's not what I meant."

"It's business, Gus."

"Sure it is."

"We'll probably be stuck indoors hard at it most of the time."

"Exactly."

She landed at Nice after dark, the aircraft skimming low over the Mediterranean, its waves silvered by the rising moon, and took a taxi from the airport. Ambler had offered her a helicopter ride, but there seemed little point at night, and anyway, Laura wanted the time to herself, wanted a chance to absorb what had, and what might be going to happen. The driver was going to take the autoroute, but Laura asked him to drive the coastal road instead; it was narrow and winding in places, and she knew that Ambler probably expected her to get in as early as possible, but her excitement was still surging, still bubbling, and somehow the sight and smell and sounds of the sea, with her window wound right down, took her back to Aegina and gave her a rare sense of timelessness and freedom.

Her first sight of the Hôtel de Paris, its enchanting, white filigree and sculpted façade exquisitely illuminated, overlooking the Place du Casino, took Laura's breath away. Since working for Ambler, she had visited many lovely and impressive places, but the setting for this perfect hotel, and the air of grace and wealth that pervaded the square and the magnificent entrance hall, was utterly overwhelming. Catching a glimpse of her reflection in the mirrored walls behind the reception desk, Laura had never felt so aware of her lack of sophistication, but no one else appeared to notice.

"Welcome, mademoiselle," a dark-suited man greeted her. "I hope you had a good journey. We have kept your suite, as Monsieur Ambler instructed us."

"Is Mr. Ambler in at present?" Laura asked.

"I believe he has left a message for you, mademoiselle. You will find it in your suite."

The excitement prickled and grew. Her suite was on the second floor, with a small balcony overlooking the port. There was a beautiful sitting room, immaculate and comfortable, a bedroom with a huge bed and long, partly mirrored closets, and a gleaming, tiled bathroom with two basins, piles of white towels and a telephone. Laura held onto the wave of pleasure rising inside her, gave the porter fifty francs—Hal Deacon had organized some currency for her, and had advised her on the proprieties of tipping—and closed the outer door firmly.

"I don't believe it," she said, her voice hushed, even though she was quite alone. "I just don't *believe* it."

She dropped her shoulder bag onto an armchair, kicked off her shoes and walked around the suite again, slowly this time, taking in every detail, every stick of furniture, every fabric.

She saw the flowers for the first time. A magnificent bowl of white roses, with a card in an envelope. She opened it.

Called away on business this evening. Hope you weren't too rushed. Please make yourself at home, and order anything you want from room service—and I mean anything. And feel free to use the telephone to call home if you need to. The maid will let you have anything you've forgotten.

I'll call you in the morning. Have breakfast on your balcony. No sense in hurrying here.

R.J.A.

Laura went to bed that night in a state of bliss. She had not left the suite, had been tempted to go down to look around, perhaps to have a drink in the bar, but a strange kind of superstition had gripped her, as if by leaving the suite it might melt into the night. She had taken the longest, most heavenly bath of her life, soaking in bubbles and using all the towels, before wrapping herself in a soft white robe and ordering, as Ambler had instructed, exactly what she wanted, a *soupe de poissons* and a wonderful chicken cooked with wild mushrooms and cream. She had switched on the television and lain down on the bed, with all the lights out and the balcony doors and windows open. It was cool now, and the breeze blew the curtains and flicked the pages of the magazines on the coffee table, but Laura could hear the sounds of life, the purring of expensive motor cars, the voices of the rich, raised in laughter and, in quieter moments, the clacking of high heels on the pavements; and it was the sound of the free world, and she only closed the windows and doors when she went into the sitting room and saw that the petals of the white roses were being blown by the wind.

The waiter came and fetched her dinner table, and the maid came to turn down the bed and to bring fresh towels, and Laura telephoned Gus to tell her that she was wrong, because Ambler wasn't even here, and then she wrote a post-card to Adam, and one to her secretary, though she tore that one up as soon as she'd written it, afraid of giving the wrong impression; and then she took one more look at the twinkling lights and the starry sky, and when she went to bed, naked between the softest, smoothest sheets she had ever known, she drifted into gentle, dreamless sleep.

He called her at nine o'clock.

"Welcome to Monaco. Had breakfast yet?"

"The best of my life," Laura said, warmly.

"Thank you for coming over."

"You're thanking me? This suite, this beautiful hotel—" The roses caught her eye. "And the flowers are so lovely, thank you so much, Mr. Ambler."

"My pleasure, Laura." He paused. "When do you think you might be ready for our meeting?"

"Is half an hour too late?"

"Not at all. I told you, no sense in hurrying here."

Laura arrived first, had another few moments to absorb the remarkable entrance hall again, the magnificent chandelier suspended from the domed, polychromed glass ceiling, the caramel leather furniture, the huge Oriental rugs.

"You look very pretty," Ambler said when he saw her, wearing the polka-dot dress, so simple, so without artifice. He was always stirred by the first sight of her, but somehow here, in this temple of sophistication, her innocence seemed so acutely touching that he had to force himself to remember the truth about her. "You had a good night, I take it. I always sleep especially well when I'm here."

"I slept wonderfully, too," Laura said, struck, as she often was, by his appearance. He was lightly tanned, and wearing a beige linen suit and a white shirt, unbuttoned at the neck. It was the first time she had seen him without a tie.

They sat in a quiet corner and ordered coffee. Laura set the buff folder she'd brought down with her on the table.

"Everything you asked for. I had the personnel files copied and reduced—I hope that was all right."

"Sure." Ambler left the folder untouched, and looked at her. "If you were going to be replaced, Laura, who would be your first choice for the job?"

Unnerved, but trying to seem calm, Laura crossed her legs.

"Am I going to be replaced, sir?"

"Just answer the question, if you can." His eyes gave nothing away.

Laura took a breath. "Anne Lockhart would be my first choice, no doubt about it." She paused. "Am I being fired or promoted, or just moved?"

Ambler gave a small smile. "None of the above."

"Then why the question?"

"No one is irreplaceable, Laura, we both know that. Every now and again, I like to check over my options at every level."

"I see."

"No," Ambler said. "You don't."

"Not really."

"That's okay." The waiter brought their coffee, and poured for them. Ambler waited until he'd gone. "I don't feel like looking at these papers right now, Laura."

"No?"

"I'd rather go shopping."

Now Laura was truly baffled. She had never known a more work-oriented man than Roger Ambler. The very notion of him setting business aside in favor of pleasure was unthinkable.

"Would you mind coming with me?"

"Shopping?"

"If you don't mind."

It was a perfect morning as they stepped out of the hotel, warm and sunny, with a gentle breeze. The square was filled with expensive cars, but Ambler steered Laura away to the left and into the Avenue des Beaux Arts. They passed Cartier, Louis Vuitton and Bulgari, strolling leisurely, and paused outside Christian Dior.

"Were you looking for something particular, Mr. Ambler?" Laura asked.

"Absolutely," he answered. "But I'd like you to do me a favor, first."

"Of course."

"Call me Roger, at least while we're here. We're on vacation now."

"We are?"

"From this moment on. Didn't I mention that?"

"No," Laura said. "You didn't."

He fixed her with one of his penetrating looks. "Do you mind?"

She took a moment before answering.

"No. I don't think I do."

He smiled. "In that case, come with me."

He took her arm, lightly, and the sudden closeness startled Laura, made her uncertain whether she wanted to draw away or move closer, but she did neither, just walked with him, allowed him to lead her along the street and around corners, and the riches of the place lapped around them, and she gazed into windows and up into the blue sky, and scarcely knew how they came to stand outside Chanel.

"Would it offend you very much if I bought you a gift?"

Laura's mind struggled for the right response, but failed to find it.

"I'll take that as a no," Ambler said, and drew her gently inside.

"You can't buy me anything in here," Laura said.

"Why not?"

"It's much too expensive."

"Not to me." He smiled. "Just try a few things on, see how they feel."

He overwhelmed her, with his charm, with his insistence, and the clothes, too, the feel of them, the extraordinary way they made her feel when she put them on, overcame her resistance. And she did want to resist, knew that she ought to say no, to stop him before she had said yes to something considerably more than a suit or a dress or a blouse or a pair of shoes, but she felt suddenly powerless, felt oddly weightless and unreal, as if she were dreaming.

Gus—she thought at one point, while a vendeuse showed her a tiny evening bag, and she heard her own voice making admiring noises. *I need to talk to Gus—I need her to anchor me, to bring me back down to earth before it's too late.* But she realized, at the same time, that it was probably already too late. She could refuse him, of course—Ambler surely wasn't the type to force himself on anyone, he certainly didn't have to—but the path back to the way it had been between them was, she thought, already closed.

They returned to the hotel for lunch, and Laura went up to change into the pale pink suit he had bought her, with shoes and bag to match, their shades so subtle, not cloying or too much, and then she went down, as he had suggested, to the Salle Empire, where Ambler sat, waiting for her, at a window table.

He rose as she approached, and this time he said nothing at all, just nodded his head and smiled.

"You approve?"

"Did you look in the mirror?"

"Of course."

"Then you know."

He suggested that they order simply, just a main course and, perhaps, dessert, so that they wouldn't ruin their appetites altogether for dinner. They ate a delicate sole, wrapped in a light pastry crust with fresh asparagus tips and a hint of cream, and they drank a Sancerre, and Ambler told her a little about the history of the hotel, and of the Principality.

"It's made up of four separate parts, four *quartiers*," he said. "Monaco-Ville, the old town, overlooked by the palace; the area around the port, called the Condamine, Fontvieille, more modern and mostly industrial, and Monte Carlo, the rock, which is where we're sitting now."

"Some rock," Laura said, gazing around at the gilt and marble and trompe l'oeil walls.

"Wait till you see the casino," Ambler said. "It's the ultimate example of *belle époque*—a gorgeous place to lose money."

Twice during lunch, Laura tried to bring up the subject of the agencies, but Ambler refused to be drawn. He seemed quite different, his body, normally so erect and alert, relaxed, even the sharp features appearing to soften a little. For some time Laura sat tensely, in spite of her enjoyment, like someone waiting for the other shoe to drop, as if she feared that at any minute Ambler might revert to her remote, on-duty employer, or worse, be transformed into an aggressive seducer demanding payment. But then, gradually, as the meal progressed, she began to realize that something entirely different was happening between them. He wanted to be with her. This man who controlled thousands of people, who was far, far richer than she could even guess, who could have any number of beautiful, wealthy women, was enjoying being with *her*. And there was something very likable about him, now that a little of the armor plating was melting away, not just the startling generosity he had shown her, but something very real, very human.

He told her a little about his roots, about his family and the early days of the Ambler Corporation.

"My father started it all, you know. Arnold Ambler—he always hated his name for some reason, even thought about changing it, but didn't want to hurt his parents. It was mostly shoes, of course, in those days, until he got into publishing, which was where he really wanted to be."

"Was your mother involved, too?" Laura asked.

"Not in an official capacity, no. My mother, Mary, was pretty much a quiet force behind my father. She leveled things out, I guess, when his ideas got a little wild, perhaps, or his ambitions for us."

"Us?"

"I have one sister, Rona." Ambler smiled. "We don't see as much of each other these days as we'd like, but we're still pretty close."

"Does she look like you?"

"In a very soft, female way, yes, she does. I think you'd like her." He paused. "And I think she'd like you, too."

"Does she ever come to London?"

"Seldom," Ambler said. "But I hope you'll meet her in New York."

"If I ever get there," Laura said.

"You'll get there."

The rest of that afternoon was spent sightseeing. Ambler took Laura up to the Grimaldi Palace, looking at the outside with affectionate disapproval. "If an American architect today suggested attaching a peaches and cream mansion to a medieval fortress, he'd probably be shot."

"Yet it's beautiful, somehow, here in the sunshine," Laura said.

"It's a pity we can't go inside," Ambler said. "The *appartements* and galleries are stunning, but they're closed to the public when Rainier's in town."

They wandered through the maze of tiny streets in old Monaco, gazed at the old houses, all shades of pinks and yellows and ochers and creams, stepped inside the souvenir shops, sat for a while drinking coffee in Place St. Nicolas, and then Ambler drove Laura, in his hired Mercedes, along the winding Moyenne Corniche, with its hairpin bends and breathtaking views, to the *Jardin Exotique,* where the gardens, crammed with cacti and flowering plants, cascaded down the steep rock face.

They were back in the hotel before six-thirty.

"Will you have dinner with me tonight?" Ambler asked.

"I'd love to."

"Not had enough of me yet?"

"Of course not," Laura said, and found that she meant it.

"If it wouldn't be too dull for you, we could stay here, eat upstairs in the Grill—there's a great view—and then I thought you might enjoy a visit to the casino."

Laura hesitated. "Are you sure you haven't anything else to do? Please don't feel you have to entertain me—I've had such a wonderful day."

"So have I." Ambler smiled. "And I assure you there's nothing else—no one else—I'd rather see tonight."

The casino stunned Laura more than anything else had. What Ambler had described to her as the ultimate example of *belle époque* was an overwhelmingly glamorous, almost decadent experience—she'd never seen so much gold, so much marble, such glittering crystal, so many painted nymphs and sensuous peasant girls—so much money being thrown away. They didn't actually throw it, of course, it was all done with the utmost propriety, gambling chips, round ones, square ones, being planted with firm delicacy by practiced fingers on the green roulette tables, until the wheel had been spun and the tiny ball had found its numbered groove, and then most of the chips were swept efficiently up by the croupiers, all of them elegant men in dinner jackets.

Ambler wore a white tuxedo with a black bow tie, and Laura wore the black velvet pants suit that she'd thought of packing at the last moment. She was aware that she was imperfectly dressed for the place and the season, and yet she felt no disapproving glances, felt more relaxed and content than she had all day. Dinner had been wonderful. They'd shared chateaubriand with béarnaise sauce and tiny *pommes allumettes,* and Ambler had ordered the most superb red wine Laura had ever tasted, and then he'd taken her arm again, and led her past the small sculpture of a horse and rider that stood near the front door of the hotel.

"See how the horse's right leg is gleaming?" he showed her. "Decades of gamblers have rubbed that for luck on their way to the tables."

"My grandfather was a gambler," she said a little later as they walked through the *salons privés.* "He lost more than he won."

"You'll be luckier."

"I don't think I'm going to play."

"Why not? It's fun."

"Because I don't have the money." Laura looked him straight in the eye. "And I don't want to gamble with yours."

Ambler looked right back. "It's just as much a part of this holiday as the hotel or dinner—it's simply entertainment, Laura. I think you should start with roulette—I'll be wounded if you don't let me teach you at least the basics."

She had to smile—there was nothing else to be done.

"Good," Ambler said. "First, we find somewhere to sit—I refuse to have to stand and lean over people's shoulders to make my bets." He found them two chairs, side by side, and within moments, Laura had a small stack of square chips before her. Looking at the monetary equivalents stamped on them, she stared at Ambler in horror.

"You're joking, surely? I can't play with these."

"Sure you can." His blue eyes sparked. "This is nothing.

In the *super privé* rooms, the roulette minimum can be five hundred francs."

Laura took a deep breath. "What do I do?"

"Okay. Now look at the table and at the wheel. Basically, you can place a variety of bets. If you put a chip smack in the middle of a single number, it's called *en plein*—if you put it on the line separating two numbers, that's *à cheval,* if you put it on the outside line opposite three numbers, that's called *transversale,* and if you want to bet on four numbers, you place your chip on the intersection between them, and that's *en carré.*" He smiled at her again, enjoying the concentration on her face. "Okay so far?"

Laura nodded. "Do I have to tell him what I want, or can I just put the chips down myself?"

"If you can reach." He paused. "There are more bets, but I'd stick with those for now—except that if you want to play it really safe, you can just put your money on red or black, or on an odd or even number."

"That's for me."

"It's up to you. Oh, and of course, there's the most basic rule of all."

"Which is?"

"No one ever really wins at roulette."

"Then why do so many people think they can?" Laura asked.

"Optimism," Ambler answered. "And most people—certainly in a casino of this class—play strictly for fun."

They played for more than an hour. Laura lost for the first forty minutes, then won three times in a row and refused both to continue or to keep the winnings. "You'll be the one wounding me," she said, firmly, holding the chips out to him.

Ambler gave a small shrug and accepted them. "I'll keep them for you for tomorrow."

"Will we still be here?" Laura asked, conscious now that she was in no hurry for the dream to end.

"It's possible."

They strolled around the square on their way back to the hotel. It was very clear again, the breeze softer, more gentle than the previous evening.

"It's so beautiful here," Laura said, quietly.

"Indeed it is." Ambler's voice was even lower.

Laura glanced at him as they strolled. "Is something wrong?"

"No." He shook his head, slowly. "Nothing at all."

He escorted her up to the second floor, walked her to the door of her suite, and now Laura expected it to happen, anticipated his arms moving around her, his head bending toward her, his lips touching hers—but there was nothing at all. He simply looked at her, his eyes more gentle than she had ever seen them, and smiled again, a warm, knowing smile.

"Sweet dreams, Laura Andros," he said.

"Thank you." Her voice almost betrayed her. "For everything."

"Good night," he said, and turned away.

Laura put the key into the lock and turned it, hardly daring to look back at him, but just before she stepped inside, she tilted her face and saw that he was standing near the elevators, quite still, watching her. She looked back, unsmiling, and went into the sitting room.

"Gus," she said, out loud. "I need to talk to Gus."

It was after two o'clock, but it was an hour earlier in England, and anyway she knew that Gus wouldn't mind being woken.

"Not sharing a room yet?" were her first words.

"Of course not."

"Don't tell me he hasn't tried."

"No," Laura said, still feeling shaky. "He hasn't."

"All work? Bloody hell."

"No work at all."

Laura told her everything.

"Christ," Gus said. "It's worse than I thought."

"What do you mean?"

"I mean, now you've got a real problem."

"I know," Laura said.

"Do you, really?" Gus paused. "You know what's going to happen, don't you? He didn't just make a pass, which would have been okay, if that's what you wanted at the time. You could have got over that, could both have forgotten it, even if you'd slapped his hands a bit. But now we know what he's really after."

"Do we?"

"He wants a mistress. A permanent arrangement."

"Don't be crazy."

"It's not a bit crazy. He'll buy you a few more things, and then he'll take you to bed, and then he'll offer to set you up in a flat—he's got company flats all over the place, hasn't he, you said he has—"

"Gus, stop it," Laura said. "That's not what's happening at all."

"Isn't it?" Gus paused again. "There's nothing wrong with it, if you want to go along with it—if I could stand the idea of letting a man near me, I wouldn't mind being a kept woman."

"Of course you'd mind," Laura said hotly. "I wish I hadn't phoned you now."

"I'm sorry, kid. Honestly. Me and my big mouth."

Laura said nothing.

"Only I didn't think you were taking it seriously."

"I'm not."

"Yes, you are," Gus said, gently. "You're falling for him."

"I'm not," Laura said again. "I've just had the most wonderful day of my life, that's all. It'll all be over soon, and I'll be home again. Back to reality."

"Yeah," Gus said. "Good night, kid. Sweet dreams."

"And you."

Laura put the telephone back on the receiver, and walked over to where the bowl of white roses still stood, freshly watered, on the table. Absently, she fingered one of the flowers, and a soft, fragrant petal fell onto the polished surface. Laura shivered a little, and wrapped both her arms about herself. For a moment, she stood very still, closing her eyes. Ambler was there, in her mind, very handsome and golden in his tuxedo, looking right at her. She opened her eyes again, and the chill was gone.

"You're wrong, Gus," she said. "This time, you're wrong."

The trouble was, she didn't really believe that.

The real trouble was, she didn't really mind.

CHAPTER 11

Laura was breakfasting on her balcony the next morning when the delivery came. She looked at the bags and boxes held out to her by the uniformed boy, and shook her head.

"They're not for me," she said. "It's a mistake."

"You are Mademoiselle Andros?"

"Yes, but I'm not expecting—"

"These are yours, mademoiselle." He took an envelope from one of the bags and gave it to her. Her name was written on it, in Ambler's hand. She took the packages from him, thanked him and closed the door, remembering only then that she ought to have tipped him. There were three bags, one very large from Chanel, two from Christian Dior, and two glossy white card boxes, light in weight. Her heart thumped a little faster, and her stomach clenched. She thought about what Gus had said last night. A small part of her didn't want to open them. A larger part did.

There was a bikini, poppy red and scanty, a swimsuit, black and red, and a short robe, beautifully cut, to accompany both. There were slim white linen slacks, a navy blue and white cotton sweater and a nautical blazer, white canvas shoes with just a touch of navy, and a roomy shoulder bag. The Chanel bag revealed a black dress, strapless silk organza with a stiff net petticoat, and the Dior bags held high-heeled black patent open-toe shoes, very delicate, and a tiny matching clutch bag. Laura had never seen more beautiful clothes.

She waited until she had unpacked the last item before she opened the envelope. She was trembling, her fingers clumsy, her breathing shallow.

> *My dear Laura,*
>   *The moment I saw these, I knew they were made for you. I offer them to you with respect, admiration and affection. Please don't reject them. You'll be needing them all over the next few days. I think they should all fit well—I confess I got the maid to tell me your shoe size.*
>   *No strings, Laura. Just gifts.*
>
>   *Roger.*

Laura sat down on the edge of the bed and burst into tears. She wept for more than five minutes, tears streaming down her cheeks and dripping onto her hotel terry robe. She knew she was idiotic for crying, yet at the same time she felt a kind of detached understanding, as though her alter ego was standing beside her, patting her shoulder and reassuring her that it was all right to react emotionally, all right to feel so moved. All right to accept.

She splashed her hot face and reddened eyes with cold water before she telephoned his suite.

"I don't know what to say," she said, her voice still a little more tremulous than she had intended it to be.

"Just say you like them."

"They're the most gorgeous—the most *perfect* clothes I've ever seen."

"Do they fit?"

"I don't know."

"Try them on. You'll need the maid to help you with the dress—tell her if it needs fixing."

Laura swallowed. "I still don't know what to say."

There was a smile in his voice. "Say you'll accept them."

"I shouldn't."

"Did you ask to come on this trip?" His voice grew stronger. "Was it your fault that I whisked you out here under false pretenses?"

"No." She smiled at the admission.

"Do you want to go home?"

Laura hardly hesitated. "No."

"Then you'll need those clothes."

Everything fitted perfectly—the dress might, as Ambler had written, have been made for her. Laura called him back and told him, her pleasure rising, her confidence surging, and he asked her to put on the navy and white outfit, to bring the bikini and whatever else she might need for a day out, and to meet him in the entrance hall in an hour. When she asked him where they were going, he refused to tell her.

"Trust me," was all he said. "You'll have a good time."

She believed him.

He took her to La Condamine, strolled with her, still at that deliberate, unhurried pace, taking pleasure in her appearance and in the sparkling excitement in her green eyes; he told her that according to legend this was the port of Heracles, the greatest Greek hero, pointed out to her the most fabulous of the yachts in the harbor, took her hand, for a while, felt it soft and firm in his, and could hardly believe his own self-control.

"I want you to close your eyes now," he said to her. "Let me guide you."

"Where are we going?"

"If I tell you, it won't be a surprise."

She shut her eyes, felt his grip, firm on her arm, felt the stone under her feet, felt the soft breeze on her face and in her hair, let him lead her, let herself relax, give in. And then they stopped.

"Okay," he said.

"Can I open them?"

"Right now."

It was a yacht. It was pure, snowy white, streamlined beauty. It looked like a rare seabird, wings tucked down, ready to sail or to soar. It was compact, small in comparison with the giants they had seen moored a little farther out, but all the lovelier, the more perfect for it. Its name, painted in deepest blue on the side, was *Laura*.

"So?" Ambler said, softly.

She stared at the yacht, at the name.

"Say something, for God's sake."

"I don't understand," Laura said. "Whose is it?"

"She's mine."

"But—the name."

"Yes."

The tears sprang into her eyes again. She couldn't stop them. She was conscious of Ambler standing close beside her, watching, waiting, but the words, if she could find them at all, were trapped inside her, strangled by the magnitude of the emotions battering her.

"You—" she began, and stopped.

"I ordered her a long time ago," he said, gently. "I only decided on her name three months ago."

Three months. Laura stared at him. It was hardly possible. It was *not* possible.

"You can't have done," she said.

"It must seem strange, I know." He took her hand again. "But you see, I've known for a long time how I felt about you, Laura."

"But you didn't know me."

"Perhaps not. But I knew how I felt." He paused. "She's ready for us. Shall we go on board?"

Laura stared back at the yacht. Back at the name. *Laura*. It was like a dream, like every fantasy rolled into one— except that she'd never allowed herself fantasies like that, because life had taught her early that they were pointless. Yet now, suddenly, she could no longer be sure of that. Of anything.

She gave herself up to it, as she had the clothes, and the game of roulette the night before, and all the rest. They boarded the yacht that bore her name, and she met the crew of three, two men—one middle-aged, the other scarcely out of his teens—and a woman of about twenty-five with short-cropped brown hair, called Jeanne. All wore white nautical caps, blue denim shorts and white T-shirts with *Laura* printed in small neat italics on their left breast pockets. Ambler introduced her to them as Miss Andros, but she knew that they heard him calling her by her first name, and she thought that it seemed to please them to have her on board.

"I'm not a yachtsman," Ambler told her, while he showed her around. "That means I can neither tell you anything much you might want to know about the boat, nor, on the other hand, can I bore you to death, which a lot of amateur sailors tend to do."

"I know a little about boats," Laura said. "My grandfather used to have a motorboat, and my friend Adam and I used to catch rides with the fishermen whenever we could." She smiled. "I've never been anywhere near anything so lovely as this."

There was a roomy deck area for sunbathing and relaxing at the stern end of the yacht, and below there was a sitting area, a bedroom with queen-sized bed and video equipment, a head with marble basin and glass-enclosed shower room, a galley with every conceivable convenience, right down to a dishwasher, and even the linen cloths were embroidered with the name *Laura*, and it was all so new, so clean. Everything gleamed and sparkled newness, from the unused shower stall to the waist-high safety rail that ran right around the boat. The crew busied themselves with moving the *Laura* smoothly out of the harbor, and then the two men seemed almost to disappear, and only Jeanne remained for a little while, to serve them glasses of kir royale, made up of champagne and cassis, before she, too, vanished.

"She's going to prepare lunch," Ambler told Laura.

"Do you think she'd like some help?"

"Definitely not. Only enough space for one down there, anyway."

Laura watched the boats in the harbor, and the traffic beyond, beginning to shrink into miniatures, watched Monte Carlo itself receding, felt the old, familiar, almost-forgotten sensation of being on the sea; the spray, the smells, the sounds, the swell, gently rocking, soothing, adding to the dreamy quality of this day that had begun, for her, when the parcels had arrived in her room.

"We're going to be lucky, I think, with the weather," Ambler said. "You have to take the rough with the smooth this time of year."

Laura nodded, slowly. "It was the same on the island."

"You were very happy there, weren't you?"

"Very."

"But not so happy later."

"No."

Ambler stood up and took off his jacket, laid it down neatly and straightened again. "You okay here for a few minutes? I have a call I need to make, and I want to check with Jeanne about lunch."

"I'm fine," Laura said. "Take your time."

She watched him stroll away, disappear down the steps. She'd never seen such a transformation in body language, never seen tension drop away so swiftly as it had fallen from Ambler's shoulders since her arrival. She thought about that question about her past just now, thought how little he had asked her until then about the years before she'd joined the agency. She could remember wondering, after their first meeting in 1983, if he would find out what she had done, if maybe he would get rid of her, but then, almost immediately, she'd been given her first promotion, and she had known that Beth Barker could not have given her away. She'd felt so bad when Beth had been shunted sideways, leaving her job free for her, and not all that long afterward Beth had resigned from the company, and Laura's guilt had grown more acute. But then she was so accustomed to guilt, had been for so long, and Beth's demotion and ultimate departure, at least, had not really been her responsibility.

"What are you thinking about?"

Ambler's voice jolted her.

"About the agency, actually."

"Here? Now?" He sat down beside her, leaning comfortably, one elbow propped on one of the big, soft cushions strewn on the white leather seating that ran right around that end of the deck. "Even I'm not thinking about business."

"Not even about that call?"

"Not even."

"Are we going anywhere in particular?" Laura asked, leaning back lazily.

"Not far—I thought we might sail around Cap Ferrat, then come into harbor at Beaulieu. There's a hill village not far from there I think you'd love—unless you'd rather just stay at sea."

Laura looked at him. "You're the boss," she said.

They dropped anchor while they ate lunch, near Cagnes-sur-Mer. There was cold langouste, thinly sliced rare roast beef, tomato salad and cheese. Jeanne served them, then disappeared again to join the other two at the bow end.

"Do you think it's warm enough to swim?" Laura asked Ambler.

"I doubt it," he said. "But I will if you will."

She went below to change into the red and black swimsuit, carrying the robe in her hand. When she came back up, Ambler had already stripped to his trunks. He was solidly built, in excellent shape for a man in his forties who lived as well as he did.

"Very, very lovely," he said, appraising her. He made no reference to the fact that she had brought the swimsuit when he had suggested she bring the red bikini, and his eyes did not linger on her for longer than a few seconds.

The water felt icy.

"I suppose this is healthy," Laura gasped, when she was sufficiently recovered from the shock to speak. "Very invigorating."

"If you call hypothermia invigorating," Ambler called back, his voice half strangled. "Deceptive, this time of year, isn't it?"

Apart from helping her onto the ladder when they climbed back onto the yacht, Ambler never touched Laura. He produced two massive white towels, handing one to her, and she half-expected him to wrap it around her, maybe even to rub her dry, but he merely watched her again, for a few moments, and then gave the order to up anchor and head, very gently, for Beaulieu.

From the sea, Eze-Village looked like an ancient fortress, perched on a mountain, but from within it was an enchanting maze of steeply sloping paths, alleyways and aged, precariously angled houses. There were galleries, and shops, of course, and cafés and one or two hotels, but it was possible to turn corners and imagine oneself transported into an earlier century. Laura and Ambler wandered into a beautiful hotel called the Château de la Chèvre d'Or, and sat on cushioned white wrought-iron chairs on the terrace, drinking mineral water, surrounded by sun-bleached stone, flowers and cacti, gazing down at the brilliant sea, twelve hundred feet below.

"This is another world," Laura murmured, trying to lock the panorama forever in her mind. "When I'm back in Earls Court, in the flat, or sitting in Oxford Street poring over budgets, I'll try and conjure this up—this view, these moments."

"I hope there'll be more moments," Ambler said, gently. "And maybe—" He stopped.

"Maybe what?"

He shook his head. "Nothing. Not yet."

Gus's words came back again into Laura's head. *He'll buy you a few more things, and then he'll take you to bed, and then he'll offer to set you up in a flat.* Maybe Gus was right, after all, Laura thought, and if that was true, she'd know it soon enough. But then Gus didn't know about the yacht, didn't know about the *Laura*. Didn't know that Ambler had shown no inclination to take her to bed—that he had hardly touched her, even though he must have sensed, must have been aware that Laura had wanted him to. Still wanted him to.

"There's a party tonight I'd like to go to," he told her as they walked back into the hotel.

"Of course," Laura said, quickly. "You must."

"I meant I'd like to go with you."

"Oh." She paused. "Are you sure?"

"You could wear the dress, if you'd like to."

"I'd love to."

He nodded. "I'll pick you up at nine."

"Here? In the hall?"

"No," he said. "I'll come to your suite."

* * *

When she heard his knock at the outer door, Laura had been ready for fifteen minutes. She could not remember ever having taken so much trouble over makeup and hair before, and she was glad that she'd splashed out in the duty-free shop at Heathrow and bought a tiny bottle of Arpège. She'd dabbed just a touch behind each ear, at the base of her throat and on her wrists, and she had used a tiny amount of hair spray, not so much that her glossy black hair would lose its natural swing, but just enough to make sure that the perky evening breeze didn't ruffle it. Ruffled hair was fine on a yacht, or sauntering through a hilltop village, but it definitely was not the right look to go with this dress.

Two or three times after the maid had come in to fasten the impossible-to-reach tiny golden buttons at the back, Laura had spun around in front of the mirrored wardrobes. She simply could not believe how she *looked*. It was a dress of dreams, not just for the dress itself, the glorious organza, the frothy petticoat, the magnificent cut—it was what the dress did to *her,* to her body, to her shoulders, to her neck, to her legs, to her arms, and, of course, to her face.

Laura, who had made it her habit to study elegant women ever since coming to London, had observed the women coming in and out of this hotel, this bastion of wealth and class, had noted those who belonged, compared with those who clearly did not, and she had noticed a look common to them all, even to the young teenagers. It was a look of effortless glamour, a kind of careless chic that seemed to have nothing whatever to do with what they wore or how their hair was done. It was in the way they walked, the way they moved their arms, even their heads; it was in their eyes, in their voices, and it appeared, at first glance, to come from an inner source, to be an inborn, almost magically natural gift of style. But Laura realized now that what had really created it was money. Not solely that, of course—for otherwise one would never see the brash ill-judged flaunting of wealth—but she thought now that it was money, and money alone, that could release that inner style, that could set it truly free.

The way that the black dress had set her free.

"Yes," he said, when she opened the door. "Oh, yes."

"You approve?" she asked, as she had at lunch the previous day.

"Christ, yes." His eyes were bright with pleasure.

He came into the room. He wore another white tuxedo, identical to the one he'd worn the night before, but Laura knew it was another one, because a woman in the casino had spilled her drink, and a tiny splash of Bloody Mary had marked his left sleeve. He probably had a wardrobe full of tuxedos in every home.

"Turn around," he said.

She turned, twirling a little, loving the feel of the skirt.

"It's the most wonderful dress I've ever seen, Roger," she said.

"That's the first time."

"For what?"

"That you've actually used my name." His smile was gently mocking. "I mean you stopped calling me sir, or Mr. Ambler, but you've avoided Roger like the plague."

"I didn't realize."

"Sure you did."

Laura felt suddenly awkward. "I'm sorry," she said. "Would you like a drink—or are we in a rush to leave?"

"No rush," he said. "No drink, either."

"Then I'll just get my bag." She moved toward the bedroom.

"Wait a moment."

She turned around. "Yes?"

He held something in his right hand, a velvet covered box, slim and square-shaped. "For you," he said, and gave it to her.

Laura looked down at it. "No."

"Open it."

"You've given me enough."

"Please." His voice was insistent. "I need you to at least look at it."

She glanced up into his face, saw the unprecedented plea in his eyes, and turned her gaze back to the box. When she opened the lid, she thought she gasped, yet perhaps she only gasped in her mind, for the room was absolutely silent. There was a necklace in the box, of square-cut emeralds and diamond baguettes, and a pair of matching earrings. She knew nothing at all about jewels, yet she was aware that these were breathtakingly fine.

"Roger, I can't," she whispered.

"Yes, you can."

"No."

"You must."

He took the necklace off its satin cushion, stepped behind her and put it around her neck, fastening the clasp.

"You put the earrings on," he said. "Please."

"Roger, this is wrong." She was trembling. "I don't understand why—" The necklace felt heavy, strange about her throat. "I don't know what you want from me."

He was in front of her again. "I want you to put on the earrings."

"That isn't what I mean."

"I know that," he said gently. "Please, Laura, put them on."

She took them out of the box, still trembling, and clipped them on.

"Now take a look."

She let him propel her over to the gilt-framed mirror on the far wall. She saw her reflection. What the black dress had begun, the jewelry completed.

"They're so heavy," she said, softly.

"You'll get used to them."

She shook her head. "That's not really what I'm trying to say."

"I know what you're trying to say, Laura. You'll get used to that, too."

"Will I?"

She felt that she was looking at a beautiful stranger. It was odd, acknowledging her own beauty that way, for she had never been narcissistic. She remembered how, after she had moved into the flat, after her escape from the dismal room in Paddington, she had often sat, naked, before her mirror, looking at herself. She remembered that she had never been able to look too closely into her own eyes, and she recognized that that had changed, gradually, with the passing of time; that the farther Lucia and Kane House had receded into the past, the more able she had become to cope with herself. It wasn't that it ever went away, or that she ever forgot it for more than a few hours, but she had become better able to push it away, into the back of her mind. Laura felt, deep down, that her changing fortunes, the better times—the agency, the flat she shared with Gus, their friendship—were less real than the dark times. Gus had told her, more than once, that she had it upside down, that those things had been misfortune, fate handing her a raw deal; but Laura knew, had always known, that Lucia Lindberg had exposed her real self, had peeled away the layers and forced her to acknowledge the dark segment of her soul. Time and work and kindness had helped the layers to heal, and the Laura Andros who had flown to Monte Carlo at the bidding of her boss was almost restored, was almost whole. And now Roger Ambler was building on those layers, was, perhaps, creating a new person altogether, and it was a fascinating sensation, too compelling to resist.

She gazed into the mirror.

"I look so different," she said.

"I knew this was how you would look," Ambler said.

She looked, curiously, into his face. "Did you plan it then?"

"I always plan everything," he said.

The party was at a villa in Cap d'Antibes, just off the coast road, on a steep, winding hill. It was a white stone house with an ocher tiled roof, all glowing under floodlights, and it reminded Laura of Chryssos, and all the time Ambler was talking to her, and introducing her to people, and dancing with her, she had a sense that her grandfather was close at hand, and the thought gladdened her. The whole evening had a dreamlike quality, created in part by the enchantment of the setting, and by the way the guests—some of them colorful, some understated, most of them possessing that innate quality she'd observed in the public rooms of the Hôtel de Paris—flowed smoothly in and out of the handsomely furnished and decorated villa and into the wondrously landscaped gardens, lit by silver lanterns. Laura noticed strangers looking at her, their faces approving and interested, and she began to feel not only that she belonged there, on Roger Ambler's arm, but that she was beautiful, too, perhaps even a little intriguing and, best of all, anonymous. Whenever Roger introduced her, he did so only by name, never once referred to the agency; one or two men and women attempted to find out more about her, but he was never drawn, just stood a little closer to her or held her arm a little more firmly, so that she felt strengthened against their curiosity, felt valued, felt secure.

"Are there many parties as wonderful as this?" she asked him once.

"Maybe," he answered, looking into her glowing face. "But if there are, I haven't noticed."

Laura had never seen so much food in her life. The snowy white tables snaked all through the gardens, laden with every kind of fish and meat, vegetable and salad, fruit and cheese, and on the crest of the slope was a long stone barbecue manned by four chefs, grilling langoustes and steaks and *poussins* and big Mediterranean prawns.

"Gus would adore this," she said. "She loves good food."

"You think a lot of her, don't you?" Ambler asked.

"She's the most important person in my life," Laura answered simply.

For just an instant, Ambler was silent, and then he smiled. "I look forward to meeting her," he said.

"You'll like her," Laura said. "She's very different."

Again, Laura noticed that he didn't question her friendship with Gus, that he never asked deeply probing questions, and she wondered if, after all, he might know more about her than she had thought. Yet that was impossible, for if he knew everything, she would not be here now, at his side.

A rich man doesn't have to know everything about his mistress. The thought was her own, but she could almost hear Gus saying the words. *He may have to know about a wife, but a mistress has no past and no future—she only needs to exist in the present.*

And the evening chilled a little.

It was late when they left the party, and Ambler, still ebullient and energized, suggested another visit to the casino, but

Laura had the sense that each of the experiences he had given her that day were so unique, so sublime for their novelty, their freshness, that it might be wiser to let it end now, while the mingled scents of bougainvillea and the barbecue and the myriad perfumes of the guests still danced in her nostrils, while the night sounds of crickets and music and animated voices still rang in her ears.

"I'd rather stop while it's all so perfect," she said to him, as he drove back toward Monte Carlo. "It couldn't get better."

He glanced away from the road, for just a second. "You mean the day, or the vacation?"

"The day, of course," Laura said.

"Good," he said, and relaxed again.

He saw her to her door again, as he had the night before, but this time he waited while Laura turned the key in the lock, and this time he stepped with her into the small entrance lobby of the suite, and every nerve end of Laura's skin quivered in expectation.

"I won't come in," he said.

Laura stood very still.

"I thought perhaps a nightcap?"

Ambler smiled. "Not tonight. I have an early meeting tomorrow."

"I keep thanking you," Laura said. "But it isn't enough." She touched the emeralds at her neck.

"Your eyes thank me," Ambler said. "Which is more than enough."

And then, at last, he kissed her. He lifted his hands and placed them on either side of her face, framing her gently, and he bent his head and touched her mouth with his, just the briefest, lightest of kisses.

"I'll call you in the morning," he said. "After my meeting."

He released her face, smiled into her eyes, then turned and was gone, the door closing quietly behind him. Laura still stood motionless, feeling the ghost of his lips on hers. She thought about telephoning Gus, but told herself that it was too late. She knew perfectly well that the hour had nothing to do with her reasons for not telephoning, knew that Gus might even be waiting to hear from her, but still Laura knew that she would not call. She always told Gus the truth about everything, and Gus was always totally honest with her.

Not tonight, she thought. She didn't want that kind of honesty tonight.

Roger played chemin de fer in one of the *Super Privé* rooms until seven o'clock in the morning. The room was lavish but masculine, all leather, even the curtains. He sat between a blond woman of about thirty-five with the best cleavage he'd seen in months, and a Saudi Arabian man wearing Giorgio perfume, and he lost for four straight hours, and he drank too much Chivas Regal, and he hardly noticed any of it.

Laura was the only thing on his mind. He had known, for a long while, that he had become perhaps overly obsessed by her, but the reality of being with her, at last, had blown everything else out of his head. After so much time, so much patience, he had been able, away from prying eyes, to observe her at close quarters, to assess what lay below the surface that had so immediately captivated him—and now, tonight, he had, with that finely judged kiss, triggered the final round of the contest he had begun playing three years ago. Until now, Laura Andros, for all his fascination, had been an item on his agenda; a major item, like a planned merger, but not wholly absorbing. Until now.

Roger remembered his sister, a few years back, taking him to task for marrying his first two wives for the wrong reasons. *More mergers than marriages,* he could remember Rona saying, and something more, about the importance of romance, passion and control. That was how it could be with Laura, he knew it. He could supply the romance, she would bring the passion, and as for the last, her youth had been one of the things that had so attracted him initially—he had known that he could mold her, build on the potential that he had instantly spotted, and, ultimately, control her.

That would be the real challenge, of course, the point where the battle for the depths of Laura Andros would begin. He could have bedded her long ago, have had her and dropped her, or perhaps kept her on the sidelines, like a toy. But a young woman who had done what she had as a young girl, would not be easily controlled. But wasn't that precisely what had fired his desire for her in the first place, what had caused those endless, unprecedented sexual dreams, what had prompted him to embark on this strange game of self-imposed celibacy while he waited for her to be ready?

There had been times, during business meetings over the past two years, observing her intelligence and ability, and yet, at the same time, her naïveté and innocence, when Roger had become confused about what it was that he might, ultimately, want from her. But now, after these last two days of being with her, free and clear of business, having watched her lovely, expressive face as he had startled her with the clothes, the jewelry and the *Laura*, Roger had finally identified the most profound need in him that Laura personified. It was the other ingredient of which Rona had spoken. It was love. He was in love with her, and though it surprised him, it pleased him, too.

He would not wait much longer. It was too draining, too costly in time and strength, drew him too much away from the Ambler Corporation, from his real world. The game had been played perfectly to this point, and now he would begin his final moves.

Roger Ambler sat at the chemin de fer table in the *Super Privé* of the Casino of Monte Carlo, losing money and drinking Chivas and thinking about the days that were to come. The blonde on his left glanced at him from time to time, appraisingly. The Giorgio-wearing Arab on his right, who had been winning ever since the arrival of the American, hoped that he would stay a little longer. But Roger was hardly conscious of the people around him, or of the room in which he sat. The image of Laura Andros, naked and descending on him, was the only thing of which his mind, and his hard, blazing cock, were aware.

CHAPTER 12

They boarded the *Laura* again at noon. The weather forecast, according to the *météo* and the yacht's captain, was unsettled, but Roger had set his sights on Cannes, and was not to be diverted.

"A little breeze won't bother you, will it?" he asked Laura, when they were already moving out of the harbor.

"I don't think so. I used to be a pretty good sailor."

"That's what I thought."

They were standing, quite close together but not touching, leaning on the guardrail, watching the port growing smaller again.

"I was thinking," Laura said, "about the office."

"What about it?"

"I can't just stay away indefinitely."

"Sure you can. Hal tells me things are fine."

"Oh."

Roger looked at her. "Disappointed?"

"Of course not."

"No one's indispensable, Laura." He paused. "Except me."

She glanced at him, knew that he meant it in spite of the humor in his eyes. There was a greater intensity about him today, she'd felt it the moment she'd seen him. She wondered what it meant, whether it was relevant to her at all, or something connected to the meeting he'd had that morning.

She had a strong sense of something coming to an end. She wondered how unhappy it would leave her.

"How much longer?" she asked.

"Not much," he answered.

"What exactly does that mean? A few days, or less?" It was unrealistic not to know.

"Hours." Turning to face her, he laid his right index finger against her lips, as if to silence her. "Not yet," he said.

They dropped the lunch anchor near Nice. The sea was flat as glass, and there was no breeze.

"It's so clear," Laura said. "The forecast must have been wrong. It usually is in England."

"The clearness means they probably got it right. When the coastline looks hazy here, that means good weather, clear means a change for the worse."

"How much worse?"

Roger shrugged. "Don't worry about it—we're never going to be that far from shore."

"I'm not worried," Laura said. "What's for lunch?"

"I like a woman with an appetite."

"You've been spoiling me—usually I eat a sandwich at the most."

"From your boyfriend's snack bar."

She looked at him. "How do you know about Ned?"

"Hal told me."

"I didn't know Hal was a gossip."

"The greatest."

Laura hesitated. "Ned's not really my boyfriend—not anymore."

"Just good friends."

"That's right." Her eyes met his directly. She wanted to know what was going to happen. As well to know. Better to know.

Jeanne served lunch. A mound of shiny black pearls on a bed of crushed ice, served with thin slivers of crustless toast, little shell-shaped pats of butter and half-lemons wrapped in muslin.

"I've never had caviar before," Laura said.

"Some people like it with egg and onion," Roger told her,

"but I can never see the point of masking the taste. It takes a little while for your tongue to really identify the flavor and the texture."

He took a slice of toast, buttered it using a tiny silver knife with a rounded blade, spooned caviar lavishly onto one edge of the toast, squeezed lemon over it and leaned toward her. "Bite it off," he said, and popped it into her mouth. It was the first vaguely intimate moment they'd shared that day. He watched her. "Well?"

"Mm."

"You need more." He spooned more onto her toast. "Your tongue needs more."

Laura let him feed her. "You're right," she said after a few seconds. "It's very different." She licked her lips. "It's good."

"Now a sip of champagne," Roger said. "They're beautifully matched." He poured for them both from the Dom Pérignon bottle in the ice bucket beside him, and handed her a glass. "To you."

They were sitting on the semicircle of white leather seating in the stern, the food on a low table before them. The sun was very warm, the air a little more sultry than it had been when they'd left the harbor.

"Laura," Roger said suddenly, "come a little closer."

"All right," Laura said. She slid across the leather toward him. "But it's okay, I can feed myself now."

His eyes were very blue. "Your taste buds," he said again, "need another new experience."

"Do they?" she asked, softly.

He took the champagne glass out of her hand and put it on the table, and then he took her face between his hands again as he had the previous night, and kissed her. But this time, it was a different kind of kiss, searching, lips parted, stronger, more forceful. Laura did not pull away. It was what she wanted, her lips, her mouth, her tongue, all of her. Her arms went around him, his hands left her face and he pulled her closer, and the kiss grew more passionate, so that their teeth grazed, and their tongues mingled, and they had to draw apart because they were out in the open and not quite alone.

"I thought—" Laura said, and stopped.

"What did you think?"

"That it was over."

Roger smiled. "No," he said. "It's far from over."

"I'm glad," Laura said.

The breeze came up suddenly, sharply, and clouds began to blow in from over the Alpes Maritimes, assembling in a cooler grayness over the Mediterranean. Laura watched, but could not hear, the captain in conversation with Roger, thought she detected a touch of disapproval in the Frenchman's face, but then Roger returned to her side, smiling.

"A little on the overcautious side, our captain."

"Is there going to be a storm?"

"Probably, but not for a while yet. He wanted us to turn back now, but we want to go on to Cannes, don't we?"

"If we can," Laura said. "I don't really mind either way."

"I do," Roger said.

"We could always go back by road, if the captain would be happier."

"The captain's happiness isn't my concern, my dear— though if you're a little nervous, that's different."

"I'm not in the least nervous," Laura said. "I used to love it when Adam and I went sailing and it got a bit rough."

Roger was silent for a moment. "Was Adam your first love?"

Laura smiled. "No—not in that way. We thought of each other as brother and sister, and anyway, we were just children."

"Some children harbor romantic thoughts."

She shook her head. "I don't think we ever did."

"How was it when you saw each other again?"

Laura was surprised. "I didn't realize you knew."

"You went to Athens in August of '83." He smiled at her disconcerted expression. "You stayed for just one night because of a flu epidemic in the Oxford Street branch."

"That's how you knew about it."

"Of course. How else?"

"I thought for a moment you might have been keeping an eye on me."

"Perhaps I was."

Laura hesitated for another instant, and then returned to his question. "It was wonderful seeing Adam again. But sad, too."

"Because it was too short."

"Not only that," Laura said. "It was sad because so much had happened since we'd last been together."

"That's just life, isn't it? Nothing ever stays the same. You both had to grow up."

"Of course we did. There were other things, too." Laura paused, treading carefully. "My grandfather's death—the sale of our house."

Until now, Laura had skimmed lightly over her childhood, telling him only that she had been orphaned at three years, that Theo Andros had sent her to boarding school in England and that he had died while she was there. She wondered, for the first time, whether she would ever want to tell Roger Ambler everything that had happened to her, and even if she did want to, whether she would have the courage to do so. She doubted it.

"I'm sorry you had to cut that vacation short," Roger said now.

"It couldn't be helped," Laura said. "And I can always go back again."

"Sure you can."

Still he hadn't really pried into her past. Just those light questions, never anything heavy-handed. She no longer believed he was simply disinterested, only that he was waiting for her to tell him whatever she was ready to. And she took it as a lead, also, an indication that she, too, should not ask many questions about his own life. Knowing too much might lose her her job. If she had not already lost it.

Roger wondered if she would ever voluntarily tell him what she had done. He guessed not. He thought no less of her for not confessing. He was still, after all, her employer, and one of the things he most enjoyed about Laura was the inner strength that he knew existed. A spur-of-the-moment unburdening now, a sudden desire for total honesty because she cared for him, would show more weakness than strength, would be unworthy of her.

That kiss had weakened him almost beyond endurance. All those months of celibacy might have been for nothing. It had to be right. It had to be perfect. Nothing else would do.

He did not intend to wait much longer.

The breeze became a wind, the temperature dropped, and Roger abandoned his plan to go into Cannes.

"We're going straight back," he told Laura. "Do you mind?"

"Of course not, I told you."

"I'm afraid our *capitaine* isn't too pleased with me," Roger said, clearly amused. "He got a little tight-assed about being in charge of his ship, and I told him the *Laura* wasn't the goddamned *Queen Elizabeth*, it was my boat, and if I don't mind being in the water during a mistral, why should he worry, so now he's sulking."

"Is it going to get bad?" Laura asked.

"It'll probably get a bit rougher, but do you imagine I'd risk my brand new yacht, let alone our lives, if I thought there was even the slightest danger?"

"Of course not."

"Glad someone has a little faith." Roger took her arm. "To be perfectly honest, I've been looking forward to a little weather." There was a glint in his eye.

It grew much rougher. The sea turned from blue to iron gray, the waves capped with white. The smaller craft, the sleek speedboats and sailboats, had almost all disappeared back into safe harbors, and the *Laura*, together with most of the other yachts in the vicinity, was hugging the coast for protection against the mistral, which came from the north, funneled through the Rhône Valley, blowing hard and cold into the south.

Roger went below for a few moments and came back up with two heavy blue and white cotton sweaters, one for himself, the other for Laura.

"You still okay?" he asked her.

"Fine," she said. "It's exhilarating."

"I'm going to have a Scotch—how about you?"

"Why not?"

"That's my girl," he said, approvingly.

They sat in the open, drinking Chivas Regal on the white leather seat, getting wet, arms around each other, while the crew busied themselves with looking after the boat, keeping dry in the pilot house as much as possible.

"Want to go below?" Roger asked, after a great splashing wave showered them with cold, salty water.

Laura shook her head. "I think I'd feel worse down there." She smiled. "I'm beginning to be glad we didn't have too heavy a lunch." She sipped at her whisky. "This is good," she said, feeling it warm her.

Jeanne appeared, wearing a hooded white oilskin with *Laura* printed on the back in larger italics than on the T-shirts all the crew wore.

"The captain would like to speak to you, Monsieur Ambler," she said, having to raise her voice now against the sound of the wind and waves.

"I'll be right there." Roger looked at Laura. "Maybe you'd better go below while I talk to him."

"I'd rather stay on deck."

"Not on your own." He rose, tugged her up with him and pushed her gently toward the steps. "Go on, just for a few minutes."

It was warm in the narrow sitting room, snug and less oppressive than Laura had thought it might be. She used the head, and checked her face in the mirror. Her cheeks were flushed, and her eyes were as bright as she'd ever seen them. She looked a mess, especially compared to the way she'd looked at the party the night before, but on the other hand, she thought perhaps she'd never looked better.

The boat rolled unexpectedly, and Laura had to grab onto the basin to stop herself from falling. She thought that the captain was probably urging Roger to let him take the yacht into port before they reached Monaco.

"Laura?"

"Coming," she called, and opened the door.

"All right?" he asked.

"Fine," she said again. "It's getting worse, isn't it?"

"He wants to take her in to Beaulieu," Roger said.

"He's probably right, don't you think?"

"I guess so." The intense look was back in his eyes. "I wanted to take her all the way back," he said. "I wanted to be out on deck at sunset."

"Why sunset?" Laura asked.

"One of my plans," he said. "Though maybe a storm's even better." He reached for her hand. "Come on—let's go back up."

The wind slapped her in the face as they emerged, taking her breath away and stinging her eyes, but the clouds directly above had broken apart, and the sun shone through with a glaring fierceness magnified by the mass of dark gray surrounding the break.

"Come on," he shouted, against the noise.

Keeping a tight grip on her hand, Roger led her toward the bow. The yacht yawed, and they both stumbled against the rail, but as soon as they straightened up, Roger went on, pulling Laura with him until they were as close to the front of the boat as they could get.

"Feel good?" he wanted to know.

"I feel great!"

"Isn't this the best?" he demanded.

The yacht rolled again, and Laura fell against Roger, and his right arm went around her, holding her close against his chest.

"Look," he said, and pointed with his left hand at a tiny rainbow just over the deck, where the strong beam of sunlight had caught the sea spray. "Better than sunset," he shouted against the wind, and an expression of satisfaction passed over his face.

"We can have a sunset any old time," Laura agreed, dizzy with it all.

"You really like it?" Roger asked.

"I *love* it."

"You want more?"

Laura nodded, her face wet with spray, her hair slicked down against her head like a black cap. "Of course I want more."

"Then marry me," Roger said.

The yacht yawed again, and they both lurched together, struck the guardrail, bruising their sides.

"Did you hear me?" he yelled.

Laura was staring at him.

"Well?" he demanded.

"I'm not sure if I heard you."

"I asked you to marry me," Roger shouted. His eyes were fierce, his features were the sharpest she'd ever seen them, accentuated by the darkened wet gold of his hair. "Say yes, Laura, and you can have it all—everything you ever wanted!"

The harbor at Beaulieu was coming closer, rocking yachts and wildly bobbing small boats, and houses and hotels, and beyond, up on the hill, Eze-Village, where they had sipped mineral water just one day earlier and gazed out over the hazy coast and the perfect azure sea.

Laura still stared up into Roger's face. It was more like a dream than ever—she expected to waken at any second, and find herself in bed in Finborough Road with Gus next door, and laugh at herself for her unconscious romanticizing.

"We've only had two days," she said. "You don't even know me."

"I know you very well," he said.

She shook her wet head. "No, you don't."

Roger smiled, his teeth very white against his tanned face. "I know all I need to know about you, Laura." The wind howled, and he held her very tightly. "I've wanted you for three years—I had to be sure about you, had to wait and see what you were made of before I could take a chance on you—"

"But you hardly ever *saw* me!"

"Let's just say I kept an eye on you—that was all I had to do. I knew how I felt from the beginning, but you were so very young—too young. You couldn't have coped then."

"And now you think I can?" Laura still stared at him, trying to read his eyes, to read her own heart, to keep some weak grip on reality.

"I know you can." He drew back from her just a little, held her at arm's length so that he could look properly into her face. "Laura, I can give you the most wonderful future. Everything you've ever dreamed of, and more besides. I'm rich and I'm powerful, and I'm in love with you, and it's all going to get better—and I've never had the right woman to share all that with, and I knew, almost from the first time I saw you, that you could be that woman, if I could only help you grow, if I could guide you—"

"All the time—" Laura could hardly believe her ears. "The promotions—you built my career because you *wanted* me?"

"Only because you had the talent to do those jobs—I'd never have trusted you with them otherwise, you know me better than that."

"I thought I did." She shook her head. "No, that's not true—I never thought I knew you at all. You were so remote, you were a figurehead who swooped down from the mountain every now and again to check on the little people. You never gave me the tiniest hint of what you were thinking."

"How could I, before I was one hundred percent sure? I didn't really make up my mind until a few months ago—"

"When you named the *Laura*?"

"Before that, before Christmas. That was why—" He stopped.

"That was why what?"

Roger shook his head. "It's not important."

They were moving into the harbor, the sway gentler now, the sea already calmed by the walls, by the land itself and the other vessels safely moored.

"You have to tell me now," Roger said, urgently. "Before we anchor. I have to know now—I won't wait any longer."

"Can't you give me any time to think?" Laura felt suddenly chilled, abruptly aware of her drenched clothes, of the craziness of the way they had stayed out in the open. "Maybe after I've got out of these—"

"No." Roger's voice was sharp, commanding. "Now or never." He drew her close again, hugged her fiercely against himself. "Yes or no, Laura."

He wants a mistress. She remembered Gus's words, and she'd believed that Gus was right, even when she had denied it. It had never occurred to her, even for an instant, that he might consider marrying her. Things like that just didn't happen, not to girls like her. A sudden surge of guilt swept her. He didn't know about her, didn't know what she had done, where she had been, what kind of life she'd had. She ought to tell him now, before it was too late—it wasn't fair to him to keep the truth from him—

But if she told him now, it would all be over. All of it, not just Monaco and the *Laura* and a glittering, secure future. Everything that had come her way since Roger had first laid eyes on her would disappear. Just as it would if she did not accept his proposal.

And why should she not accept the most irresistible offer any woman had ever been tempted with? Marriage to Roger Ambler would mean so much more than the luxuries that his wealth could provide—it would mean safety, genuine security. It was her chance to bury the past, forever.

"Laura—"

Out of the corner of her eye, she could see the crew scurrying about, knew they had arrived, knew that she was running out of time.

"I don't know if I love you," she said at last, able to speak more quietly now that they were out of the great howl of the wind. "It's the easiest thing in the world to be *in* love with you—you're the most attractive, the most generous, the most remarkable man I've ever met—"

"You will love me," Roger said, with assurance, though the urgency was still in his eyes and in his voice. "You're beautiful and talented, and you're soft and you're tough, too. You'll make me the perfect wife I've always hoped for, and I'll make you a damned fine husband." He reached for her left hand, raised it to his lips and kissed it. "And you're much too clever to say no to me—and that doesn't mean I think you'd say yes just for what I can give you, because I know what you're made of—"

"Roger—"

"Just say yes, Laura. Don't say anything else, but for the love of God, say you'll marry me."

For just one moment, one long, painful moment, Laura closed her eyes. She conjured it all up again, the tormented weeks at Osborne, the fear and the anger and the awful, enduring guilt, and the trial and Kane House with all its deprivations and innate brutality, and the terror of being outside on her own, the months in the damp, infested room in

Paddington. And she knew that with just a single word, she could escape it forever.

So she said it.

"Yes."

CHAPTER 13

It was like being caught up in a tornado. She had never seen anyone make things happen the way Roger did. All that unfamiliar relaxation she had observed after her arrival in Monaco had vanished almost immediately once she'd given him the answer he wanted. They had spent one more night at the Hôtel de Paris, a lavishly romantic evening in the Salle Empire followed by another visit to the casino, and Roger had not left her side for an instant, and Laura had been more baffled than ever when he brought her to the door of her suite and left her again, right after another long, passionate embrace that she knew had left him as breathless and shaky as it had her.

"We're leaving at six," he told her. "Can you be ready?"

"Of course," she said. "I don't think I could sleep anyway."

"Are you going to call Gus?"

"I think I'll wait till I see her."

"You're not going to London," Roger said. "We're flying to New York."

"We are?"

"That's where we're getting married."

"But I have to go home—I have to go to the office—"

"Anne Lockhart's already taken over." He smiled at her startled face. "Hal tells me the move's gone smoothly."

For the first time, Laura felt a ripple of anger.

"That's my job, Roger," she said. "I should have been consulted."

"You were. Lockhart was your number-one choice, remember?"

Her mind flashed back to their first meeting downstairs. *Am I being fired or promoted, or just moved?* she had asked him. *None of the above,* he had answered.

"You're a very sneaky man, Roger."

"A sneaky man very much in love," he said.

They flew to London in time to catch the morning Concorde. Laura stepped into the slender white steel bird and sat on her pale gray leather seat beside her fiancé and accepted more champagne and caviar, and watched him fall almost instantly asleep. The flight took less than four hours, and he woke only once, instantly, crisply awake, to squeeze her hand and glance through a sheaf of papers from his briefcase, before closing his eyes again.

"I'm sorry, sweetheart," he said, as they arrived at Kennedy. "I guess I've programmed myself either to work or sleep while I'm in the air."

They drove into the city, sitting in the back of a long, black limousine with darkened windows, a tiny television set and a bar. The rugged-looking chauffeur's name was John, he wore a gray uniform with a cap, and for the first ten minutes of the ride he brought Roger up to date with news, local weather, a brief report on the general good health of Rona and Nelson Howarth and their girls, before, without being asked to, he pushed a button that closed the window between himself and his passengers, sealing them off into a private space.

"You're very quiet," Roger said.

"I'm trying to absorb everything," Laura told him. "There's so much to take in."

He took her hand again, laid it, encased in his, on his right thigh, a move of affection, not seduction. "You'll have plenty of time, sweetheart. There'll be nothing you can't cope with."

"I feel—"

"How do you feel?"

"Out of control," she said.

"Only if you want to be," Roger said. "Would you rather go to London?"

"Of course not."

"Then stop worrying, and enjoy the ride."

He brought her to the Plaza Hotel, checked her in, came up with her to her suite, overlooking Central Park, and told her that he had to go.

"Aren't you going to stay with me?"

"I wish I could, but I have to get to the office. You have a good look around, ask for anything you need, and take a nap."

"When will you be back?"

"We'll have lunch."

She put her hand on his arm, held on to it. "Roger, I don't know where I am—I've seen New York in films, but—"

"I told you to stop worrying," he hushed her. "Just stay put—it'll only be for a few hours. Take a stroll around the hotel, if you like, get familiar, but don't go outside until I get back." He put his arms around her. "You're not just a tourist, Laura. Manhattan's going to be your home—your number-one home, anyway. You'll have family, you'll have all the help you need getting to learn the way things work here."

"You will stay here tonight?" she asked.

"And kill our wedding night?" He shook his head. "I'll be home tonight, in my bachelor's bed, thinking about you."

Laura smiled. "And when exactly is this wedding night to be? Do I get a say in that, or is it one of your many secret plans?"

"Don't you like the way I organize things?" he asked, still holding her.

"How could I not?"

"Then that's okay, isn't it?"

He brought his face down to kiss her, and Laura kissed him back, more fervently than she'd ever kissed him or Ned, and there'd never been anyone else, and Roger touched her body intimately for the first time, sliding his hands down her back to her behind, and squeezing her buttocks lightly but firmly, drawing her to him so that she felt his erection and shivered with pleasure.

"Leave everything to me, my darling," he said, very softly, gazing into her eyes. "I'm a master planner. You won't be disappointed."

He released her, and walked over to a mirror on the wall of the sitting room, took out a handkerchief from his trouser pocket and wiped her pale pink lipstick from his mouth. Then he held up the handkerchief and kissed it, before he put it back into his pocket, and left the room.

He returned, as he had promised, for lunch, which they ordered in the suite from room service. Everything on the table, from the side salad to the fillet steak that Roger had asked for, was three times larger than it ever was in England or had been in Monaco.

"This is America." Roger shrugged. "You'll get used to it. I don't eat this way every day—if I'm in the office, I grab a sandwich, or often I don't bother eating anything until the evening."

Laura peeled a king-sized shrimp and dipped it into the red sauce that had accompanied it. "These are delicious," she said.

"How are you feeling?"

"Marvelous."

"Some people say that flying Concorde cuts out jet lag, others say they feel just as lousy. I never suffer from it at all."

"Maybe I don't either," Laura said, though she still had a heady feeling of unreality.

"That would be useful, since we'll be traveling back and forth to Europe all the time." Roger paused. "Did you call Gus?"

"Not yet."

He raised an eyebrow. "Why not? Frightened to tell her the news?"

"Of course not. It's just that—" She stopped.

"Go on."

"There are so many things I need to think about. There's

the flat—and of course there's Gus to consider. I can't—I won't just leave her in the lurch."

"I wouldn't ask you to."

"She can't afford to keep the flat on her own," Laura said.

"I don't suppose she can. Didn't you tell me she has a market stall?"

"She has two stalls now—but she still couldn't afford all that rent."

"The rent will go on being paid," Roger said, easily. "Or Gus could move into something a little more upscale, if you'd like her to."

Laura flushed. "I wasn't asking you to do anything, Roger—I just meant that I need to take time to work things out."

"Consider them worked out." He swallowed the last piece of his steak, wiped his mouth and tossed the napkin onto the table. "We need to get something cleared up right away, if we're to be married." He looked at her penetratingly. "You haven't changed your mind about that?"

She shook her head. "Of course I haven't."

"Then just try and take this in. I have a great deal of money, maybe more than you can imagine, maybe not. You have many things more valuable than mere money that I will be asking you to bring to our marriage, but you don't have the cash. Okay so far?"

"I suppose so."

"Marriage is a bargain. It's give and take, do you agree?" He went straight on. "It's no hardship to me to buy you things, sweetheart, or to use my money to make you happy. I want you to be as happy as possible—that part of our bargain's easy for me. Unless you fight me every step of the way, which will be a big pain in the ass but won't ultimately change the fact that I've got it, and I want to spend it on you."

Laura sat back in her chair and shook her head. "You're amazing."

"So are you."

"I'm not."

"I say you are." He studied her with undisguised admiration. "You're so young and so beautiful, and you're smart and you have dignity."

She leaned in to the table again. "The young part," she said. "Are you sure that isn't going to be a problem?"

"Not for me."

"But I'm not quite twenty-four, Roger, and you're—"

"Twenty years older." His gaze held hers steadily. "Is it a problem for you? Do you think I'm too old for you? Any number of people are going to tell you I am."

Laura waited a moment before answering. "I hadn't even given it a thought until now. I just loved being with you—it never occurred to me that the difference could matter." She smiled. "But then again, I didn't know that you were going to propose marriage."

"What did you think I intended?"

"I wasn't sure."

"You thought I just wanted to make love to you. Another notch in my belt."

"Gus thought you might want a mistress."

"Did she now?" It was Roger's turn to smile. "She wasn't all wrong. I guess a lot of men hope they'll find a woman who can be both wife and mistress at the same time."

Laura felt a new frisson of excitement touch her. "And you think I can be those things?"

"Don't you?"

"I don't know."

He spelled out the arrangements he'd already made. They would be married, if she agreed, in the garden of his house in East Hampton, Long Island. The same Episcopalian minister who had married Rona, his sister, had agreed to look after things for them, his brother-in-law would be his best man, and it would be an intimate affair, Roger reassured Laura, nothing that she needed to feel apprehensive about.

"We'll fly Gus over, of course," he told her. "And anyone else you want to be there," he added, as Laura jumped up from her chair and flung her arms around his neck. "Did you think I wanted to cut you off completely?"

"No, no—but it's all been so unreal, so *wonderfully* un-real, that I didn't know what to think. Thank you for thinking about Gus," she said, kissing him. "But there isn't anyone else, not really—"

"What about Adam?" he asked.

Her eyes grew even brighter. "I didn't like to ask."

"Why not? Because of the cost?"

"That, and I thought you might not want him to come."

"Because I asked if he was your first love? You said that he wasn't. I believed you."

"And it was true—Roger, we were just like brother and sister."

"I know you were." He grinned at her. "I'm just teasing you, darling. Don't take it to heart."

"I never imagined you as a tease," Laura said, going to sit on the sofa. "But then I never imagined a lot of things."

"At the agency, you mean?" He watched her nod. "That's all over now, Laura. Forgotten. History."

"I know it is, but—"

"I want you to forget it." He was suddenly serious. "I mean it. I don't want you to think about working for me, I don't want you to talk about it, not to anyone."

"But I'm not ashamed of it."

"Nor should you be." He was still unsmiling. "But you're my fiancée now, and you're going to be my wife, and that other part of your life is finished. Is that okay with you?"

Laura nodded slowly. "Up to a point."

"What point?"

"I was proud of my job, Roger. I enjoyed it, and I did it well. I'm not going to bury it as if I were ashamed of it. I won't talk about having been one of your employees, if you'd rather I didn't—I can understand why you might not want me to do that. But I'll always remember it, and I want to be free to talk to my friends about anything, and to you, most of all."

"Anything?" Roger said.

"If you're going to be my husband"—Laura went on—"I hope you're going to be my best friend."

"I hope so, too," Roger agreed. "And is there anything particular you want to talk to me about now? Anything you want to tell me?"

Laura felt the flush start at the base of her neck. She looked at him evenly, without flinching.

"Not right now," she said.

It was interesting, Roger thought, how exciting he found the fact that she was going to continue lying to him. A part of him—the romantic part, he supposed—hoped that she would surprise him by confessing everything before the wedding, before he committed himself to her. But most of him knew perfectly well that if Laura had not told him by now, she never would, and as he had known from the beginning, that inner hardness was one of the main reasons he was so attracted to her.

He thought of her kisses, such fresh, giving, yearning kisses. He thought of the way her buttocks had felt under his hands, the way his own body had reacted to her, and he imagined how her breasts would feel to his fingertips, how sweet her skin would smell, how she would taste. He thought about the way she would make love to him, about the things she would do. The things that a girl like her would be willing to do on her wedding night, with all inhibitions tossed away.

No one would believe that he had waited for that night to bed his bride—even Laura, he knew, could scarcely believe it. But he had always known it would be worthwhile. Perfection was always worth waiting for.

He took her to meet Rona that evening, before dinner, at the Howarths' duplex apartment on Park Avenue and Eighty-second Street. Nelson Howarth was out of town, and would not return for two more days, but Rona was poised and avid for her first glimpse of her brother's chosen partner.

She opened the front door herself, both hands outstretched. "My dear Laura, you are very welcome—you don't mind if I call you Laura, do you?"

"Of course not," Laura said, staring in fascination at the glamorous creature before her who was at one and the same time almost a duplicate of Roger, and yet one of the most feminine women she had ever seen.

At forty-one, Rona Ambler Howarth was everything she

had ever wanted to be. She was able, without too much difficulty, to present within an hour of breakfast, an image of effortless, immaculate beauty. She had a husband she loved, admired and respected, two daughters who were, thank the Lord, easy to adore. She had the most desirable of Manhattan homes, another on the Island and a third residence, an apartment in Geneva. She still had overall control of Zero Publishing, her beloved company. She had heaps of money, piled up in accounts, stocks, investments, antiques, fine art and, of course, in the Ambler Corporation, which she had always been content to let her darling brother take care of. And best of all, she was a thoroughly happy woman.

She had wondered, ever since receiving Roger's call from Monte Carlo two days earlier, whether that happiness might be going to become a little tarnished by the arrival into their midst of an unknown girl eighteen years younger than herself and named Andros. Rona prided herself on not being imperious or especially affected, but in truth she had a natural aptitude toward snobbery, and marriage to Nelson Howarth and the first appearance of her name in the *Social Register* had sharpened that aptitude considerably.

"I'm crazy about her," Roger had told her on the telephone without prevarication, "and I'm going to pin her down before she gets away."

"Why might she want to get away?"

"She doesn't know it herself yet, but she has a very strong will. It's hard to know how she might react if I give her enough time."

"Wouldn't it be better to find out?"

Roger's voice had been patient but very firm. "Rona, darling, you told me after Patricia divorced me that I should aim for love, passion and control."

"But from what you're saying, you're not too sure if this Laura can be controlled—not that I'd approve if you brought home a spineless girl." Rona had paused. "I imagine you've picked her because she's young enough to be molded?"

"I picked her, as you so perceptively say, over three years ago, and I've been molding her ever since."

"My God, Roger, you've never said a word."

"I wanted to be sure I'd got it right this time, sis."

Rona had laughed then. "Well, if you haven't after three years of planning, then I guess you never will."

Her first viewing—she couldn't help but think of it that way—of Laura Andros was, Rona thought later, more interesting than anything else. The girl was lovely to look at in an unusual way. The day or two in the Mediterranean sun had lent her skin a slight glow, but Rona couldn't help but be relieved that Roger had not brought home the olive-skinned, aggressively foreign-looking beauty she had imagined. Laura's good figure, wonderful hair and remarkable eyes meant that she'd be a joy to shop for and to work on. Her oval-shaped face spelled gentleness, the unusual pointed chin signified strength, and her slender fingers, wrists and neck meant that she would wear jewelry well.

"You've very, very lovely," Rona told her as she led the way into the smaller of her two sitting rooms and invited her brother and his clearly nervous fiancée to sit on the chintz slipcovered armchairs. "But of course I knew you had to be special to have had such a dramatic impact on Roger." She looked intently at Laura. "I'm so very glad to have the chance to meet you, my dear. My brother's happiness is of great importance to me."

"I'm sure it is," Laura said. "I often wish I'd had a brother or sister."

"You had Adam," Roger said. "He was Laura's best childhood friend, while she was still living in Greece. We're both hoping he'll get here for the wedding."

"That would be nice." Rona paused. "I was hoping you'd both have dinner with me, but Roger thought that having to cope with an entire evening's grilling after a long journey might be too tiring."

"So we'll just have a drink instead," Roger said. "I'll do the honors."

"Thank you, darling." Rona looked back at Laura. "Who else have you invited to the wedding, Laura, dear?"

"I haven't had too much time to think about it," Laura said, a little wryly, "but I'm hoping that Gus—that's my flatmate in London—will come."

"Gus is short for Augusta," Roger explained. "Augusta Pietrowski."

"Is that a Polish name?" Rona asked.

"That's right," Laura said. "I have no real family to invite, I'm afraid."

"Roger told me," Rona said gently. "I was sad to hear of your losses. We still miss our parents very much, but at least we were both adults when they passed away." She brightened. "Nelson and our girls are longing to meet you. Anna and Susan were very cross with me for making them go to bed at their usual time, but they're only eight years old, and they do have school in the morning."

"Roger's talked so much about them," Laura said. "I'm looking forward to meeting them, too."

They stayed until half past eight, by which time Laura had agreed, gratefully, to let her future sister-in-law help her shop for the wedding, starting the next morning. Rona waited until she was certain that they were not about to return for any reason, and then headed straight for the telephone.

"Nelson, she seems absolutely fine," she told her husband, who was staying at the Connaught Hotel in London. "A pretty thing, with a dear little accent—unworldly, of course, but nothing that can't be fixed."

"That's all good news, isn't it?"

"Of course it is, but I still think we ought to find out a little more, for Roger's sake."

"Surely he's done all the checking that needs doing, Ro?"

"I'm certain he has."

"Then why do we need to do anymore?"

"Because he's known about her for more than three years, Nelson, and he's never said a single word to me. You know he usually tells me everything."

"So you think that means he must be keeping something from you."

"I'm sure of it, and it troubles me," Rona said.

"What about his right to privacy, Ro?" Nelson asked his wife. "You don't usually pry into his affairs."

"Nor would I this time, if it were just an affair—that's

precisely the point." Rona held the receiver tightly against her ear, as if that might guard against eavesdroppers. "I just have a feeling about her, Nelson. I liked her—I really did. But there's something there, in the background. Maybe it isn't important, but I'd just like to be sure."

"What if there is some skeleton in her closet? Do you intend to tell Roger that you've been spying on Laura?"

"I'm not spying," Rona said defensively. "I'm just trying to help him, that's all." She paused. "Will you try, my darling, for me?"

"You know I will." With a small sigh of resignation, Nelson Howarth took his gold Cross pen from the breast pocket of his jacket. "All right, Ro. Give me all you know."

Rona picked Laura up at ten o'clock in the morning. They met in the Fifth Avenue lobby, and Rona, wearing a pink light wool Chanel suit and almost-flat shoes, linked arms companionably with Laura.

"We have a chauffeur to make life easier," she told her, "though I thought we might start with a stroll to Bergdorf's— that's still *the* store, Laura, darling, no matter what anyone else tells you."

Laura allowed herself to be steered toward the revolving door and down the red-carpeted steps outside, facing a lovely fountain in the center of a spacious square.

"Aren't the tulips gorgeous?" Rona said. She began to walk briskly, drawing Laura along with her. "We'll show you the city another time," she said, "but right now, Fifth Avenue, Fifty-seventh Street and, of course, Madison Avenue, are all you really need to know about."

"What are we going to buy?" Laura asked.

"A wedding gown, of course. I know Roger's being romantic, but I do think it's a pity he's rushing things quite so much—we simply don't have time to have your gown designed. But don't worry, dear, Bergdorf's has heavenly dresses, and with your lovely figure, I'm sure we'll have no problems at all."

"I'm not worried," Laura said, busy gazing around as they walked.

"That's good." Rona tucked her arm even more firmly

into hers. "But you have to promise to tell me if it seems as if I'm trying to take over—Nelson tells me I can sometimes be bossy."

"But I'd be lost without you," Laura said truthfully as they slowed down on the corner of Fifty-eighth Street so that she could take her first long look at a Fifth Avenue store window. "I'd be going to all the wrong places—I don't know the first thing about New York." She smiled ruefully. "Come to that, I don't even know where I'm going to be married or where we're going to live."

"You poor darling," Rona said with genuine sympathy.

"The poor darling doesn't even know where she's going to live!" Rona accused her brother later on the telephone. "It really is too bad of you, Roger, forcing us all to race around like this."

"Poor darling Laura," Roger countered, "is going to live on the sixtieth floor of the most desirable building in Manhattan—"

"Plus the house on the Island, plus San Francisco and the Paris apartment, I know, I know," Rona persisted, "but put yourself in her shoes—she doesn't know anything about them, she hasn't even *seen* them."

"I'll take her to Trump Tower tonight—blow her away with the lights." Roger paused. "What do you think of her, sis?"

"I think she's an absolute darling. A little shy, but at her age if she weren't just a tiny bit anxious about all this, she'd be positively bumptious. Mind you, she certainly comports herself very well."

"So she should, given all her training."

"Training?"

"Rona, I've told you she was my London area manager for the agencies."

"I know you've told me," Rona said, "but just because you gave her a good job—"

"I gave her a good job, as you call it, because she was qualified and well-equipped to handle it. As a matter of fact, she's not going to be an easy act for her successor to follow."

"If she was important to you in London," Rona suggested, "maybe you should have left her there?"

"I'd hardly want to leave my wife in London."

"Of course not, but you could, perhaps, have put off marriage for a little while and just enjoyed"—she paused, delicately—"seeing her occasionally."

"No, sis, I could not have done that." Roger was growing impatient. "I told you before that I know what I'm doing this time."

"She's certainly different from Suzy and Patricia—"

"And you like her? So far as you can tell."

Rona was nothing if not honest. "I like her very much."

"Then please just help her get ready for this wedding, and leave the angst and pop psychology to the gossips—there'll be no shortage of them once our engagement's been announced."

"So long as you're prepared for that, darling."

"I'm prepared for everything, sis."

Nelson Howarth's lawyers in London reported back to him in the forty-eight hours he had requested. Only just back from England himself, he called Rona from his office.

"There's nothing wrong with Laura Andros, Ro," he told her.

"There must be."

"Nothing untoward at all." He glanced over the faxed report again. "If anything, the information's a little sparser than it might be—"

"Sparser? What do you mean?"

"Just what I say. The facts are scanty, few and far between. I have the obituaries for her parents—good people, nothing there; a little stuff about her grandfather—reading between the lines, I'd say he was a gambler, but that's not the end of the world—"

"But what about Laura?"

"Early education by a tutor in Greece, then boarding school—a place called Osborne College—then a shorthand and typing course—" Nelson scanned the pages once more. "Her work history, her address, and that's it."

"That isn't normal," Rona said. "It's just a résumé."

"It isn't abnormal either, dear."

"What about boyfriends? Hasn't she lived with anyone?"

"Only this Augusta person—" Nelson paused. "She's twenty-three years old, Ro, and she's a nice girl from a decent family."

"But I have this feeling," Rona persisted. "Maybe she's covered something up."

"Maybe there isn't anything to cover up, Ro."

"Maybe."

In London, Gus was finding the news hard to absorb. Laura had finally called her on her second afternoon in New York, telling her that her plane ticket would be delivered to the flat the next day, and that the plan was that she would stay with her at the hotel until the wedding.

"You're crazy, kid."

"You've said that already."

"I mean it. This is over the top, this is really weird. People just don't do this kind of thing—men don't act like this."

"I don't suppose many men do."

"But Roger Ambler's different from other men?"

In her suite at the Plaza, Laura smiled into the receiver. "You wouldn't believe how different, Gus."

"You're right, I wouldn't."

"Gus, I can't explain properly over the phone. It's too romantic, too wild to describe in a few words." Laura was gripped by sudden anxiety. "Gus, you will come, won't you? I can't get married unless you're here."

"Maybe that's a good reason for me not to."

"No, it isn't," Laura said firmly. "You have to come, and I have to get married."

"Why? You can't be pregnant—or at least, you wouldn't know if you were."

"I'm not pregnant. I told you, we haven't even slept together."

"That's the weirdest part of all," Gus said. "You're sure he's not gay?"

"He's had two wives already."

"That doesn't make him straight, and it doesn't make him much of a safe bet for marriage, either."

"He married them both for the wrong reasons," Laura said. "He's told me about them—they were terrific women, but they weren't right for him."

"And you are?"

"Gus, why shouldn't I be?" Laura was growing hurt. "Why do you find it so impossible that a wonderful man, who just happens to be successful—"

"Filthy rich, you mean," Gus interrupted.

"—who happens to be filthy rich and successful—"

"And almost twice your age."

"For God's sake, Gus, can't you try to be happy for me?" Laura took a deep breath. "Are you coming to my wedding or not? It happens to be important to me for you to be here with me—you're my very best friend in the world. But if you don't want to come, I'll be marrying Roger just the same."

"Of course I'm coming," Gus said, quietly. "But don't get any ideas about bridesmaids or anything like that, okay?"

Laura smiled with relief. "Somehow, I've never seen you as the bridesmaid type."

"At least you haven't flipped completely."

Roger was in Chicago for meetings with Tom Bailey when Gus arrived at Kennedy, but he made one of his limousines available to Laura for the day.

"Do what you like with your friend, go where you like. Your credit cards won't be ready until after the wedding—there wasn't much point rushing them through with the wrong name—but any decent store or restaurant won't mind calling the office to check if you charge something to me."

"I do have money of my own, Roger," Laura told him. "So does Gus."

"She's our guest, sweetheart. It'll be my pleasure to look after her while she's here."

The passengers flowing through the arrivals area of the TWA terminal building looked alternately weary, energized or simply unmoved. Most of the men wore sober suits or jeans, many carried raincoats over their arms, but the clothes worn by the female passengers ran the gamut from downright sloppy to first class chic.

Gus, Laura thought, when she caught her first glimpse of her, looked like Gus, only more so. Gus looked unique. She wore the multilayered dance look that was acceptably in vogue these days, especially when designed by Alaia or Kamali, but Laura knew that Gus's scarlet leotard, emerald dance skirt and baggy seersucker jacket, incorporating red and green in its stripes, had been assembled in a variety of market stalls with Gus's brilliant eye for cut and color.

"You look fantastic!" Laura threw her arms around her. "Heads are turning all over the place—Gus, you were made for New York."

"More to the point, were you?" Gus, still much taller than Laura even in her flat dance slippers, planted a kiss on her friend's dark head. Her own hair, tamed just a little more than usual in honor of the first class seat that Roger had insisted on buying her, was a rich burgundy shade that clashed dramatically with her leotard. "I'm glad to see you, kid."

"Not as glad as me." Laura bent down and retrieved Gus's battered Gladstone bag. "What have you *got* in here— rocks?"

"Makeup, books and booze, actually." Gus grimaced. "I certainly needed all that free drink on the plane—I've never been so scared in my life. Why didn't you tell me flying was so petrifying?"

"I like it," Laura said.

"You always were strange." Gus looked around. "So where's this limo you've told me so much about?"

"One of them"—Laura said with a grin—"is parked right outside."

"And are they ready for Gus Pietrowski? The groom's family, I mean—I daresay you've prepared the man himself for me, haven't you?"

"No one could ever be prepared for you."

Laura kept telling Gus that having her in New York made her situation seem suddenly more real, but Gus had never felt so much part of a dream, of some bizarre fantasy. Maybe under different, less crucial circumstances, she might have simply sat back and enjoyed the buzz, the hype, the glamor and prosperity, all so aggressively shoved right into the face of the misery and the slums, but her best friend had been lured into this alien craziness by a man she hardly knew, and that knowledge seemed to concentrate all Gus's energies into watchfulness and suspicion.

"Wait till you see it at night," Laura told her, "especially from where we're going to live. It's like being in space, surrounded by zillions of stars, with crisscrossed landing strips below."

"God, Laura Andros, you sound like one of them already—did they wash your brain as well as your hair at that swanky place?" Rona had taken Laura to Kenneth on Fifty-fourth Street, by way of an introduction, so that they could take a good look at her before the wedding to plan exactly what they would do to her on the day. "By the way, your hair doesn't look too different, I'm glad to say."

"They said they liked the way it was, so they just trimmed it a bit—it's nice and shiny though, don't you think?"

"Your hair's always been shiny, kid. Don't let them con you."

"No one's conning me, Gus," Laura said, quietly. "If anything, it's the other way round, wouldn't you say?"

The Trump Tower apartment measured three and a half thousand square feet, with views to Central Park and the city that had been achieved by knocking two units into one. There were four bedrooms, four bathrooms and a gleaming expanse of open-plan sitting and dining areas with a cocktail bar that was almost a room in itself, and a study with banks of computers and fax machines.

Gus hated it. She disliked the restrained public areas, all masculine browns, the way that the uncompromisingly male, almost corporate style had been drawn on into Ambler's apartment itself, all bronzed mirrors, sculptures, Italian marble and muted leather. She was appalled by the fact that Roger had told Laura never to open a window because it would interfere with the air-conditioning system, just as she had felt that the concierge, the doormen and elevator operators, for all their short tailcoats, white gloves and courtesy, were no better than glorified guards. It felt like a prison to Gus, an opulent, cold-hearted jail.

"Where's the real kitchen?" she asked Laura, as she was shown into a gadget-lined room little more than galley-size.

"This is it," Laura said, "though there is a utility room for the washing machine and dryer, and another freezer."

"But there's no space in here—how can you cook a decent meal?"

"I don't think Roger ever thinks about cooking. He says that Trump Tower is known as a 'reservations' building, because most of the people who live here don't have to bother to cook—the ones who really care have created their own kitchens." Laura paused, abruptly embarrassed. "Awful, isn't it?"

Gus ran a finger over the microwave oven's glass door. "I'm not sure awful's the word for it. It's unreal—like something in a shop window, only you're perched up in the sky." She gave a small, involuntary shudder, but seeing Laura's disappointed face, she tried to cover it up. "It's fantastic, kid, really amazing."

"You don't like it."

"I don't have to live in it."

"We won't be here all the time—Roger says he wants me to travel with him. And there's a house, on Long Island—that's where we're having the wedding."

"Not forgetting the flat in Paris," Gus added, mockingly.

"Gus, do you hate me?" Laura asked suddenly.

"Course I don't hate you. Why ask that?"

"I mean do you hate me for what I'm doing?"

"Marrying a filthy rich old man, you mean?"

"Roger isn't old."

"Old enough," Gus said, then relented. "Of course I don't hate you for marrying him, not if he's what you want. It's just that—" She hesitated.

"Go on."

"Well, look at us. This place has everything—it's a sodding palace, but we're standing talking in this poky little kitchen." Gus paused again. "Think you can get used to this? Get to feel at home?"

Laura waited a moment, biting her lower lip. "You want honesty?"

"Always."

"When I got to the Hôtel de Paris in Monte Carlo, it took my breath away. When I saw the suite he'd reserved for me—all that space, all that luxury—I couldn't believe it was real. And that went on happening—the shops he took me to, the things he bought me, the yacht—" She paused. "I got used to it so fast, Gus, you wouldn't imagine how *easy* it was to get used to."

"So you think you can cope?"

Laura brushed her hand over the immaculate marble worktop. "Yes, I think I can. I'll miss you like hell—I wish, more than anything, that Roger would say we could live in London, or that I thought you might want to come over here—"

"Don't hold your breath, kid," Gus said, gently.

"He can protect me, Gus," Laura went on, quietly. "He makes me feel secure—not just his money, though it's the money that gives him his power, I know that." She looked hard into Gus's cool gray eyes. "I've never been able to get away from the past, you know that, don't you? It's always been there, just behind me, just over my shoulder, breathing down my neck. The fear and the guilt."

"It won't go away just because you're in New York."

"It isn't the geography," Laura tried to explain. "It's a different world—a fresh beginning. It's like Roger's re-made me."

"You didn't need re-making."

"Maybe." Laura shrugged. "Maybe if things hadn't gone the way they did, I'd have been fine the way I was."

"But things were going pretty well for you before he got you to Monaco, weren't they? For us both."

"Yes, they were," Laura said slowly. "But mostly because of Roger. If it hadn't been for him, Gus, I'd never have been promoted."

"Did he tell you that?"

"Not in so many words, but I know it's true."

Gus looked steadily at her friend. "He's a manipulator."

Laura smiled. "I know he is." She paused. "You haven't asked me if I love him."

"I don't need to."

"He knows I'm not sure about that," Laura said. "I told

him that before I accepted his proposal—that I'm in love with him, that it was the easiest thing in the world to be *in* love with him. At least I haven't lied to him about that."

"Just don't lie to yourself about one thing," Gus said.

"What do you mean?"

"Don't kid yourself you'll be leaving the guilt behind. It's here with you right now—I just heard it in your voice. It's perched there on your shoulder, the same way it was in Finborough Road, the same way it was in Kane House."

"I feel safer with him, Gus," Laura said. "That's something, isn't it?"

"I hope so."

Rona came to fetch Laura for a fitting of her gown at eleven-thirty the next morning, but Gus, jet lagged and in no mood to attack Fifth Avenue, stayed in the suite, now extended to take in a second bedroom on the other side of the sitting room. At a quarter past twelve, Roger, just back from Chicago, arrived.

"I know you're Gus," he said. "You couldn't be anyone else."

"How do you do?" Gus, wearing a hotel bathrobe, gave him her hand, liking, against her will, the firm, cool squeeze of his grip. "Laura's gone to try on her wedding dress."

"With my sister." Roger stepped into the sitting room. "Do you mind if I wait for her?"

"I don't know if they're coming straight back. Might be hours."

"I'll come in for a while," Roger said. "It'll give us a chance to get acquainted."

"I'd like that," Gus said.

"I thought you might." Roger closed the door. "Why don't we order some coffee, and you can quiz me about my intentions."

"I already know they're honorable, don't I?" Gus said. "Since I'm here for the wedding."

"I guess you do." Roger paused. "Maybe I've got some questions for you. After all, I don't think anyone knows more about my bride-to-be than you, do they, Gus?"

"I'll order the coffee." Gus picked up the telephone.

"On second thought"—Roger halted her—"I think I'll have a drink. I don't, usually, before lunch, but it's been a rough twenty-four hours."

"What would you like?" Gus asked, the receiver still in her hand.

"Don't worry, I'll fix myself a Bloody Mary from the bar. What can I get for you?"

"My body thinks it's barely breakfast time."

"Vodka and tomato juice are great for jet lag, trust me."

"They say your wedding day," Rona said to Laura, while they were alone in the changing room, "should be the happiest day of your life, but I think too many brides are exhausted by the time they reach the altar."

"That's because they've usually had to make all the arrangements." Laura stared into the mirror, loving every tiny pale appliquéd flower, loving the way the short, creamy gown accentuated her narrow waist. "Not many brides could be as lucky as me."

"So you think you will be happy?"

"How could I not be?"

"I'm glad," Rona said. "I know your life hasn't always been easy."

Laura let her hands play, for a moment, with the silk of her skirt. "I don't think anyone's life is always easy, is it?"

"Not everyone has to cope with the losses you had to."

"I was very small when my parents died," Laura said. "Too young to understand. And thanks to my grandfather, I had a wonderful childhood."

"But then you lost him, too." Rona spoke softly. "All those years at school in England, with no family to take care of you. Where did you stay during the vacations?"

Laura felt her throat tighten. "I stayed at school."

"That must have been very hard."

"I grew accustomed to it." Laura took a breath and turned slowly around. "Do you think the dress will be ready in time? We still haven't seen the veil."

Rona looked intently at her for a moment, but her sigh was hardly discernible. "Everything will be ready, dear. You can trust Roger to make sure of that." She smiled. "Trust is everything, isn't it, Laura?"

Laura returned her gaze as evenly as she could. "I suppose it is."

"You could write a book," Roger said to Gus, as he mixed their third Bloody Mary. "Have you ever thought of doing that?"

"Who wants to read about a market stallholder?" Gus was sitting back comfortably on the sofa. The drinks had made her more relaxed than she had meant to be, though she didn't suppose it mattered.

"I was thinking of the rest."

"The rest?"

"Your life in that home, for one thing. A lot of people might want to read about that. They like survival stories."

Gus peered up at him as he handed her her fresh drink.

"I didn't know you knew about that."

Roger sat down in an armchair and crossed his legs. "Nothing to be ashamed of, is there?"

"I'm not ashamed."

"I didn't think you were." He raised his glass. "To you, Gus. For being Laura's best friend." He sipped at the drink. "For helping her survive."

"She's got guts," Gus said. "Always did have."

"You don't mind talking about it, do you?"

"Not really." Relaxation was beginning to give way to sleepiness.

"Laura doesn't seem to feel that way," Roger said lightly.

Gus shook her head. "It's harder for her. She's always had a lot of guilt." She had one more swallow of Bloody Mary, and put down her glass on the end table beside her. "Laura thinks you don't know about it."

"I didn't," he said. "I don't, really, other than what you've told me."

Gus sat up straighter, and her head spun a little. "I haven't told you anything."

"Not much anyway."

She stared at him. "You conned me."

"No, I didn't."

"You bastard."

"I'd like to hear more," Roger said, easily. "If you feel like telling me."

Gus felt sick. "I warned Laura she didn't know what she was getting into. I told her to be careful."

"I know you did." Roger gave a small smile. "That's why I understand your motives in telling me about her, Gus."

"I didn't tell you."

"Sure you did. You don't want to lose Laura—you'd like her to be happy, of course, but somewhere closer to home, with someone more—familiar. You can't help being jealous of me."

"I'm not jealous." Gus stood up, her legs shaky. "Just because I'm not as trusting as Laura doesn't mean I wouldn't be glad for her if she found a decent man." She became suddenly aware that her bathrobe had fallen open a little way. Feeling vulnerable, she wrapped it more tightly around herself.

Roger remained seated. "You may not like to admit it to yourself, but I think you were hoping—I'm sure you still are—that I'll call off the wedding."

"Will you?" Gus asked.

"Of course not. What kind of man do you think I am?"

"I'm not sure." Gus stared down at him. "Will you tell her now, what you do know?"

"I think that might distress her, don't you?" Roger paused, and his voice was quite gentle. "She wants to put the past behind her, that much I've learned. I think she'd be very hurt if she thought you and I had spoken about it. I love Laura very much, Gus. The last thing in the world I want to do is hurt her. I don't think either of us wants to do that."

Gus said nothing.

"Why don't you sit down?" Roger said.

She sat.

"Has Laura told you that we won't be taking our honeymoon for a few weeks because of my schedule?" He didn't wait for her to answer. "I was wondering if you'd care to stay for a week or so after the wedding? We'll have plenty of space, and I think Laura might find it easier to find her feet with your support."

"You want me to stay?" Gus was baffled by the new twist in his manner.

"If you don't mind."

"But why? I thought you'd want to get rid of me."

"Why would I want that? You're Laura's closest friend. I recognize the fact that it may be tough for her settling down in a brand-new world, and I don't always have time for the most important things in my life."

Gus felt a little steadier. "You really do love her, don't you?" She heard the surprise in her voice.

"If I wasn't crazy about her, I wouldn't be marrying her." Roger's expression was perfectly serious. "Will you stay, Gus, after the wedding? I know it would mean a lot to Laura, and that's who really matters, isn't it? To us both."

"I'll stay." Gus looked at him. "For Laura."

"And will you tell her about our conversation?"

"I'm not sure."

"I don't want her hurt, Gus."

"You think I do?"

"I'm sure you don't. Which is why I'm hoping you'll keep it between us."

"For Laura's sake," Gus said, ironically.

"She thinks I'm one of the best things that's ever happened to her," Roger said, "and from what I've heard about her life, I have to say I'm too honest to disagree. If she found out now that I knew about the past she's chosen to keep a secret, she'd feel guilty for not having told me herself, and I suspect she'd be very angry with you, which would be a pity for you both."

"What about honesty between husband and wife?" Gus asked. "Or don't you believe in that?"

"Ultimately, of course. But right now, Laura's too fragile. I believe it would be cruel to dig into old wounds. When she's ready, she'll tell me. If she's never ready, it won't change the way I feel about her." Roger paused. "I know you don't trust me, Gus, but Laura does. That's very important to me, and I believe it's important to her. I don't think you really want to risk spoiling that for her, do you?"

Gus looked around the plush sitting room, at the fresh,

crisp cleanness of what money could buy, thought about the frenetic, alien city outside. She was out of her depth now and she had no answer to give Roger Ambler.

"No." He smiled. "I didn't think so."

CHAPTER 14

They were married in the early afternoon on Wednesday, the fourteenth of May, in the back garden of the house in East Hampton that Roger and Rona had bought a few months after their father's death in 1973. The previous morning, Adam Demonides had arrived from Athens, and had been whisked by John, the chauffeur, with Gus for company, to A. T. Harris on Forty-fourth Street so that he could rent morning dress for the wedding, and Roger had taken Laura to the offices of his attorney, Brian M. Levy, and had her sign a prenuptial agreement.

"Please don't be offended," he had said to her.

"I'm not."

"It's just something that's done, these days—it's almost part of the wedding ceremony." He had laughed. "They talk about committing people who don't have any kind of an agreement drawn up, and this one is the simplest—it's really basic." He smiled again. "It's just in case you were to walk out on me right after tomorrow."

"And try to keep half your property."

Laura's voice had been perfectly even. She knew enough to have expected this—she read the *Daily Mail*, she watched American miniseries. Rich men who married poor girls, and vice versa, had to protect themselves in the greedy eighties, though she knew from reading articles about Marvin

Mitchelson and his famous clients that prenuptial agreements were made to be broken.

"I accepted the gifts you gave me in France," she went on, softly, aware that Levy, the smooth, bespectacled lawyer, was listening carefully, "and now that we're to be married, I seem to have accepted the fact that I'm going to be sharing your life and, with it, some of your possessions."

"That's as it should be, darling," Roger said. "I know you were hesitant about taking things from me at first, and the last thing I want to do is imply you might be marrying me for what you can get out of me—"

"But in a way, I must be," Laura interrupted him gently. "By marrying you, I'm also marrying what you are, which includes your money—there's no way around that. I'm not a hypocrite, Roger. I grew up never having to think about money, having everything I wanted, and I'd be liar if I said I wasn't looking forward to having that again." She paused. "But if you were to want to end our marriage—because I can't imagine that I'd be the one to want to leave it—then I would expect to leave with what was mine, and only mine."

"That's pretty much what this agreement states, Miss Andros," Levy said.

"So you don't mind?" Roger asked her.

Laura looked at the lawyer. "Where do I sign?"

"Now this I like," Gus told Laura before the ceremony, when they were getting ready in one of the bright, sunny bedrooms upstairs. Rona, who had spent at least twelve out of the past twenty-four hours shepherding the bride-to-be through a lavish routine of massage, manicure, pedicure and waxing of areas which Laura had never dreamed of waxing, had finally left the two friends alone together for a while. "Why can't you live here instead of in that tower?"

"It's so big," Laura said. "It's beautiful, but it's huge, don't you think?"

"At least it's on the ground. And it feels more human than the apartment."

Laura looked at Gus's face. "Would you be happier if we could stay here until you go back to London?"

"Much," Gus said, definitely. The city excited her, but it gave her a nervy, intense feeling that she didn't care for. It was the way she'd felt about town centers in the bad old days, when she'd climbed out of the window at the children's home, when she'd got out of Kane House because of that restless itch deep inside her. She hadn't pinched anything—not so much as a pack of cigarettes— since she'd moved into the flat with Laura. She was afraid of the feeling Manhattan gave her.

"I'll talk to Roger later," Laura promised, softly.

"Do you know where you'll be tonight yet?"

"He won't tell me." Laura looked at the reflection of her face in the dressing-table mirror. She looked pale, but her makeup, applied by one of the stylists sent from Kenneth, was perfect. "Not even a hint. He loves secrets."

"Doesn't he just?" Gus said.

Laura turned around, aware that they could have only moments before Rona returned to help her into her gown and fix her veil. "Do you still think I'm doing the wrong thing?" she asked.

"Who am I to know what's right or wrong?" Gus said, warily.

"Do you still think I don't know what I'm letting myself in for?"

"Probably, but you know that yourself." Gus came over and rested a hand on Laura's shoulder, one of her rare unsolicited touches. "Cold feet?"

Laura shook her head. "No." She smiled. "Not really."

"Then I suppose you must be doing the right thing." Gus hesitated. "I think he's a bit of a bastard, but I think you know that, too—and anyway, most of them are. But he's nuts about you, I can see that much, so maybe you'll be okay." She paused again. "You can always come home if it doesn't work out."

"It will," Laura said.

The gardens were laid out on several levels, with gentle slopes and perfectly maintained pathways and broad smooth stone steps linking and unifying the separate sections, the rose garden, the orchards, the pool area with its summer-house and the Japanese sunken garden.

The chairs for the wedding guests had been set out on the spacious lawn closest to the house in three dainty rows of eight across, four seats on either side of the pale green carpeted aisle that had been created with care so that the heels of Laura's cream silk-covered shoes should not sink into the grass.

When Laura walked down from the house on Adam's arm, she saw, through a haze, twenty-four intrigued faces turned toward her of which she recognized only Gus, Rona, Nelson and the two girls, Hal Deacon and Brian Levy, and her stomach lurched with sudden terror.

"You're all right, *moraki mou*," Adam whispered, squeezing her arm more tightly. "Last chance to change your mind," he said.

"Too late now," Laura whispered back.

Adam stopped walking. "It's not too late."

Laura looked straight on, focused on Roger, saw his golden head glinting in the May sunshine, his face tilted back toward her. And she drew on Adam's arm, lightly but decisively.

"Come on," she said. "I'm getting married."

Later on, when she thought back to the afternoon, Laura remembered it in a kind of fog, as if she were looking, through gauze, at a slow-motion replay of another person's wedding day, not her own at all. She remembered some of the guests, the way they had watched her when they thought she wasn't looking, the way their eyes had veered away quickly when she had caught them. She had been glad of some of them, of Gus, of course, so stunning in the long, ribbed white cotton cardigan dress which they'd found together in Saks and which accentuated the sinuous thinness of her body and had a scarlet-piped slit in the right side that showed off her legs in a way that Laura could tell Rona strongly disapproved of. It had been wonderful having Adam with her, too, though in some ways that had been a strain, for he hadn't fitted in the way Gus had managed to; even if she did stand out in this genteel gathering like an exploding firework, Gus knew how to challenge people without saying a word, but Adam was too polite, too gentle, too different from the Howarths and their like to settle comfortably into the formality of the Long Island afternoon.

"Of course, we're always deliciously informal out here," Laura had heard a snooty voice telling Adam, and suddenly a vivid memory of their childhood at Chryssos had flashed back into her mind, a picture of them sitting on the rocks on their little beach, with lessons over for the day and no one to nag at them or pull them into line, just perfect freedom with the sand and the sea and the pine forest and their lovely, soothingly shabby villa behind them. And Laura, newly married into yet another new world, had looked around at the impeccable lawns and meticulous flower beds, had thought of the glazed-chintz curtains inside and the Aubusson rugs and the Meissen bowls filled with roses, and a vast longing for the past and for its innocence had swept over her.

Hal Deacon had been friendliness itself, bringing congratulations from Oxford Street and the other branches, but Laura had seen something else in his eyes, behind the smiles, something cooler and less pleasant. Brian Levy, the attorney, had oozed charm and offers of help, and then there was Roger's secretary, a silken woman of about thirty-five called Pamela, and the family doctor, an older, white-haired man named Saul Parrish; and all the Howarths, of course, Rona, exquisitely slender in soft yellow linen, her husband, gently courteous, and the twin girls, blond as their mother and uncle and identically charming with their pageboy hairstyles and their nonmatching dropped waist dresses.

One guest came late, too late for the marriage service, almost too late for the reception. Laura saw him from a distance, as she stood talking to Adam in the rose garden, her right hand gently waving away a bee. Roger was shaking the newcomer's hand vigorously, clearly glad to see him, and Laura found her eyes drawn to him because he looked, at first glance, so different from the other wedding guests. He was a head taller than Roger, dark and lanky, with a curiously natural, easy elegance that seemed to make his beige linen suit, well-cut as it was, an irrelevance, as if one looked at him and knew that he would look just as good in jeans or overalls or even nothing at all.

"Who is he?" Adam asked her.

Laura shook her head. "I don't know."

"He looks an interesting man."

Laura focused on Adam again. "Do you really have to go straight back?"

"I'm afraid so—I can't afford to lose my job." He put a finger inside his shirt collar and tried to ease it. "At least I don't have to wear a tie in my office. Without air-conditioning in Athens even the bosses work in short shirtsleeves."

"I wish things were better for you," Laura said, softly. "I wish you could stay here and never go back."

"I don't think your husband would think that such a good idea."

"Roger wouldn't mind. He knows we're just friends."

"Does he?"

"Why do you say that?"

Adam shook his head. "Just the way he looked at me when I gave you to him." He smiled. "I think he would have snatched you from me if he could."

Laura looked back toward Roger, still in conversation with the new arrival. "I can't imagine Roger being jealous," she said. "He's so confident, I can't imagine him needing to be."

"He's crazy about you, little one," Adam said. "You give him cause, you'll see how jealous he can be."

Roger introduced Laura to the man a few minutes later.

"You've heard me talk about Thomas Bailey," he said. "Known to some as Cowboy Bailey. Tom's taught me all I know about the newspaper business."

"How do you do?" Bailey took Laura's hand and shook it firmly. "I'm sorry to be so late, but you are the most beautiful sight I've seen in a long, long time. Roger, you're a lucky man."

"Thank you." Laura smiled. "I'm happy to meet you." Bailey had a longish, pointed nose, eyebrows that sloped down a little at the outside edges, giving him a quirky, semi-doleful, semi-humorous expression, warm, soft brown eyes, and dark hair that flopped a little over his forehead. It was a mobile, intelligent face that lit up when he smiled, and it was impossible not to like him instantly.

"Tom's just flown in from Chicago," Roger said.

"I'd have been here on time if I could," Bailey said, apologetically, "but there was a small crisis at the paper I had to handle."

Glancing down, Laura saw with amusement that even with his elegant suit he was wearing boots. "I hope there's enough food left for you, Mr. Bailey."

"Tom, please," Bailey said quickly.

"There's no shortage of food, baby," Roger said, grinning, as if the notion of running out of food was absurd.

"I imagine newspapers have one crisis after another," Laura said.

"And Tom gets involved with them all," Roger told her. "This man's an idealist, my darling. He eats, sleeps and breathes newspapers."

"Where are you people heading for your honeymoon?" Bailey asked. "Or is it a federal secret?"

"Nowhere just yet," Roger said.

"We've just had a holiday," Laura added.

"All three days of it." Roger put an arm around her shoulders and kissed her cheek, careful of her veil. "Baby, that was no holiday, but I can promise you our honeymoon will be." He grimaced. "If I can ever find the time to take it."

"Laura will have to make sure you do," Tom Bailey said, and Laura noticed that the smile he gave her was very gentle and particularly sweet.

"You liked Tom, didn't you?" Roger asked her later, as they drove away from East Hampton.

"I liked him a lot," Laura said. "Though we didn't speak very much."

It was almost eight o'clock in the evening, and Roger had whisked Laura, with the smallest of a set of Louis Vuitton suitcases, into the Porsche that he kept at the house, the only car he liked to drive himself. He had not told her where they were going, and Rona, though dying of curiosity, was sure he had not shared the secret with anyone. Laura had felt great sorrow at her parting with Adam, and she had felt guilty about abandoning Gus to the big house empty of all but servants, but when Roger had held open the passenger door of the shiny red car and she had slid gracefully in, aware of how well her going-away outfit—a long, slim sleeveless tunic of white linen, with narrow matching pants and a wide-brimmed hat—suited her, all the negative emotions had disappeared in a billowing cloud of anticipation.

She had no idea where they were going. Roger drove fast but smoothly, they took one highway, then another, crossed a bridge, but it was dark by then, and she might have been anywhere, so Laura just gave herself up to it all, the way she had given herself up to Monaco and the gifts and the yacht and his proposal, and she knew that tonight, at last, the waiting that had begun that first evening in the Hôtel de Paris, would be at an end, and she thought that she was ready, more than ready.

They were in Manhattan, she knew that much, in a part of the city she had not seen, in a quiet, narrow street a block from a river, with elegant town houses, their windows curtained and private, and trees on both sides.

"Which river are we near?" she asked Roger, when he had parked the car and came to help her out.

"It might be the East River, or the Hudson, or it might be the Tiber or the Sumida."

"Where is that?"

"Tokyo," Roger said. "Come on, Mrs. Ambler."

Laura stepped out of New York City into old Japan. She saw, briefly, bamboo, reeds, painted screens and two women in kimonos, their hair traditionally dressed and their faces very white. They were escorted, wordlessly, to the second floor where a padded door was unlocked with an ornate key, and then, after a few softly exchanged words between Roger and the woman who had brought them up, they were alone.

Laura stared around. The suite was stark but beautiful, lacquered ebony, creamy screens dividing room from room, with bowls of flowers, fragile works of art in themselves. Silently, conscious of Roger's watching eyes, she walked around, saw the long, low table surrounded by cushions, saw the futon, creaseless and fresh, the small padded wooden pillows, and the exquisite little flower arrangement beside the bed: a white lily, petals open wide, a tiny blood-red flower placed in its center.

She returned to Roger.

"What is this place?" she asked.

"It's our place, for tonight." His eyes were very blue. "I began looking for it in January. I found it two weeks ago."

"Just before you called me to Monaco."

"Do you like it?" he asked her.

"It's like being in another world," Laura said.

"May I tell them to begin?"

"Begin what?"

"Our night."

It began with dinner. Intricate tiny packages of raw fish on tiny beds of rice with seaweed, little lacquered bowls of aromatic broth and meats and vegetables, served to them by two young women, their dark heads dressed with flowers and combs, their kimonos lovely. Roger and Laura ate with chopsticks, and drank sake out of tiny silver cups, and in a while, one of the older women played a three-stringed instrument, like a miniature guitar, and the music reminded Laura of a sad, haunting bird, and when Roger took her hand and kissed its palm, her eyes filled with tears of pleasure.

Dinner over, Laura waited for them to be alone again, but though the bowls and every tiny trace and crumb of food was cleared away, two of the women remained with them in the room.

"They're waiting for you," Roger said.

"Why?"

"To prepare you."

"For what?"

"For our first night."

Laura's eyes widened. "How?" she whispered.

"You'll see," he said, smiling. "Enjoy."

They took her hands and drew her into the bedroom, parted another set of dividing screens and coaxed her through with them. She saw a table, covered with towels, and a raised round bath surrounded by steps.

"All for you," one of the women said.

"For your pleasure," the other added, and laughed, a tiny, tinkling laugh.

"My God," Laura said, and shook her head. It spun a little, from the sake, added to the afternoon's champagne. It occurred to her, for a moment, to run, to refuse, to tell Roger to ask them to leave her alone, for she knew that they were waiting to undress her, perhaps even to bathe her, and the only time she could remember standing naked before complete strangers was at the police station after she had killed Lucia Lindberg—

"We can leave you, if you prefer," the older woman said, intuitively.

"But it will be nicer if we stay," the younger said. "For you."

Laura took a deep breath, smiled, and left the past behind.

"Please stay," she said.

They massaged her with fragrant oils, everywhere, their hands practiced and deft and gentle, and when they were done, Laura was almost too limp to move from the table, and they had to assist her into the bath, where they washed every part of her in the steaming, moisturizing water as if she were a baby or, perhaps, an empress.

"What now?" she asked, as they wrapped her in a huge, soft towel.

"Now you go in there," the older told her, and Laura saw that she was pointing to a small area screened off from the rest of the room. "And when you're finished there, we make you ready."

Laura wondered, while she was peeing in the tiny bathroom, what Gus would make of this were she a fly on this particular wall. She was certain, by now, that this was some kind of fantastic brothel, and she remembered what Roger had said to her at the Plaza about some men hoping they could have both wife and mistress in one woman. *Or whore.* The thought sent a shiver through her, part excitement, part fear.

They washed her again, between her thighs, and then showered her gently with cool water, and then they rubbed her dry and applied a lotion that left her smooth and exhilarated.

"Now we dress you," the younger said, and when Laura turned around, the older was holding a white silk kimono out to her, and when she opened it out, she saw a beautiful fragile leaf embroidered on the back.

"The color of your eyes," the older said. "Created by your husband."

Laura thought about the lovely silk and lace nightgown she'd bought with Rona in Bergdorf's for this night, but then she thought about Roger and all the trouble he had taken, and she let them put it on her, trying to study the way they fastened it, but knowing that she would never be able to do it that way again.

They brushed her hair with bristle brushes so that it gleamed, and looking into the mirror, Laura saw it might have been her hair that had inspired Roger, for it did look almost Japanese with its geometric bangs and shining jaw-length bob.

"You want makeup?" the older asked.

Laura looked at herself.

"No," she said. "Thank you for everything, but no. Nothing more."

In the bedroom, Roger, standing by the screen, stepped away from the peephole through which he had observed the massage and the bath and the shower. He, too, wore a kimono, and his was the green of the leaf on Laura's, with his own embroidery stitched in white.

He could hardly believe the time had come. It occurred to him, for just a moment, that this might have been an error, that perhaps after five months of celibacy, five months of longing, he might fail her and himself. But then he remembered the soft, curved peach of her ass, and he looked down at himself, saw the hugeness of his erection and smiled at his own foolishness.

The screen slid aside. The two women came through first, bowed to him and vanished. And then came Laura.

* * *

She looked at him, saw how handsome he was, how flushed his face was from sake and anticipation. The lights had been dimmed a little, for which she was grateful, but she was still afraid.

"All right?" he asked, gently.

"A little nervous," she said, and her voice was hardly more than a whisper. "It was wonderful, but so—" She stopped, anxious not to say the wrong thing.

"So different," Roger said.

"It certainly was." She smiled.

"I meant it to be."

"You succeeded."

"Are you ready?" he asked.

Laura glanced past him toward the dining room. "Have they gone?"

"Gone, and the door is locked. We're alone." He paused. "Are you ready?"

"I think so."

He held out his arms, and she walked into them, felt his strength and his heat, felt his penis already pushing against her kimono. The preparations had aroused her in ways she had never experienced before, had brought to life every nerve end from her scalp to the soles of her feet. She wanted him to undress her, she thanked God that she wanted him, for she'd thought she would, but it had been such a strange courtship, with just those long, searching kisses and so little touching, and she'd been frightened of finding herself suddenly frigid.

Roger ran his hands over her shoulders and down her arms to her hands, then put her a few inches away from him and cupped her breasts through the silk, round and firm, nipples springing erect.

"I can't believe I waited," he said.

"Nor can I."

"You didn't want to wait?"

She closed her eyes, felt his hands on her breasts. "In a way, no. In another, I'm glad it's happening this way."

"I wanted it to be special," Roger said.

"I know you did."

He picked her up, suddenly, lifted her easily in his arms and then, bending, placed her on the futon. He knelt beside her, slipped a hand inside her kimono, shivered a little as he touched her silken flesh, then stooped and kissed her once, a long, urgent kiss, mouth open, and then he sat up again, on his knees, and looked down at her.

"Take it off," he said.

"I'd like you to do it," Laura said, softly.

"You can have your turn later," he said. "Take it off."

She unfastened it, sat up a little, let it slip from her shoulders, exposing her breasts, watched his lips part, his pupils dilate, and then pulled it away from beneath her and set it aside, close to the lovely white lily with its tiny floral spot of blood. She had expected to feel shy, but the sake and the Japanese women and their skills had prepared her perfectly; she felt that she was unfolding, like a flower. She looked down at the dark tangle of pubic hair that they had anointed with the rest of her, and she felt Roger's eyes on her, too, and she lay back and waited.

"Turn over," he said.

"But I want to see you," she said.

"Please, darling, turn over."

She turned, saw a small lacquered box that she thought had not been there before, heard the rustle of silk and knew that it was Roger's kimono, and then she felt his weight beside her on the futon, and she drew in her breath, waiting for his touch.

He touched her buttocks with both hands. Cupped them, stroked them, then ran his hands down between her thighs, making her shudder. She felt one of his fingers finding her, felt it, strong and bony, locate her vagina and slide into its warm moistness. She began to turn over, but he stopped her, with a hand on her back.

"Stay," he said.

The finger stayed inside her vagina, probing, and then he straddled her.

"Oh, Christ," she heard him say. "You are so perfect."

She felt him pushing her thighs apart, felt his knees between her legs, opening her wider, and then he was grasping her tight buttocks and she felt his mouth on them, kissing, licking, biting a little, and then suddenly she felt his penis, knew it was his penis, and it was pushing into her, and she struggled for a moment, tried to resist, for this wasn't the way she had expected it to be, and it was so big, so *big,* and it hurt so much that she cried out in pain—

And he withdrew.

"I don't believe it," he said. "You can't be."

"What?" she cried, and struggled over onto her back. She saw that his face was quite contorted, his eyes startled.

"You can't be a virgin."

"Why not?"

"Jesus," he said.

"It doesn't matter," she said, anxious at the shock in his face. "It didn't hurt so much—please don't stop."

"I'm sorry, darling." Quickly, he lay down beside her, put his arms around her. "I didn't realize—I never thought for a moment—"

"But I thought that was why you waited," Laura said.

Roger laughed, a short, slightly bitter laugh. "I waited because I wanted you to be my wife, not because you were a virgin." He shook his head. "I was sure—"

"Of what?"

He shook his head again. "It doesn't matter."

"Roger, please, tell me."

"I told you it doesn't matter." He laughed again, and the bitterness had gone. "And it doesn't, it really doesn't—in fact, it's better this way, much better than I could have imagined."

Laura smiled with relief. "Thank you," she whispered, and wrapped her arms around him tightly. "Kiss me, please," she said. "Let's start again."

He made love to her, the way she had expected him to. He kissed her, her mouth, her breasts, every part of her, so that she began to glow again with wanting him. He took as much time as he thought she might need, not wanting to rush her this time, intent that it should be as pleasurable for her as it could be. *Poor little virgin,* he thought. All that pent-up lust, all that suppressed violence, just waiting, locked up the way she had been, just waiting to be released. He asked her if she was ready for him, he kissed her cunt, wet her with his tongue, and then he penetrated her, tore her hymen, heard her sweetly stifled cry of pain, and then, gradually, he felt the beginnings of her enjoyment. He felt her arms snake around him, felt her pushing against him, learning to draw him farther into her, discovering the rhythms of sex, felt her starting to seek what she needed—he saw the blush spreading over her body, her breath quickening, knew that she was seeking but failing, and he climaxed then, poured himself into her, for he knew that there were many more hours to come that night when he could show her the way to her own orgasm, and he wanted to empty himself into her, wanted to do that over and over again, for he wanted her to give him babies, wanted her to give him a son.

They rested for a while, lying very close together, and Laura felt a great relief, almost a sense of triumph, for even if she hadn't reached orgasm, even though the extraordinary arousal he had touched off in her had not been fulfilled, sex was more wonderful than she had hoped, the closeness, the panting, groaning closeness of it.

"I never thought about the pill, or anything," she said, suddenly. It was the first time she had considered contraception.

"I'd hate you to take it," Roger said, not opening his eyes.

"You wouldn't mind then—"

"It's what I want," he said, "more than anything."

She found his hand and held it tightly, and something very like love swept over her for the first time, something quite different to the emotions she'd felt till now which had, she supposed, been a kind of intense infatuation.

"I want that too," she said, realizing with a rush of surprise that she did.

He opened his eyes.

"I want you," he said.

"Already?"

"Oh yes."

He kissed her breasts for a long time, sucked on her nipples, felt her quiver and sigh, felt her squirm, felt her body become ready for him again. She watched him make love to her, studied the concentration on his face, such an absent, blunted intensity, as if the man she had known until then was set aside, like a shell, and this exposed inner being, so focused on desire, on instinct, on their physical bodies, was the real man.

"Kiss me." She wanted his mouth on hers. He slid down on the futon. "No," she said, urgently. "My mouth, kiss my mouth." He moved swiftly, covering her body completely with his, and it was a different kind of kiss, wholly intimate, wholly abandoned, exploring, almost bonding—

He turned her over, suddenly, his hands strong and determined.

"Kneel." His voice was husky, darker. "My way this time," he said. "You'll like it."

He grasped her buttocks, spreading her open, and entered her, thrust hard into her vagina with a grunt of pleasure. Laura felt a fresh shock of pain, knew that she had not been ready, not for this, and he was like an animal now, like a bull or a great dog, not a man, not a lover, and she tried to struggle free, but he held her with one arm and with the other hand he found her clitoris and began to play on it with such skill that soon, against her will, she was learning his way, too, and her body, if not her mind, was spiraling toward orgasm, and moments later they came, together, and she felt, for a few instants, as if he were stabbing her to death. *Was this how it felt to her?* flew through her mind, and she gave a groan and gripped his penis inside her for one more moment, wanting the agony, and then they both collapsed back onto the futon, lying apart this time.

"Now that," he said, after a while, "was fantastic."

Laura, lying on her back, licked her dry lips. "I liked it even better the first time," she said, shyly.

"You came this way, didn't you?"

"Yes, but—"

"You'll get used to it."

"I loved us being face to face," she said.

"That's okay," he told her, easily. "We'll do it that way, too." He paused. "There are many, many ways, darling Laura, and you're a fast learner." He found her hand and kissed it. "I knew you'd be a natural," he said.

* * *

They slept for an hour, and then Roger woke Laura with a
drink of cool water, and though it was the middle of the
night and she was tired, he coaxed her into the bathroom,
into the big round bath, and he washed her with a bar of
soap and the hand shower, played it over her breasts and ass
and between her thighs, and then, when she was fully awake
and aroused again, he gave her the soap and asked her to
wash him.

"My cock, too," he said.

Laura washed him, felt the blush on her face, felt him
grow erect in her hands, and then she took the hand shower
and rinsed him carefully. He helped her out of the bath, and
they toweled each other dry, and then he pushed her down
onto her knees.

"Now you can suck me."

She froze.

"Come on, baby," he cajoled her. "I'm clean enough to
eat." He bent and put his right hand behind her head and
pushed her face closer to him. "Come on, Laura, you have
to try it—you'll love it, I promise."

Gingerly, she kissed it. It was so immense, face to face.
Face to cock, she thought, and had a sudden urge to laugh.

"I don't want to do this," she said.

"Sure you do. Just try it—just take me in your mouth and
suck me a little."

She opened her mouth, took him in a little way, and Roger
pushed her head gently, so that he filled her and she was
frightened, suddenly, that he would choke her and she tried
to pull away, but he strengthened his grip and pushed at her.

"Just relax, baby—don't fight it, accept it."

With a jerk, she pushed him away, hard. "I told you I
don't *want* to."

"Okay, okay," he said, backing off. He pulled her up and
put his arms around her. "I'm sorry, I didn't mean to upset
you."

"I don't want to be forced to do anything," Laura said,
still angry.

"Don't be mad at me," Roger said, soothingly, "not tonight. Come back to bed."

They went back to bed, and he made love to her again, and this time he lay on his back and Laura found that she loved the freedom of being on top, of being able to feel in control, and when they had both climaxed, they rested again, and Roger turned to her so that she was on her side and he was snuggled up against her back, a perfect fit, and for a moment she thought that he was going to try to take her from behind again, and she stiffened, but he told her not to get tense, that they were going to sleep now, that it was only the first night and they had a lifetime to come.

The two young Japanese women came back, in the morning, with jasmine tea and sweet buns, and the day was sunny and bright, and sleep had restored them both, and Roger made love to Laura one more time, very tenderly and carefully, wanting her to leave the house feeling good, and later, when they were dressed and ready to leave, he picked up the black lacquered box that she had seen next to the bed, and put it into his Vuitton bag.

"What's in there?" Laura was curious.

"Playthings."

"What do you mean?"

"The ladies provided them for last night." Roger smiled. "But I thought you'd had enough excitement, so I've bought them for later."

"Show me."

"Are you sure?"

"Of course." Intrigued, she watched him take out the box and open it. Her eyes widened. "My God, what are they?"

Roger smiled again. "The thing that looks like a cock is a dildo, a very special one made of ivory." He didn't touch it, just looked at her face, saw the flush rising from her neck. "The two balls joined by the cord are called love eggs— they're for you to play with on your own, if you like."

"How, for God's sake?"

"You put them inside you, into your vagina, and then any movements you make, even walking around, can turn you on."

"I don't think so."

"We'll see." He put one hand into the box and touched a short string of plastic beads. "These are pleasure beads, sometimes called Thai beads. I don't think you're ready for those yet, but you will be, in time."

"What do they do?" Laura changed her mind. "No, don't tell me, I think I'd rather not know."

"You'll find out." He shut the box and returned it to his bag.

"I don't think so," she said again. "I think I like the real thing."

"I'm not going to force you."

She looked at him. "Have you used those things?"

"Not the love eggs."

She tried to laugh. "Nor the dildo either."

"Why not?" He saw the shock on her face. "Don't knock it till you've tried it. Sex is full of potential, my darling, lots of fun and games."

"What about love?" she asked softly.

"Of course love." Roger stroked her cheek. "But one need not preclude the other."

She asked him, in the car, whether they might live in the house so long as Gus was in America.

"Sure we can, though I assumed she'd rather be in the city."

"I don't think she likes Manhattan. I think it scares her a little."

"Does it scare you?"

Laura shook her head. "No. Which is strange, in a way, because Gus has always been braver than me."

"On her own territory, maybe. Some people can exist almost anywhere—I think you're one of those people. Others, like Gus, need to feel in control."

"I've been out of control since I left London," Laura said.

"No, you haven't," Roger said. "You just prefer to think you have."

"But you've been pulling all the strings."

"Are you sure?"

The first fortnight of their married life was almost uninterrupted bliss. Had Gus not been with her, Laura knew that she might have found the daylight hours a little lonely, since

Roger had plunged back into business the day after the wedding, but as it was, he managed to find time to meet her at odd hours in spite of work, either for lunch or for a bowl of strawberries and cream at the Plaza or for a glass of wine at some appropriate location near to wherever he was engaged in meetings. And while Roger was unavailable, Laura and Gus explored Long Island, driven by John, who had also been asked by Roger, if Laura was willing, to give her driving lessons so that she could handle the Mercedes convertible sports car he had already bought for her.

"You're going to be unbearable," Gus told her one afternoon, as they sat by the pool sunning themselves. "He's going to spoil you rotten."

"He already is." Laura popped a raspberry in her mouth and grinned. "But what can I do? I'm helpless."

"I hope not."

Laura heard a serious note in her friend's voice and turned to look at her. "Gus, I'm only joking, you know that."

"I'm not talking about Roger spoiling you," Gus said. "I think that's great—you deserve the best."

"So what are you talking about?"

"Nothing, really." Gus shrugged. "I suppose I'm afraid he'll take you over, change you."

"Maybe that wouldn't be such a bad thing," Laura said lightly.

"Oh yes, it would, kid. You don't need changing."

"I don't think Roger wants to." Laura gazed out beyond the blue pool toward the bank of rhododendron shrubs, awash with vivid pinks and reds. "I think he intends that I get used to a lot of stuff that he's used to."

"Money," Gus said.

Laura smiled. "And what it can buy."

"And is that so important?"

"To him, yes, I think it is. Maybe the most important." Laura paused. "There's all this kind of thing, and then there's the power. It's different for us—we've gone through rough times, and we know we can survive. But Roger was born to it."

"So were you."

"But it isn't the same, because I didn't keep it."

"Don't you feel as if you've won it all back again?" Gus asked, frankly curious. "As though it was all stolen from you before, and now it's yours by right?"

"No," Laura said. "No, I don't think I feel that at all."

"How do you feel? Now that it's done."

"Lucky," Laura said.

On the nineteenth day after the wedding, a Monday, Roger, who normally left the house long before Laura was even awake, stayed to have a cup of coffee with her and Gus in the sunny primrose-papered breakfast room. He waited until Gus had finished her toast, before he asked her if she might leave them alone.

"Just for a few minutes, if you don't mind."

Gus gave one of her shrugs. "I don't mind. It's your house."

Laura was surprised. "Why did you do that?"

"Like she said, it's my house." Roger put down his cup. "And I'm afraid I have to talk to you."

"What about?"

"About Gus."

Suddenly tense, Laura waited.

"There's no easy way to tell you this, baby, so I'm just going to tell you the truth. One of the maids, Gardner, was tidying Gus's room yesterday—she says she has to straighten up most days—"

"Is that all?" Laura was relieved. "Gus has always been untidy. I'm sure she'd never expect anyone to clean up after her."

"That isn't all," Roger said, and his face was grim. "Gardner found something in the room, tucked behind a stack of underwear." He kept his voice low and discreet. "It was an antique mirror."

"So?" Laura knew what was coming, did not want to know. "So she has an antique mirror."

"It doesn't belong to her, Laura."

"How do you know?" She tried to pick up her cup, but her hand was trembling a little, and she had to put it down again.

"Because it's mine. Or rather, it's Rona's."

"Maybe it just looks like Rona's mirror."

"I'm afraid not. This one lives—or rather, it did live—on a windowsill in one of the guest rooms on the other side of the house. It isn't there anymore. It's in Gus's closet, hidden in her underwear."

Laura had grown pale. "There must be an explanation."

"Obviously, there is. With her record, I'm afraid it isn't too hard to see what it might be."

For a moment or two, Laura was too startled to speak.

"You know?" she said, at last.

"She told me herself."

"When?" Laura could not believe it. "What did she tell you?"

"About her past. Her very sad past. She told me the day I first met her, at the hotel, while I was waiting for you to come back from a fitting." Roger reached for Laura's hand across the white tablecloth. "I hate having to tell you this, darling. I know how you feel about Gus, and I like her a lot, too. But we've talked about her not being able to fit in here, and I guess this little—lapse, shall we call it—?"

"She doesn't steal anymore," Laura said staunchly. "She hasn't for years. Why on earth would she start now?"

"Stress. Finding herself out of her depth, perhaps? I'm not an expert in these things." Roger paused. "Except that I do think it would be for the best if Gus went home."

"You'd throw her out?" Laura stared at him.

"Not for a minute," Roger said calmly. "Not if you still want her to stay. I don't give a damn about the mirror. That isn't the issue here at all."

"Then what is the issue?" Laura felt close to tears.

"The issue is what's best for Gus. You said yourself that she hasn't done this for years, so it must be the upheaval of flying over here, of being out of her own safe territory, that's driven her to steal again. Surely the answer must be to let her go home." He paused again. "Don't you agree?"

"I don't know."

"Think about it. Take your time." He stood up and kissed the top of her head. "I'm sorry to spoil your morning."

"This has spoiled a lot more than my morning," Laura said.

"I know. Believe me."

Laura looked up at him, saw the sympathy on his face. She had to ask. She was afraid to, but she had no choice.

"What else did she tell you?"

"Wasn't that enough?" Roger asked.

Laura found Gus in her room, flipping through the pages of the latest *Vogue*.

"How could you?" she asked.

"How could I what?"

"How could you tell Roger?"

"Tell him what?" Gus put down the magazine. "What am I supposed to have told him?"

"About your past. His word, not mine. Why in God's name did you do that?"

Gus stood up. "He tricked me."

"Don't be stupid." Laura had never thought she could be so angry with Gus. "And then, on top of that, to steal from him—I can't believe you could do that to me—to *yourself*, for pity's sake."

"I don't know what you're talking about," Gus said slowly. "I admit I let something slip when I was alone with him that first day, while you were out with Rona."

"I know you did. What I can't understand is why."

"He already knew, Laura."

"Knew what? About you?"

"About us."

"What the hell are you talking about?"

Gus sat down again, on the edge of the bed. "He kept giving me Bloody Marys—I'd never had one before, and on top of my jet lag, I suppose I got a bit drunk." She shook her head. "But he knew. About me being at Kane and in borstal."

"You said he knew about us."

"He certainly knows you were at Kane."

"I don't believe you." Laura stopped pacing and stared at Gus. "You tried to put me off marrying Roger, and when that didn't work, you thought you'd try and put him off me. The stealing's your problem—I could forgive that—I can even *understand* that. But not trying to destroy my marriage."

"I didn't." Gus shook her burgundy head, her gray eyes appalled. "I don't see how you could even begin to think I'd want to do that."

"Then why did you tell him?"

"I'm not even really sure that I did tell him. He tried to confuse me—he knew he was getting me drunk. He conned me into thinking I'd told him, but then I realized he already knew." She looked at Laura, pleading. "He's playing us off against each other, don't you see that? He knew the truth all along, at least about me, and he's just decided now's the time to use it. He's the kind of man who uses things."

"Don't be ridiculous. If Roger had known anything like that about me, do you honestly think he'd have considered marrying me?"

"I don't know."

"Yes, you do. The same way that I know." Laura's mouth trembled. "I never dreamed you might be jealous, Gus. I never thought you could do anything so awful."

"You believe him then?"

"I don't seem to have much choice, judging by the evidence." Laura went over to the walk-in closet and opened the door. "Where do you keep your underwear?"

"Is that what I'm meant to have pinched then? Knickers?" Gus's voice was suddenly very hard. "Take a look. Pity they don't have name tags on them the way they did at Kane."

"I'm not looking at your bloody underwear," Laura said, rifling through the pile of Marks and Spencer polyester. Her right hand found it, and with a sinking feeling in her stomach that was almost a physical pain, she withdrew it. It was matte silver, very ornate and clearly very old. "Try and explain this, Gus. Please."

"I wish I could."

"Not nearly as much as I do." Laura had never felt such sorrow.

"If I tell you I've never seen that mirror before in my life, will you believe me?"

"How can I?"

Gus got up, came over and looked at it. "It's nice, isn't it? Just the kind of thing I might have fancied."

"Can't you just admit it? Please, Gus." Laura's anger was gone. "How can we help you if you won't admit it."

"We?" Gus shook her head again. "If it's 'we', there's no chance."

"He's my husband."

"And I'm your best friend."

"I thought you were."

Gus left the next day. Laura wanted to go with her to the airport, but Gus was adamant that she wanted to go alone, and that she was only accepting the ride in Roger's car because otherwise she would miss the flight. She wished she could buy her own plane ticket back to London, but of course they all knew she couldn't, not if she was going to be able to manage when she got home. When Laura told her that Roger had offered to take over her portion of the rent on their flat, Gus said that a common stallholder couldn't very well afford to be proud, but just as soon as she was able, she'd be moving into somewhere more in keeping with her means.

The farewell was pure agony for them both. Once Gus knew for sure that Laura believed she had stolen the mirror, she shut up like a clam, became silent and cold and unyielding, yet no amount of surface ice could freeze out the pain within. Laura understood what she had done, and knew, too, that there was no way for her to make amends for her betrayal of her friend. She had accused Gus of treachery, but if she had only taken time to think, she would have known that Gus would never deliberately have hurt her, and that the lapse with the mirror had, just as Roger suggested, only come about because of the strange tensions and newness of her surroundings. But it was too late. The damage was done, and Laura knew that she had lost the best friend she had ever had.

Gus spoke only briefly, just before she left the house. She had packed only what she had arrived with, leaving her wedding outfit and the other items that Laura had bought her on the bed in her room.

"It's better like this," she said to Laura, standing wretchedly in the entrance hall beneath a portrait of Arnold and Mary Ambler. "Me going back where I belong. I shouldn't have come at all."

"That's not true, Gus, I don't know what I'd have done without you." Laura was biting back the tears. "I only wish—"

"Too late wishing now. You don't believe me about the mirror, and maybe I shouldn't blame you for that, but I do." Gus's voice was cool and dignified. "What really gets me most, though, is that you believed him about the other thing, too. The more I think about it, the more sure I am that I didn't actually tell Roger anything he didn't already know about our past. He just wanted to make me feel I did."

"You're wrong," Laura said.

"Maybe I am, maybe not. It doesn't really matter anymore."

"You matter"—Laura's voice was choked—"to me."

"No, I don't."

Laura felt as if Gus had struck her, almost wished that she had. "Will you be okay?" she asked, weakly.

"I expect so."

Laura tried to touch Gus's arm, but she stepped quickly away, and Laura flinched. "Oh, Gus, I'm so sorry."

"I know."

"When will I see you again?"

"Never, I should think."

"Can you try to forgive me?" Laura had not experienced such a sense of helplessness in years. "Or at least to understand."

"I don't think so." Gus's tone was still cool, but the wounds were clear in her gray eyes. "You made your choice, kid."

"Oh, God," Laura whispered, "I'm so scared."

The front door was open. Outside, standing diplomatically out of earshot, John waited by one of the black limousines.

Gus stooped to pick up her bags, and her frizzy burgundy hair bounced.

"You're right to be scared," she said.

CHAPTER 15

Laura came to live in Trump Tower. It was easier, in the Manhattan chaos, to forget about Gus for hours at a time, though the guilt never really went away. She knew that she had had to make a choice, and that with her marriage not yet three weeks old, she had had to choose her husband. So far as Gus's final warning words to her went, Laura decided to block from her mind the disquieting possibility that Roger might, after all, know about her own past. It was *not* really possible, she reminded herself, for as she had told Gus, he would never have married her if he had known.

She saw quite a lot of Rona and Nelson and their girls. It was so many years since she had been part of a family, and though Laura often sensed that Rona had reservations about her, her sister-in-law treated her with a warmth and kindness that went much further than mere duty to her brother, and Laura was frankly grateful for that. Anything Laura needed, Rona said regularly—any problem she ran up against which she felt, for any reason, she couldn't go to Roger with—Laura could come to her. They were family now, Rona said. Family was everything.

Laura wrote to Adam, to Helen Williamson and Ned, afraid of cutting herself off completely. She missed Gus in so many ways. She had high hopes that Roger, in time, would become the best friend that she believed a husband could be, but in these early weeks of their marriage, they were still too different, too far from the kind of unity that went further than romance, good conversation and sex. While Gus had been with them in East Hampton, the sexual side of their marriage had become more relaxed than Laura had dared to hope it would after their wedding night, with Roger seeming to accept that Laura was happier with a more orthodox, somewhat tamer relationship than he might have ideally wished for. Once Gus was gone, however, and they had set up their matrimonial headquarters in the Manhattan apartment, Roger became more demanding, but by now Laura felt more able to compromise. It troubled her still that her husband's preference was to make love to her from behind, but at least Roger recognized now that her own preference was unquestionably face to face, with the emphasis on tenderness rather than adventure.

In many ways, it had quite swiftly become plain that the courtship was over. Roger, now completely back in harness, was simply too preoccupied on the whole to be able to devote more than a few hours at any one time to Laura.

"That's why we're so keen for you to learn the ropes," Rona explained to her, when Laura came to tea at her duplex, "so that you can get on with playing your part effectively."

"My part?" Laura queried.

"As Mrs. Roger Ambler," Rona said. "You must know that it isn't quite the same as marrying a lesser man. It isn't the same at all."

"You're talking about being supportive."

"In many ways, perhaps more than you can imagine, dear." Rona poured pale Earl Grey into fragile teacups. "Roger mixes with an enormous variety of people, from his shoe salespeople to senators. I expect your own position with Ambler Agencies has trained you to mix with the salesmen and most of the employees, but I doubt that it's equipped you for the people who really matter." She peered more closely at Laura. "Why the smile?"

"Forgive me," Laura said, "but that sounded so snobbish."

Rona put down her cup. "I have never been a snob, but I'll forgive you for the insult," she said, benevolently.

"I didn't mean to insult you, Rona," Laura said sincerely.

Rona was not to be diverted. "We have to be realistic, Laura. My brother needs more than just a wife to welcome him home at night—though goodness knows that's important. He needs a wife who can deal with just about anything."

"What sort of anything? Entertaining, you mean? Dinner parties?"

It was Rona's turn to smile. "That trips so lightly off your tongue, my dear, but it's taken some women a lifetime to entertain really well. It's far easier when you've been brought up to it, of course, but even then not everyone has what it takes."

"Do you think I have what it takes?" Laura asked steadily.

Rona took a moment before answering. "I'd say that any young woman capable of captivating my brother so—wholeheartedly—certainly has the potential to become a first-rate Manhattan hostess."

"Do you believe I went out of my way to catch Roger?"

"Not exactly, no. I sensed, when we first met, that you were too much in shock to have plotted your ascent."

Laura stirred her tea. This was the first time she and Rona had clashed, and though it was the gentlest crossing of swords, it was nevertheless a moment not to be underestimated.

"That makes me sound like a social climber, which I'm not."

"I know that," Rona said, gently. "I'm aware of your background. It was one of the reasons that I chose not to try to obstruct the marriage."

"Roger's wealth, of course, is new to me," Laura admitted.

"I could tell you were honest, too. That was another reason."

"I'm not sure if anyone could have stopped Roger, even you."

"That, to be candid, was the main reason," Rona said.

And thankfully, at precisely the same instant, both women laughed.

The next time Roger and Laura went to stay in the house on the Island, he gave her a gift of a small silver handgun, tiny enough to slip into an evening purse.

"What's this for?" It lay in its box, on their bedspread. She didn't want to look at it, let alone touch it.

"Protection." He picked it up. "It has your initials on the handle, see?"

Laura shook her head. "I don't need it."

"You don't have to carry it around with you. The apartment in the city's secure enough, but I want you to be able to defend yourself out here, just in case."

"I really don't want it."

Roger looked at her. "You're very pale. Are you okay?"

"I just don't want to have a gun. Weapons make me nervous."

"They make me nervous too," he said, lightly, "especially when someone else has them and I don't." He paused. "We'll lock it away, somewhere just you and I know about, okay?"

Laura nodded. "Okay."

"I'd like to show you how to use it first."

"I could never use it."

"Sure you could, if you had to."

Laura looked down at the little silver gun. It looked innocent, like a child's toy. "No," she said. "Put it away."

"But wouldn't it be more sensible to learn—"

"Please," she said, more urgently.

Roger smiled. "You really do have a thing about weapons, don't you?"

They put it away.

"You're not still on the phone?" Laura complained one evening in early June, waiting for him to be ready for dinner. He had come into the apartment just after eight, and by nine-fifteen he had still not emerged from his study, and so Laura had knocked on the closed door and gone straight in.

"Just a moment, Ted, my wife's talking to me." He pressed the privacy button. "Laura, baby, never interrupt me in the middle of a call."

"But I've made dinner."

"Why?" he asked.

"Because I felt like it. It's been ready for over an hour."

"Why didn't you tell me?"

"Because you've been on the phone."

He released the silence button. "Ted, I'm sorry, but believe it or not, Laura's waiting to give me dinner." He listened for a moment, then laughed. "I know, but she's European and old-fashioned."

He ended the call and stood up.

"So why did you cook? We always go out to eat."

"I'm sick of going out. I wanted some time alone with you. Anyway, Rona's always saying I need to practice entertaining."

Roger laughed again. "That means you need to practice hiring the right caterers."

"Surely that's straightforward enough," Laura said, determined not to be put down, "so long as I just use the ones Rona does."

He came around his desk and kissed her hair. "Have I told you lately that I'm crazy about you?"

"Mostly in bed."

He reached down and squeezed her behind. "Well, I'm crazy about you in and out of bed, okay?"

Laura smiled. "Prove it."

"I thought you said dinner was ready."

"I meant prove it by letting the answering service take your calls."

"Can't be done, not tonight."

"It can't be done any night," Laura said, frustratedly. "Even in restaurants either you bring that awful cellular phone or the maître d' interrupts us every ten minutes."

"That's what comes of marrying a mogul," Roger said.

"Is that what you think you are?" Laura asked. She had only just begun feeling confident enough to tease her husband occasionally, and she thought that he seemed to like it, so long as she didn't take it too far.

"Don't you think I am?"

"I think you're just a guy who makes shoes and engines and finds jobs for people and helps run a few newspapers."

"You do, do you?" He put his arms around her. "The hell with dinner."

"On one condition."

"What?"

"The answering service." Laura smiled into his eyes. "I know I'm only a small part of your entourage now that you've put the ring on my finger, but there are times when I'd prefer to have your full attention." She paused. "Such as when I've been slaving over a wonderful dinner."

"Christ," Roger sighed, going back to the telephone. "Henpecked already."

Tom Bailey came to lunch the second Sunday in June, when he was in New York. Roger told Laura to order something in, since Tom was easy to feed and liked informality, but Laura remembered how much she'd liked Bailey, and was in the mood to make a traditional British Sunday lunch, and so they were given rare roast beef, Yorkshire pudding, roast potatoes and acorn squash, because Laura couldn't find the parsnips she'd wanted.

"That was gorgeous," Bailey said, his voice lazy and contented, his down-sloping, brown eyes warm with pleasure. "One of the things I miss most about England is the Sunday roast."

"You've spent time in England?" Laura asked.

"Tom's a great Anglophile," Roger said. "He studied at Oxford, and he's never been the same since."

"But no one"—Bailey's mind was still on food—"has cooked for me like that since Julie died."

"Julie was Tom's wife," Roger explained. He lit a cigar, clearly a compliment to her lunch, since he tended to smoke only after the most excellent meals. "She was a wonderful cook, wasn't she, Tom?"

"She was wonderful in most ways," Bailey agreed.

"I'm so sorry," Laura said, softly. "When did she die?"

"Ten years ago," Bailey said. "A lifetime."

Laura smiled at him. "I'm flattered to be compared to her."

"So long as it's only your cooking," Roger said. He paused. "You know, if you're really determined to use the kitchen here, maybe we should think about enlarging it."

"I can manage," Laura said. "But thank you."

"Let me know if you change your mind, baby."

It was fun having Bailey in the apartment. He was a long,

sprawling man, and Laura could see now why Roger said they called him Cowboy. It was more than his boots and jeans, it was his easy manner. Laura couldn't imagine Tom Bailey letting anyone snub him, or caring if they did, for that matter. She noticed that Roger had spotted the fact that she liked their guest, and she noted, too, that he didn't care for that liking to go too far. They had discussed animals for a while during lunch, because Bailey had just adopted an abandoned mongrel dog which he'd called Sam, and for some reason horses had come up in the conversation and Laura had said that she hadn't ridden in years, but that she'd like to try again.

"I'd be happy to take you riding one day when I'm in town," Bailey told her. "You can ride in Central Park, I believe, though of course there must be some good stables close to your place on the Island."

"I don't mind where we go," Laura said.

"Horses are dangerous," Roger said.

"A lot less dangerous than cars," Bailey pointed out. "And a heck of a lot less damaging to the environment."

"Tom's only an environmentalist when it suits him," Roger told Laura.

"I'm not an environmentalist at all," Bailey said. "I just like horses."

"I don't trust them," Roger said.

Laura went riding with Bailey the next time he was in town, which was a few days before her birthday. Roger must have told him, because he'd brought her a gift, a beautiful jade cat.

"I'd have brought you a live pup," Bailey said, "but I don't know if you're planning to work or not, and dogs need a lot of company."

It was the first time Laura had really stopped to think about returning to work. She found Tom Bailey a breath of fresh air, and was a little surprised at the thought, since, after all, her whole life ought to have felt more than fresh at this point. She supposed it was the fault of the city. She loved Manhattan in many ways, its excitement and energy and stylishness, but Bailey brought with him a sense of open space and spontaneity, and even though she never felt confi-

dent enough to coax her horse into anything faster than a
canter, she experienced a pleasurable feeling of freedom during their ride in the park.

"I don't want you to go again," Roger told her, later that
evening, as they dipped paper-thin slices of beef into gently
bubbling broth at Mitsukoshi. They both loved Japanese
food, though every time they entered one of the more classic
Japanese restaurants in the city, Laura, remembering their
wedding night, felt a strange kick of nervousness in the pit
of her stomach.

"Why not? I had a wonderful time."

"I told you before, it's dangerous. I don't want you to go."

Rebellion kicked its heels. "It isn't up to you."

"No, it's up to you. I'm just telling you what I want."

"It's really very safe, darling," Laura said. "You can't go
crazy, not in Central Park. It's very ordered, and the horses
were perfectly trained."

"I had a friend once who was paralyzed after a fall,"
Roger said. In fact, the friend had been more of an acquain-
tance, and the fall had been from a ladder, not a horse at all,
but he had an idea the story might give his point of view an
added fillip.

"How terrible," Laura said.

"So you can understand why I'd be much happier if you
didn't ride?"

"Of course I can." The horseback riding hadn't been all
that important to her, but she found that the other notion that
Tom Bailey had woken in her was. "Roger?" she said.

"What?"

"I think I'd like to go back to work."

"Whatever for?"

She saw that she had startled him. "I've always worked.
I like it."

"But that was before."

"Before I married you? But I'm still me."

"Of course you are, baby, but you don't need to work anymore."

"I may not have to, but I'd like to." Laura paused. "Aside
from any other considerations, I'd prefer to go on earning
my own money."

Roger smiled, and drank some broth. "If you need more pocket money, you only have to ask, you know that."

"I don't always like asking, Roger." She watched him carefully, anxious not to offend him. "Don't misunderstand me, darling, please. I'm so grateful for all that you give me, all you do for me—and it isn't just the money, it's the fact that I'm used to being fully occupied. You know how motivated your staff have to be to get on." She raised her chin, the small gesture of defiance almost subconscious. "And I think I got on pretty well, even if you did arrange some of it."

"I told you in Monaco that you wouldn't have gotten your promotions if you hadn't deserved them."

"Well, then?"

"You can't work for the Ambler Corporation anymore."

"I suppose not, but—"

"And you can't work for an opposition company." Roger sipped his sake. He could see that she was determined. "I guess you could look around a little, see what's available."

"You don't mind then?" Laura was pleased.

"I want your happiness," he said, and paused. "It would have to be something that could accommodate our traveling. I want you with me, Laura, as much as possible."

"I want that, too."

"Good."

Laura's birthday, on Midsummer's night, coincided with a charity ball being held at the Metropolitan Museum for which Rona had told her she needed a full-length gown. It was crimson silk chiffon, very décolleté and slender, but with enough fabric in the skirt to make dancing a joy. The charity, for handicapped children, was one that both Roger and Nelson Howarth supported handsomely, and midway through the evening, the band played "Happy Birthday" for Laura, and the crowd on the dance floor cleared a space for Roger to lead her into the center to start off the next waltz.

"Happy?" he asked.

"Very." She felt the weight of the bracelet he'd bought her, square-cut emeralds and diamond baguettes to match her necklace and earrings. Expensive gifts were of tremendous importance to Roger, she realized now, signifying love as well as generosity. "It's been a wonderful day."

He drew back from her a little, to look into her face. "Are you sure you're perfectly happy?"

"Why wouldn't I be?" Laura smiled into his eyes. "I still sometimes feel as if I'm in a dream—this is that sort of an evening, don't you think?"

The waltz ended, and Roger held her close for another moment, before he began to lead her off the floor. "I still feel there's something worrying you. I wish you'd tell me what it is."

Laura stopped, before they reached their table. "It's Gus," she said.

"What about her?"

"I can't seem to get her out of my mind. I want so much to speak to her, but whenever I try to call, the answering machine is switched on, and it's still playing my old message—she hasn't even changed it."

"Gus doesn't strike me as the type to bother with a machine."

"She isn't." Laura let her anxiety show. "Roger, I know that she probably just doesn't *want* to talk to me—and I can understand that—but I'm scared something's happened to her. I've called and called, and I've written letters. I just need to know that she's okay."

"So what do you want to do about it?"

"I'll have to go to London. I have to know."

"Of course you do."

Relieved, Laura kissed his cheek. "I thought you might mind my going."

"You have to. I know how important Gus is to you." He thought for a moment. "Can you bear to wait a few more days?"

"I suppose so. Why?"

"Because we're going to Paris next Wednesday."

"We are?"

He smiled. "I was planning to surprise you—whisk you off to JFK with your bags already packed. But under the circumstances, I guess you ought to know."

"And from Paris I could skip over to London."

"We'll both go."

"That would be wonderful," she said, gratefully.

"I'm a wonderful husband."

Though Paris, Laura quickly realized, was one of those rare cities in which it was truly possible to live and love and have a fine time with hardly any money, it was certainly an even more heavenly place in which to be rich. Having the funds to dine at the Ritz and shop in the Faubourg St. Honoré did not preclude one from strolling in Saint-Germain and sitting in the Luxembourg gardens, but then again, having one's very own spacious and immaculate *appartement* near the Bois de Boulogne to go home to, was definitely an added bonus she wasn't going to dismiss.

She loved the apartment, one of eight in a grand, gray stone house, on the top floor, with its own private roof terrace. Its gentle, traditional decoration and furnishing were in absolute contrast with the Trump Tower apartment, the height of elegance, yet still managing to be comfortable. It was a place in which Laura felt she could kick off her shoes after several hours of walking, and curl up on the silk brocade sofa with a good book; a place of peace and lightheartedness with a huge pale marble bathroom created for laziness, and a well-equipped and spacious kitchen which made Laura think, with a pang, of Gus who would, she was certain, have approved of it as thoroughly as she had disapproved of their New York galley.

Roger was constantly on the go for the first two days, but Laura didn't mind a bit. She was thoroughly content to be a tourist in Paris, and when they were not together she insisted on doing without the chauffeur-driven car he wanted to provide for her. She wanted to meet Paris on her own terms, she told him, and would not, for once, allow him to talk her into his way of doing things. She would take cabs whenever she needed to, but otherwise, with the insane traffic jams that seemed to clog up every street in the city at all times, she preferred to walk or, perhaps, to take the Métro.

Rona telephoned on the third morning.

"Roger's gone out," Laura told her, after they had exchanged pleasantries.

"It's you I want to speak to, dear," Rona said. "I have to tell you—confess may be a better word—about a little arrangement I've made on your behalf with an old friend."

"What sort of an arrangement?"

"Her name is Hélène de Grès," Rona said, "and her husband was Hubert de Grès, the head of one of the top banking families in France. Hubert died two years ago, and Hélène has gone into a kind of social retirement, but in her day, she was the finest—and I mean the *very* finest—hostess I have ever encountered. Now I know that you're a very independent girl, Laura, and that you certainly don't want—or need—to be seen to be working too hard at learning how to do things—"

"Rona"—Laura interrupted her fondly—"what are you trying to tell me?"

"Hélène has offered to give you a few hints."

"Hints?"

"On giving dinner parties, on simply being 'at home,' on throwing major events. Hélène de Grès knows everything there is to know, and she's agreed to give you three days."

Irritation crept into Laura's voice. "Rona, I'm sure you can give me all the help I need when I need it. This is my first time in Paris, and my first time here with Roger—I can't say that I dreamed of spending it learning how to fold serviettes."

"I don't imagine you did—and they're called napkins, by the way, not serviettes." Rona's voice grew a touch firmer. "Believe me, Laura, I'm doing you the greatest of favors by introducing you to Madame de Grès. You'll adore her, and what's more, you'll enjoy her."

Inwardly, Laura sighed. "I'll have to speak to Roger."

"Well, of course you will, and if he's against the idea, then we'll have to make our excuses, but think of it this way—if you had tried to take on the job of area manager in your first week with Ambler Agencies, do you honestly think you could have coped?"

"Certainly not."

"Then what makes you think you can jump straight into the big league without the slightest training or advice? Being

Mrs. Roger Ambler is a job in itself, make no mistake about it."

"You keep calling me that, Rona. I think of myself as Laura Ambler." She paused. "Does it really matter so much if I don't become a fabulous hostess for my husband? Who will it matter to?"

"It'll matter to Roger the first time you bungle the seating arrangements and end up slighting one of his guests."

Our guests, Laura wanted to say, but held her tongue. She'd come into this marriage with open eyes, or she'd believed that she had. If Rona Howarth and this Hélène de Grès were part of the package, she'd just have to put up with them or start making enemies. Laura knew better than to do that.

"How do I contact this Madame de Grès?" she asked.

"She's expecting you this afternoon. I'll give you the address—it's a simply wonderful house in Neuilly."

"You assumed I'd agree?"

"Only because I know what a clever girl you are."

"Thank you, Rona."

If Rona noticed the irony in Laura's tone, she made no comment.

Laura had never seen ceilings as high as those in the de Grès house, at least not in any private home. They were beautiful, ornately carved ceilings, hung with massive, gleaming chandeliers. Twin staircases, carpeted in powder blue and meeting on a broad landing dominated by a huge antique mirror, led to the salon where Hélène de Grès was waiting to meet her.

She was a tiny woman, with wavy brown hair and sharp eyes. She wore a black linen suit, and just a light touch of perfectly applied makeup.

"How do you do, my dear?" She gave her hand. "I am so very glad that you have come to me, and quite flattered. May I call you Laura?"

"Please." Laura felt gauche and uncomfortable. She understood already why Rona had sent her here. Her job had not, after all, prepared her for this new life. If she felt ill at ease in the friendly company of this one stylish lady, then perhaps she did need a little help for the times to come when she might be faced with entertaining ten, or perhaps a hundred, less amiable strangers. "It's very kind of you to agree to meet me," she said.

"Dear Rona has always been most complimentary about my parties," Madame de Grès told Laura. "When Nelson first brought her to Paris, my late husband was engaged in writing his memoirs for the Howarth publishing firm, and Rona and I got along famously from the beginning. She is an enthusiast, don't you find?"

"Very much so."

"I enjoy that in a woman—in a man, too, of course." She peered more closely at Laura. "Rona tells me that your husband is somewhat older than you. Has he married before?"

"You've never met Roger?"

"Alas, no."

"He's been married twice before." Laura felt her cheeks grow warm.

"So he, too, is an enthusiast."

Laura laughed. "I suppose he must be."

"She has a book," Laura told Roger later that evening, as they drank martinis on their roof terrace. "It's more of a bible, really—the kind of thing great secretaries pass on to their successors—only hers is everything any woman ever wanted to know about how to get her guests angling for another invitation."

"I take it you liked her."

"She's one of the most impressive people I've ever met. I was nervous at first, but now I can hardly wait for tomorrow."

"So it's all set?"

"Do you mind? It's just for a few hours during the afternoon for the next two days. Only she's kept her diary free for me, so it would be terribly rude to back out."

"Very rude." Roger shrugged. "The only pity is that I'll be flying over to London tomorrow morning, and I know you wanted to come along to try to see Gus."

Laura came back to earth. "Does it have to be tomorrow?"

"I'm afraid so. I guess it can't be helped."

"I'll have to telephone Madame de Grès."

"You can't do that. You said yourself that you can't back out now." He set down his martini glass on a little white iron table. "I should have a couple of hours to spare tomorrow between meetings. I could try to check Gus out for you—at least make sure she's not sick or in any kind of trouble."

"I can't ask you to do that."

"Sure you can. You're my wife—I'd do anything for you."

The following afternoon, Laura learned about the importance of the New York *Social Register,* at least to those in it and to those who strove to get into it. She learned about the hard study that sometimes went into the compilation of a guest list and the seating plan that followed acceptances. She learned the value of becoming the perfect guest, first because popularity was enjoyable and led to future invitations, second because the more one was invited, the more one could learn, and third because it would make her husband even more contented than Madame de Grès assumed he already was. Some things could be learned, some required good instincts. You could be taught when to send flowers, what to write on a formal card, which topics of conversation to avoid when encountering a sensitive guest, but you had to learn for yourself how many minutes and how many charming smiles you could bestow on a male fellow guest before you risked making an enemy of his wife.

Roger did not return until late. Laura was waiting up for him, sitting curled up in a negligee on the sofa in the salon, the door open so that she could be sure of hearing him when he arrived, even if she had dozed off.

"Hello, darling." He bent to kiss the top of her head, and dropped his briefcase on an armchair before going straight to the cocktail bar and pouring himself a cognac. "Want one?"

"Please." Laura was wide awake. "How was your day?" She was dying to ask him about Gus, but she wanted to be seen to put his interests first.

"Good." He put the glass stopper back into the heavy decanter and came to sit beside her. "Hal sends his best and says to tell you that Anne Lockhart is going great guns, but they still miss you."

"I bet."

"Do you care?"

"Not really."

Roger leaned back against the soft cushions. "I've been shopping today."

"What did you buy?"

"Nothing yet, but let's just say I'm on the verge of buying myself a little slice of British history in the making." He raised his cognac glass. "Let's drink to it."

"What are we drinking to?" Laura asked, curiously.

He looked at her in the soft lamplight. "It's top secret, baby."

"Don't tell me if you don't want to." She understood confidentiality.

"I want to. I just need to know that you understand it's to go no further than this room."

"Of course."

"Then here's to the *Saturday Courier.*"

"I've never heard of it."

"That's because it doesn't exist, yet. But it's going to, believe me, and when it does, I'm going to own the controlling interest."

"Wasn't Tom Bailey talking about a British Saturday paper when he came to lunch?"

Roger laughed. "That's just the bee in Tom's bonnet, as they say. His brainchild, and that's where it's going to stay, in his brain."

"Why?"

"I told you when I first introduced you to him. Bailey's an idealist. He's very bright, and very talented." Roger shook his head. "But he has this insane idea he won't let go of, for a paper that's going to tell it how it is."

"What's so bad about that? It sounds fine to me."

"It may sound fine, but honesty above everything just isn't practical. Ideals seldom are." He tried to explain. "A lot of editors go in to bat for the truth, and there's no shortage of high-integrity journalists, even proprietors, who want to tell the truth the way they see it."

"The way they see it," Laura echoed.

"You got it. If a reporter hands in a story, just the bare bones, that's all it is, a report. A good writer can give it a slant, something extra, and a strong editor will stamp his paper's attitude all over it. The trouble with Tom is that he has a puritanical streak in him. No one's going to want to read the kind of paper Tom wants to publish—they'd be bored to death by page two. He and his father fell out years ago because of his high-and-mighty notions."

Laura was surprised. "That doesn't sound like Tom."

"Maybe lofty's a better word." Roger swallowed some cognac.

She couldn't wait a moment longer.

"Did you get a chance to try Gus?"

"I said I would."

"And did you reach her?"

"She's not answering the phone."

"We know that." Laura was very tense. "I thought you might try to call in at the flat."

"She wasn't there."

"Oh." She wanted to weep.

"So I went to that market near Hampstead."

"You went to Camden Lock?"

"And there she was, selling Indian silk and junk earrings to unsuspecting American tourists."

Laura sat up straighter. "Did you talk to her?"

"Well, I didn't go there to buy—sure I talked to her. She's fine." He saw the anxiety in her face. "She really is okay." He shook his head. "You know, seeing her there helped me understand what happened when she was in New York. Talk about a fish out of water."

"She must have been surprised to see you there."

"Not all that much. She knows you've been trying to speak to her, and she knows I get to London regularly—I guess she knew it was only a matter of time before one of us showed up."

Laura put down her glass on the end table beside her. "So she really doesn't want to talk to me anymore."

"I think she'd love to talk to you, deep down, and maybe one day she'll be ready to."

"But not yet."

"Maybe not ever," Roger said gently. "But you don't have to worry about her anymore. She's in good shape, and I've taken care of the apartment rental for a while, so that should help her get ahead of the game."

Laura looked up, surprised. "Gus let you do that?"

"She didn't like it much, but she's no fool. She talked about paying me back someday, and I agreed that we could call it a loan if it made her happier." He laughed as Laura threw her arms around him. "I'm glad to see I've made you happier, too."

"You're so good to me." She hugged him tightly.

"You sound surprised."

"I think I am, a little," Laura said, honestly. "After what happened when Gus was on the Island, I didn't expect you to be so generous."

"I think it was seeing her in her world, seeing how totally different it was from ours—I guess it helped me understand her a little more."

"I love you," Laura said.

He smiled. "I love you, too, baby."

"Coming to bed?"

"Soon. You go ahead. I have some papers I have to sort through."

"Don't be long."

He took his cognac and briefcase into his study, a smaller, less fully equipped room than his workplace in Trump Tower. He sat at his desk for a while, contemplating his deceit. What he'd told Laura was, at least, half true. He had contacted the landlord of the flat in Finborough Road, and he had paid the rental for another three months. But Gus had not been at the flat, and he had not gone to Camden Lock. He had no interest in Gus Pietrowski, except in the way in which she had still been affecting his wife by causing her anxiety, and Laura's fears had now been laid to rest. There was a slight risk, of course, that she might, one day, find out that they had not actually met, but Roger felt confident that he could deal with that easily enough if the time came by saying that he'd had someone else check to see that Gus was okay, and he'd simply embellished the story a little to make her feel better.

He laid out some papers on his desk. That irritation was in the past now, that period in his wife's life was over. Rona had unwittingly kept Laura from going with him to London, and now he would just have to avoid taking her there for the foreseeable future. There'd be a lot of trips over if the *Courier* got off the ground. He was aware that Laura hadn't asked as many questions as he'd hoped about the new paper, but if he'd wanted a big reaction he oughtn't to have mentioned it before giving her the news about Gus. Laura enjoyed the things that money bought, but she cared more about people and feelings. He found it gratifying to know for sure that she had not married him solely for what he could give her.

He put away his papers, and went to bed. He had an idea that grateful sex with Laura might be worth having.

CHAPTER 16

In early September, Laura received a letter from Adam Demonides giving her the good news that he was going to be
married, and the even better news that his bride-to-be was an
American named Fran Gallagher, and that they were coming
back to live in the United States.

"He says they met on the plane, when he was going back
to Athens after the wedding," Laura told Roger that evening,
when they met at the New York Hilton before the annual
dinner dance in honor of the Ambler Shoe Corporation. "She
was studying archaeology for the summer, and they fell in
love right away—isn't it wonderfully romantic?"

"Very romantic," Roger said, smiling at one of the re-
gional managers whose face he knew well but whose name
eluded him for the instant.

"Not as wonderful as the fact that they'll be practically
neighbors, at least when we're on the Island."

"Where did you say they're going to live?" Roger asked,
paying attention for the first time.

"Montauk. Apparently, Fran's family own a chandlery
there, which will be perfect for Adam because he can be
near the sea again. Montauk's not too far from East
Hampton, is it?"

"Not too far." The news disquieted him. He had believed
himself rid of Laura's past. "When are they coming over?
When's the wedding?"

"I don't think they've set a date yet, but Adam says they'll be flying into New York at the end of this month."

"What a pity." Roger had always prided himself on his ability to think on his feet. "We'll be away."

"Where?"

"I thought it was time we had our honeymoon."

"You didn't say anything."

"You should know by now how much I like surprising you."

They landed at Coolidge International Airport in Antigua exactly three days before Adam Demonides and Fran Gallagher were scheduled to arrive at JFK. Even from the plane, Laura glimpsed white beaches and waters of the most incredible turquoise she had seen since those around Aegina on the best days of summer, and on the ground, driving in the back of a Rolls-Royce south toward St. John's, the island's capital, she felt memories of childhood stroking gently at the back of her mind. Once they reached the St. James's Club, however, the past seemed far away again, for Roger had brought her to the nearest thing to paradise, and there was no time for memories, however pleasant, for every image, every taste and every scent of the present was too precious to waste. There were two tranquil beaches, palm trees everywhere and green hills that overlooked the Caribbean, any number of glorious spots in which to sunbathe, tennis courts and stables, glass-bottomed and sailing boats, even a deep-sea fishing boat for use by the guests. Laura and Roger woke later than they were accustomed to most mornings, and though Roger was never away from the telephone for longer than a couple of hours at any one time, Laura had not seen him so visibly relaxed since their days in Monaco. They sailed and swam and played tennis together and shopped in St. John's, and Laura took lessons in waterskiing and scuba diving while Roger read the streams of faxes that came in daily.

And then there were the nights. Candlelit dinners, usually of locally-caught fish, visits to the casino, strolls along the beach, and then to bed. A soft breeze blew in the evenings, cooling the island, and after Laura and Roger made love, they lay naked on their king-sized bed feeling the gentle air from the open doors stroking their bodies and lulling them into sleep. For the first week, they were very happy. And then, in the early hours of the eighth day of their stay, Roger got out of bed and produced the black lacquered box that Laura had not seen since their wedding night.

"Time for a little adventure," he said, and opened it.

Laura lay on her back and was silent.

"Remember these little toys?"

"I remember."

"I've waited over four months. I knew you needed time to relax with me, to get comfortable. You are comfortable now, aren't you, baby?" He sat on the edge of the bed, looking down at her.

"Very." Remembering what was in the box, Laura didn't feel in the least comfortable. She felt like covering her nakedness, but knew that would offend him, and he was right, he had waited months, and she supposed there hadn't been anything too terrible, too deviant-looking, in the little box, no leather, no whips or chains or anything. Better, maybe, to give him what he wanted rather than risk him going elsewhere for it.

"So what's it to be? A little extra spice?" He took out the pleasure beads and laid them on the sheet beside her. "Just a little taster."

"Taster?"

"A sample of the real thing."

Laura eyed the beads. "What do we do with them?"

He ran a finger over them. "We put them inside you."

"We do?"

"They'll give you sensations that nothing else will."

Laura couldn't imagine, looking at them, that they could do anything much more than tickle her and fall out. She said nothing.

"You don't get it, do you, baby?"

"Maybe not."

"They don't go in your pussy." He smiled. "They go in your ass."

Laura sat up. "No, they don't," she said.

"Sure they do."

"No," she said again. "They do not."

"Why the hell not?"

"Because I don't want them to. It's my ass, isn't it?"

"If you insist."

"I'm sorry," Laura said, a little more gently. "That kind of thing just doesn't appeal to me."

"What about what I want, baby?"

"If you want to use them, go right ahead."

"But I want you to have the pleasure."

"It wouldn't give me pleasure. It would embarrass me."

"You'd enjoy it." He lay down, took her hand, drew her down with him. "You might enjoy the real thing even more."

Laura snatched her hand away. She pulled at the sheets, tried to cover herself up. Her cheeks were burning.

"I must say I'm surprised," Roger said. His voice was suddenly cool. "Knowing what you've been in the past."

Laura froze. All the heat turned to ice.

"Knowing what kind of place you were confined in." He was speaking very clearly. "Everyone knows the kind of thing that goes on in those places, Laura. No one escapes."

"I did." Her mouth was suddenly very dry.

"Even if you did, you must have seen things that most little girls don't get to see. That's why I can't quite understand why you pretend to be so naïve and shrinking."

Laura scrambled out of bed, found her caftan-style dressing gown and wrapped it around her. "How long have you known?"

"You know how long. Gus told me—or as good as told me."

She stood with her back to the door, staring at him. "She told me she thought you already knew. About me, as well as her. Why didn't you tell me you knew? Why did you pretend it was only Gus you knew about?"

"I didn't know that much." Roger had sat up, too, his knees drawn up, a pillow resting on his lap. "I'll admit I got curious after Gus let it slip. Can you blame me? I found out everything then."

"Before or after the wedding?" Her legs felt like jelly.

"Do you think I'd have married you if I'd known?"

"I'm not sure what I think anymore." She couldn't believe

how calmly they were discussing it. It was like talking about
an old parking fine she'd hidden from him. "How did it
make you feel, finding out?"

"It made me feel many things," Roger said. "I felt very
sad for you. And shocked, too, of course. After all, you were
such a little-miss-perfect on the surface, weren't you? The
ideal up-and-coming corporate woman, albeit with a less
than honest personnel file."

"Didn't you feel betrayed?" Laura asked softly.

"A little. Hell, I felt a lot betrayed, what man wouldn't?"

"So why did you stay with me?"

"Because it didn't stop me loving you." He smiled. "I
guess it excited me, too."

"And that's why—" Laura stopped.

"The sex? Sure, why not?" He shrugged. "It's all part of
getting to know your partner, of understanding their needs,
what they're made of. Could be I might understand you better than you do yourself, what do you think?"

"I don't know." Laura felt suddenly drained, as if she
might fall if she didn't sit down. "I don't know what to
think."

He saw how white she had become. "You're worn out,
baby," he said, gently. "Come back to bed."

"I can't."

"Sure you can." He smiled again. "I promise I won't lay
another hand on you tonight. And these things"—he picked
up the pleasure beads and placed them back into the box on
his bedside table. "Gone."

It felt almost like getting back into bed with a stranger.
She lay down without removing the caftan.

"That's my girl," Roger said. "Get some sleep." He turned
out the light.

Laura lay stiffly in the dark for a few moments. There was
a clear foot of space between them.

"What you said before," she said, very quietly, "about the
kind of thing that goes in places like Kane. Nothing like that
happened to me—Gus protected me from all that."

"Did she?" There was irony in his voice. "I guess that
shouldn't really surprise me."

"What do you mean?"

"It isn't hard to see what I mean, Laura." He paused. "Gus probably wanted you for herself, even then. She still does."

"That isn't true." If she hadn't been so deathly tired, if they hadn't been on an island in the Caribbean with nowhere for her to go to, she might have got out of bed again and left.

"I know love when I see it," he said.

"Do you?" Laura asked.

He woke her at dawn, making love to her with such tenderness that she was filled with renewed gladness and optimism. It might be all right, after all. It might even be better than before, now that all the secrets were out. She watched his golden head in the pale morning light as he kissed her breasts, and she knew that even if he had known about her all this time, he had only kept his knowledge from her so as not to hurt her. Having him inside her, filling her, made her feel so good, so wanted, feeling his ejaculate flooding her as he climaxed was so welcome this morning because she knew it signified that he still wanted her to bear his children, in spite of what he knew.

"Good morning," he said, moments after he had collapsed beside her.

"Good morning." Laura smiled at him.

"Enjoy that?"

She kissed his shoulder. "It was a lovely way to be woken."

He went to the bathroom, closing the door. She heard the sounds of showering, and she dozed, peacefully. The door opening woke her again. She opened her eyes as he came toward the bed. He had another erection.

"My way now," he said. He got onto the bed and turned Laura over onto her stomach. She felt him tremble with excitement, heard his shallow breathing, and she knew that this time there would be no foreplay and no love to speak of. It was a part of their unspoken bargain, the compromise that had been struck after their wedding night, once her way, once his, and she had grown used to it, and it was only the lovelessness of it that troubled her now. But then, at the last moment, she heard him fumbling in his bedside drawer, heard something being torn, and as she felt the new roughness of the way he grasped at her buttocks to spread her open, she realized what he wanted.

"No," she said, and tried to move, but he held her too tightly.

"I've put on a rubber," he said. "There's nothing to worry about."

"Roger, for Christ's *sake*," she cried, softly, but he was pushing into her, and it hurt so much, for he was huge and she felt the membranes tearing, and she was so revolted she felt sick. "Stop it," she begged him, "please *stop!*"

"I can't stop. Just enjoy it."

Laura knew then that this was her punishment, and she remembered that he had made her feel like that the first time in the brothel, and maybe it was true, maybe it was her punishment for taking a life, and certainly it was his revenge for her deceit. And so she just lay there, taking it, feeling the ripping in her rectum and the sickness in her stomach, and time had stopped, it might have been minutes or hours or a lifetime until he gave a cry of what sounded like triumph and agony at the same time, and he pulled himself out of her and got off the bed and went back into the bathroom. And Laura pulled the sheets up over herself, right up to her chin, rolled onto her side, and wept silently.

"I'm sorry," he said, when he came back. "It must have hurt you."

"It did." She didn't look at him.

"Did you enjoy it at all?"

She wanted to scream.

"No," she said, quietly. "It was painful, and it disgusted me." She took a breath, steadying her voice. "And I said no. And it's against the law."

"So's killing," Roger said.

And Laura said nothing more.

They had lunch in their suite, on the patio. Laura was afraid to be alone with him, but she couldn't face sitting in a public place with him either, with so much left unsaid. Roger ate cold lobster, his appetite unaffected. Laura played with her food, hardly able to swallow.

"We have to talk," she said.

"If you like."

"Don't you want to ask me about it? About what happened at Osborne?"

"I know most of it," he said. "I have the court transcripts."

"How?" She felt fresh shock.

"I have my ways. You know that."

"I don't understand," Laura said. "I feel suddenly that I don't know you at all. I don't know what you feel about me, where the past fits into the present, into us."

"There is one thing I would like to know," Roger said.

"Yes?"

"How did it feel? Killing someone."

Laura stared at him for an instant, then looked away.

"You must remember," Roger said. "Something like that can't be easy to forget. Though I expect you might want to."

"You're right," Laura said. "You don't forget. Not ever. But you try damn hard." She forced herself to look back at him. "I don't want to remember that, Roger. Please don't make me."

"I won't make you." He snapped a red claw, and extracted the lobster meat with a two-pronged fork. "I guess I'm a little intrigued."

"You make it sound as if I'm an exhibit, some kind of freak."

"I don't intend to." He dipped the flesh into mayonnaise and ate it.

Laura took a sip of mineral water. "If you have those transcripts," she said, softly, "you'll know pretty much how I felt."

"Oh, I know you didn't mean to do it, and you don't have to tell me how guilty you must have felt."

"Then I don't understand what it is you want to know."

Roger sat back in his chair. "You've been through something that most of us don't ever experience, unless we go to war, maybe, and I escaped Vietnam. You've taken a life—I know you didn't mean to, but that's what happened. I'd like to know what that feels like."

The midday sun was very hot, but Laura felt chilled.

"It's a turn-on for you, isn't it, my past?"

"I guess it is."

"That's why you thought I'd like rough sex."

He smiled. "You don't know what rough sex is."

She flushed darkly. "What you did to me this morning was quite rough enough."

"I know. I'm sorry."

"I don't ever want you to do that again."

"Okay," he said. He sounded agreeable. "I think I can understand your reluctance to let go. You let go once, with a knife in your hand. That's enough to inhibit anyone."

Laura stood up, rattling her chair. "Is this why you married me?" Her fists were clenched and there were tears in her eyes. "To hold the past over me, to torment me with it?"

"No, it isn't," he said steadily. "I married you because I was in love with you. And to protect you."

"You have a strange idea of protection," she said, bitterly.

"Don't you think I have some small right to be a little harsh, Laura? You lied to me, or at least you neglected to tell me the truth about yourself. Some men in my position might take that pretty badly."

"Most men would. That's one of the things I don't understand."

"You don't trust my love."

Laura sat down again, still close to tears. "I feel you're playing games with me. One minute, you're kind and loving, and the next—"

"What?" Roger showed anger for the first time. "Do I hit you? Do I curse at you, abuse you?"

"No, of course not."

"All I've done is to be honest about my needs. We've both lied to each other—maybe I should have told you what I knew. But that's all over now, and I want to be open with you, with my wife, and in my book admitting the kind of thing that turns you on sexually is a part of being honest."

"And if I hate what turns you on?"

"Then I'll try not to want it too much." His anger had

gone, and he gave a small, soft laugh. "Once in four and a half months isn't that bad, is it?"

"I suppose not." Laura felt numb now, as if she could no longer focus clearly on what was right or wrong, as if there was no black or white, just a fuzzy kind of gray.

"And will you at least try to have a little more fun with me?"

"That depends on what you mean."

He laughed again. "I'm not planning to tie you up or have you whip me. I just like trying different things every now and then—is that so bad?"

"No."

"And this is our honeymoon, after all." Roger reached across the table for her hand, and squeezed it. "I do love you, Laura. I love you in spite of what you might have done in your past—maybe I love you more because of what you must have been through."

"I'm not sure I deserve to be loved," Laura said.

"Sure you do." He still held her hand. "Be a good wife to me, that's all I ask, and I'll look after you, I'll protect you from the past."

For the first time, Laura thought of New York.

"Does anyone else know? Rona?"

"No one. I said I'd protect you." He let go of her hand. "And I don't want you to tell anyone else, ever."

"Who would I tell?"

"You'll make friends. Just don't think you can trust them. Not with something like that."

"I could trust Gus," Laura said.

"You're better off without Gus," Roger said. "And you can trust me, that's the important thing to remember."

They returned to New York. They were both disappointed, in their own ways, though neither of them had given up hope of making a success of their marriage. The hoped-for sexual feast for which Roger had starved himself for months had proved something of a damp squib; there was a certain amount of pleasing sexual tension in playing teacher to an unwilling pupil, but unless the teacher could unleash hitherto unsuspected delights in that pupil, the pleasure was necessarily limited. Nor had Laura become pregnant yet. His first two wives had disappointed him, too, in both those areas; sex with Suzy had been fun for a time, but had soon paled, and the only position Patricia had ever wanted to do it in had been on top—and so far as babies went, Suzy had used a diaphragm and Patricia had swallowed the Pill together with her multivitamins and minerals every morning.

Roger had no intention of giving up on Laura. After all, it was early days in their marriage and she was still only twenty-four. He still believed that a girl like Laura had to have a wildness buried within her that just needed to be released. When he thought about the things he still wanted to do with her, he thought about the way they tamed frightened creatures at the circus. He was a great believer in training, in conditioning. It worked in business, especially in the agencies; he only had to walk into any one of the Ambler branches in the States or in Europe to see his men and women motivated almost to the limits of rationality. It worked best when they were young enough. And Laura was certainly that.

So far as Laura was concerned, the fairy-tale romance had gone with the honeymoon. Roger still went out of his way to make romantic gestures, but what had seemed to her before, for all his worldliness, to be genuine and artless, now appeared calculated, possibly even cunning. She knew that she had disappointed him, was guiltily aware that Roger had not exactly accused her, as most men surely would have, of marrying him under false pretenses, and to try to assuage her guilt she began to work harder than ever at being the wife he wanted, at least out of the bedroom.

When Laura told Roger, in mid-November, that she was planning a trip to Long Island so that she could meet Adam's fiancée for the first time, he insisted on taking over the plans for the reunion. There was no need for Laura to go out there, he said, when they could come to Manhattan; he would send a car to pick them up and bring them to Trump Tower.

"I rather hoped we could spend a few days together," Laura said.

"They can stay in the apartment. God knows there's enough space."

"But are you sure you want them here?"

"Why wouldn't I?" Roger asked. "Adam's your oldest friend, after all, and since he did me the favor of giving you away at our wedding, I'd like the chance to show him and his fiancée a little hospitality."

"That's very nice of you." Laura would much rather have gone to Montauk, but she knew she couldn't say so without offending her husband. The ease that had begun to permeate their relationship before Antigua, had vanished. Roger was good to her, on the whole, and she felt it necessary to respond with gratitude and politeness. She felt, at times, more like an employee than a wife.

"Do you think they'd like a party, to celebrate their engagement?" he suggested.

"I don't think so," Laura said. "They wouldn't know anyone, after all."

"Are you sure?"

"I think it might embarrass Adam."

"Whatever you say."

She liked Fran at first sight. She had red-gold hair, lightly tanned and freckled skin, long slim legs, strong arms and a wide, expressive mouth that smiled a lot of the time, especially when she looked at Adam, whom she clearly adored.

"Isn't she wonderful?" Adam kept saying to Laura right through the days and evenings they spent in each other's company. "Can you believe how lucky I was to find her?"

"Fran's lucky, too," Laura kept telling him.

"Don't you think we're perfect together?"

"Perfect."

Roger, of course, was busy most of the time, shuttling as usual between his Manhattan office and White Plains, the old headquarters of the Ambler Corporation from where the shoe and machinery empires were still taken care of, and conducting his daily meetings on conference phone lines with the San Francisco office, the hub of his computer businesses. Still, he managed to make himself free every evening of Adam's and Fran's stay, taking them all out to dinner every night at a series of glittering locations, ignoring the fact that Laura had said they might be happier at less formal establishments.

"They can eat burgers and kabobs any night of their lives," Roger said. "While they're with us, let them live a little."

Laura saw what he was doing. Before Antigua, she might have thought he had the best intentions, but now she knew better. For reasons she could not begin to understand, he was jealous of her relationship with Adam, and for reasons she understood slightly better after sharing his world for five months, he resented every minute he had to spend with two young people he considered to be out of place in their circle. He was, therefore, endeavoring to see that they felt so uncomfortable and ill at ease during their stay that they would have no wish to return. Laura had no choice but to let him control things while Adam and Fran were at Trump Tower, but she drew the line at allowing him to manipulate her out of her oldest and dearest friendship.

Three weeks after Adam and Fran had gone back to Montauk, Laura called Roger at the office to tell him that Fran had telephoned to invite them to stay with them for a weekend.

"I suggested they might want to come to our place in East Hampton, but Fran's family really want to repay your hospitality."

"That's very good of them," Roger said, "but it's out of the question."

"Why is it?"

"I'd have thought that was obvious, even to you."

"Well, it's not," Laura said. "I think it's a lovely idea."

"For one thing, we don't have a free weekend."

"I looked at your diary. There's nothing much marked in three weeks' time."

"Forget it, Laura," Roger said. "We're not going."

"Why not?" she persisted, determined to force him into honesty.

"Because people like the Gallaghers and Demonides are not our kind." The gloves were off. It was time she understood her position.

"They're certainly my kind," Laura said.

"Not anymore."

"You are such a *snob*," she said angrily.

"And proud of it. I'm sorry, baby, but you did push me on this."

"Only because I knew damn well what you meant, and I was just hoping that I might be wrong."

She put down the receiver. It was the first time she'd ever hung up on him. She felt quite good about it.

Three Fridays later, while Roger was in Chicago for the day, Laura took the Long Island Railroad to Montauk, where Adam and Fran greeted her with open arms. She entered the Gallagher home—a white clapboard building that housed the chandlery on the first floor and the family on the second and third—with a sense of immediate warmth and pleasure. Stuart and Betty Gallagher, Fran's parents, had tea ready for her, a real tea, with home-baked scones and preserves, and the house, with its slightly sloping walls and open fireplaces, comforting in the early November damp, filled Laura with a longing for something she could not quite define.

When John, Roger's chauffeur, arrived soon after ten that evening, with the message that she was needed back in Manhattan, Laura sent him back alone, with sincere apologies for his long wasted journey but with only the clearest and entirely unapologetic message for her husband. She'd left the Gallaghers' phone number in the apartment; if Roger needed to speak to her he knew where she was, unless, of course, he was suddenly able to join them.

"He won't like that, I think," Adam said, when John had left. "Maybe you should go back in the morning?"

"Why should I?" She was still angry at being sent for, like a parcel, or a schoolgirl. "We were both invited for the whole weekend. He chose not to be free, but that doesn't mean I have to shut myself away from my friends." She flushed a little, not having intended to admit so openly that Roger had snubbed them.

"Just don't worry if you change your mind," Fran told her, kindly. "I mean, we all want you to stay, of course, but you don't have to consider our feelings for a moment, if that's what you were thinking."

"I'm thinking of myself," Laura said. "And I'm hoping Roger may see my point, when he cools down."

She had expected him to be at the office in White Plains on Monday afternoon when she got back to Manhattan, and she was consequently startled to find him in the apartment. As the front door closed behind her, he was already standing on the cool marble floor of the entrance hall, and Laura could see that he had been poised for this moment, and that he was intensely angry.

"Because of you," he said, "I have been forced to cancel three meetings." There was no hot fury, his voice was cold and measured.

"Why did you have to do that?" Laura faced him, though inwardly she quaked a little, acutely aware that she stood on what might be the brink of their first major fight.

"To stop you fostering any false illusions that you might have won some kind of victory this weekend."

"I didn't know it was a battle," Laura said. "I accepted an invitation that included you—"

"Which I asked you not to accept."

"You tried to order me not to go."

"So you thought you'd thwart me, like a spoiled teen-ager."

"Which was why you sent John to get me, to humiliate me."

Roger stepped closer to her. There was no rage in his eyes, just that cold implacability. "The humiliation was all mine, as you were well aware when you sent him back alone."

Laura looked down at the bag at her feet. "Do you think we could fight about this later? I'd like to take a shower, and I have to change—I told Rona I'd go to one of her charity teas."

"Your shower can wait," Roger said, "since I've waited for you."

"Don't be childish," Laura said angrily, "and stop trying to order me around."

"Just one order." Still there was that icy, matter-of-fact clarity. "One command, if you prefer." He paused for effect. "You are not to see Adam Demonides again."

"I beg your pardon?" Laura couldn't believe her ears.

"You heard me perfectly well."

"You're actually standing there telling me not to see my oldest friend?" She was shaking with fury. "You don't surely expect me to obey you, do you?"

"There's no doubt in my mind," Roger said, calmly. "Lord knows, I haven't demanded too many things of you."

Laura stared at him. "You're not jealous. You *can't* be jealous. Adam's engaged to Fran—they adore each other."

"Why the hell would I be jealous of a penniless little Greek?" His blue eyes were mocking. "I know you better than that, Laura. You're much too clever to risk the security of this marriage for someone so worthless—which is why I know you will do as I tell you."

"And if I don't?"

"There will be consequences."

"What kind of threat is that?"

"No threat." Roger turned to walk away toward his study, then stopped, without turning back to face her. "A guarantee. Believe it, Laura."

She knew she ought to push him, to fight the battle to its end, no matter how unpleasant it might be, to establish her rights for once and for all as well as trying, if possible, to accommodate his wishes, perhaps even his fears, but she was afraid to take it further. She knew that she was dealing with the powerful side of Roger Ambler from which the smaller fish in his pool hid, knowing they could never survive confrontation. She was his wife, and, as such, she did, of course, have plenty of rights of her own, but her past rose up to block her, to blunt her claws, and she kept silent.

A week later, Laura began to search for employment. She had been checking the classified section of the Sunday editions of the *New York Times* for several weeks, ever since she had first raised the subject of her working, and now she set about scheduling interviews with the best of the agencies she had circled, excluding, of course, the Ambler Agency near Columbus Circle. By the following Tuesday, she had landed a job working as a public relations aide to an Italian retailer of small leather goods setting up four new upscale boutiques, one in the CitiCorp Center, one on Sixth Avenue, and two in New Jersey malls.

She broke the news to Roger that evening, bringing him a Bloody Mary in his dressing room shortly before they were due to go to the Howarths' for dinner. The atmosphere between them for the last few days had been courteous, if not warm, and she sensed he had been almost relieved that she had apparently, for the time being at least, backed down over Adam and Fran. She knew he didn't want her to go out to work, but she knew, equally, that he had no desire to make her unhappy. She needed some measure of independence, and it was up to her to persuade him to see that. Besides, he owed her one.

"I'm really excited about it," she told him, her stomach taut with nerves. "And since the hours are so flexible— almost part-time really—it means it won't interfere too much with the things we want to do together."

"You haven't accepted the job, have you?"

"Not officially, but I've as good as told the agency yes."

"But you've signed no contracts?"

"Not yet."

He took a long swallow of his drink and handed it back to her, turning away to check his tie in the mirror. "Then you shouldn't have too much trouble telling them you've changed your mind."

Laura's jaw felt stiff. "Why would I do that?"

"Because it isn't suitable."

"What's wrong with it?"

"There's nothing right with it." He turned back to her, and his eyes were friendly, not angry at all. "You still haven't grasped your position as my wife, have you?"

"I think I'm beginning to."

"No, no, baby, don't get all resentful." He reached for her hand and held it in spite of her. "I'm not playing the heavy husband for the sake of it. I need you with me, Laura. I need you as my companion, as my hostess, not just as my lover—I need a partner, a woman who's *for* me, not just with me."

"But I can still be all those things, Roger, even if I take this job."

"No, you can't." He released her hand. "Think about it honestly, and you'll see that I'm right. The moment you take a salary from these people, you belong to them first, during the hours you work for them, and those hours will grow and grow, believe me, especially if you're good at your job, which you would be." He tapped his chest with his right hand. "I know the way businesspeople think, Laura, better than you do, and while you belong to them, you can't belong to me."

"I don't want to belong to anyone," Laura said softly.

Roger shook his head. "I used the wrong word."

"Did you?"

"You know what I mean. Don't pretend to be obtuse." He looked down at her dress and smiled. "Have I told you I love the way you're always ready on time, the way you don't play those 'keep him waiting' games the way some women do?"

"That's my agency training," Laura said.

"I told you I always knew what I was doing."

She almost hated him for that. She wanted to stand and fight, on equal terms, the way most husbands and wives would be able to. She wanted to be free to lose her temper and scream at him, to let go and tell him everything she really felt about his blatant, ongoing manipulation of her. But she couldn't do any of those things. Not because she feared what he might do. He might lose his own temper, might even hit her, might tell her to leave, might, ultimately, divorce her. All those things were at stake in many less than perfect marriages, she guessed, especially where one partner had the upper hand. But those things were not really what Laura feared. She was afraid to let go, terribly afraid to get too angry, in case she lost control. She had never forgotten her grandfather's advice to her. *Give way when you have to, but never let others trample on you.* But standing up for herself was what had destroyed her teenage years, what had cost Lucia Lindberg her life. She could not afford to lose her temper, could not afford to lash out the way normal women might.

And Roger knew that. It irked him that Laura feared loss of control when they were in bed together, but in other ways it suited him well, and he used it to his advantage, just as he felt able to use, without actually having to say as much, the knowledge that he could, at any time, expose her past. Though that, in reality, was a weapon he was unlikely to want to use, since it would, at the same time, cause him to lose face.

Theirs was an interesting marriage, a silent, softly-spoken battle of wills. Laura gave in on some things and resisted on others. She did not take that job or any other, but she continued to speak to Adam at least once each month, always making a point of reporting to Roger that they had spoken, and so long as she made no mention of actually seeing Adam, Roger made no complaint. Laura continued to work hard on the superficial aspects of their partnership. In a way, she had begun to see it as her new career. She had learned to shop with the best of them, to have her hair done twice, sometimes three times each week, to slip into Kenneth or Elizabeth Arden for several hours at a time, to take the "right" aerobics and stretch-and-tone exercise classes and to nibble at lettuce leaves while the happy women that Rona had once described, in a discreet whisper, as "poor ignorant creatures," munched their way through pastrami sandwiches and chocolate fudge cakes.

Laura didn't realize that she had gone back to the habit of looking at her reflection without really looking into her eyes until one afternoon in February of 1987, strolling through Saks, she caught an unexpected glimpse of herself in a wall mirror and stopped, for a moment or two, to look at the expensive-looking stranger who stared back at her. She could hardly see Laura Andros anymore in that glass. The woman who stood there, carrying her Rizzoli and Bergdorf Goodman shopping bags, her hair exquisitely cut, her makeup perfectly applied, was a clone of many of the other wives of highly successful men she had met over the months at Rona's many charity functions, to which she now, almost invariably, was invited in her own right. The woman in the mirror was Mrs. Roger Ambler; the clothes and the beauty treatments were her shield, her armor, as much as her name. Laura stepped in closer to the glass and forced herself to look at her eyes. She looked past the subtle eye shadow and perfectly separated mascaraed lashes, past the unwavering pupils. There was vulnerability there, still, and perhaps a touch of pain.

She looked away, quickly, and walked on.

CHAPTER 17

In the third week of March that year, 1987, Roger had the last of a series of major arguments with Tom Bailey over the incursions they were both on the point of finalizing into the British newspaper industry. While Ambler's paper, the *Saturday Courier*, was scheduled for launch in a year's time, Bailey's own weekly, the *Saturday Journal*, now seemed likely to beat Ambler's to the punch, with Bailey having already resigned from the editorship of the *Chicago Courier* and set up headquarters in London's Dockland, from where he would both control and edit his paper.

Up until now, the two men had found themselves able to dust themselves down after their heated exchanges, and to shake hands with some degree of mutual respect still intact, but on this particular occasion when they parted, they knew their friendship was at an end. Bailey had believed that with the disparate styles of their two planned papers, there might be room in the British market for them both, but there was no longer any doubt that their rivalry was set to be more ferocious than either man had anticipated. With the UK already heavily loaded with weekly newspapers, the challenge of tempting readers away from familiar territory would be massive, and there was no guaranteeing which way a potential reader might turn—to the *Courier* for tough sensationalism, or to the *Journal* for its assurances of integrity above all else. Suddenly, Bailey and Ambler had become two stags preparing to lock horns over the same slice of territory, and it was a war that neither of them relished. "Cowboy" Bailey, still holding out for his dream paper, hoped to try to win by the fairest possible means, but while his ideals were more firmly entrenched than ever, he was far from naïve, and winning had to be his ultimate aim. Roger, by now more galvanized than ever by the power-winning potential and sheer glamour of this latest venture, intended to stop at nothing to make the *Courier* the clear victor.

"So what happened?" Laura asked Roger the night after his showdown with Bailey.

"What happened is the son of a bitch told the London *Times* that I'm a danger to the industry because I don't have the passion for journalism that he does."

"Tom said that?" Laura could hardly believe it.

Roger's face was still dark with anger. "He as good as told them that a paper on which I have any influence won't have any heart or guts, because I take on businesses solely to wring profits out of them." He picked up the *Times* and read from the article. " 'When a major investor, whose greatest strength has always been his willingness to stand back and let the experts run his businesses, suddenly announces he intends to have hands-on influence over something as unfamiliar to him as a newspaper, then that paper is headed for trouble.' "

"Do you think Tom really said all that?" Laura asked. "Papers misquote people all the time, don't they? Or quote them out of context."

"The bastard didn't even try to deny it."

"I'm sorry," Laura said.

"Not as sorry as he's going to be," Roger said grimly.

"I meant I'm sorry because you were friends."

"Friendships are overrated, Laura. I've told you that before."

Roger grew harder to live with. He made frequent trips to Britain—always without Laura, though he continued to take her along on many of his other business trips—and returned in a heightened state either of excitement or of irritation. Whether his meetings—with Gordon Harrington, the *Courier*'s editor-in-waiting, or with the print unions, or with the builders of the new, fully computerized plant outside Coventry—had gone excellently or had disappointed him, Roger's appetite for sex, rather than affection, grew more voracious, his demands on Laura more aggressive. He was intensely disappointed by her failure to become pregnant; he insisted she go for physical checkups, he grew suspicious that she might be using contraception, even searched her closets and dresser drawers for evidence of the Pill. He bullied her increasingly into the sexual play that he thrived on but which she still disliked, sometimes by plying her with champagne to relax her, but often simply by becoming so sullen or belligerent when she refused that she gave in, just for a quiet life. He made her watch when he used the ivory dildo on himself, he nagged at her to let him watch her use the love eggs, and Laura knew that he only made love to her normally when he thought she was most likely to conceive, and even then she no longer thought of it as lovemaking, only as fucking. She began to be repelled by his advances, the sight of his erect penis began to fill her with disgust and even fear. He forced her to perform fellatio on him one night, and after he came in her throat she had to run to the bathroom to vomit. It was almost a whole week before he spoke to her again.

"You forget how much you owe me," he said to her sometimes, and Laura knew then that she was in much deeper trouble than she'd previously wanted to understand, because a part of her believed that he was right. She was glad, in a way, that she couldn't talk to Gus anymore, because she realized now that Gus had seen through Roger from the beginning. Laura began to consider leaving him, but that same guilt-driven part of her brain told her that she might simply be getting what she deserved. Perhaps the sex was just something she had to come to terms with, to put up with, in payment for what he gave her—not the luxuries, for Laura knew that whatever else she might be, she was not a whore—but the security and respectability, the citadel of Trump Tower, the shelter from the dark of the past.

Adam and Fran's wedding was set to take place on June 24, Midsummer Day and also Laura's twenty-fifth birthday.

When the invitation arrived, Roger told Laura that Rona had already made elaborate plans for a surprise birthday party for her at the Howarths' Manhattan duplex. Laura suspected that Rona was about to be pressed into throwing a party that she had probably not even considered, but there was no way of finding out, and in any case, at least Roger had taken the trouble to find an excuse rather than simply ordering her to refuse the Gallaghers' invitation.

Eight days before the wedding, Adam came into the city to buy a gift for Fran. He called Laura on the off chance that she might easily slip away to meet him. They shopped together in Macy's, wandering through The Cellar so that Laura could show Adam the pretty dinner service she'd been hoping to give them as a wedding present, and then she helped him to choose a cream silk and lace negligee for Fran, before they slipped into a coffee shop on Sixth Avenue for a sandwich and the first face-to-face conversation they'd had in more than six months.

"You don't look well," Adam told her.

"I'm fine," she said.

"You look strained." His black olive eyes peered intently at her. "Is he making you unhappy?"

"Of course not." Laura smiled as brightly as she could manage. "I want to hear everything, Adam—about the wedding, about Fran, about the chandlery. You look wonderful."

"I am," he said. "I'm a very lucky man."

"Is Maria coming over?"

"Did you think she'd let me get married without her? She's so excited." Adam held up his crossed fingers. "If things go well with my residence, and if she likes it, I'm hoping she will come and live with us."

"That would make everything perfect." Laura thought back with deep affection to the black-haired woman who'd cared so well for Chryssos and for her grandfather.

"What's wrong?" Adam asked.

"Nothing." She picked at her sandwich.

"You don't eat, there are shadows under your eyes, and your smile isn't coming from your heart."

"Of course it is." Laura shrugged. "If I look a little tired, it's because we had a late night at the opera."

"I suppose you won't tell him that we met today?"

"Probably not." She shook her head. "Not wanting me to see you is the one thing Roger's done that I find impossible to really forgive."

"And I admit I find it hard to understand why you let him stop you," Adam said frankly. "You were always such a fierce child when anyone tried to prevent you from doing what you thought right."

"That was before," she said, softly.

"You're still the same girl, Laura."

"Am I?"

Fran Gallagher telephoned the following evening, her voice distraught.

"Adam's been arrested."

"What for?" Laura couldn't believe it. "Fran, for God's sake, what *for*?"

"Drugs! They found pot in his room."

"I don't understand."

Fran sounded almost hysterical. "They came hammering on the door less than two hours ago with a search warrant, and they tore Adam's room apart, said they'd had some kind of tip-off about him."

"But Adam doesn't take drugs."

"Of course he doesn't—and he'd sooner die than have anything to do with them, but they found marijuana hidden in a suitcase under his bed. He says he knew nothing about it, and I know he's telling the truth."

"He wouldn't lie." Laura was outraged. "Someone else must have put it there—when did he last use the suitcase? Maybe it was planted on him at the airport?"

"He's been here nine months, Laura. And they said someone tipped them off." Fran paused, fighting to control her thoughts so that she could be of some use to Adam. "It's possible that someone could have come into the house—it's easy enough to get upstairs from the store."

"But who? And why?"

"That's not important right now," Fran said, urgently. "That's why I called you. Adam isn't a citizen—we aren't even married yet—"

"You think they could deport him?"

"I don't *know*—but he needs a good lawyer. I thought that you—I thought that maybe your husband—"

"Of course," Laura said quickly. "I'll try to reach him."

"Isn't he home?" Fran sounded more desperate than ever.

"He's in California, but I'm sure I'll be able to contact him. Fran, try not to worry—Roger has the best lawyers."

"I wasn't sure whether to call—I know he doesn't want you to see us."

"Roger will want to help," Laura said, decisively. "He might not like me seeing too much of Adam, but he won't want to see him in jail."

It was while she was standing in the big, mirrored sitting room punching out the telephone number of the San Francisco apartment that the thought struck her with such an impact that she had to put down the phone and sink into a chair. He had told her last November, after she'd snubbed him and stayed on in Montauk with the Gallaghers, that if she ever saw Adam again, there would be consequences. *Consequences,* he had said. She had seen Adam yesterday. Had spent almost three hours with him, had eaten lunch with him. Surely it wasn't possible that Roger was having her watched?

"Please, God, tell me he didn't have anything to do with this," she prayed out loud, staring at the telephone on the solid marble table. But she knew it was entirely possible that Roger might have done exactly that. He had the means at his disposal. He had the power. Wasn't he always telling her how useful that power could be?

Slowly, she put out her hand and picked up the receiver again. There was only one thing to be done, and that was to speak to him exactly as she had intended to, to place Adam at his mercy.

He answered promptly.

"How nice," he said. "I was going to call you a little later."

"Roger," Laura said. "I need your help."

Adam was back in the Gallaghers' home within twelve hours, all charges against him magically dropped. On the telephone from San Francisco, Roger was matter-of-fact and noncommittal about the help he had clearly given, but when he got back to New York, the picture became chillingly clear.

"Just a small example," he told her, as she got into bed beside him, "of what I can do when I put my mind to it."

"I'm very grateful," Laura said.

"I'm not talking about having the charges dropped."

For a moment, she could not speak.

"I didn't think you were going to admit it," she said, finally.

"So you did know?"

"I hoped I was wrong."

"And you know why?"

"Because I saw Adam."

"I did warn you." He shifted over toward her, saw her edge away, and was filled with fresh anger. "I hope you realize that this was just another warning. That Adam could always be a few phone calls away from being thrown out of the country."

Laura raised her chin. "They'll be married in less than a week."

Roger shrugged. "There's always jail."

"Why would you do something like that to him? He's a stranger—he's never hurt you."

"To keep you in your place," Roger said. "I'll admit, I didn't think it would have to be like this—I thought you were brighter, and I thought you'd be a better wife."

"You mean you thought I'd let you fuck me any way you wanted."

"Don't flatter yourself. If I want to, I can get all the fucking I need."

Laura was staring at him. "How else have I been such a bad wife?"

"I thought you'd be loyal," Roger said, frankly. "I thought you'd be with me, on my side, no matter what. I thought a girl like you—someone who'd done what you had, who'd been where you had been—would be grateful."

"I've been grateful," Laura said.

"Not in your heart." Roger's eyes were sad and cold at the same time. "You won't ever see him again," he said, quietly.

Laura did not answer.

"You know what will happen if you do." It was a statement.

Still she said nothing. Something else had come back to her, something else that she had to ask him.

"What about Gus?"

"What about her?"

"The mirror. She didn't steal it, did she?"

"Sure she did." Roger lay down. His navy blue cotton pajamas looked as if they'd just been freshly pressed, and his hair was immaculate.

"She said she didn't."

He gave a small sigh. "Do we have to start all over again with Gus?"

"Of course not," Laura said, and turned out her bedside light.

She knew, from that moment on, that she was going to leave him.

It wasn't easy, working it all out. She couldn't simply walk out of Roger's world without careful planning. For one thing, she wasn't sure where she could go to. Instinct drew her toward London, labeled it home, though she had only spent six years of her life there. If she left the marriage of her own accord, the prenuptial agreement she had signed in Brian Levy's office made it clear that she would have no financial claim whatever on Roger; but something more than self-blame, a leftover sense of pride and independence that had been buried during the period of their marriage, seemed to be reawakening in Laura, making her feel that she did not want anything more from her husband. She would not, therefore, have much money to speak of, had not greatly increased her savings during her years at the agency, and she had, therefore, to make one immediate stand against Roger's tyranny by taking a job and saving every cent earned for her leaving of him. It would be her secret bottom drawer, her hope chest, only instead of the old-fashioned collection of items accumulated in anticipation of marriage, Laura's hoard would be in readiness for divorce. She wanted to leave Roger—she *would* leave him, of that there was no longer any doubt—but she was afraid of slipping back down into the darkness of the Paddington bed-sit, with its cockroaches and damp, and its way of making her feel that she was no one, less than no one. It was only Gus who had saved her from that before, and Gus would not be there for her this time because Laura had betrayed her.

There were others to consider, too, in her plans to go. Adam might be married to an American citizen now, but as Roger had pointed out, even if the authorities couldn't readily deport him, there was always jail. And then there was Maria, getting older and depending on her son and daughter-in-law. Who could say how many ways there were for Roger to punish her?

"I can understand Laura wanting to work," Nelson Howarth told Roger one Sunday afternoon when they were all seated around the dining table in the East Hampton house, finishing their lunch. "In fact, I think it's admirable. Too many young women are content just to be wives, or to fill their hours with charitable works because it's the thing to do."

"Rona has her charities," Roger said, popping a cherry into his mouth.

"In addition to Zero," Rona pointed out quickly, and smiled at Laura. "I suppose I have to understand, too, dear, since I'd be lost without my company, even if I don't have to go into the office these days unless I want to."

"Last time we talked about my getting a job," Laura said to Rona, "you thought it was the wrong thing for me to do."

"That was before I saw how important it was to you. We're all of us different, aren't we?"

"Seems I'm outvoted," Roger said, dryly. "So I'd better make my suggestion right away."

"What's that?" Rona asked. "Or can I guess?"

"If Laura insists on working, it might make sense for her to join Ambler."

"Go back to the agencies, you mean?" Laura was startled.

"Of course not," Roger said. "I'm sure we could find something else appropriate for you."

"I daresay you could," Laura said, slowly, "but I don't think it's a very good idea."

"Laura's right," Nelson agreed. "The agencies would be one thing—she has a fine track record there—"

"It's out of the question." Roger was adamant.

"What would you have her do?" Nelson inquired. "Sell shoes or computers, or make machinery—or do you mean to create some fictitious executive position that's just going to make her look foolish?"

Laura felt a rush of warmth for Nelson, followed by a renewed stab of guilt. She had not anticipated help from her in-laws in preparing her escape from her husband.

"What about Zero?" Rona said, stirring her coffee.

"What about it?" Roger was starting to sound irritable.

"Only that publishing's such an acceptable area for someone in Laura's position to work in. Even you could approve of that, darling, couldn't you?"

Approve. Laura swallowed down her urge to tell Rona what Roger could do with his approval. "Is there a vacancy at Zero, Rona?" she asked, instead, quite calmly. "I'm not really qualified, you know."

"I know that, dear, but you read a great deal of fiction, and you're literate and articulate. We can always use an extra reader for all the unsolicited manuscripts we're constantly swamped with."

Laura's thoughts circled in her head. The idea of taking a salary from the Ambler Corporation in order to save up to leave Roger was too underhanded to contemplate, and she supposed that receiving her paycheck from his sister was not much better, and yet she knew that it was the best possible plan she could hope for. She thought she could do the job, she knew she would work hard for the money she would earn, and Roger would probably put up with it because, as Rona had implied, publishing was respectable, and because reading and reporting on books was something she could fit into his schedule.

"Well?" His voice nudged her.

She looked directly at him. "What do you think?"

He shrugged. "If you like the idea."

"I love the idea. If Rona really means it."

"I always mean what I say, dear, you know that."

Laura smiled at her. "In that case, I say yes, please."

On one hand, her life improved so markedly after she started at Zero that she might almost have given up her plans to leave, but on the other hand, Roger himself made that impossible. Since the episode over Adam, he had become so possessive of Laura that she often felt almost unbearably stifled. He seldom stood in the way of her work, even buying her her own laptop computer to make it easier for her to compose her reports while traveling with him. He insisted she accompany him everywhere he went, with the exception of his trips to Britain, but even when he was thousands of miles from New York, Laura had the sense that she was being spied upon. From time to time, she spoke on the telephone to Adam or Fran, but only when Roger was with her, lest he might suspect some sort of collusion and take new revenge on her friends.

The battles over sex were silent now, her resistance mostly in her head, her body acquiescent, almost numb. She lived in constant fear of becoming pregnant, yet she dared not go to a physician for a prescription, certain that Roger would, somehow, learn about it, but there was, mercifully, no pregnancy, and it occurred to her that perhaps, with no children in three marriages, he might be infertile, though that possibility had never even been mentioned when he had sent her for checks on her own fertility. As the months passed, and her savings account began to swell a little, Laura lay on her back or on her stomach or in whichever position he chose, and allowed her mind to wander forward, imagining the little flat she might be able to afford, and where it might be, and fantasizing about making up her quarrel with Gus, and feeling free again, to be herself and not her husband's property.

She disliked Roger by now more than she had disliked anyone since leaving Osborne, but she did not hate him. If she contemplated hatred at all, it was always focused clearly upon herself, for she acknowledged, more and more as time passed, that she was the real traitor in the match. He never struck her, or beat her; he continued to give her everything that money could buy; if she observed a vulgarity in him now that he had concealed from her in their early days together, that was no more than probably happened in any number of marriages as familiarity began to breed contempt. He did not respect her, but she could not entirely blame him for that. Much of the blame was her own, and she accepted it squarely. She despised herself for marrying him, and for failing to stay the course, and for scheming to leave him.

In the last few weeks, he began to disturb her sleep, waking her in the middle of the night to take her roughly, often sodomizing her, ignoring her whimpers of pain and seeming to grow ever angrier when she just lay still and took what he doled out. Laura thought, more than once, that she might die if he touched her again, but she was half-dead anyway, and a few more times would not matter, because she would be gone soon, away from him, and she couldn't wait much longer, because even the damp bed-sit, even the gutter, might be better than his body pumping at her, and with her gone, really gone, maybe he wouldn't trouble Adam anymore, and even if he did, she couldn't protect him forever by staying, she couldn't stay . . .

They went to Paris at the beginning of December, planning to stay until the New Year, but Laura knew that she would leave before Christmas, would not endure the mockery of accepting more gifts and acting out her gratitude and comparative contentment. On the seventeenth, Roger flew to New York, leaving Laura in the Paris apartment because she told him she was feeling unwell, and she did look pale and tired, and he wanted her to be fit in time for the seasonal festivities.

She waited until she knew his flight was airborne before she packed three suitcases of her belongings. She had known for weeks precisely what she would take and what she would leave; the Chanel suits and Ralph Lauren outfits were symbols that she might need in the future and that could last her for years; the fur coats and evening gowns she left behind, taking only her old favorite, the short strapless black silk organza dress he had given her in Monte Carlo, for those early days of delight were still alive in her mind, a reminder that she could not, did not regret it all. She left all the jewelry in the wall safe except for the diamond solitaire ring he had given her one day before their wedding; she had considered leaving that, too, but she would not pretend to be too naïve to realize that the value of that large, pure stone might mean all the difference to her, while it would mean nothing at all to Roger.

She left two notes, one for Rona, sincerely regretful, attached to a parcel of manuscripts that she had been assigned to read for Zero Publishing, and she left Roger's note, carefully sealed, on the desk in his study.

> *Dear Roger,*
>   *I doubt if you will be truly surprised by my leaving. It may even be a relief to you, if you permit it to be. If we'd both been honest from the beginning, our marriage might have stood a chance, but more probably we would never have let it happen. We're too different, and I think you believed I was someone I'm not, another kind of person altogether. I know I'm as much to blame for that as you.*
>   *I hope you will forgive me, but I know you may choose not to. Please don't try to change my mind. Please just let it be. I'll find a lawyer, who will contact Brian Levy. I won't try to challenge our prenuptial agreement. I know how much you have given me. I don't want any more.*
>   *I'm sorry I couldn't be the woman you hoped for.*
> *Laura*

In the British Airways arrival area at Heathrow, she went to a hotel reservations desk and found a modest place with vacancies near Victoria Station. She had too much luggage to take the tube into town, found it hard to bear the friendly inquisitiveness of her taxi driver, but later, when she had been alone in her drab hotel room for a few hours, she regretted her reticence and longed for someone, anyone, to talk to.

She put on a pair of jeans, a black turtleneck sweater and her lined Burberry raincoat, and went out for a McDonald's cheeseburger, something that Roger would never let her do. She could have gone to a far better hotel, could have sat snugly in a luxurious room and eaten room service, but she had to make her money last; there was no way of knowing how long it would take her to find a job. Being out in the hurly-burly of Victoria raised her spirits, took away the doomed sense that had gripped her for a while in the confining hotel room. It was not a life sentence, she could come and go as she pleased, and she had no one to answer to. She was free. But although there was relief in this new freedom, there was no joy. She was too alone for that.

Back in the hotel, she gathered her courage to try to telephone Gus, but the number was unobtainable, which meant either that she no longer lived in Finborough Road or that the phone bill hadn't been paid. In a way, Laura was glad not to be able to speak to her right away, for she didn't know what she would say, how she would begin, and it might be easier face-to-face. She resolved to go to the flat tomorrow evening—there was more chance of finding Gus home in the evenings. She could have gone tonight, but she was too cowardly, she needed a good night's rest before facing up to the rejection that was bound to come.

The cheap hotel bed sagged, the pillows were hard. Laura slept little, woke often from her fitful dozing to wonder where she was, and when she did manage to drop off into sleep, she dreamed that she was being made to watch Lucia Lindberg and Roger making love on a futon in a Japanese room. Apart from being blond, the girl didn't really resemble Lucia at all, yet in the manner of dreams, Laura knew that it was her, and when she struggled back up to wakefulness, she determined not to sleep again, and it was a relief when morning came, and she could put on one of her suits and get herself ready to go out and start organizing her new life.

Since Roger had seen to it that Laura had not returned to London since their marriage, her account in an Oxford Street bank near the Ambler Agency had not been closed. Laura's first step was to pay in the dollar check she had withdrawn from the American account she'd opened especially to accommodate her salary from Zero Publishing. Her new surname and the lack of a permanent address caused a few complications, but Laura was able to produce her passport and marriage certificate, and she knew that her appearance spoke in her favor, and when she asked the assistant manager if she could place her diamond ring into the bank's vault for safekeeping, she could see from the tiny flicker in his eyes that he had noted its value.

Gus was not at the flat that evening. The woman who had been their neighbor before Laura had gone away came to her front door to say that she had not seen Gus for months, and that she had left no forwarding address. The first edges of disquiet began to gnaw at Laura, but the next morning, when she went to the market at Camden Lock and still found no trace of Gus, the disquiet turned to alarm. She asked around, but no one had any information to give her, and, dispirited, she wandered out of the market back out to the main road and went into a café to sit and think.

She was gazing into the froth on her cappuccino when a man sat down opposite her. He was middle-aged, dark and rough-looking, and when it became apparent that he was staring at her, Laura looked deliberately away, and began to think about paying for her coffee and leaving.

"You were asking questions in the market," he said.

Laura looked up. "I was." He smelled of raw fish and beer.

"Looking for the girl with the Polish name, the punk, weren't you?"

"You know her?" She couldn't keep the eagerness from her voice. "Do you know where she is?"

"Depends who's asking."

"I'm a friend. We used to share a flat—I moved away."

"So did she."

"But where to? I have to find her."

"I got a problem with my memory," the man said.

Laura realized suddenly that he wanted money. Quickly, she fished in her bag for her wallet, pulled out a ten-pound note and held it out. "Please," she said, urgently.

"It's starting to come back to me," he said. "But it's still a bit vague."

Laura waited a moment, then took out another five pounds. "That's it," she said. "Either you know, or you don't."

"She's in the nick," he said.

Laura's stomach lurched. "Which one?" She held firmly onto the money. "Where is she?"

"Holloway." He paused. "At least she was." He held out his hand.

"You're sure?" Laura watched his eyes carefully.

"Some of the others could have told you, if they wanted," he said.

"Why didn't they?"

"Take a look at yourself," he said.

She gave him the money.

Laura had hoped not to have to ask Helen Williamson for help, but there was no one else, so she wrote to the principal of Osborne College that evening, asking for a recommendation to a lawyer who could be trusted to work swiftly and effectively without overcharging. The reply came to the hotel, delivered by special messenger with a Christmas card and warmest wishes, on the morning of the twenty-third. The solicitor's name was Mary Lloyd, she worked in a Holborn practice, and she was awaiting Laura's call and would do her best to get her the information she needed before the holidays.

At four o'clock on Christmas Eve, Mary Lloyd telephoned to tell Laura that Gus was serving six months in Holloway for shoplifting and assault.

"Are you there, Mrs. Ambler?" Mary Lloyd's voice was gentle.

Laura stirred herself. "Do you have any more details than that?"

The solicitor checked her notes. "Miss Pietrowski was remanded in custody on October fourth and sentenced on November fifth. She's unlikely to serve more than four months, which should bring her release forward to February." She paused. "I gather it's not her first offense."

"No. Gus was in a borstal years ago."

"Actually, she was in Holloway last year."

Laura's mouth was very dry. "Are you sure?"

"From June to September, 1986."

"But my husband—" Laura stopped. "There's no doubt?"

"None at all. That's all the information I have. Is it enough?"

"More than enough." Laura was beginning to tremble. "Thank you so much for your help."

"I understood you might be seeking advice regarding marital difficulties," Mary Lloyd said.

"Yes." Laura was gripping the receiver so tightly that her knuckles were white. "I'll be in touch soon."

"Merry Christmas, then, Mrs. Ambler."

"And to you," Laura said.

She put the phone down and went to the window, drawing aside the cheap flowered curtains to stare out into the dark. It was raining and windy. Traffic was flowing ceaselessly, brakes squeaked, people walked, heads down under their umbrellas.

She had not hated Roger until now, but suddenly everything else that he had done—even what he had done to Adam and Fran—paled into insignificance by comparison to this. At the time when Roger claimed to have met with Gus in London in June the previous year, she had been in prison. He had not seen her, nor had he, presumably, paid her rent on the flat.

"Oh, Gus," she said, out loud.

Hatred rose in her, feeling like the most acute pain, and for a few moments she allowed it to rise, knowing it was safe to let herself feel it now, with Roger thousands of miles away. She could no longer doubt that he had planted the mirror in Gus's wardrobe in the East Hampton house, or at least that he had arranged to have it put there. He had wanted Gus out of her life, that was all he had wanted—he hadn't cared what it might do to Gus, just as he hadn't given a damn what might have happened to Adam had the drug charges against him not been dropped. He had wanted only to control her life, to manipulate her into and out of friendships as he chose. And she had let him. She had believed Roger instead of Gus, and because of that Gus had come back to London alone and wounded, and had gone straight back to her old ways and trouble.

Her fault, after all. Laura knew that it always came back to that. If she had been a better friend to Gus, she would not be in prison now. If she had been a better wife to Roger, he might not have felt the need to get rid of Gus. The "ifs" ran on and on, a pointless, useless litany of excuses.

Across the street, someone else lifted a curtain to look out of a window, and Laura saw the lights of a Christmas tree and wondered if there would be any semblance of Christmas in Holloway. At Kane House, they had always made a small effort with a plastic tree and paper decorations and enforced carol singing, but how much Christmas spirit could you hope to get into a prison cell?

She hated herself so much she wanted to die.

In the first week of January, Laura went to visit Gus. It took all her courage to walk into the prison, all her willpower not to turn and run. She remembered Gus shuddering when she first saw Trump Tower, remembered her likening of that gleaming pile of luxury and security to a prison, and that irrational comparison seemed more bizarre than ever to Laura now that she felt the walls of Holloway closing around her and realized that Gus had come to this only a matter of weeks after Roger had flown her to New York.

When she got her first glimpse of Gus, Laura was so shocked that she could hardly breathe, let alone speak. They sat facing one another, a table between them, in a room full of other inmates and visitors. Gus had always been thin, but now her shoulder blades stuck through her pale skin, the shadows beneath her eyes were dark, almost panda-like rings, her lips were chapped and her hair, frizzy as always, was, for the first time Laura could remember, its natural brown. She was smoking, and the fingers that held the hand-rolled cigarette were trembling. There were marks, like scars, on her neck.

"What are you doing here?"

"I'm back." Laura's voice was hoarse with anxiety, and she cleared her throat. "I've left him."

"How'd you know I was here?" Gus's accent seemed more pronounced than it had been when they'd last met.

"I went to the market."

"Why'd you leave him?"

"I found out you were right."

"That's crap." Gus drew hard on her cigarette. "You knew that before he sent me packing."

"Maybe." Laura's throat was tight with the effort of not breaking down. "I didn't want to believe it."

"You shouldn't have married him."

"No."

"You didn't love him." Gus's words were matter-of-fact, not especially harsh, yet each one felt to Laura like a slap.

"No," she said again. "It wasn't fair to him."

Gus took another drag on the cigarette. "Still on your guilt trip, I see."

Laura was conscious of time being wasted. She wasn't here for herself, what had happened to her didn't matter now. What mattered was helping Gus.

"Is it really awful here?"

"No, it's a fucking health farm, can't you see?" Now Gus's gray eyes were very hard. Laura couldn't remember her ever looking at her that way before. "They offered me the Ritz, but I turned it down."

"I don't have anywhere to live yet." Laura kept her voice down. "But I'm looking."

"Park Lane?" Gus mocked. "Or Knightsbridge—better for Harrods." The cigarette finished, she stubbed out the last shreds.

"He told me he came to see you," Laura said, her eyes burning. "He said he'd paid the rent for you for a while. He said you didn't want to speak to me, that was why you never took my calls or answered my letters."

"And you believed him."

"Yes."

"And I'll bet you're really sorry now."

"Yes." It was almost a whisper.

"And you want to make it up to me, but you don't know how."

Laura nodded, unable to speak.

Gus stood up. There was a large bruise on her left forearm. "You can't make it up to me."

"I have to." Laura couldn't stand yet, didn't trust her legs to support her. "You have to let me try."

"I don't have to do anything." There was a faint hint of a wry smile on Gus's thin lips. "Forget about me. You managed pretty well for long enough."

"Never," Laura said. "Not for a single day. And since I found out what happened, I can't sleep, I can't eat, I can't do anything for worrying about you."

"That's your problem."

Laura stood, leaned against the table. "Can I come and see you again?"

"No," Gus said.

"But I could bring you things—there must be things you need."

"I've got everything."

"Please," Laura said, desperately.

"Forget it."

Laura came out of the prison, went back to Victoria, fell onto the bed and slept for five hours. Then she got up, took a shower, went out to buy herself a large notepad, some ballpoint pens, a copy of the *Evening Standard* and an inexpensive pocket calculator, and then she got herself another cheeseburger and a large cup of coffee and sat down at a corner table in McDonald's.

There was no way on God's earth that she could, or remotely wanted to forget about Gus. Their friendship was the rock upon which her whole adult life had been founded; without Gus, she believed she might not have survived at all. Laura knew that she had betrayed that friendship, but there was no time now for tears or self-recrimination. It was time to be practical. It was time to *do* something.

She ate her burger quickly, stirred more sugar than she usually used into the dark coffee, opened the spiral notepad and took the top off one of the pens. On the top of the first blank page, she wrote and underlined two words: *Home* and *Money.* Then she sat back to think. The most important thing was not to panic. There was some sort of an idea, stoking tantalizingly at the back of her mind. Laura remembered that during her days at the agency, she had sometimes come up with outstanding schemes for motivating her teams of counselors or appealing to their clients. What she had to do when one of those ideas started to tickle, Laura recalled, was just to try to relax and allow it to come forward in its own time, ready to be formed.

Several minutes later, she wrote another word. *Contacts.* After a second cup of coffee and an apple pie, she turned the page and made two columns, one headed by the word *Skills,* the other by *Experience.* She closed her eyes for a few more moments. And then she began to write in earnest.

On February 10, when Gus emerged from Holloway, Laura was waiting for her, a taxi parked just along the road.

"I don't want this," Gus said.

"Please."

"I don't need you."

"I know you don't," Laura said, softly. "Just please give me another chance. I need to talk to you, to show you things."

"They've fixed me up with a room," Gus said.

"I know they have. And I'll take you there, later, if you still want me to. Only please come home with me now."

"You got a place then?"

Laura nodded. "Will you come?"

"You going to hassle me if I don't?"

"Definitely."

Gus shrugged. "Go on then."

The flat was on the third floor of a large block built in the early thirties about five minutes' walk from Chalk Farm tube station and about ten minutes from the market at Camden Lock. The view from the living room and one of the two bedrooms was of the pleasant, tree-lined road, and the second and much smaller bedroom's window overlooked gardens.

"I haven't unpacked my things yet," Laura told Gus. "I wasn't sure which room you'd prefer."

"I told you they've found me a room."

"I know, but at least take a look." Laura went ahead of Gus into the smaller room. "I had a feeling you might like the garden view, but on the other hand, maybe you need space more."

"After living in a cell, you mean."

"You know that's what I mean." Laura came out and went into the large bedroom. "There's more wardrobe space in this one, too, so whoever takes the other room would have to keep some stuff in here."

Gus followed her in, moving slowly, almost stiffly, as if she'd lost the habit. "You might have to advertise for someone to share."

"If you don't want to move in."

"How can I?"

"Easily. Just stay."

"I've got no money," Gus said.

"At the moment."

"I've lost my pitch."

"No, you haven't," Laura said. "At least, you've got another one."

Gus turned her head slowly to face her. "You've been busy."

"Very." Laura sat on the single bed near the window. "Do you think you might be interested?"

The day had begun overcast, but now the sun, breaking through, illuminated Gus's face, showing up the weariness, accentuating the shadows.

"I'd like to tell you to sod off," she said.

"I don't blame you," Laura said.

"Why would you, when you can blame yourself?" Gus shook her head. "You never really change, do you, kid?"

"In some ways, I think I've changed a lot."

"You've just learned a lot, that's all." It was warm in the room, and Gus unbuttoned her black greatcoat.

"Why don't you take it off?" Laura suggested. "We could at least have a cup of coffee while you think about the flat."

Gus took the coat off.

"Just dump it on the bed."

Gus draped it over her left arm, like a visitor only staying for a moment or two. "Let's have that coffee then."

Laura stood up. "Does that mean you are thinking about it?"

"I want to hear about this pitch you claim I've got."

"That's only the half of it," Laura said.

She explained everything to Gus, from the temporary work she'd been doing during the workweek and the publishers' manuscripts she'd been reading in the evenings and on weekends to keep the money coming in, to the negotiations she'd been engaged in over the market stall, and the divorce proceedings she had asked Mary Lloyd to commence on her behalf.

"So you won't be getting anything out of him?" Gus asked. They were sitting in the small living room on the faded chintz sofa that had come with the flat, and they were on their third cup of coffee.

"I've had enough already, wouldn't you say?"

"Some great clobber. What about all the jewelry?"

"I left it behind—except the diamond ring." Laura flushed a little.

"Don't tell me you feel guilty about that?" Gus shrugged. "At least you had the sense to keep it, that's a start, I suppose."

"I thought it might help to raise funds," Laura said, "for my other idea."

"So what is it?"

"It only works if you're involved."

"I thought you had me back in the market?"

"That's only part-time."

"So what's the rest?"

"I want us to open an agency."

Gus looked blank. "Makes sense for you, I suppose, but what's it got to do with me?"

"Not an employment agency," Laura told her. "Not really an agency at all—more of a management company for small, independent caterers—a cross between an agency and a cooperative, I suppose." She went on. "I know London's full of caterers, really good cooks doing directors' lunches and private parties, and I suppose it's the same in most parts of the country."

"So why would they need you?"

"To maximize their success—organization and support, mostly." She had it all worked out. "Often they work in pairs, usually two talented women, sometimes men, of course, having to waste precious time on running their businesses instead of concentrating on what they're best at."

"And that's where you'd come in," Gus said.

"I thought we could take on a cross-section of the best—or at least the second-best, because the top people wouldn't need us, and we couldn't cope with the demands they'd make. We'd be offering our people the same free hand they'd have on their own, but under our umbrella they'd let us handle their admin and take care of the things they wouldn't otherwise have time for—backing, marketing, expanding their contacts, helping them to stay efficient." Laura saw Gus shaking her head. "What?"

"You keep saying 'we,'" Gus said. "What do I know about any of that?" Her eyes had grown harder again. "I'm a shoplifter—I used to be a stallholder in a market. Neither of those things qualifies me for this."

"You're a fantastic cook," Laura pointed out. "You've got a brilliant imagination and great, original taste in more than just food—and your intuition's a thousand times sharper than mine about people."

"If I'm so sharp," Gus asked quietly, "why have I just spent over three months in the nick?"

"Forget that right now," Laura said. "Think of the good times running the stall—think how competitive those markets are, how successful you were, how often you advised me when I came home with agency problems."

"Think how easily I blew it all."

"Because I let you down."

"You didn't tell me to come back and start pinching again. You didn't tell me to bash the store detective that caught me, not to mention the policeman I kicked in the balls."

"You didn't?" In spite of herself, Laura smiled.

"I bloody did." Gus was serious. "Is that the kind of woman you want working for you?"

"I want you to be my partner, Gus."

"Don't be daft."

"There's no one in the world I'd trust more."

Gus smiled for the first time, a wry, sad smile. "I don't know what you said about intuition, but I must be a better judge of character than you." She shook her head. "I'm a loser, haven't you worked that out by now?"

"And what am I? Look at the opportunities I've had and messed up." Laura knew she had to get Gus to listen to her. If she went away now, back to whatever sordid little room the authorities had found for her, back to being on the dole, that would be the end of her. "Gus, you've always told me that I'm a survivor, but the truth is we both are. We're good together—we're at our *best* together. I'm the one that blew it—I let my boss seduce me, I fell for him hook, line and sinker for all the wrong reasons—I let him blind me, for God's sake, and I paid for that, believe me—"

"I do," Gus said.

"Then please don't punish me anymore."

"I don't want to punish you at all."

"But if you go off now—" Laura was growing desperate. "If you won't forgive me and come back and try again, it'll never come right again for either of us."

"Who says I'm going anywhere?"

Laura said nothing, hardly dared to.

"I always wanted to live around here, all the time I was working the market. It's pretty, and cleaner than most, safer too—and if there is a chance I could have my own stall again—"

"I told you, it's all fixed." Laura's whole body was tensed.

"I don't know about this other idea though," Gus said. "You've got to think it through properly—"

"I have," Laura said.

"What about the money?"

"I'll go to the bank and borrow. Our overheads wouldn't be too high—we could operate out of the flat. There'd be a lot of traveling around to begin with, and there'd be advertising—and we'd have to buy a decent computer—"

"I don't know anything about computers."

"I'd teach you—it's easy."

They grew hungry, and Laura heated up a chicken casserole she'd made the way Gus had always loved it with plenty of herbs and garlic, and they shared a bottle of red wine, and for an hour or two it was almost the way it had been before, though they were both full of tension, were both keeping most of what they'd been through locked up inside themselves.

"I've already sounded out a couple of people," Laura told Gus, later, after they'd called to say that Gus would not, after all, be needing her room. "I talked to Liz Browning, who used to cater for Ambler Agencies—mostly when we held seminars, or had client parties, that sort of thing. She thinks it's a great idea and would be happy to join. And I spoke to Ned."

"Your Ned?" Gus was startled. "I thought he'd be the last person who'd want to talk to you."

"Ned's not the kind to hold a grudge," Laura said. "He got married a few months ago to a girl named Kerry from New Zealand. We've kept in touch with Christmas and birthday cards, and the odd postcard. He's still got the snack bar in Duke Street, but he always fancied getting into catering."

"Is he good enough?"

"I told him he'd have to take a course."

Gus raised an eyebrow. "You wouldn't have done that in the old days."

"No, I don't suppose I would." Laura ventured a smile of some pride. "I've even lined up a potential client—a pretty substantial one. A friend—or rather, an ex-friend of Roger's, who's going to be launching a new national newspaper this spring—"

"At the same time as Ambler's?"

"That's why they fell out. He's a lovely man—I don't think you met him, but he was at our wedding. He lived in Chicago while I was in New York, but we got on really well when Roger let us."

"Jealous, was he?"

"I never thought about that at the time," Laura said. "It honestly didn't occur to me that Roger could possibly think he had to worry about me looking at another man."

"Have you spoken to Roger since you walked out?" Gus asked. "He must have been spitting feathers."

Laura shook her head. "Mary Lloyd—that's the solicitor who helped me find you—she's been in touch with his lawyer to ask for a divorce, but I've asked her to keep my address to herself."

"He could find you if he wanted to."

"I know he could," Laura said. "I'm just hoping he'll accept it's all over, and leave me alone."

"He won't though, will he." It wasn't a question. "Ambler's not that kind of man." Gus paused. "And I shouldn't think he'll like you trying to do business with one of his rivals, either."

"I expect not," Laura said, softly.

"Are you sure you know what you're doing, kid?"

Laura shook her head again, slowly. "I'm just trying to keep it all together," she said. "I've learned a lot, like you said. I'm not about to waste it all, and I'm not going to let either of us go under again."

"That's good." The doubt was still in Gus's voice.

"But?" Laura looked at her old friend. "But what?"

"Just be careful," Gus said.

PART THREE

CHAPTER 18

Thomas William Bailey III felt he had come home. He realized that in terms of birth and roots, and family and loyalties, he was thousands of miles away from home. He was well aware also that to every one of the people surrounding him now on a daily basis, he was a foreigner and an outsider, and he was equally aware that there were going to be many times over the next few years when he would miss his homeland fiercely. But Britain was where Tom Bailey had chosen to make his stand. He had a hazier, long-distance notion that if he could make his *Saturday Journal* a success here, then he might be able to go back to the States and try to repeat it over there, but right now he was in London, and everything was only just beginning.

He was thirty-eight years old, and he had wanted to publish his British weekly paper ever since he'd studied at Oxford in the late sixties and had hatched his earliest dreams of breaking away from his father's and grandfather's parochial influences, and creating a newspaper that a whole nation could depend on. The Bailey family had owned the *Mercury* group of newspapers—an empire that encompassed papers in Illinois, Indiana, Missouri, Ohio, Michigan, Iowa and Minnesota—for three generations, and the papers were as successful today as they had always been, but they catered mostly to farmers, men and women whose everyday lives revolved around wheat, corn, hay and hogs. Tom had fought a long battle to talk his parents into letting him go to Oxford, and they had only given way because of their supreme confidence that their son would be only too glad—after sampling the claustrophobia of a little island compared to the big, open country that he had grown up so close to—to come back to the family estate in Kenilworth, about thirty miles north of Chicago. All the Illinois Baileys, before Tom, had been hooked on the considerable power they wielded in the heartland of America, but as Tom began to travel, and to open his mind and heart to learning and experience and to those people he encountered along the way, he realized that he could take the wide open spaces with him wherever he went, and that there could be riches in the world of newspapers that had little to do with money.

His period as editor of Roger Ambler's *Chicago Courier* had been a time of further education and growth for Tom, who had long ago made up his mind that being the proprietor of his dream paper—even a hands-on proprietor—would not satisfy him because he intended to be its editor, to work, day in, day out, alongside his staff. The Chicago job had followed several years of reporting, feature writing and news editing in an array of papers on the East Coast, all jobs that Tom had thrived on, and for the few precious years that he'd had Julie by his side, she had encouraged him to do whatever he felt he had to do, while Thomas Bailey II and his second wife, Gloria, sat back and waited, with unshakable arrogance, for the prodigal son to return to the fold in time to keep their old empire secure.

It was Nancy Whittaker, Tom's maternal grandmother and a woman of vast inherited wealth in her own right, who had finally ensured that Tom need never go back to the *Mercury* traditions that he had found so confining. Nancy had always adored her grandson, respected the grit that had compelled him to scramble off the Bailey estate and fend for himself, and the gentleness that had made it painful for Tom to hurt his father and, especially, his mother, Frances Whittaker Bailey, her daughter. Her son-in-law thought that Tom was immature, perhaps even a little crazy, but Nancy realized that his visions, if a touch unrealistic, were infinitely worthwhile; and when Frances died of Hodgkin's disease, Nancy had made Tom her sole heir before she, too, had passed away in her sleep, leaving him wealthy enough to realize his dreams.

"From everything you've ever told me about your dad," Tom once said to Ambler, while they had still been friends, "you'd think you and I might have been mixed up at birth. Lord knows you have much more in common with my father than I do, and I think Arnold and I would have seen eye to eye on most things."

Tom was sorry about the way things had turned out with Ambler. He had always known that the fact, on its own, that Roger had poached his idea for a Saturday weekly, was more than enough to severely damage their friendship; yet what had ultimately sent it crashing had been Ambler's final realization that Tom's commitment to his *Journal* was every bit as ironclad as his own to the *Courier.* For years, when Tom had talked about his goal of guaranteeing the truth of his printed words, Ambler had responded with a friendly mockery that Bailey had accepted without rancor, but once Tom had resigned his editorship with the Chicago paper and moved to London's Dockland to begin assembling his workforce of undeniably gifted men and women, a declaration of war had become inevitable.

The call from Laura Ambler in January had taken him by surprise. Tom had heard that she and Roger had separated, and though it wasn't really in his nature to take pleasure in the misery of others, he couldn't help feeling that Laura, who had struck him as an independent but vulnerable young woman, might be better off without her power-hungry, ever ambitious husband.

"We're going to have some kind of facility in the building," he had told her, in response to her questions about how he was going to feed his staff. "But no one's been contracted yet, and if there's a way around cardboard food served by faceless uniforms that isn't going to be more expensive, I'd be happy."

"Do newspapers tend to have boardroom lunches?" Laura had asked him.

"Only the sandwich kind," Tom told her. "There's no time

for three-course meals and fancy silverware—and even if we're Christ-knows how far from Fleet Street, nothing's going to stop half our journalists escaping for the kind of gossipy liquid lunch that seems to get them through the day."

"What about looking after the reporters when they're stuck somewhere, staking out a story for hours or even days?" Laura asked. "Or do they just have to fend for themselves?"

"You've got it." Tom had smiled into the telephone. "Though I'm all in favor of taking care of my people as best I can. I don't believe in encouraging ulcers or cirrhosis." He paused. "Do you think you might have someone on your books who could take care of our launch party in May?"

"I'll make sure I have," Laura had assured him, determining that if her brainchild hadn't taken on flesh by then, she'd do the catering for Bailey's party herself. "Perhaps we could meet in a month or two to talk over details?"

"I'll look forward to that." Tom had paused again. "How are you finding being back in London? It must be a little strange."

"I'm getting there," Laura said.

"I'll bet you are. Let me know if there's anything I can do—help get this company off the ground, whatever."

"How about some free advertising?"

"I'd certainly give you a special rate," Tom said.

"I was only joking." Laura was appalled.

"I know you were, but I'm not. It sounds like a good project to me."

One week after Gus's release from Holloway in February, Laura called Bailey again to invite him to lunch.

"I have to warn you I have an ulterior motive," she said.

"That's okay."

"It's nothing too huge," Laura said, uncomfortably.

"Is it something we could settle on the phone?" Tom asked.

"Oh. Sure."

"Only so we could free ourselves from business and enjoy the lunch," he said, easily. "Don't worry if you'd rather talk about it face-to-face."

"No, that's okay." Laura paused. "I need a reference, for the bank."

"For your funding?"

"That's right." She took a breath. "The problem is I don't have a house or anything to sign over to them as security."

"And I'd warn you against it if you did," Tom told her. He fished around in the chaos strewn over his makeshift desk for a pen; since he had declared his office the lowest priority in the *Journal* building, the decorators had taken him at his word, and the room, though bright and airy with a fine view of the Thames, still resembled a building site. "Okay, tell me—bank, address, the manager's name—and a phone number if you have it."

"You're sure you don't mind?"

"I said I'd help if I could." He took down the details. "Do I still get that lunch, or only if I get results?"

"When and where?" Laura asked.

"Better yet, how about dinner?" Tom thought. "Better still, why don't we go riding again?"

"Horse-riding?"

"You liked it in New York, didn't you? Before Roger intervened."

"I loved it," Laura said, delighted. "But I wouldn't know where to go."

"No problem," Tom said. "We can ride in style, in Hyde Park, or we can really have fun a little way out of town."

"Fun, please, anytime."

"A woman after my own heart," he said. "How about Sunday morning?"

"You're going on a date with him?" Gus said.

"It's not a date, it's business."

"On horseback?"

"It's instead of lunch." Laura grinned. "I told you they called him Cowboy Bailey in New York."

"He sounds a lot more fun than Ambler."

"Don't start, Gus."

"Watch yourself though, all the same."

"Don't *start*, Gus."

* * *

He picked Laura up from the flat and drove her north out to Hertfordshire, where Tom was given a handsome gray gelding and Laura a scrawny, but obliging chestnut mare. They rode out slowly from the stables, Tom enjoying the cold, dry February morning air, Laura concentrating a little too hard on trying to relax.

"Okay?" Tom asked her.

"I think so," Laura said, feeling precarious as they crossed a narrow road to get into the open fields. "If you want to go faster, don't take any notice of us—my horse knows a lousy rider when she meets one."

"Just take your time," Tom said in his easy voice. "I'm happy to walk all the way if that's what you want. Life's too much of a gallop most of the time right now anyway."

They got safely off the road and into an open field. "I think I could speed up a little now," Laura said.

"If you're ready. We're here to enjoy ourselves, not win the Derby."

Laura began to genuinely relax, felt the mare beneath her relaxing too, seeming to become aware that she was in for an easy morning. They headed into a forest, not the dense kind of woodland where you had to duck every few minutes to avoid low branches, but a lovely, spacious, sweet-smelling forest with dappled glades and sudden shafts of pure sunlight, and Laura had not felt so glad to be alive for a long, long time.

"Thank you," she said, later, as they sat in a pub between Radlett and Elstree, eating ploughman's lunches and drinking cold beer. "That was the best morning I've had in months, maybe more."

"Me, too," Tom said. "I should have brought Sam. He'd have had a fine time."

"Sam?"

"My dog."

"Of course," Laura remembered. "The mongrel you adopted. He came over with you?"

"And spent six months in quarantine." Tom shuddered. "That was one of the toughest decisions I've ever made, but I figured Sam had probably been through worse, and it was the only way we could get to stay together in the long term."

"And he's all right?"

"They let me visit him—I must have driven them nuts, calling them up all the time to make sure he was eating and getting enough exercise. Sam loves coming riding, he barks at the horses and goes crazy."

"You should have brought him."

"Next time."

Laura heard from the bank two days later to say that her loan had been approved and that confirmation would follow within a week. She wanted to call Bailey right away to thank him, certain that he must have brought a degree of influence to bear, but she didn't want to risk embarrassing him, so she went to a garden center, planning to have some kind of indoor plant sent to him with a note of thanks; but remembering that Bailey had told her he'd just moved into a house with a garden in Cheyne Walk, Chelsea, she ended up having a small American red maple tree delivered to his house with a whimsical message to Sam, telling him it was to help him feel at home.

A photograph of a grinning black and white dog with pointed ears and a bushy tail arrived in the mail two days later with a note on the back in sloping writing: *Tom planted it. I christened it. We hope you'll come sit under it soon. Love, Sam.*

Gus was much quieter now than she had been in the old days. She had told Laura right away that she didn't want to talk about her time in prison, and Laura had respected that, but as the weeks passed she began to wonder if locking all the pain up inside her might not be doing Gus much more harm than good.

"I miss the way it was," she said, one evening at home at the beginning of April. They were in the sitting room and *Cagney and Lacey* was on the television in the corner, but Laura knew that neither of them was really paying much attention.

"The way what was?" Gus asked, her eyes still on the screen.

"Us. We used to talk about everything."

"No, we didn't."

"Pretty much." Laura paused. "I know you said you didn't want to talk about how it was for you in Holloway—"

"That's right," Gus said. Her eyes left the television and met Laura's.

Laura saw the wall going up, but kept on.

"The thing is, I haven't really talked either, about what it was like, with Roger."

"I'm not stopping you."

"It might be easier, for me that is, if we could both open up."

"No," Gus said, sharply, then softened a little. "I'm all right the way I am, thanks to you, but I can't talk about it. It's the way I cope, you know that. It doesn't mean I can't listen to you if you need to let off steam."

Someone took a shot at Cagney. They both focused for a moment, saw that she hadn't been hit, looked away again.

"I don't really need to." Laura shook her head. "It feels like it was a dream now, anyway—all of it, good and bad."

"That was what was wrong with it from the start," Gus said. "It never did seem real. I don't believe in fairy tales."

"Nor do I. Not anymore."

"He was a bastard. I knew that before you went to France. So did you."

"If I did," Laura said, "I pretended I didn't."

Gus looked at her. "Want to tell me what he did? To you, I mean, not to me or Adam." Laura didn't answer. "He didn't bash you, did he?"

"No."

"Didn't think so." She paused. "Was it the sex?" She watched Laura's face.

Laura could hear her own soft breathing. "He said he knew what went on in places like Kane." Memories of the Japanese whorehouse and of Antigua, the bedroom that had become a battleground, flooded back, and she flushed deep pink. "He said, more or less, that I married him under false pretenses because I didn't tell him what I'd done, but I think that's what excited him. I disappointed him."

"Bastard," Gus said again.

"I told him that you protected me from all that at Kane."

Laura looked at her. "You're right about you not talking. You never said much about the borstal, when you came to Finborough Road." She looked away again, back toward the television. "How did you get those marks on your neck?" she asked quietly, tensely.

Gus was silent.

"I'm sorry," Laura said, and her voice cracked a little, "but I just keep on imagining, and I can't stand it because it was my fault."

"You'll have to go on imagining then." Gus stood up. "I'm going to bed."

"Gus, please."

"No."

"I'm sorry," Laura said again.

"Me too. I know it might be better for you if I could share it with you—better than imagining, maybe. But I'm never going to talk about it, to you or anyone. It's finished."

"Okay," Laura said softly.

"If you can't accept that, kid, then I'll have to go."

"No. Please. It's all right. I won't ever ask you again."

"We've got to move forward now," Gus said. "Think about the future, the business and all that. Right?"

"Right."

Two weeks later, on a Saturday afternoon when Gus was at the market, Laura heard the buzzer and went to answer the door.

"Rona."

"Laura."

They looked into each other's eyes for a long moment.

"May I come in?"

"Of course." Laura stood back. "I'm sorry." She closed the door.

"I've startled you," Rona said.

"Yes, you have. Please, sit down."

Rona, who had never looked out of place in all the time Laura had known her, looked curiously inappropriate in the flat. She chose the armchair closest to the window, sat down and crossed her legs gracefully. Laura noticed that the faded chintz cover looked even more shabby than it had before.

She remembered the first time she had seen the Howarths' duplex apartment; Rona's fabrics had been chintz, too, yet they were a world apart, like pure silk and polyester.

"This is very nice," Rona said.

"Thank you." Still in shock, Laura tried to rouse herself. "Would you like some coffee?"

"No, thank you."

"Or tea? I'm afraid we only have tea bags."

"No tea, no coffee," Rona said, pleasantly. "Just a little chat."

"What brings you to London?"

"Don't you mean, what brings me here, to your home?"

Laura sat on the sofa. "I didn't know you knew my address."

"We've known it since the day you moved in."

"I see." The afternoon was bright, but the light in the room felt suddenly dimmer, the atmosphere more oppressive. Laura did not ask Rona how they had known.

"I received your note of regret, with the manuscripts," Rona said.

"It had to be that way." Laura's heartbeat had quickened. "I hated doing it to you, when you'd been so kind."

"I'm sure you did." Rona paused. "Roger's told me everything."

Laura waited.

"The whole story."

"Which story in particular?" Laura asked.

"The only one that counts," Rona answered. "Your sordid little past. Which you hoped to conceal from us." The pleasantness was gone.

"I admit I didn't tell Roger," Laura said, "but I realize now he knew about it when he married me."

"That is simply not true."

"I believe it is. He tried to make out that it was Gus who let it slip, but she told me he knew all along."

Rona's pale, beautifully made-up face, became tauter. "And of course you would choose to take the word of a thief over your husband."

"Gus is the most truthful person I know," Laura said. "I only wish I'd believed her sooner, about everything."

"I have neither the time, nor the inclination, to waste on a common, social-climbing murderess." Rona stood up. "I've come here to tell you two things."

Laura stayed where she was.

"Firstly, my brother doesn't ever want to set eyes on you again. He'll never take you back, even if you go down on your knees and beg him to."

"I don't want to go back to him," Laura said, evenly. "I'm sure you know my lawyer has been in touch with his about a divorce."

"Secondly"—Rona swept on as if Laura had not spoken at all—"I'm here to warn you that if you ever—*ever* try to besmirch your husband's name, or the rest of my family, in any way whatsoever, you'll have me to answer to, and I don't think you have the slightest idea how tough I can be."

"I think I can imagine." Laura managed a smile. "Though I'm not sure what you're afraid I might say."

"None of us is in the least bit afraid of you, Laura," Rona said. "But you might be wise to watch your tongue. After all, you lied about yourself for long enough. I wouldn't like to see you making the mistake of becoming honest now, just to try to embarrass Roger, and I promise it would be a great mistake for you."

Laura got up too. "What exactly are you threatening me with, Rona?"

"No threats, my dear. Just a little advice."

"I think you'd better go now," Laura said.

Rona glanced around the small sitting room. "No wonder you wanted the Ambler fortune so badly." She looked back at Laura. "I tried to warn him when he first brought you to New York, but he wouldn't listen to me. Nelson had you checked by our London lawyers, but someone had, shall we say, cleaned up your records."

"I expect that was Roger. No one else could have done it."

"How dare you?" Rona's blue eyes, so like her brother's, glinted with anger. "How *dare* you try to drag a man of Roger's standing down into your gutter!"

Laura walked out of the room, and opened the front door. "Please go," she said.

Rona got as far as the doorway and stopped.

"When I think of what we did for you, how we all tried to help you, I'm sickened."

"I know how much you did, Rona. And I think I was properly grateful."

"So grateful that you waited until your husband was on a flight over the Atlantic before you walked out on him."

"I had my reasons," Laura said, softly. "I could go into them, but I wouldn't want to cause you embarrassment."

"The only person you'd embarrass would be yourself." Rona walked out into the whitewashed, linoleum-covered hallway. "Let's face the truth, my dear. You simply couldn't take it—you couldn't cope with our standards."

"I can't argue with you there."

"Good afternoon, Laura," Rona said.

"Good-bye," Laura said, and shut the door.

She waited until she was certain Rona had gone, and then she poured herself a large glass of wine, and burst into tears. Her eyes were still red from crying when Gus came home. She listened to Laura repeating every word of the encounter.

"Bitch," she said.

"I can't really blame her," Laura said.

"Why not, for God's sake?"

"She's his sister. I'd expect her to be loyal to him."

"Well, she's gone now, anyway. Good riddance."

"Has she?"

"Of course she has. You wouldn't catch her coming somewhere as sleazy as this a second time."

"It isn't sleazy," Laura said, on the verge of tears again.

"To Rona it is."

"That doesn't matter anyway—what she said doesn't really matter either."

"So what does?" Gus asked.

"The fact that she knew where I was living. That she says they knew from the day I moved in." Laura's eyes were anxious. "He's obviously having me watched, Gus."

"No, he isn't. Why would he?" Gus shrugged. "He probably had someone check up on you when you first got back to London, that would make sense. But you heard Rona, he's finished with you."

Laura poured herself another glass of wine. Her hands were shaking. "I didn't want to think about what he might do to punish me for running out on him. I liked believing he might leave me alone, that he might even be glad I'd gone."

Gus sat down on the sofa beside her. "The only way Roger Ambler could have punished you, would have been to stop you getting any of his money, but you told him you didn't want any, which probably made him furious."

"That would make him want to punish me more, wouldn't it?"

"Course not. He's got bigger fish to fry than you."

"He's got the *Courier* to launch." Laura's eyes were still anxious. "Which means he'll be over here more than usual."

"He's always come to England. It hasn't worried you up to now."

"Yes, it has." Laura took a sip and put down her glass. "I'm always imagining I see him in the West End. I was in the bank the other day, and I was so sure I'd seen him outside in the street that I didn't dare go out until he'd gone."

"You're getting paranoid," Gus said.

Laura forced a smile. "You know what they say. Just because I'm paranoid doesn't mean they're not out to get me."

The business was starting to come together. After hours and hours of trying to come up with original or effective names for the company, they decided to call it simply Laura Andros Associates.

"We can't use my name," Gus had insisted. "Andros & Pietrowski sounds like a Marx Brothers act. This is businesslike, and we could have just LAA on the top of the headed paper in one of those fancy prints you showed me on that bloody computer."

Gus pretended she hated the computer, claiming it went against all her principles to understand a machine, but Laura had woken up late one night to find Gus tapping away on it with her headphones over her ears, creating a press release that Liz Browning, the former Ambler Agencies caterer, had suggested they issue as soon as possible. Ned Archer, as Laura had asked, was taking a course in catering dinners and cocktail parties, and Kerry, his wife, who loved good food as much as Ned did, had agreed to give up her own job and work with him. Laura, on one of her bolder and less paranoid days, had picked up the telephone and called Hélène de Grès in Paris to tell her what she was doing, just in case she had any suggestions to offer; not only had Madame de Grès been kindness itself, but she had also put Laura in touch with two young sisters named Colette and Claudine Mireau who were, Madame claimed, extraordinarily fine and attractive cooks, and who would be delighted to spend at least one year living and working in England.

"I think we should take some courses, too," Laura told Gus.

"I can't see me going back to school," Gus said.

"You'd love it—and you never know when we may get called on to replace one of our people at the last moment. We've got to know what we're doing, don't you agree?"

"Suppose so."

Tom Bailey's *Journal* launch party, on Friday, May 20, the night before the first edition of the paper was due to be published, was set to be the debut, too, of Laura and Gus's company, with Liz Browning and her team planning to create edible miniature newspapers and mock headlines made out of canapés and whatever else they could come up with that would stay within the budget and help Bailey make the kind of gentle, controlled splash Laura knew he hoped for.

Laura found the message from the bank on their answering machine late on the Monday afternoon before the party. She had just put down the receiver when Gus walked in.

"What's up with you? You look terrible."

"That's a lot better than I feel."

"I'm shattered." Gus collapsed onto the sofa. "What's happened then? Tell me all about it."

"It isn't funny."

"It can't be that bad, surely."

Laura was very pale. "The bank want their money back."

"Of course they do."

"They want it now."

Gus sat up. "They've only just lent it to us."

"Seems they've changed their minds."

"But they can't."

"Apparently they can." Laura played nervously with a strand of her hair. "He's behind this."

"Roger, you mean?"

"Of course Roger. Rona made it pretty clear that I can't do anything without them knowing about it. He must have found out we were catering Tom Bailey's launch."

"But that doesn't make any sense," Gus said. "I know Bailey's his rival, but if we weren't doing it someone else would be, so what's the difference to him?"

"The difference is that he gets to kill two birds with one stone." Laura's nervousness was turning to anger. "Or at least he gets to inconvenience Tom, to force him to replace us—but he gets to finish us in one fell swoop."

"Can't we go somewhere else for the money?"

"Depends how he's got this bank to drop us, doesn't it?" Laura said.

Gus stood up, all her fatigue wiped out. "You think he's told them about you? But I thought Rona said they wanted it kept quiet."

"She did, more or less," Laura agreed. "And there are all sorts of things Roger could have told them to put them off—he could have told them I married him for his money—"

"Why would that put a bank off?" Gus said. "Surely their best clients are mad keen on money."

"But he might have said I was dishonest."

"He wouldn't have to invent things about you when your partner's a convicted thief."

"Gus, don't," Laura said.

"It's true though, isn't it?"

Laura felt sick.

"So what are we going to do about it?" Gus sat down again.

"I don't know."

"How much have we spent so far?"

Laura shook her head. "Never mind that—what about the party?"

"You'll have to tell Bailey."

"I know."

"Are you going to call him or face him?"

"Call him. It'll be a waste of his time if I go and see him."

"Shame," Gus said.

Tom Bailey returned Laura's call just after ten that evening. When she told him what had happened, he was silent for a moment and then he asked her if she had any idea at all what might lie behind the bank's withdrawal.

"Not an idea with much foundation," Laura said. "Or at least not with any real evidence."

"But you have your suspicions?"

"Yes."

"You're aware that Roger's over here now?"

"I assumed he must be, with the *Courier* launch a few weeks away."

Tom's voice was gentle. "I don't want to put words in your mouth, Laura, but would you say that he's an angry man right now?"

"Pretty angry. Roger doesn't like being crossed, as you know." Laura gripped the receiver tightly. "My main reason for calling you was to apologize, Tom. And to try to give you what time I could to reorganize things for Friday. If you could give me the name of your assistant so I don't have to bother you—and if Gus and I can be of help, you only have to ask, though we haven't done our training yet and I don't think we're up to—"

"That won't be necessary," Tom said.

"Oh. Right." She bit her lip. "I'm so sorry. I know this is the last thing you need right now."

"It isn't your fault."

"I'm afraid it must be," Laura said miserably.

"Why don't you leave this with me now, and we'll speak again tomorrow."

"Only if there's a way we can help."

"I'll let you know."

The telephone in the sitting room rang at twenty past ten next morning. Gus was out at the market, and Laura, having hardly slept during the night, was feeling ragged. Fifteen minutes later, having run all the way, she was pulling at

Gus's sleeve trying to get her attention away from the earrings she was trying to sell to a Norwegian tourist.

"Gus, it's okay!"

Gus went on talking to her customer, telling her that the clips were nickel-free.

"Gus, will you *listen*."

"Excuse my colleague," Gus apologized to the Norwegian girl. "I can let you have another quid off the price—they really suit you."

Laura waited while the sale was completed. The market was pretty quiet, and Gus seemed to be one of the few stalls with any customers at all.

"Where's the fire?" Gus asked.

"No fire."

"What's all the excitement then?"

"Are you sure you want to know?"

"That the bank's changed its mind, you mean?"

"What makes you think that?"

"They have, haven't they?" Gus saw from Laura's eyes that she was right. "I knew he'd do it."

"Who?"

"You know bloody well who."

"You think Tom did it?" Laura asked.

"Course he did. Stands to reason. He's just as rich as Ambler, isn't he?"

"I don't think so."

"Real money. You said he'd inherited a fortune. I bet Ambler's cash is all tied up in the company."

"Corporation," Laura corrected. "Anyway, I doubt if you're right, but who cares? The bank manager said that there'd been some kind of error, and he apologized—he actually *apologized,* Gus. He told me to carry on as if yesterday had never happened."

"I hope you made him sweat a bit."

"I did not."

"You should have. I would have."

"If I'd been with him," Laura said, "I'd probably have kissed his feet."

"You might do better kissing the cowboy's."

Laura ignored her. "I'd better get back. I left a message for Liz—I should be there when she calls."

Gus grinned. "He'll be wanting payment."

"We'll just have to give him the greatest party ever then, won't we?"

"He'll be wanting more than that."

"That's just tough," Laura said. "I've learned my lesson."

The party was a smash hit. The first edition of the *Journal* looked impressive, with its front page mostly given over to Tom Bailey's policy of printing hard news and unadulterated facts in the spirit of unbiased truth, and to the unprecedented guarantee that would sit, every Saturday for the duration of the newspaper's life, just beneath its name:

Absolute honesty, or your money back.

Neither Laura nor Gus had any role to play on the evening itself, but Tom had insisted they come, though he had seen fit to warn Laura that Roger had been sent an invitation, too. Laura had told Gus that she couldn't go, and Gus had said that if she didn't face him now, she never would, and what was more, Tom Bailey would think she was a coward, and she'd be missing out on meeting at least a year's potential and influential clients, *and* it was about time she got out and had some fun. So Laura had gone with Gus, and Roger hadn't shown anyway, which did not surprise Tom at all, though it did disappoint him a little for it confirmed what he'd pretty much realized already, that now that the *Saturday Journal* was on the streets, swords had been drawn.

The festivities were being held on the roof of the *Journal*'s building. Conscious of the foregone conclusions of doom that had been circulating around the newspaper community almost ever since his declaration of intent had first been publicized, Tom had realized that people needed to be convinced that a commitment to honesty did not preclude fun or entertainment. A marquee, lined with newsprint and some specially commissioned cartoons by Klug, the *Journal*'s political cartoonist, had been erected in case of rain, but in the event, with the day's sunshine tapering into a clear, mild evening, it stood open all along one side so that the guests could enjoy unimpeded views over the river. Those present, apart from staff and freelance writers, included competitors from tabloid and broadsheet papers—though few journalists from the Sundays, since most of them were still sweating over their last-minute pieces—politicians, actors, bankers and backers. Laura and Gus, straining to pick up scraps of useful gossip and, hopefully, compliments for the food and organization of the party, heard at least a dozen people saying that the *Journal* couldn't last, because though it was clear that Bailey had honorable intentions, in the first place he was an American and in the second, he was apparently a gentleman, so how could he hope to survive? Anyway, although the two new Saturday papers might have the advantage of beating the other weeklies to the draw on a lot of stories, they would be laying themselves open, like bodies on a slab, to being dissected by their potent rivals every Sunday morning—and besides, what was a weekly newspaper without Saturday sport?

"They're saying Tom doesn't have a chance," Gus whispered to Laura, at about eleven o'clock.

"I think some of it's sour grapes," Laura whispered back. "I've heard people say he's snapped up some of the best writers in the business." She moved even closer to Gus, to be sure that no one else heard her. "David Giles, the features editor, has been turfed off three other papers because of his principles, but I gather he's absolutely brilliant."

"Have you seen the sports editor? When I heard it was a woman, I thought she'd be big and butch, but she's gorgeous."

"Her name's Sandra something," Laura said. "She's Irish, and she plays football and cricket."

While Laura had dressed carefully, in a cream linen dress, straight cut with a short skirt, hoping to look attractive but suitably executive, Gus had revived some of her old punkiness, though she had toned it down so that what had sometimes appeared aggressive now simply looked sparky and original.

"One of us ought to make sure we talk to the diary editor," Gus said. "We might get a mention next week."

"I think he's called Rupert something." Laura peered around.

"If it's a bloke it had better be you."

"Don't be silly, Gus."

"I'm being realistic. You look dead sexy tonight."

"I wanted to look businesslike."

"I don't know about that, but you look rich."

Laura winced. "I don't, do I?"

"Don't be such a snob." Gus grinned. "You can't give money a bad name just because Ambler had so much of it."

Tom Bailey thought that Laura looked sexy, too. In fact, even tonight, when he was being stretched in more directions than he could count, he kept finding his eyes, and his thoughts, coming back to her, however much he reminded himself that it was inappropriate. It wasn't just that she was beautiful—though he did find her quite fiercely lovely, with that curtain of silky black hair and the white skin and those intense green eyes, and that delectable, curiously accented voice; it was also the mixture of inner courage and vulnerability that he had first noticed in New York when they'd gone horseback riding together, and he remembered, too, that the plucky aspect of her character had surprised him that day, for it had been so much less evident in the Trump Tower apartment with Ambler, and he realized now that many things about Laura had perhaps been suppressed by her husband.

It was the inescapable fact that she was still married to Roger Ambler that was keeping Tom from asking her to have dinner with him. He recalled that in New York, when Ambler had insisted that Laura did not ride again, he had experienced a certain relief, for he had recognized even then that he was attracted to her—more attracted than he had been to any woman since Julie. Maybe after the divorce was through, maybe once the dust had finally settled, he might feel differently—though by then, of course, Laura would have been seized upon by any number of eligible men. But in the meantime, in spite of the rift between himself and Ambler, Tom still felt there would be something improper about inviting his ex-friend's wife to share anything more intimate than lunch or an innocent morning's horseback riding.

He was a graceful man, Laura thought, observing him through a sea of champagne-swilling people. He was so tall that he had to stoop to talk to most of his guests, and twice she had seen him accidentally bump into someone, and yet there was still that gentle, humorous grace about him. He was impeccably dressed tonight, in a suit that was probably Italian, with a floral silk tie that was probably French, and glancing down at his feet, she saw that he was not even wearing the accustomed boots that had given him his nickname; yet still his dark brown hair flopped onto his forehead, and still it seemed to Laura that, in spite of the fact that Tom Bailey was decidedly in command of the evening and more than a match intellectually for anyone at the party, he looked like an American who belonged on a ranch, and probably on the back of a horse, rather than here on this English rooftop, among a whole bunch of men and women who would drink his champagne and then gladly watch him, metaphorically at least, tipped over the edge.

She recognized that she was attracted to him, and she thought that the attraction might be mutual. But she knew that there was nothing either of them would do about it, because she was still married to Roger, and because Tom Bailey was a decent man. In any case, it was too soon for her, she was still too wounded by the experience, and as she had told Gus, she ought to have learned her lesson by now, and this was not the kind of man for a girl like herself, who had been through what she had been through, who had done what she had done. And besides, Bailey had already helped her and Gus twice, and he had been able to do that because of his power and his money, and Laura was bitterly aware that those were the things that had attracted her to Roger Ambler, and she was afraid, now, of the seduction of wealth.

CHAPTER 19

Roger Ambler had never been a man to let emotion get the better of him. All through his adult life, even through the losses of his parents, through his first two divorces, he had remained able to prioritize. The Ambler Corporation had always come first. It had to, because it was the biggest and best part of his life. It was him.

By the middle of June, the anger that had been building inside him since he had returned to Paris before Christmas and found Laura gone, was showing signs of taking on uncomfortable proportions. The fact that she had left him at all had shocked him, and the added insult of her note in which she'd made it clear that she would not even try to break their prenuptial agreement, had aggrieved more than relieved him. The knowledge that marrying Laura Andros had been a gross judgment error—the private awareness that he'd wasted five years on an aberration—had really stung him.

"How could you?" Rona had asked him, over and over again. "How could you have been so foolish as to marry a girl like that? And why, in God's name, didn't you *tell* me about her?"

He had assumed Laura would be easy to forget. He had concluded, swiftly, that he was better off without her. He had also resolved that the time would come when he would make her pay. Since she was no dumb bimbo—she would almost certainly have made a more enjoyable wife if she had been—Laura must know that he would not let her off scot-free. But she would just have to wait for her punishment. And in the meantime, he would get on with the real business of being Roger Ambler, and leave her to sweat it out.

It was her connection with Tom Bailey that had really begun to goad him. Roger had been forced, lately, to admit that Bailey had been another error of judgment. He had never given the younger man enough credit. He had assumed that all that enthusiasm and idealism would knock him out of any kind of race against the hard men who powered the British newspaper industry, and yet there Bailey was, his *Journal* more than a month old and still arousing interest. And there was his estranged wife, the murderous, conniving little bitch, running her own company with her thieving Polish weirdo friend and doing well to boot, only because Bailey had stepped in to bail her out. Roger knew that he could have done more to stop Laura's little venture, but experience told him to bide his time, reminded him that the more ground she gained, the higher she managed to climb and the more respect she won, the more damage he would ultimately be able to inflict on her. And in any event, Laura was no longer of sufficient importance to waste valuable energy on.

The *Courier* was on the streets too, now, and most of the smart money was on his baby to kick the *Journal*'s ass to kingdom come before starting to take on the real competition. With the king's ransom he had personally poured into the *Courier*, they had royal color spreads, the raunchiest, hardest-hitting gossip column in the land, the hottest contests with the most extravagant prizes, a pull-out sport section that had already won praise for its practical layout and they had, in the space of one month, scooped the other weeklies on two minor political scandals. Though the *Saturday Courier*, of course, and the northern newspaper group that had provided Roger with his entry point into the UK, were just a minor part of his corporate world. Ambler Shoes was going from strength to strength, still swallowing up smaller manufacturers and retail outlets throughout the United States; Ambler Computers was expanding all the time, and while Roger knew they would never be a match for IBM or Apple or Digital, they were still considered com-

ers to be reckoned with; Ambler Machinery continued to
cause concern, had never wholly recovered from the strikes
that had almost crippled the company during the seventies,
but that frailty was more than adequately compensated for
by the agencies, which Roger still liked to regard as the human side of his corporation.

His critics said that his holdings were too disparate, that
there had never been any passionate focus to his career, and
that that would always keep him from becoming a major
force. Roger didn't give a damn what they said. Even Arnold
Ambler, whose ambitions had been dwarflike and plodding
compared to his son's, had shared Roger's belief that eggs
were best placed in separate, secure baskets. Sure, he would
never be a Sulzberger or Thomson, or a Conrad Black or a
Murdoch, but Roger was something that the majority of his
jealous, carping critics would never be. He was very, very
rich.

The *Saturday Courier* was the closest he had ever come to
being passionate about any commercial venture. So far as
Roger was concerned, if a business did not pull its weight,
he closed it down. But in the case of this newspaper, he
knew already that he would give it a more than average
chance. For one thing, he could not contemplate failure so
long as the *Journal* still survived. And for another, in the
same way that Arnold Ambler had wanted Zero Publishing
because he'd believed there was honor in books, Roger
wanted the prestige of being the proprietor of a British
newspaper.

It was dignity, he supposed, that he wanted, however
much he might deny that publicly. And perhaps a measure of
respect, not solely from those who needed or feared him.
Laura had humiliated him in a hundred different ways, by
rejecting him, by failing to give him children, by running
out on him and choosing comparative poverty over his
wealth—and now she had deliberately sought to humiliate
him further by going to Bailey for help.

His life was filled with boardroom meetings, with power
dinners, with stock markets and the expansion of his offshore bank accounts in Switzerland and Luxembourg and
Liechtenstein, with introductions to high-ranking politicians

in the United States and in Britain. He had asked Rona to organize the redecoration of both the Paris and Trump Tower apartments, to rid them of the memory of Laura's presence. Available women were back on his scent, parading themselves at every opportunity, and when Roger was staying at discreet hotels around the world, he made up for the disappointments with Laura by fucking his way through the best range of young, tight-assed prostitutes he could buy.

He did not miss Laura at all. But neither did he forget her.

CHAPTER 20

On the last Thursday night in September 1989, Gus was raped. She was walking back to the flat from Chalk Farm tube station when two men dragged her off the pavement into the front garden of a small, dark house. They stuffed her own scarf into her mouth to stop her from screaming, and then they pushed her, kicking and scratching, down onto the grass, pulled up her skirt, tore down her tights and panties and took her one at a time. One of them held a Stanley knife close to her right ear and knelt on her chest so that she could hardly breathe, while the other man raped her, and then they changed places and did it again.

Gus lay very still when they had gone, afraid they might come back. She could still smell them, their body odor and their semen and the cheap aftershave one of them had worn. She could still hear them, their grunting, their cursing, their abuse. No one had seen the attack. She was hidden from the road by bushes, and the house that the garden belonged to appeared deserted. No one came to help.

When she felt sure they would not return, she got up off the grass, put the torn panties and tights into her bag, pulled down her skirt and began to walk home. She was in pain, but she hardly noticed it. There was blood trickling down her legs, but she didn't notice that either. Two girls, walking on the other side of the street, stared at her. She knew she was covered in grass and dirt, but it made no difference to her.

Had Laura been awake when she got in, Gus might have told her, but Laura was already asleep in bed, so Gus put all her clothes into a bin liner and stuck that into the rubbish bin, and then she ran a bath, as hot as she could bear it. She knew she was doing what they told women not to do after they had been assaulted, knew she was washing away evidence, but she did not care about that. She no longer cared about anything.

"You all right?" Laura asked next morning, at breakfast.

"Fine," Gus said.

Laura glanced at her for a moment, and Gus thought that perhaps, after all, something did show, and in her mind, silently, she cried out for Laura to ask her what was wrong with her, but then Laura just went on drinking her coffee, and Gus said nothing at all.

Five days later, after she and Gus had spent a morning together doing their company accounts, because Laura was insistent that they keep that side of the business up to date and accurate at all times, Laura went off to a meeting with Ned and Kerry Archer. When she returned to the flat, there was a message on the answering machine telling her that Gus had been admitted to the Middlesex Hospital.

She wasted no time trying to phone, just ran frantically downstairs and flagged down a taxi on Chalk Farm Road, praying all the way there. Gus was okay. At least, she had cut one leg quite badly, a staff nurse told Laura, and they were keeping her in for observation because she had struck her head, but otherwise her injuries were all minor.

"Which is almost miraculous, considering," the nurse, a young woman with brown curls, round cheeks and a Glasgow accent told Laura before she was allowed in to see Gus.

"Why? I don't know what happened to her."

"Your friend tried to commit suicide," the nurse said, gently.

Laura stared at her. "I don't believe you."

"I'm afraid it's true. Apparently she tried to jump in front of a tube train." She paused. "At Tottenham Court Road."

"You mean she fell?"

"No. There's no doubt. Someone saw her get ready to do it—a young man waiting for the train. He got there just in time to drag her back. He saved her life."

They were in the sister's office, a small cubbyhole of a room with white walls and an orange curtain on the windows. Laura sank down onto one of the chairs.

"I can't believe it."

"It must be a shock, I know."

Laura looked up at her. "We were together all morning. We were doing the books—Gus was fine."

"Is that what she likes to be called? We've been calling her Augusta—it was on a donor card in her bag." The staff nurse sat down on the other chair. "She gave you no indication then, of what she might do?"

"None at all." Her voice was low, almost a whisper.

"She hasn't seemed particularly down? Nothing's happened?"

Laura shook her head, still hardly registering what she had been told.

"Have you known Gus long?"

"Since we were kids."

"You know she's tried it before, don't you?"

Laura was silent. Memories came back, Gus returning to Finborough Road in the early days, the scars on her wrists.

"It was seven years ago. Things had been pretty terrible for her. She promised she'd never do it again." *I want to live.* She remembered Gus saying that, either before or after they went to fetch her things from the squat she'd been living in.

"I gather she has no family," the nurse said.

"None. I'm her family."

"That's good. She's going to need you."

"Has she said anything? About why?"

"Only that she wanted you to think it was an accident. Other than that, she's said nothing to give us any clues. Except that—" She stopped.

"What?" Laura knew there was more. "Except what?"

"She's quite bruised," the nurse said.

"From the fall, you mean?"

"No, not from that. She has quite a few nasty bruises. Some of them are on her thighs. On the inside." The staff nurse paused. "It looks as if someone may have been violent with her. Do you know if Gus is seeing anyone?"

"You mean a man?" Laura was staring again, in fresh horror. "Gus never dates men." She shook her head quickly. "I don't mean she's gay, either—she just doesn't go out with men."

"Anyway"—the nurse glanced at the clock on the wall—"that's all I can tell you. I thought you ought to know, for Gus's sake. The bruising may be completely irrelevant."

"Or it may not be," Laura said. The thought that someone might have hurt Gus was too painful to cope with. "What happens now?" she asked.

"She'll be seen by a psychiatrist—that's routine, in suicide cases. She's bound to recommend some counseling, but that'll be up to Gus, of course."

"Can I see her?"

"Certainly."

They both stood up.

"Don't press her too much right away," the nurse advised. "Though it's up to you, of course. She's quite shaken up, and the doctor in casualty gave her a mild sedative."

"Maybe she won't want to see me."

"I expect she will."

"I know it's silly," Laura said, "but I feel scared of seeing her."

"That's quite normal," the nurse said. "It's a bit like swimming—better once you're in. Just be yourself with her—just let her know you're on her side."

"She'll know that."

"All the same, it won't hurt to confirm it."

Gus was always pale-skinned, but now she was ashen. She had always been thin, but now, in the skimpy hospital gown, she looked suddenly frail, her crazy hair a shock of red on the pillow. There was a dressing on her forehead, and her injured leg was hidden under the bedclothes. There were no tubes, no drips, nothing to alarm, yet inwardly Laura felt herself recoil.

"I'm sorry," Gus said. Her voice was hoarse, and Laura thought she might have been crying. "I botched it."

"Thank God." The curtains around the bed were drawn, giving them privacy. There was a plastic chair against the wall, and Laura moved it to the side of the bed and sat down. She took Gus's right hand and held it, gently. "Can you tell me why?"

"Not in here." Her lower lip was chapped, as if she'd bitten it. "Maybe at home. I ought to tell you, I suppose."

"Only if you want to. Though I wish you would."

"It wasn't your fault," Gus said, suddenly, as if it had just struck her that Laura might think it was. "Nothing to do with you—with us."

"How are you feeling?" Laura asked. "Does your head hurt?"

"Bit of a headache, nothing much. My leg's throbbing a bit." Gus shut her eyes for a moment. "They gave me something, some kind of dope."

"Just a sedative, the nurse said."

"What else did she say?"

Laura hesitated. "She said you were bruised."

"She'd be bruised, too, if someone rugby tackled her on a tube platform."

"He saved your life."

Gus winced. "Poor bloke. I swore at him."

"The nurse said some of the bruises had nothing to do with what happened today," Laura said.

Gus didn't answer.

Laura kept hold of her hand. "Did someone hurt you, Gus?"

"I told you, I don't want to talk about it." Gus took her hand away.

"Okay."

"They said I've got to stay here tonight."

"Just for observation."

"Could you get me some stuff? Toothbrush, bit of makeup, that sort of thing. And something to wear—I ripped my jeans."

"I ran out of the flat without thinking," Laura said. "I'll go and get it now. What else? Something to read?"

"If you like."

Laura knew Gus wanted her to go, but she stayed where she was.

"They noticed the old scars, Gus."

"I know. They're going to send a shrink to talk to me."

"The nurse told me."

"I won't talk to him," Gus said.

"I think she said it would be a woman."

"I won't talk to any shrink, and I won't talk to a counselor, either."

"Then you'll have to talk to me," Laura said.

"Maybe."

Laura took Gus home next morning. She never spoke for the duration of the journey, and when they got into the flat, she limped straight into her room and lay down on the bed.

"I think I'll take a nap."

"Good idea."

Laura let her sleep for two hours. Every now and again, consumed by the fear that Gus might jump out of her bedroom window, or that she might have a hoard of sleeping pills, she put her head around the door, then quietly shut it again. Gus lay on her back, on top of the covers, her eyes closed, yet Laura felt she was not really asleep.

At lunchtime, she knocked on the door before opening it.

"I've made some soup," she said. "Fancy some?"

"If you like."

"Do you want it in there, or will you come out?"

"In here."

"Wouldn't you rather come out?"

"Okay, I'll come out." Gus sounded tetchy.

"Good," Laura said.

She watched Gus finish a bowlful of vegetable soup, and refuse a second serving. She had no real appetite herself, was too nervous for food.

"I'm not going to talk," Gus said.

"Not if you're not ready."

"Stop being so bloody gentle." Gus stood up abruptly from the table, almost knocking over her chair. "You're acting like one of them."

"One of who?"

"The nurses, the doctors, all soothing and patronizing."

"I'm not patronizing," Laura said.

"I know you're not." Gus sat down again, in the armchair by the window. She stared out into the garden. "I was raped."

Laura felt a tightness in her chest. She waited.

"Last week," Gus went on. "On Thursday night." She licked her dry lips. "They must have followed me from the station. Two of them."

"You didn't say anything," Laura whispered, aghast.

"You were asleep," Gus said, simply. "And then, in the morning, I couldn't talk about it. I couldn't stand to."

Laura didn't know what to do. She wanted to get up and go to Gus, to put her arms around her, but something stopped her, blocked the closeness.

"That wasn't the reason," Gus said, quietly. "That wasn't why I wanted to die. Not just the rape."

"Then what?" There was pain in Laura's voice.

"That's what I can't talk about. Not yet."

Suddenly, Laura thought she knew.

"Was it something that happened in prison?" she asked.

And Gus stood up and left the room.

She didn't come out again until almost six o'clock. She looked at Laura, who had been sitting on the sofa for most of the afternoon, waiting, not knowing what else to do but wait.

"It started in borstal," she said, and sat down in the armchair.

Laura sat up. Gus's voice was so quiet it was hard to hear.

"Or I suppose it started before that, at home."

"Your father."

Gus nodded. "He didn't—you know. He had a go once, but I told him I'd kill him if he ever touched me again, and he believed me." She could see him still, in her mind, after so many years, crouching naked by her bed, a thief in the night, disgusting, sickening. She blinked, to clear away the image, and went on. "I got bashed a lot in the borstal. I thought I was so tough, but I soon learned. Three of them had a go at me one night, held me down and . . ." Her voice trailed away.

"Don't go on if it's too hard," Laura said, softly.

Gus swallowed. "Might as well. I don't mind you knowing." She paused. "It was more humiliating than anything, I suppose. They just used their hands, didn't have anything else, didn't know much more. They were just kids, like me."

"Not like you," Laura said.

"Maybe not." Gus's eyes were quite dry, but she pulled a tissue out of her sleeve and wiped her nose. "I got sharper after that, learned to look after myself, got up to their level, you know? And they never got me again, but that didn't stop the nightmares."

Laura waited a few moments.

"What about Holloway?"

"It was worse there."

Laura sat in silence.

"It was only a couple of them. Most of the women were okay, but these two were right bastards." She stopped again. "They used things—"

"Gus, don't."

"I want to." Her gray eyes were full of pain. "It's all in my head, anyway—it's never really gone away, I just kidded myself it did." She twisted the tissue in her hands, her fingers shredding it. "They used whatever they could get—I never knew where they got half of it. And they liked hurting you more than anything."

Laura felt sick. She thought about Ambler and his little black box. She thought about telling Gus, but it wouldn't help her, and it wouldn't wipe the memories out of her mind, so what was the point?

"And then there was last Thursday night." Gus looked at Laura, then looked away, out of the window again. "They had a knife."

"For God's sake, Gus, you have to tell the police."

"What for?" Gus asked harshly. "It wouldn't mean it hadn't happened."

"You know what for. To stop them doing it again."

"They wouldn't catch them. I can't even describe them."

"Maybe you could, if you really tried."

"I don't want to try," Gus said, still hard. "Anyway, I kept my eyes closed most of the time. And it was dark." She paused. "They grabbed me right off the pavement and dragged me behind some bushes in a garden. It's a house just round the corner, not far at all, I was nearly home."

"And I was in bed asleep." Laura shook her head. "Oh, Gus, I'm so sorry."

"You didn't rape me."

"But I was *asleep*."

"Don't be stupid," Gus said. "Don't you want to know what they did?"

"Only if it's going to help you."

"They got me on the ground—on the grass, my feet in the flower bed, the soil was really cold under my heels. One of them got on top of me, kneeled right on my chest and held the knife next to my face, and the other pulled down my tights and my knickers and did it." The tissue was all shredded, on the carpet, but Gus's fingers went on working. "My first time with a man, kid." Her voice was hoarse again, as it had been in the Middlesex. "My first real fuck. And then they changed places, and there was my second."

Laura stood up then, went to her, put her arms around her, but Gus pushed her away, got up and limped into the bathroom. Laura heard her throwing up, over and over again, and she stood in the sitting room, hands clenched into fists of helpless rage, and she knew there was nothing she could do to help her, because there was nothing she could do to change anything that had happened. After a long time, Gus came out of the bathroom, and her face was almost as white as it had been yesterday in the hospital, even though she'd put some makeup on that morning.

"I'm sorry," she said, "about what I did. I know I promised you I'd never do it again, but I didn't think I could stand it anymore, not after—" She couldn't go on, and the tears were starting at last, welling up in her eyes, choking her. "I wanted to do it so you'd think it was an accident—I didn't want you to know, but I screwed it up—" She wiped her eyes with the back of her hand.

Laura went to her again, tried to embrace her again, but Gus couldn't bear it, couldn't stand to be held. "Gus," she said, and she was crying, too. "Gus, please don't say you screwed up."

Gus opened her bedroom door. "I could have taken pills, but I know you, you would have blamed yourself, and it wasn't anything to do with you."

"If I was such a great friend, you would have been able to tell me."

"See? You're doing it already—for Christ's sake, Laura, you didn't rape me—you had nothing to *do* with it—you've got such an *ego*—"

"I'm sorry." Laura swallowed her own tears. "I'm just selfish, that's all. I don't want to lose you—you're my best friend in the world."

"I know that."

"Then let me help you."

"How?"

"I don't know yet. We've got to tell someone what happened. We've got to at least report it to the police, in case those men are still around."

"You tell them if you want." Gus's chin went up. "But I'm not going to go through it all again, and I won't let one of their doctors touch me—you tell them that."

"If that's what you want."

"And I don't want to talk to anyone else about it either, so don't start getting ideas about calling a shrink."

"What about one of those victim support groups?"

"No one." Gus was adamant. "No one."

"All right," Laura said. "I won't call anyone."

Laura brought Gus her dinner on a tray, and soon after, Laura went to bed too, but she couldn't sleep at all, and in the middle of the night, a little after three, she heard a strange and awful sound, and she realized that it was Gus sobbing, and it tore at her almost more than her dreadful stories had done. She got out of bed and went to Gus's door, but then the sound stopped, and she didn't feel it was right to intrude, and she lay down on the sofa so that she would hear if the weeping began again, and dozed until it was light.

Gus agreed to make a statement to the police, but for six days after that she never spoke at all, and Laura grew terrified of what she might do. And then, with unnerving suddenness, Gus seemed to return, but she never mentioned either the rape or any of the past horrors, and Laura didn't dare bring up the subjects. They went on almost as normal. Laura Andros Associates was up and running now, and doing better than either of them had hoped, and Gus participated in the business much as she had done before, and continued to run her stall at Camden Lock, but she never went out after dark unless she had no choice, and Laura felt that she was only partly there, and that she was deeply depressed.

In the eighteen months that had passed since the launch of Tom Bailey's *Journal,* Laura and Tom had seen one another at regular intervals, usually for lunch, generally taken on the run, and from time to time they had gone horseback riding, trying out different stables in different counties. They had become good friends. Laura had met Sam, Tom's dog, and Tom had told her that the red maple tree that she had bought for them was flourishing, and that one of these days she must come to the house in Chelsea and visit it, but that day had not yet come. It made Laura happy to be just friends with Tom. She was aware that he still thought her attractive, and especially aware that had she been interested in getting involved with any man, there was no one she'd have picked above Tom, but as it was, she had been bitten the once, and she was in no rush to make the same mistakes again.

One morning in early November, more than a month after Gus had tried to throw herself under the train, Tom called Laura to issue her with an advance invitation for a Thanksgiving dinner at his house.

"There's a catch," he said.

"I have to cook?"

"Not quite that big a catch, but I did hope you could have one of your people take care of the evening. Liz would be my first choice, but if she's got a booking already, I trust you to choose." After a shaky start the previous year, Ned and Kerry Archer had taken on all the day-to-day catering requirements for the *Journal,* though Tom still preferred Liz Browning to take care of more distinguished events.

"Sounds perfect," Laura said, grabbing her diary. "That's

the twenty-third, isn't it? Or is it the thirtieth, I'm not sure, I'm ashamed to say."

"Last Thursday in November," Tom said. "Do you think Gus might be free, too?"

Laura hesitated. "I'm not sure."

He caught the note in her voice. "Something wrong?"

"Nothing. Not with me, anyway."

"What's up with Gus?"

Laura didn't answer. Suddenly, she had the greatest urge to confide in Tom Bailey. All her instincts told her she could trust him, and yet she knew she would be betraying Gus if she did.

"Laura? What's the matter? Is she sick or something?"

"Or something," Laura said. She paused a moment longer. "She's very depressed."

"Depressed about something, or just blue?"

"Definitely the first."

Tom got the message. "And I shouldn't be asking."

"On the contrary, I think I want you to ask. But I'm less sure that I should be answering."

"Because it's Gus's business. I can respect that." Tom paused. "But I know how much you guys depend on each other, and so I guess you're trying to help her now, am I right?"

"I don't seem to know how to help her, that's the trouble," Laura said.

"Which is your business. And since I hope I'm your friend, too, maybe I could try to help you out with that?"

"Maybe you could."

They met for lunch the next day. Because they were nearing the end of the week and the craziest time for the *Journal*, Tom asked Laura if she wouldn't mind coming into the office and making do with one of Ned and Kerry's sandwiches. With Annette, his secretary, primed to allow only the most urgent calls through to Tom, they shut the door and sat in the gray leather armchairs near the picture windows with their wonderful river views.

"Did you ever see such a long couch?" Tom asked.

"No, I never did," Laura agreed.

"I had to have it custom-made for my cat naps. It's odd, I can get by at night with hardly any sleep, but I have to be able to put my feet up for the odd ten minutes during the day."

"It would have to be pretty long then." Laura smiled at him. He was wearing jeans, a black turtleneck sweater and his cowboy boots. He looked like almost anything but the owner-editor of a weekly British newspaper.

"So let's talk about Gus," Tom said. "Or rather, why don't you talk, and I'll just listen. That's if you want to."

"I want to," Laura said.

She kept it brief and uncolorful. Without telling him where these events had taken place, she told him that Gus had endured three separate episodes of sexual abuse in her life, under different circumstances, and that at the end of September, she had been the victim of a rape, and that this had led to her trying to commit suicide.

"She opened up to me after I got her home from hospital," Laura told Tom, "but it was almost as if she felt obliged to explain to me what she'd done. And she talked about botching the attempt, as if she was sorry that man had saved her life."

"And you're afraid she may try it again?"

"I'm terrified she may try again." Laura paused. "It isn't the first time, Tom. She cut her wrists once, about seven years ago, after—"

"After?"

Laura shook her head. "I can't tell you that—anyway, I'm not even sure. It was during a period that Gus and I were apart." She stood up, too restless to sit still any longer. "She won't talk about it at all now, and I just feel she's so depressed, so *lost,* and it scares me."

Tom, too, stood up. "Just wait a few minutes, will you?"

"If you're too busy, I can leave—"

He was already at the door. "I'm not too busy—just give me a little while, okay?"

"Of course."

He came back almost a quarter of an hour later. Laura was pacing.

"I'm sorry. It took longer than I thought."

"Don't worry." Laura made herself sit again. "My time isn't anywhere near as valuable as yours."

"I'm not sure that's true." He sat on the long couch, close to her chair. He had a piece of notepaper in his right hand. "I've been speaking to a friend of mine—she's a doctor, a consultant at one of your teaching hospitals, with about a million contacts."

"You didn't—"

"No names, nothing too specific. I just told her we were talking about a young woman with a history of sexual abuse from childhood on, culminating in a rape, resulting in a suicide attempt." Tom held up the piece of paper. "She can't recommend this place highly enough. It sounds ideal—somewhere for Gus to go to where she can talk to experts in her own time, without too much pressure—"

"It won't work," Laura interrupted. "I'm sorry, Tom. Gus wouldn't agree to go anywhere, she's made that more than clear. I meant it when I said I thought she only told me anything about it because she felt obligated. She refused to talk to the doctors or nurses at the Middlesex, and I don't think she said so much as good morning to their psychiatrist."

"Maybe if you tried again now?"

"I think it might do more harm than good. I think she might leave the flat, and then God alone knows what she might do."

"Christ," Tom said, and tossed the piece of paper onto his coffee table.

"I'm so sorry," Laura said again. "I've taken up your time, and now you've bothered a busy doctor—"

"Will you stop apologizing?"

She fell silent.

"I'd like to get my hands on the bastards who raped her," he said.

"I know," Laura said. "But there's no real hope of anyone getting their hands on them. And anyway, we wouldn't be going back far enough to repair all the damage."

"I guess not." Tom looked grim. "There's only one sure way to heal all that, and that's time and space, and people who care." He was quiet for a few moments. "So if you're certain Gus won't talk to a therapist, we'll just have to take care of her ourselves."

"Not we," Laura said. "It's down to me."

"Why not we?" Tom asked. "I know I haven't seen that much of her, but I've grown fond of Gus—she seems a pretty special person. I'd at least like to try to help." He paused again. "We could make sure she spends as little time alone as possible, without crowding her. Do you think she might like to come riding with us?"

Laura found she could hardly answer. She just looked at him, into his warm brown eyes. "Why are you so kind?" she asked, curiously. "You're the busiest man I know, and yet you always make time to help me out."

"Some things are more important than business, wouldn't you agree?"

"I would." Laura paused. "Some people wouldn't."

"You're talking about Roger."

"Yes."

"I'm not Roger."

"No," Laura said. "You're not."

"Anyway," Tom added, "when have I ever helped you before?"

"How about the bank loan?" she said, steadily.

"Who said I had anything to do with that?"

"No one." Laura kept looking at him. "Some things don't need to be said."

He smiled. "I guess they don't."

They both tried to do whatever they could to give Gus a sense of security. If she knew what Laura and Tom—when he could manage the time—were doing, she gave no indication, nor did she object. It was a little like leading an acquiescent child around from treat to treat and then safely home again, and that was so entirely unlike Gus that as the weeks passed, Laura grew increasingly despondent.

And then, four days before Christmas, the police telephoned to say that they had arrested two men on suspicion of a series of rapes in the Hampstead area, and that they needed Gus to attend an identification parade.

"But I don't know what they looked like." For the first

time in almost three months, Gus looked terrified. "I told you then I had my eyes closed most of the time."

"Most of the time, perhaps." Laura spoke gently, carefully. "But maybe if you were to see them again—"

"I couldn't. They can't make me."

"No, of course they can't. But think how good it would be to see them locked away so they couldn't hurt anyone else."

Gus looked hunted, like an animal. "Why can't someone else do it?"

"I suppose they will be."

"Then they won't need me."

"Apparently they do."

For several minutes, Gus said nothing, and Laura, too, sat in silence.

"Would you come with me?" Gus asked, at last.

"Of course I would." Laura paused. "Does that mean you'll do it?"

Gus didn't answer.

"Gus?"

"Maybe," she said.

Laura went with her to the police station in Rosslyn Hill. The officers were all kind to Gus, offered her cups of tea and chairs at each stage of the procedure, but Gus was as taut as stretched elastic, and Laura was afraid she would snap, and couldn't they just please get on with it so that she could get her home safe and sound again? But they'd arrived a little early, and the gathering of the men who would take part in the parade was running a little late, and so they had to sit in a small, bleak office furnished with only a bare, ink-stained desk, a pair of gray steel filing cabinets and two chairs.

"It'll be fine," Laura said, softly.

"Yeah," Gus replied, and her jaw was clenched so tightly that the word came out almost like a grunt.

"They can't hurt you, Gus."

But of course they'd already done that.

When Gus saw the lineup of men, she began to tremble from head to foot. The inspector supervising the parade let her smoke, but she couldn't even hold the cigarette, and one of the other officers present took it gently out of her fingers.

"Take as much time and care as you wish," the inspector told her. "Walk past the line at least twice, please."

There were fourteen men in the line. Gus looked for a long time.

"I don't know," she said, at last.

"Are either of the persons you saw on this parade?" the inspector asked.

"I don't *know*," Gus said again, and her eyes were a little wild. "They all look like ordinary blokes—they all look the *same*." She paused. "Maybe if I could hear them speak."

"You cannot identify any persons on the parade by appearance only?"

"That's what she said," Laura said through gritted teeth. She longed to get Gus out of the narrow, oppressive room, away from those men, but more than anything, she wanted Gus to be able to identify the rapists and to start to put it behind her.

"They didn't say much, but I might remember their voices."

"What would you like them to say?"

Gus didn't answer.

"It might help to have them say something your attackers said that night," the inspector said.

"Vocabulary wasn't their strong point," Gus said. "Mostly they just called me fucking bitch, things like that."

"Anything else?"

"They said I was ugly."

"What did they say, exactly? Do you remember?"

"Yes, I remember."

"Are you okay, Gus?" Laura asked.

"Stop struggling, you ugly cow." Gus's mouth turned up in a semblance of humor. "That's what one of them said."

Laura closed her eyes.

"Is that what you'd like them to say now?" the inspector asked.

"Yes."

The men were asked if they were willing to say the words, and they agreed, but it made no difference.

"No go," the inspector said outside the room, and shook his head. "I know it's been hard for you, Miss Pietrowski. I'm sorry it didn't work out."

"Me, too," Gus said.

Laura looked at Gus. She was chalky white. "Are you all right?"

Gus nodded. "Can we get out of here?" Her voice was throaty.

"Of course we can," Laura said.

The only time Gus spoke about it for the rest of that day was just after Laura poured her a glass of wine at seven o'clock that evening.

"I don't think I could have gone to court," she said.

"No," Laura said. "At least that's something."

"Except I don't know if they're still out there."

"If they are, they're not anywhere near here," Laura said. "You said you thought they followed you from the tube—they could be anywhere in London."

"I don't mean they'd come after me," Gus said. "I'm not scared of that."

"Good."

At three in the morning, Gus started screaming. Laura ran into her room, and found her huddled in the corner on the floor, eyes wide and terrified, arms flung up cradling her head as if to protect herself.

"Gus, it's all right!" She got down onto the floor beside her, and tried to put her arms around her, but Gus flinched and pushed her away so hard that Laura almost fell. "Gus, you've had a nightmare, it's okay now—" She put one hand out, carefully, touched Gus's shoulder, wanting to bring her back from her night terror or whatever it was that had driven her from her bed. "Gus, darling Gus, you're all right—"

Gus began to cry. She covered her face with her hands, and she began to sob, great wracking sobs that shook her whole body.

"That's better," Laura said. "That's good." She watched her uncertainly, not knowing whether to try to hold her again or not. "Let it out, that's right, let it go."

Gus went on crying. She sat there, still hunched over in the corner of her bedroom, and she went on and on, and Laura began to feel afraid all over again, because it was going on too long, and they weren't the normal, healing tears she had hoped for, and she didn't know what to do for the best; and finally, when it was almost four o'clock, and Gus was still sitting on the floor, weeping, Laura left her for a few moments and went to telephone Tom.

"I'm sorry—I know it's the middle of the night—"

"What's up?" His voice was husky from sleep.

"It's Gus—she's falling apart."

Laura had told Tom about the identification parade, had called him afterward to tell him how brave Gus had been, and they'd both shared the same hope that even though she hadn't been able to pick out the men, it might still represent a closing of the episode.

"What's happening?" Tom asked, fully awake now.

Laura told him precisely. "I don't know what to do. I think she needs a doctor, but I don't have one—and anyway, they'd probably just give her something to make her sleep, and I'm not sure that's right."

"You think this might be some kind of breakthrough?"

"Or breakdown."

"I'm coming over," Tom said.

"You can't. It's four in the morning—"

"Would you rather I didn't come?"

"No," Laura said quickly. "I just don't want"—she paused—"I could really use your support."

"Do you mind if I call the friend I told you about a few weeks ago? The doctor?" Tom asked. "To get some advice."

"Please. Anything you think may help."

She put down the phone, and went back to Gus.

Tom brought the doctor along with him. He introduced her as Christine Morfield. She was about forty-five and pretty, with short fair hair and blue eyes, and she wore jeans and an anorak and not a trace of makeup, and Laura knew that Tom must have got her out of bed, too, and her gratitude knew no bounds.

"How is she?" Tom asked.

"The same. The sobbing stopped before I called you, but she's been crying ever since. It isn't even really crying—she's just sitting on the floor, and the tears are rolling down her face."

"May I go and see her?" Dr. Morfield asked Laura.

"Of course. Though I'm not sure how much she's registering."

Tom looked at Laura. "You're really scared, aren't you?"

"I've never seen her like this."

"We'll get her back," Tom said.

The doctor prescribed two kinds of pills, one to calm Gus's nerves, the other an antidepressant.

"They're both mild—I'd rather start that way."

"Laura hoped that wouldn't be the way you'd want to go," Tom said.

"Mightn't it just suppress it all again?" Laura asked.

"Not necessarily," Dr. Morfield said. "What I hope will happen is that Gus will get all the rest she needs after her ordeal—she's back in bed by the way—and then, as the antidepressants kick in—which may take a week or more—she'll find herself better able to face up to her fears."

"And then?"

"Then I'm afraid it's mostly up to Gus, as you know." Christine Morfield gave a small shrug. "It's possible that she may be one of those people who are so averse to talking to strangers about personal problems that they're genuinely better off getting over things their way. Perhaps Gus will find herself more able to share things with you two."

"Perhaps," Laura said.

"You look exhausted," Tom told her. "Why don't you get some sleep too? And then in the morning, you can pack whatever you need for yourself and Gus."

"What for?"

"You're coming to stay at my place over Christmas," he said.

"We can't do that." Laura was stunned.

"Give me one good reason why not."

"It's not fair on you."

"It's what I want, so that's no reason at all."

"Gus may not want to."

"I'll talk to Gus myself in the morning." Tom paused. "Anything else?"

Laura shook her head, hardly able to think.

"Good." He turned to Christine Morfield. "Figure she'll be okay now for what's left of the night?"

"She'll be fine for a good deal longer than that." The doctor looked at Laura. "But I'd recommend taking Tom up on his offer if I were you. Getting Gus into different surroundings might do her the world of good."

That day being Saturday, the *Journal* was out and Tom was free as a bird. At ten o'clock, he called Laura to say that he was on his way, and that if she hadn't packed yet, now was the moment to start.

"Gus is still sleeping," Laura said.

"Don't wake her. We'll figure out what to do when I get there."

He brought Sam with him.

"Never underestimate the power of a good dog," he told Laura. "If Gus is reluctant to listen to me, I think Sam may tip the balance."

Laura woke Gus gently, brought her a tray of tea and toast and honey, and Gus said she wasn't hungry, but then she ate both slices of toast, and Laura ran a warm bath for her, and put out her favorite baggy jeans and her snuggest scarlet pullover, and when Gus was dressed, she came out and Tom told her that they were all going to stay at his house for the holidays.

"Don't be daft," Gus said, but her voice was still a little fuzzy.

"Listen to me," Tom said, very gently, very firmly. "No one's ever going to hurt you again if Laura and I can help it. It's time you let yourself off the hook, Gus—open up as much as you want to, or not, if you don't—cry if you need to, and then just relax."

"I feel bloody relaxed already, after what the doc gave me."

"That's just for today. You're going to relax after that because you're going to be having a damned good time, okay?

We're going to have an honest to God, Grade A schmaltzy Christmas—carols, Midnight Mass, the whole shebang."

"We are?" Gus looked cagily at Laura.

"It's all news to me," Laura said.

"I suppose that's yours?" Gus noticed the black and white dog sitting near the front door. "The famous Sam." The dog pricked his pointed ears and wagged his bushy tail.

"He's here for extra persuasion, if you need it," Tom told her. "But you don't need it, do you? You're too smart not to know when you're beaten."

Laura didn't know how he'd managed it in such a short time, but everything at the house in Cheyne Walk was ready, as if Tom had always planned to have two young women to stay for Christmas. It was a narrow, three-story terraced house with a small back garden and a view of Albert Bridge and the Thames. Laura and Gus had separate rooms on the top floor, divided by a beautiful cozy bathroom, their beds had feather duvets and handmade American quilt covers, their towels were all white and pink, and all the furniture and knickknacks in the rooms were antique, a mixture of European and North American, the kind of items families collected on vacations.

Downstairs, despite the smallness of the rooms, there was a feeling of space and snugness, with log fires in the sitting room, dining room and den. Gus was enthralled, as far as the leftover effects of the sedative would allow her to be, by the kitchen, with its big gas stove that looked well-used but gleamed with cleaning, its even bigger refrigerator, very American, with an ice dispenser, its old-fashioned walk-in larder, and last, but certainly not least, its enormous oak table, the heart, so far as Gus was concerned, of her dream kitchen.

"She looks better already," Laura said to Tom, in the hall. It was a narrow but practical hallway, with hooks for raincoats and three pairs of Wellington boots immediately below, and a small antique mahogany table near the front door with a leather box stuffed with unopened mail.

"Didn't you tell me that Gus loves cooking?"

"She's always hankered after a kitchen like yours," Laura

said. "I'll never forget when she came to look at the apartment in Trump Tower—she was so appalled by how tiny Roger's kitchen was, and when I told her that most of the people there never bothered to cook because they went out to dinner, her face was a picture."

"Quite right, too," Tom agreed. "She can do as much cooking while you're here as she likes. Though Christmas dinner's all taken care of."

"Do you have a cook?"

"What for? I spend most of my life at the *Journal*—I do get to go out to restaurants more than I'd choose to, and when I'm lucky enough to spend time at home, I cook for myself." He grinned. "I'm not too bad, either."

"What happens to Sam when you're out?"

"I have a Spanish housekeeper called Grazia who comes in most days to clean up—she does most of my shopping, too, and runs errands. And sometimes Sam comes to the paper with me." Hearing his name, the dog came around the corner and sat at Tom's feet, wagging his tail, and Tom bent down to stroke his ears. "He's a great old boy, aren't you, Sam?"

"He can't be that old," Laura said. "Not the way he chases around when we go riding."

"Actually, being adopted, I don't know his real age, but I do know I wouldn't change him for all the pedigrees in town."

Gus emerged from the kitchen. "If you two want to go off and do something, don't worry about me."

"I was just going to say that to Tom," Laura said. "You must have things you were going to do today. Please don't give us a second thought."

"I have two gorgeous women under my roof," Tom said, "and you want me to go out and leave you? No chance."

Gus looked at Laura. "This is a nice man."

Laura smiled. "I think you're right."

"Have we met any of those before?" Gus asked.

"Not for a good long time," Laura said.

They spent the rest of that day quietly. Tom talked Gus into letting them give her lunch on a tray in her room, and they left her in peace to nap for a couple of hours while they strolled in the garden, and Tom showed Laura her red maple tree, and Sam danced around their heels, barking for Tom to throw rubber balls for him. They sat, after that, in the sitting room, near the fireplace, and it was the very first time that they had done that in private, just sat quietly, talking about nothing in particular, and Laura knew that the attraction was getting harder to deny by the minute, and felt less and less sure that there were any sound reasons left *to* deny it.

"Do you think Gus might like to help decorate the tree?" Tom asked. The Christmas tree in the corner of the sitting room was almost ceiling-high and a big box of baubles and a coiled-up string of tree lights sat beneath it. Laura looked into the box and noticed it was littered with fresh pine needles.

"I'll bet this tree was already decorated, and you pulled all this stuff off just so that we could do it again."

"That would be a pretty silly thing to do, wouldn't it?" His eyes were smiling.

"I think it would be a very kind thing to do," Laura said.

They did the tree together, in the late, dark part of the afternoon, and then Tom handed the kitchen over to Gus on the understanding that if she got too tired or changed her mind about being in charge of supper, she wouldn't hesitate to say so. Gus pottered for almost two hours, in a state of near bliss that she would never have dreamed could have been possible less than sixteen hours ago. She knew what Tom was doing, knew that this was supposed to be some kind of therapy, was aware that she was being what she hated almost more than anything else, a bloody nuisance, but for some strange reason—perhaps the atmosphere in this house, perhaps the natural, genuine niceness of the man himself—she didn't seem to care. When Laura came in to remind her to take one of the pills that the doctor had prescribed for her, she didn't even object to that, just swallowed it without argument and went on with her cooking.

"This can't last, you know," Laura said to Tom. "It's too extreme a change, after yesterday, after last night."

"It's just a beginning," Tom said easily, "and not a bad one at that. Last night everything must have closed in on her, all the darkness, all the fear. Even if today only serves to remind her that it's possible to climb up out of the dark—even if she has nightmares tonight, or gets down again tomorrow or the next day—it's still worthwhile."

"I think she started feeling better when you told her just to let herself off the hook—that's exactly what she is doing, even if it is only for a while. Or maybe yesterday was so dreadful that last night was a kind of culmination of everything." Laura paused. "Or is that just wishful thinking?"

"Probably," Tom said. "I don't think it's possible to get over the kind of things that have happened to Gus in one, or even a series of lows. But I do think that if things get better for her, generally, if she starts feeling safer, maybe the lows will get less severe, more bearable."

"I think you're in the wrong profession," Laura told him. "You'd make a great psychologist, or maybe a social worker."

"Don't you like my newspaper?"

"I love it."

"Really?" Tom was pleased. "What do you like about it?"

"Your editorials, more than anything—no, I mean it. I think I'd buy the *Journal* every week even if I didn't know you, mostly because of them." Laura considered. "There's nothing I don't like in it—though I admit it's sometimes a bit frustrating having to buy one of the other tabloids just to keep up with some of the juicier scandals."

"You enjoy a good scandal, do you?" Tom looked amused.

"I suppose it depends who's being hurt by it. I do like the fact that the *Journal*'s kept its word about not printing purely sensational stories and not twisting people's words."

"I think I just have more respect for my readers than that." He paused. "What do you think of the *Courier*?"

"I don't buy it. I did, of course, in the beginning, out of curiosity."

"It's a good paper."

"It's so absolutely different from yours, it's hard to understand why Roger felt—probably still feels so competitive about it. It's far more like a weekly *Sun*, while the *Journal*'s—" She stopped.

"What?"

"I don't know." She shook her head. "Maybe that's what's so great about it. It isn't like any other paper I've ever read. It's so straight, but it isn't dry, like the *Telegraph*." She smiled. "Lovely cartoons."

"My favorite page," Tom said.

"I don't believe you."

"Haven't you noticed who the *Mutt* strip is based on?"

"Sam?"

"Of course Sam."

"No wonder it's your favorite page."

Early on Christmas Eve, while Laura went off to try to find a gift that she and Gus could give Tom next day, and to meet the Mireau sisters, who were catering a three-day event in Richmond, Tom and Gus did their holly gathering and bought cooked lobsters and a sixteen-pound turkey with all the trimmings, in Harrods food hall. That night, after demolishing the lobsters and drinking two bottles of champagne, they all went to Midnight Mass in a church just around the corner from Tom's house. And on Christmas Day, after Tom had sent Laura and Gus out for a long walk in Battersea Park, across the river, so that he could take command of his own kitchen, they all sat down to a dinner so fine that both Gus and Laura noted that on a professional level, they had better maintain their very highest standards when working for Tom or for the *Journal*.

Exchanging gifts beside the tree after dinner, they found that everybody had bought knitwear; Tom had bought cashmere turtlenecked sweaters for both Laura and Gus; Laura had found a navy blue guernsey for Tom and a bright red knitted coat for Sam, and her present to Gus was an emerald cashmere ski hat with matching long scarf and gloves, while Gus had given her a long, winter-white lambswool jacket with *LA* embroidered on both pockets.

A walk seemed appropriate.

"You two go on," Gus told them. "I'm too tired."

"You've got to come," Tom said. "It's a gorgeous night."

"You'll have a better time without me."

"We'll have a lousy time without you," Laura said, and then blushed for no particular reason.

They walked along Chelsea embankment, arm in arm, three across, Tom in the middle, with Sam's leash wrapped around his right wrist, and whenever they encountered other pedestrians, they sidestepped out into the street and then back again, and one couple eyed them with clear disapproval, and Laura began laughing and found she couldn't stop, and the other two caught it, and pretty soon they were all laughing like hyenas, even Gus, and though Laura was still making too much noise of her own to take time to think about it, she registered the fact that she couldn't remember the last time she'd heard Gus really laugh.

"Here's when we all get to make a wish," Tom said, pulling them all to a halt, still three in a row, squarely facing the river opposite the Festival Pleasure Gardens.

"Why?" Laura asked.

"Because it's Christmas night, and there's a kind of a moon—and somewhere up there is the Milky Way—or is it the Plow?"

"An astronomer you're not," Gus said.

"There are stars, aren't there?" Laura said, rebukingly. "Where's your imagination, Gus?"

"Will you both shut up and wish," Tom said.

They all three closed their eyes, swaying slightly, until Sam barked, and they opened them again.

"You tell me yours and I'll tell you mine," Laura said, her voice husky from the laughter.

"You know wishes can't be told," Tom said. "Not if you want them to come true." He was very conscious that Laura, on his right side, was leaning slightly against him, and that he was only barely resisting the urge to draw her even closer.

Very gently, Gus extricated her arm from Tom's.

"I've got some thanking to do." She stood between them and the river.

"No, you don't," Laura said.

"You can't stop me thanking Tom."

"No." Laura knew she was still leaning against him, and had no willpower to pull away.

"You're a good man, Tom Bailey," Gus said, softly. "I don't know that I've ever met a good man before."

"I'm nothing special," Tom said, a little embarrassed.

"I reckon you are—and Laura will tell you I don't say things like that."

"She doesn't," Laura confirmed.

"And you've made me feel all right—almost good." Gus paused. "I was feeling very dirty, you see. Like it was all my fault, after all—and I thought it was Laura always blaming herself for everything. I didn't know I was doing it, too." She paused. "I don't know how much Laura's told you about me, the things I've done."

"She's told me nothing," Tom said. "And I'm not interested in what you've done, unless it helps you to talk about it."

"Not really."

"Then don't."

"Anyway, all I wanted was to thank you for Christmas—and for doing so much for me." Gus stopped again. "And there's just one thing I would like to ask you both."

"Go right ahead," Tom said.

"What is it, Gus?" Laura asked, still leaning.

Gus stepped back a pace, so that she was resting against the stone parapet, the river dark and quiet behind her.

"It's a bit awkward," she said.

"You can ask us anything," Tom said.

Laura stood up straighter. "Gus, what is it?"

"It's quite simple, really."

"*What's* simple?" Laura asked.

Gus grinned. "When are you two going to stop pissing about, being just good friends, and start being what you both want to be?"

Laura, her cheeks scarlet, was grateful it was night.

"Shut up, Gus," she said.

And Tom just smiled, and said nothing at all.

CHAPTER 21

A t two o'clock in the afternoon on New Year's Eve, three days after she and Gus had returned home, Tom telephoned Laura.

"Sam's missing." His voice was tight with tension.

"What happened?" Laura was dismayed.

"We went for a walk this morning in Battersea Park, and he took off after something, the way he does—I didn't even see what it was—and he never came back."

"Oh, Tom. What can I do?"

"Could you come over? I know you're probably busy, but—"

"I'm on my way."

It was the first time Laura had seen Tom look miserable. His mouth was set tightly, and his eyes were red, and she thought he'd probably shed a few tears, and all she wanted to do was hug him, but they had to go out and search for Sam, that was the most important thing. Finding Sam was the only thing that was going to help Tom.

They looked for four hours, walking in the park until it closed at dusk, and then around the perimeter, sometimes splitting up, sometimes together, calling Sam's name over and over again. Tom was carrying his mobile phone in case the police called, and every time it rang, Laura saw the flash of hope on his face, swiftly extinguished as he abruptly ended the calls.

"We're not going to find him, are we?" he said, soon after seven, his voice hoarse from shouting and from the sheer misery of worrying about good old Sam, cut off from his protection, perhaps in pain or worse.

"Yes, we are," Laura told him.

Tom shook his head. "You don't really believe that."

"I do believe it," she said, decisively. "I think he's got himself lost, but I don't think he's been run over, or else we'd know, and I can't imagine many dog thieves wanting to steal him, no offense to Sam."

He looked down at her. "You think we should go on looking?"

"I think we should go back to the house, just for a while. And I think you should let me make us both something hot to eat—and I think a stiff drink wouldn't hurt. And then we can try again."

"If he hasn't come home."

They drank hot whisky, and after she had telephoned Gus to let her know what was happening, Laura heated up some canned soup and made omelettes, which they ate without appetite, simply in order to give themselves more strength. They went back out again at nine o'clock in Tom's new Land Rover, because Tom said that Sam loved riding in it, and the seats were higher than in his old Jaguar, giving them a clearer view of the streets and gardens. Everywhere they went, they saw people on their way to New Year's Eve parties, in cars, walking, in the backs of taxis, even on bicycles. They drove around for about an hour, and then they went back to the Albert Bridge Road entrance of Battersea Park, just in case, and by now their voices were growing increasingly dispirited, and Laura hated to admit it, but she was starting to wonder if Sam hadn't, after all, met with an accident.

Very quietly, they drove home. Tom parked the Land Rover and then, as if it was the most natural thing in the world, he slipped his left arm around Laura's shoulders, and she put her right arm around his waist, and they walked, slowly and wearily, into the house.

"Almost midnight," she said, glancing at her watch.

Tom shook his head. "I'm supposed to be at a party in Knightsbridge. I forgot all about it."

"Does it matter?"

"Not at all."

"Come on," Laura said, walking into the den. "We should at least raise a glass to the New Year, and to Sam."

"I don't feel like champagne," Tom said. "I'm sorry. It's not much fun for you."

"I didn't come for fun," Laura reminded him. "I came to try to help."

"You've helped just by being here."

"I'm glad."

"I just wish I *knew*, for sure, you know?"

"Of course I know. It's awful thinking about all the things that might have happened—" She caught herself hastily. "Not that I think they have, but I know you can't help—" She stopped.

Tom gave a wan smile. "You have a vivid imagination, too?"

"The worst," Laura confessed. "If Gus gets home late, I'm always certain she's been run over by a bus. Even when I was married to Roger, if one of his flights got delayed, I was sure I'd been widowed."

"You're not married to him anymore," Tom said.

"Not for much longer, anyway—legally, I mean."

"I'm glad."

The grandfather clock in the dining room began to strike. Tom went over to the window, and opened it. Whether it came directly from Westminster, carried on the night air, or whether it came from the television sets and radios of people partying at home in Chelsea, the sound of Big Ben took over the clock in Tom's house, drawing them on, like it or not, into the nineties, into a brand-new decade. Tom turned to face Laura, and she was crying, and looking up at him Laura saw that his eyes were wet, too, and she went right to him then and laid her head against his chest, and felt his arms go around her, and they were strong, and she had never been so glad to be with anyone in her entire life.

"It's a horrible beginning to the year," she said, softly. "I'm so sorry."

"It's not all bad," Tom said, "is it?"

For a moment, they thought the doorbell was part of the New Year chimes, and then suddenly, at precisely the same instant, they both broke free and ran for the front door.

A uniformed police constable stood on the mat.

"Oh, my God," Laura said.

And then they heard a car door, and a second man was getting out of the police car double-parked outside, and he was holding something in his arms, and Tom and Laura both held their breath, and then the bundle started to wiggle madly, and the policeman let it go, and Sam, barking joyfully, hurtled up the garden path and almost sent Tom flying. And Laura was weeping freely now, and Tom was hugging the black and white dog, and the officers refused the offer of a celebratory drink because they were on duty, and all hands were needed at Trafalgar Square; but a small boy had brought Sam into his local police station in Battersea, and so far as they could ascertain, the dog's friendly nature had persuaded the boy to try taking him home, until his father's less friendly nature had persuaded him to hand the dog over.

When the front door closed behind the policemen, Tom and Laura stood in the long hall, looking at each other, while Sam danced around, his claws making scratching sounds as he skittered on the parquet floor.

"Happy New Year," Tom said.

"It is now," Laura said.

"Thank you," he said, very tenderly.

"I didn't find him."

"You tried. And you were here. And you never once told me I should stop looking."

"Why would I do that?"

Sam, sensing something different in the air, stopped dancing and sat.

"You remember what Gus said on Christmas night?" Tom asked her.

"Yes," Laura said.

"I reckon she had a point."

"Yes." Laura's voice was very soft.

They were standing a foot apart.

"Think it's time we stopped kidding ourselves?" Tom asked.

"Do you?"

"Yes," Tom said. "I do."

"Okay." A tiny, chill, warning doubt nudged at her.

He closed the space between them. He put his arms around her. He held her for several seconds, not too tightly, until she put her arms around him too. And then they drew back, just a little, just enough to look into each other's faces. Tom kissed her. It was a very gentle kiss. His lips were dry and warm and firm. Laura kissed him back, and heard him, felt him, sigh, a long, drawn-out sigh of pleasure and relief. And the doubt disappeared.

Sam barked. No one took any notice. He barked again. Laura stopped kissing Tom.

"He's right," she said, a little breathlessly. "We should be making a fuss of him. After all, we owe him."

Tom smiled. "I guess we do."

They did not go to bed that night. Once the euphoria was past they were almost too exhausted to move, stayed downstairs in the den, very cozy, with Sam snuggling close on the sofa. Laura remembered the first days in Monte Carlo with Roger, half fearful, but wanting him to touch her. She knew now that she had not known what wanting a man, really, deeply wanting him, felt like. Tom fell asleep for a while, on the sofa, and Laura watched him, his long, slim body, his even longer legs and strong arms. His face, lean and kind, the cheekbones high, the nose a little crooked, the jaw a little stubbled, the mouth beautiful. She wanted him so much that she could almost have cried out loud, and yet she knew she was still afraid. Of sex, for one thing. Not that anything about Tom Bailey could be compared to Roger Ambler. But Roger was the only man Laura had ever experienced sex with, and he, too, had been gentle in the very beginning, in Monaco, even though she knew, now, that it had all been part of a plan, of a carefully structured game. Tom Bailey

was too straight for that kind of game playing. Laura had the
sense that although there would be a lot to learn about this
man, depths that would be fascinating to discover, so far as
feelings went, what you saw with Tom was what you got.
There was no hidden darkness in him. As there was in her.

That was why she had felt that small frisson of warning. That was the true fear. That getting involved with this
good, kind, decent man might not be fair to him. She was
afraid of hurting Tom—and yet she wanted him so *badly,*
and maybe, just maybe it might be all right after all . . .

She had telephoned Gus after Sam had been brought home,
to wish her a happy new year, and at eleven in the morning, she called again.

"I'm sorry," she said. "I never came home."

"I did notice," Gus said.

"We were so wiped out from looking for Sam, we just fell
asleep."

"I'm sure you did." Gus's voice was good-humored.

"It's true." Laura smiled.

"So?"

"So I'll be home later."

"You don't have to, not on my account."

"I know that."

"No, you don't. You think you've got to come back in
case I get down."

"You sound pretty up to me."

"That's because I'm glad, about you and Tom."

"What about us?"

"I'm not stupid," Gus said.

"No," Laura agreed. "You're not."

The following Thursday, Laura received her decree absolute,
stating that her divorce from Roger was final, and that both
parties were free to marry again. She felt not an ounce, not
a grain of sadness, only relief. It seemed to her that a gesture
of celebration was called for. Tom was heavily embroiled at
the *Journal,* and Gus was at the market. She supposed her
being drawn toward Battersea must be meaningful—she
found, increasingly, that she believed in fate. She was not at

all sure, however, if she was doing the right thing by going to the Dog's Home. Until she found Zoë, a beautiful German shepherd-retriever cross, and then Laura knew that she was absolutely right.

She called Tom at the office, found out what time he thought he'd be home, and at ten o'clock that evening, she was waiting outside his house, Zoë beside her.

"I thought Sam might like her," she told him, plunging straight in.

Tom crouched down to take a closer look. "Hello, beautiful." He fondled her ears. Zoë thumped her tail.

"She is lovely, isn't she?" Laura said. "Her name's Zoë. If you don't want her, it's all right, because I fell in love with her right away, and we'll take her—Gus won't mind."

Tom looked away from the dog into Laura's face.

"You didn't buy her as company for Sam at all," he said. "You bought her in case something does ever happen to Sam."

"Maybe. I couldn't stand seeing you so unhappy. I know no other dog would ever replace Sam, I know he's unique, but so's Zoë, probably." She looked at him anxiously. "Do you think Sam will mind? If he does—or if you do—I will have her."

"There'd be no point," Tom said.

"Why not? I run the business mostly from home, these days. I'd be there for her."

"I hope not."

"Of course I would. I know how to look after a dog. I mean, I've never really had one to look after. We had dogs and cats at Chryssos, but Maria did most things for them, and it was so safe there, they almost ran wild, but I do know enough to take care of—"

"I meant I hope you wouldn't be at home—at your place—to look after Zoë, because I hope you're going to be here, with me, with us."

They were both still crouching on the front step. It was cold and windy and dark, and crammed between them on the stone, Zoë was starting to whimper, and from inside the house, Sam was alternately barking and jumping up at the front door.

"I'm in love with you, Laura," Tom went on. "I love you."

The warning tried to elbow its way back into Laura's mind, but she pushed it away again.

"I want you to marry me."

She stared at him. "It's too soon."

"No," he said. "It isn't. But if you think it is, then come and live with me until you're ready. I don't want to be without you, Laura. We've wasted too much time as it is."

"I don't want to be without you, either," Laura said, and she knew it was true.

A middle-aged woman wearing very high heels walked past the house, her shoes clicking on the pavement. She paused, briefly, regarded them with suspicion, then walked on.

"What about Gus?" Laura said. "I don't want to leave her alone, not now."

"Nor should you," Tom said. "There's plenty of space in my house."

"I couldn't ask that of you."

"Why not?"

"Because it's one thing inviting us both for a few days, but to live?"

"I've told you before, I'm very fond of Gus. And I'd be worrying about her, too, all alone, so neither of us would ever get a wink of sleep unless she was with us."

"What if she doesn't want to? She's very proud."

"I'll tell her she can take over the kitchen. Unless you mind."

"We can share the kitchen," Laura said.

"Whatever you say." Tom paused. "Two suggestions."

"Yes?"

"One, I kiss you."

"I agree."

He kissed her.

"Two, we go inside before Sam breaks down the door."

They went inside. Sam took one look at Zoë, and froze. He seemed to go rigid, they couldn't tell if it was from fear or hate. Zoë made another small, whimpering sound, and ap-

proached him. Sam growled, from deep in his throat. Laura
and Tom watched apprehensively.

"What have I done?" Laura whispered.

"Just give them time," Tom whispered back, holding her
hand tightly.

Zoë gave a little bark, higher pitched than Sam's. Sam's
hackles rose, his pointed ears grew even more pointed, his
bushy tail grew stiff with tension. Zoë put her face close to
his, stuck her nose in his left ear, and Sam jumped, apparently shocked.

"Come off it, Sam," Tom said. "She's gorgeous."

Sam barked, his deepest, most impressive bark. Zoë sidled
up to him again, and when Sam snapped at her, she lay
promptly down and rolled over onto her back. Sam stared at
her with deep suspicion, then sniffed cautiously at her belly,
then thrust his nose farther down, between her back legs.

"No manners," Tom said.

Zoë wagged her tail, still lying on her back. Sam made a
new sound, neither bark nor growl. It seemed to them to be
a sound of interest, perhaps even of fascination.

"We should feed them," Laura said.

"Good idea."

"Has Sam been neutered?"

"Certainly not."

"Would you mind having puppies?"

"No, would you?"

They watched the dogs alternately scrapping and playing,
and, after a while, settling together, and then, without saying
a word, Tom took Laura by the hand and led her up the
stairs to his bedroom. For just a very few moments, Laura
remembered the Japanese whorehouse and the bizarreness of
her first time with Roger, and then it was gone, he was gone,
and there was only Tom, Tom and his love for her, laid out,
openly, uncompromisingly, for her, just for her.

"Is it all right?" he asked, before he undressed her.

"Yes," Laura said, and it did seem wonderfully all right,
all the fears gone, all the doubts banished. She wanted to
tear at his shirt, at the buckle of his belt, she wanted so
badly to see him naked, could not believe how desperately

she wanted to see him, for she had grown, through the months of her marriage, to hate the sight of her husband's body.

Tom gave a small gasp when he saw her, for she was just as lovely as he had fantasized she would be, and he had thought that was almost impossible. Her breasts were round and perfect, like pale, pink-nippled apples, her whole body was creamy and soft and sweetly curved.

"Words fail me," he said. "I don't know how to express the way I feel about you—the way you look right now, the way you are."

"I feel the same way." Laura drank in the sight of him, knowing that if she were an artist she would paint him, if she were a sculptor she would mold him in clay, and he was so real, so solid, and how was it possible when, so far as she knew, most penises were similar in appearance, that she could have grown to be repelled each time she was forced to look at Roger's, and yet now, tonight, she could look at Tom, and feel nothing but anticipation and longing to have him inside her.

They made love slowly, gently, then more urgently, more wildly, and they both wanted to kiss each other wherever their mouths could reach, and it seemed to them both that their passion was all the more remarkable because it had been founded on such intense affection, and they both knew they loved each other, but they knew, at the same time, that they *liked* each other too, and that was so splendid they wanted to laugh and to cry with happiness at one and the same time. They grew wet with kissing and with perspiration and ejaculate, and there seemed no end to their love-making, they just wanted it to go on and on, wanted to hold on to each other forever, never to let go, twining their legs, grasping with their thighs, embracing with their arms, caressing with their hands, loving with their eyes. It was so different, so *different,* Laura wanted to tell him, because Tom seemed to want to watch her, to look at her all the time, except when his eyes were closed in ecstasy, and he made her feel loved, and it was the most wonderful feeling in the world.

The bedroom door squeaked as it opened, but neither of

them took any notice, until a few moments later, Sam jumped up onto the bed, looking intrigued, followed seconds later by Zoë, whose deep brown eyes stared at the two humans on the nice big, soft bed; and their nakedness, and the scent of them and the presence of Sam seemed to satisfy her, for she lay down across the end of the bed, draping herself over Tom's and Laura's bare feet, and for an instant Sam raised his hackles, but then they almost swore they saw him shrug before he, too, lay down to sleep.

"Sam's all wet," Laura murmured softly.

"I know," Tom said, "and it isn't even raining."

"It must be Zoë. What a hussy."

"Like her mother."

"She's not my daughter, we're just good friends."

"We're going to stay good friends, too, aren't we?" Tom looked at her.

"I hope so," Laura said.

And the fear came back.

When Tom woke up at around four, the dogs had left the bed, and so had Laura. Sitting up, he saw that she was standing at the window, gazing out into the small, narrow garden.

"Laura?"

She stirred, but didn't turn around.

"Laura, are you all right?"

"We have to talk," she said, still not turning.

Tom smiled. "I should say we do."

"No, you don't understand." Her voice was strained. "I have to talk to you." She paused. "There are things I have to tell you."

Tom pushed back the duvet and got slowly out of bed. "It's cold out here," he said. "Why don't you get back in, and we can talk in comfort?" He put one hand on the back of her neck, just below the line where the sharply cut black hair ended. Laura turned and looked at him.

"You've been crying." Tom looked distressed. "What's the matter?"

She shook her head, saying nothing.

"Darling, what is it?" He put his arms around her, and for a moment she leaned against him, and then she pulled away.

"You can't marry me," she said.

"Sure I can."

"No." Her voice sounded stiff. "You can't."

"Why not?" Tom looked at her, puzzled. "I told you, if you'd rather, we can just live together for a while, make sure you really want to."

"Oh, I want to," Laura said. "That isn't the problem."

"Then what is?"

She tried to smile. "I have a deep, dark secret."

"One of those," Tom said lightly. "I guess we all have one or two of those hidden away." He hugged himself against the cold. "I still say there's nothing we couldn't talk over in bed before we freeze to death."

"I think we should go downstairs."

"Okay." Worry put new creases in his forehead, but he spoke steadily. "I'll go ahead and light a fire in the den—see what those dogs are doing." He put on a terry robe and left the room.

Laura went into the bathroom, looked into the mirror, forced herself to look right into her eyes. They were full of pain and fear.

"Last chance to back out," she said. "Tell him, and it's over."

But she knew she had no choice. She had lived with deceit, and she could not bear to do that again, not with Tom. She pulled on the jeans and pullover she'd been wearing when she'd arrived, and went downstairs to the unmistakable smell of dog mess. Tom was still mopping up, a bottle of Dettol in his hand.

"God," she said. "Was that Zoë?"

"Hard to tell."

"I'm sorry. That's all you needed."

"No big deal," Tom said, dropping the soiled cloth into a rubbish bag. "I've let them both out in the garden. They were overjoyed to see me."

"Didn't you push her nose in it, or whatever you're supposed to do?"

"Of course not. Poor baby, first night in a strange place."

Laura looked around the kitchen. "Don't bother lighting a fire in the den. It's nice and warm in here."

"You sure?"

She nodded.

"How about a drink? You look as if you might need one."

"I do." She sat down at the big table.

He disappeared for a moment, came back with a bottle of cognac and two glasses. "I may as well tell you before you start, that nothing you say is going to change the way I feel about you."

"We'll see." Now that the moment had come, Laura was starting to tremble, and her stomach felt twisted in knots. She took the glass of cognac with both hands, gratefully. "You'd better sit down." She took a sip, and stood up.

He sat. "I love you," he said.

"And I love you."

"Why don't we just leave it at that?"

"I wish we could. Believe me, I wish we could."

Tom looked up at her. "Why don't you sit down too?"

"I need to stand."

He waited a moment. "This is obviously very hard for you—and I don't know what you think is so awful, but whatever it is, why don't you try saying it real fast, like ripping off a Band-Aid?"

Laura turned away.

"I killed someone."

The kitchen was deathly silent.

"Her name was Lucia Lindberg. I was twelve years old, and she was thirteen. We were at school together, and she and her friends used to bully me, did awful things to me." Laura's voice was low and very clear, hardly shaking at all now, as if it was detached from her. "I became very frightened—I should have told someone, but I was scared. I saw a knife one day, in the riding stables. Just an old, rusty pocketknife, the kind that folds down."

There was a thump at the back door, as Sam and Zoë tried to get back in, followed by scratching. Tom didn't move. Laura still didn't look at him.

"I carried it with me everywhere after that, I felt safer. Until we went to see the Westbury White Horse—a chalk horse in Wiltshire." Her voice began to lose its control. She walked over to the wall near the oven, and leaned against it for support.

"You don't have to go on." Tom's voice sounded hoarse.

"I do." Laura waited a moment. "They thought I'd told the principal what they'd done to me. I told them I hadn't, but they didn't believe me. They said they were going to punish me. Lucia had said before that if I told, I'd have an accident. A really awful accident, I remember she said."

The dogs began to whine outside the door.

"I took out the knife, to make them leave me alone—" She stopped.

"But they didn't," Tom said.

"No. There were five of them, and Lucia told them to get me over to the edge of the escarpment, so I struggled, and Lucia came at me, and—" She could hardly breathe, her throat felt so tight and her heart was pounding so hard. She closed her eyes, and she was back there again, on the brink of the steep drop, Gerry holding her, Priscilla and Freddy staring at her, and Lucia—

"Laura—" Tom started to get up.

"No." Her voice stopped him. "I have to tell you."

He sat down again.

"She came at me, and I brought up my arm, and the knife was in my hand, and she ran right into it." Laura's voice was hard now, it was the only way she could tell it. "And she fell. Right over the edge. She fell onto her stomach, onto the knife. She was dead."

Tom sat very still.

"So that's why you can't marry me," Laura said, more softly now. "They called it manslaughter. But I'd been carrying the knife around all that time, and so it looked as if I'd meant to do it—"

"It was self-defense. An accident."

"Yes." She couldn't leave it at that. "But I'd wished her dead."

"You were only twelve. A lot of kids wish people dead, but that doesn't make them responsible for accidents."

"It was my knife. I wanted to frighten her."

"Because she'd frightened you."

"They found me guilty."

Again, that silence.

"I was sent to a community home. Kane House. That's where I met Gus." Laura paused. "She was there for shoplifting. Gus had had a terrible childhood—no childhood at all, really. Her father beat her mother, and her mother got cancer, and Gus started pinching things because her mother needed them and her father was no use."

"Did her father abuse Gus?" Tom's voice sounded hoarse again.

"Yes, I think so." Laura licked her dry lips. "But that's not what I'm telling you about." She looked at him at last. "Do you mind if I do sit down now?"

"I wish you would."

She sat, at the opposite end of the table.

"I took Lucia's life, Tom." She sat very straight. "No matter how it happened, whatever they'd done to me, that's the truth of it. I saw her parents in court, during the trial, and I saw what I'd done to them, as well as to their daughter." For the first time, her mouth quivered. "My grandfather had a heart attack after he heard what I'd done, and I never saw him again—he was too ill to come to England, and he died two days after the trial, and I felt I'd killed him, too." She swallowed hard. "So you see, you really can't think about marrying me, Tom. I'm not the kind of girl that someone like you can marry."

Outside the back door, Sam barked. Slowly, Tom got up and opened it, and both dogs came flying into the kitchen, paws muddying the white tiled floor, greeting both Tom and Laura. Tom crouched to fondle first Sam, then Zoë. His jaw was tight, his eyes very dark.

Laura stood up. "I'll get my bag and coat." She paused. "Would you mind if I call a cab?"

"I'd mind very much."

"Oh. Okay."

Tom straightened up, and looked at her.

"How long did you have to stay in that place?"

"Until I was seventeen. If I'd been older, I'd have gone to prison. I'd probably still be there."

"If you'd been older, it wouldn't have happened. You'd

have known better than to keep it all to yourself, and someone would have helped you."

"Maybe."

Tom shook his head. "You poor kid." He paused. "And
Gus, too. No wonder your friendship's so important to you
both."

"I don't know what would have happened to me if it
hadn't been for her. She seemed very strong. She protected
me."

"I'm sure you helped her too."

"Helped her get kicked out of Kane House into a borstal,"
Laura said, bitterly. She told him how they'd run off one day
to Bristol. "A man—a disgusting old kerbcrawler—kept has-
sling me, and when he touched me, Gus hit him with a lump
of paving stone."

"So Gus was punished instead of him," Tom said. "Some
justice."

"Yes."

"Why don't you sit down again?"

"I think I ought to go."

"I don't."

Laura sat down, on the edge of the chair, as if she were
going to get up again almost immediately.

"Did Roger know?"

She nodded. "I'm not sure exactly when he found out. I
didn't tell him, but then later I realized that he'd known for
a long time. Gus thinks he knew before he married me, but
I still have problems believing that." Laura hesitated, unsure
of whether to go on or not. "Though it excited him, apparently, what I'd done, where I'd been."

"Did it?" Tom said grimly.

"It was wrong of me not to have told him."

"I can understand why you didn't."

"Can you?" Laura paused. "I should have told you
earlier."

"Why exactly have you told me?"

"Because I love you. Because it would have been too unfair to let you go on thinking I was someone else."

"Someone else?"

"An ordinary person. Not a murderess."

"You shouldn't think of yourself that way, Laura."

"It's what I am."

"No, it isn't."

Laura stood up again. "I'm going to go now. Back to Gus. If you won't let me call a cab, I'll take a bus."

"You won't find one at this time."

"Then I'll walk."

"I don't want you to go."

"I have to."

"Then I'll drive you."

"No," Laura said, urgently. "I don't want you to."

Tom got up, defeated. "I'll call a cab."

"Thank you."

Sam and Zoë came to the door with Tom, both whining as Laura left. She bent down and hugged them both, just holding back the tears, and then she let Tom embrace her briefly, but she wouldn't allow him to come out of the house in his bathrobe, and she wouldn't answer when he asked what she was doing that night after the *Journal* had been put to bed.

"This is dumb," Tom said. "Your leaving now. We need to talk."

"I've told you everything. There isn't any more."

"Maybe I have some things I'd like to say."

"The only thing you should say to me is good-bye."

"Why?" His sloping eyes and voice were tired. "Because you were incredibly unlucky when you were just a kid?"

"I'm bad news," Laura said. "Ask Roger Ambler."

And she walked down the path to the waiting cab. She wept all the way back to Chalk Farm, noiselessly, the tears flowing, without sobs, down her cheeks, and she saw the driver watching her in the rearview mirror, but he never said anything, and she supposed he assumed he was witnessing the end of a love affair, and she supposed that when all was said and done, he was right.

Gus woke up when Laura closed the front door, and came out of her room into the hall, eyes bleary with sleep.

"How come you're home?"

"I told Tom."

"What about?" She paused. "Oh."

"I'm going to bed."

"How did he take it?"

"It's all over," Laura said.

"Who said that? Tom said that?"

"He didn't have to."

Gus was wide awake now. "In other words, you're assuming it's over."

"How could it not be?" Laura asked. "Even if he tried to accept it now, he'd come to regret it, or change his mind when he's had time to think about it."

"I doubt that, knowing Tom," Gus said.

"He's as straight as an arrow, Gus. He has a reputation to consider."

"Bollocks."

Laura smiled, for the first time in hours. "I'm exhausted. I'm going to get some sleep. I'm sorry I woke you."

"Are you okay?"

"No," Laura said. "But I'll live."

Gus woke her at nine.

"Tom's on the phone."

"Tell him I'm not here."

"He knows you're here. He's already called twice."

"Tell him I've emigrated."

"Don't be daft. He wants to talk to you."

"I don't want to talk to him."

"Why not, for God's sake?"

"Because I've said all there is to say." Laura turned over on her side, her face away from the door.

"Surely he's entitled to have his say, too?"

"Of course he is. But not now."

"I'll tell him you'll phone him later then."

"Tell him what you like, just leave me alone."

She drifted back into sleep, and dreamed that she was standing in a church, only it was so big that it might have been a cathedral, and Tom was waiting for her near the altar, and when she looked down to check that her dress was okay, she saw that she was wearing a kimono, and she looked to her left to see who was holding her arm to give her away, and it was Roger, and she wanted to shake him off, but his grip was too tight.

"Why are you giving me away?" she asked him. "You're not my father."

"I'm not going to give you away," he said. "We're going to share you."

"What are you going to do with that whip?" she asked, and she looked at his left hand, and he was holding a huge bullwhip, and he was wearing a tall red top hat and tails, and he looked like the ringmaster in a circus.

"I'll bring the whip and the cowboy can bring the spurs," Roger said.

And when Laura looked toward Tom again, at the far end of the cathedral, she saw that he was wearing a Stetson and real cowboy boots with spurs that gleamed in the light, and Lucia was beside him, and she was wearing a white shroud, with a veil over her face, and Laura shrank away in horror.

"Time you got what's coming to you," Roger said, softly, his mouth close up against the side of her face, and then she felt his tongue dart inside her ear, and she cried out in revulsion and tried again to get free of him, but he was holding her more tightly than ever, and his fingers were pinching into the flesh of her left arm, and she cried out again for him to let her go—

Gus woke her again.

"If that's what sleep's doing for you, you'd be better off awake."

Laura stared at her, and around the familiar bedroom, and sagged back against the pillow. "I had a nightmare."

"Obviously. Want to talk about it?"

"No."

"All right. Tom's been on the phone again. I said you'd call him right back, so you'd better get up and get on with it."

Laura struggled back up and swung her legs out of bed. "I thought he had a paper to edit."

"All the more reason for you to put the poor bloke out of his misery and let him get on with it."

"But he's only calling to say good-bye."

"Didn't sound like it to me," Gus said.

"Then he's trying to be kind."

"Which is more than I can say for you."

Laura telephoned Tom.

"I wanted to know if you were okay," he said, relieved to hear her voice.

"I'm fine." She heard voices in the background, and phones ringing.

"When am I going to see you?"

"Why would you want to?" She heard someone yelling.

"You know why."

Laura shut her eyes for an instant against the longing, then opened them again and hardened her voice. "You're better off without me, Tom, and if you take some time to think about it, you'll know I'm right."

"I've thought about it, and I don't want you any less than I did."

"Roger wanted me too," she said nastily.

"I've told you before, I'm not Roger. And I'm not just talking about wanting, I'm talking about love."

Tears threatened again, but she sent them away. "It wouldn't work, Tom. Believe me, it wouldn't, no matter how much you may mean that now."

"You don't know what you're talking about, Laura," he said, "because I'm not sure you've ever been loved before."

"Maybe I don't deserve to be loved," Laura said, and put the phone down.

He came to the flat late that evening, but Laura refused to see him.

"You're crazy," Gus told her after he'd given up and gone.

"Maybe I am."

"That's the best man I've ever laid eyes on."

"I don't doubt it," Laura said.

"Then for Christ's sake what is *wrong* with you?"

"Do you think it's right that a man as decent as Tom Bailey should have children by a convicted killer?"

"Oh, for God's sake, play another tune." Gus was growing angry. "You're always telling me I should have gone to a counselor, but if anyone here needs counseling, it's you. I trust Tom Bailey as much as I mistrusted Ambler, and I'm telling you that if you don't get round there soon and let him take you back, it'll be the biggest mistake you'll ever make."

"I'm never going to see him again."

"Then you're a bloody fool."

The phone rang at four o'clock in the morning. Laura heard it, and waited for Gus to answer it, but when it went on ringing she threw off her bedclothes and stomped out into the sitting room.

"Tom, you're wasting your time."

"You have to come and get your dog." He sounded angry.

"Zoë?" Laura was startled. "What's wrong with her?"

"Nothing, unless you count shitting everywhere in the house and tearing the place apart. She's a one-dog wrecker, and she's a lousy influence on Sam—I'm sorry, but I can't cope with her, and you did say that you'd have her."

"I will."

"Then do me a favor and get over here."

"Now? It's the middle of the night."

"Listen to this, will you?"

Laura listened, and heard the sound of a dog howling.

"It sounds like a werewolf," she said, dubiously.

"I think she is a goddamned werewolf," Tom said.

Laura had never heard him so angry. She realized she had no choice but to go. "I'll have to telephone for a cab," she said. "And I need to get some clothes on."

"Don't bother to dress formally," Tom said, coolly. "She'll probably only shit on you on the way back anyway."

All the lights in Tom's house were switched on when Laura got to Cheyne Walk. She asked the driver to wait.

"I don't understand," she said, when Tom opened the door. "Zoë seemed fine when I was here."

"Maybe she's meant to be your dog."

Laura stepped into the hall. Tom closed the door.

"Where is she?"

"In the garden, with Sam. Probably digging up what's left of my plants."

"I'm sorry," Laura said. "I'll go and get her."

"It's okay, I'll get her in a minute. I should at least offer you a drink before you start back."

"I don't need a drink."

"But I do," Tom said.

"Fine, you have one."

"Come into the den."

"I'd rather get going," Laura told him. "I've asked the driver to wait."

"I'll tell him you're going to be just a few minutes more." Tom was out of the front door before Laura could argue. As he came back in, she heard the sound of a car driving away.

"That was my cab." She was indignant.

"He had to leave."

"Why?"

"Because I told him to." Tom smiled at her consternation. "I did pay him."

"There was no need."

"Come and have that drink. Please." He opened the door to the den. "I have some things to say to you. Don't you think you owe me that much?"

Laura went into the den.

"Have a seat. Cognac?"

She nodded, and sat in one of the armchairs.

"First of all, two anecdotes." Tom poured their drinks and handed one to her. "You might call them confessions." He sat down in another armchair, and his expression was quite somber. "Ready?"

"Sure."

"When I was eight years old, I had a fight with a friend of mine. His name was Charlie Hooper, and we got in a lot of scraps. Charlie was much smaller than me, and it made him extra belligerent—I guess he felt he had to prove something." Tom took a swallow of his cognac. "Anyway, this time we fought in the treehouse we'd built together in one of the big old oaks on my parents' estate. I took a swing at Charlie, and he fell right out of the tree and broke his arm." Tom paused. "If he'd fallen a little differently, he could have broken his neck, and I guess you could have said that I'd killed him."

"It's not the same," Laura said. "You hadn't been carrying a knife around with you."

"I knew how dangerous a treehouse could be. I knew that taking a punch at someone up in an oak tree was a stupid thing to do. You can be sure that if Charlie had died, I'd have thought of myself as a killer, too. And so would his mother and father."

"Maybe you would, but no one would have put you on trial."

"Which brings me to my second confession."

"I don't see where this is getting us," Laura said, wearily.

"But I do." Tom drank some more cognac. "When I was in high school, I smoked a little dope. Not much, none of my crowd were heavily into it, but we'd hang out in each other's houses and on the streets, and now and again one of us would get hold of some marijuana from one of the older kids, and we'd pass the odd joint around."

Laura looked at him, thought painfully how much she wanted to be close to him again, put away the thought with an effort.

"One night, when I was the one who'd bought the stuff— just enough for one joint—we went to a drive-in movie. There were five of us, all squeezed into one car. We drank a little beer, and we passed around this joint, and it was stronger stuff than any of us had had before, and we all got a little higher than we intended."

"What happened?" Laura asked.

"On the way home, we had an accident. The kid driving lost control on a bend, and skidded into a tree. He cut his arm, and the two boys next to him on the passenger seat got a little bruised, but all in all we got away with it." Tom looked at Laura. "Suppose someone had been killed that night, who do you think would have been responsible?"

"You all smoked the marijuana."

"But I supplied it, at least I bought it." He paused. "If someone had been killed, I might have been the one in court charged with manslaughter, not to mention possession."

"I suppose so," Laura said.

"Answer me one question. If Charlie Hooper had broken

his neck, or if one of those kids had been killed in that car wreck, do you think it would stop you marrying me now?"

"Of course not."

"Because those things that happened then—the mistakes I made when I was a kid—don't change who I am now, am I right?"

"No, they don't," Laura answered quietly. "But if someone had been killed, and if you had been convicted of being responsible—even if you hadn't been jailed—I think that would have changed you, Tom." She paused. "We get scarred. Kane House scarred me, but not nearly so much as looking over that escarpment and seeing Lucia lying there below, and knowing she was dead."

Tom fell silent.

"Are you beginning to understand?" Laura asked, gently.

"Your feelings?" He nodded. "I can understand them, of course. But you're wrong, very wrong, to believe that what happened makes any difference to the way I feel about you."

"How can you say that?"

Tom sat forward, his eyes holding her. "You were a child, all alone in a strange country. You were being bullied—terrorized might be a better word, by the sound of it." He paused. "Your greatest sin was probably not telling anyone what was going on, but children make those mistakes."

"You forget one thing," Laura said. "Charlie Hooper was your friend, and so were the kids in that car. You liked them. I hated Lucia."

"I know, and you wished her dead. But you didn't mean it, did you?"

She shook her head. "No."

"It seems to me that you did more than pay for your misfortune." His eyes were still fixed unwaveringly on her. "And you've gone on paying, haven't you?"

"I suppose I have," she said, very softly.

"Don't you think it's time to cancel the debt? Don't you think it's time to start living your life without all that guilt hanging over you?"

"Maybe."

Tom smiled. "I guess that's all I'm going to achieve right now."

Laura nodded, slowly. "It's more than I thought you would."

"Is it enough, do you think?"

She gave a small smile. "Enough to start me thinking again."

"Haven't you done enough thinking?"

She considered. "I think I've done more blocking than thinking."

Tom stood up, and held out his hand. "Maybe we should go find those two dogs." Laura gave him her hand, and he helped her up.

She looked around, noticing the room for the first time since she'd arrived. "I don't see any of the chaos you mentioned."

Tom's grin was shifty. "That's my third confession."

"Zoë hasn't done any damage, has she?"

"She's an angel." He shrugged. "Well, she did chew one of my boots, and she stole most of the sandwich I had when I got in tonight."

"But you don't really want me to take her away."

"Sam would never forgive me." Tom paused. "But I think Zoë does really need you—it was you she chose in the Dog's Home, after all, not me."

Laura looked up at him. "And the howling?"

He grinned again. "You were right about the werewolf. There was a Hammer horror movie on when I got home—I made a tape of it."

"You could at least try to look contrite," Laura said. "I was in bed when you called."

"Just paying you back for last night. You got me out of bed, remember?"

"That was different."

They went into the kitchen and looked out through the window. Sam and Zoë were sitting side by side on the lawn.

"Do you want me to take you home?" Tom asked. "I will, if you want me to, though I think it might confuse Zoë."

"I don't know," Laura said. "I'd hate to give her a complex."

"You could always have one of the guest rooms."

"I don't know," she said again. "I think that might confuse me."

"Do you want to call Gus? In case she's worried."

"She won't be. Gus thinks you're the greatest thing since sliced bread."

"Do you think we'll be able to talk her into moving in with us then?"

"That's assuming you've talked me into it first."

"I'm only thinking of Zoë and Sam," Tom said.

"Of course you are."

Chapter 22

In January 1991, eleven months after Laura and Gus moved into Tom Bailey's London home, Roger Ambler married for the fourth time. His bride's name was Jillian Long, and she was the tall, slender and aristocratically lovely daughter of Senator Franklin Long, whose wife, Tina, though more than twenty years older than Rona, had long been a close friend of both the Howarths.

When, less than six months after their marriage, Jillian became pregnant, Roger was triumphant, but as his wife began to balloon, from her formerly trim arms all the way down to her previously dainty ankles, he found it increasingly difficult to bring himself to look at her, let alone make love to her. He accepted this with equanimity, on the basis that he had learned that it was not, as he had once believed, possible to have everything. He had always gotten most of the sexual gratification he needed on his travels, and while he tended toward caution in Manhattan these days, marriage did not mean that everything else had to change. In the meantime, Jillian was going to make him a father—maybe even give him a son—and the Ambler Corporation was in pretty fair shape, considering that recession was now sinking its teeth into most of the West. Ambler Machinery had been sold to Matsuhama Inc., wiping out the jobs of almost four hundred American employees, and Rona had finally given in and allowed Zero Publishing to be taken over by Penguin USA,

but the demise of those two companies had long been anticipated, and Roger and Rona were both well pleased with the
deals they had struck.

Roger spent more time in Britain than he had ever done.
As time went by, he disliked the English more and more,
acutely aware that many of those he regarded as his business
peers still looked down on him, probably even sneered at
him behind his back; and yet perversely—or maybe partly
because of that—his control of the *Courier* continued to give
him greater satisfaction than any of his other ventures ever
had. There was no need for him to be as personally involved
as he was in the day-to-day running of the newspaper, especially as Gordon Harrington, his editor, was very much Roger's man, but Roger thrived on coming up with new
gimmicks to attract a greater readership. Since the paper had
started running Roger's latest venture, a Rogue's Gallery
with a *Crime of the Week,* complete with Identikit pictures
and a weekly reward offered for public assistance leading to
arrest, their circulation figures had increased considerably,
only boosted by controversial criticisms that the paper was
encouraging latter-day bounty hunters and even vigilantism.

"The *Courier* despises crime," Roger said in an interview
on LBC, London's commercial radio talk station, "unlike
that bunch of hypocrites over at the *Journal.*"

He was referring to a recent low-level crusade by Bailey
to try to persuade the Director of Public Prosecutions to re-
open an old murder case, after a letter had been received at
the *Journal* from a man claiming to be guilty of a crime for
which another man had been imprisoned for the past seven
years. The intensity of the rivalry between the two new
weeklies was being kept alive chiefly by Ambler, but that
was more because of Tom and Laura than business. Though
the *Journal* was nowhere near as popular as the blatantly
flamboyant *Courier,* it had nevertheless lately gained some
ground by running a two-page consumers' protection spread,
alerting its readers to unreliable companies and focusing on
safety issues, especially those potentially endangering children. The *Courier*'s circulation, however, was still way
ahead of the *Journal*'s, which might have appeased Roger a
little, but Tom Bailey had rubbed salt into old wounds by

choosing to take Laura, of all women, as his lover, and Roger was not likely ever to forget that.

He had begun having Laura watched the day after he had returned to Paris in December of 1987 to discover that she had left him and gone to London. The private detective he had employed had been instructed to send bimonthly reports with photographs, where useful, and Roger had seen no reason to terminate the arrangement since then. The reports had made dull reading for the most part until Laura's relationship with Bailey had begun to heat up, and with it, Roger's anger. Bailey clearly turned his ex-wife on in ways he had never done, and that offended Roger intensely. He had a folder of photographs of Laura and Tom, strolling hand in hand in the street, embracing on the doorstep of Bailey's house in Chelsea, walking with Gus, arms linked—the cowboy, the killer and the thief, all pals together—and he even had a series of shots of the lovers romping in the hay at a riding stables. They were the ones that had fired the realization—Roger didn't know why the hell it had never occurred to him before, why he had been so goddamned *trusting*—that this liaison had more than likely begun while Laura was still married to him, after she and Tom had gone horseback riding in Central Park, an activity he had so quickly put a stop to.

Roger took out the folder of photographs from time to time and looked them over. He was meticulous about protecting the negatives, even kept them in his safe at the office in White Plains. He was not certain yet what he was going to do with them, especially the ones of Laura, half undressed, face rapt, rolling in the straw, but he knew that the day would come when they were bound to come in useful.

On March 15, 1992, Jillian gave birth to an eight pound, four ounce boy they named Roger Franklin Arnold Ambler, to be known as Roger Jr. and, more often than not, little Roger. Big Roger was beside himself with pride and filled with gratitude to Jillian. Daily, he watched her exercising, watched with anticipation as her formerly slim body shed the padding that had devoured it. But though Roger wanted

Jillian again, her libido seemed to have disappeared and showed no immediate signs of returning.

On April 20, while on a visit to New Orleans, Roger allowed himself to be picked up by a boy in the bar of his hotel. He liked looking at handsome boys, had a small collection of erotic photographs locked up in the desk in his study at Trump Tower, but actually fucking a boy was a temptation he had never let himself succumb to before. This one, however, was beautiful, golden-haired, soft-skinned and very young, and Roger found that he wanted him more than he'd ever wanted anyone in his life. He took the boy up to his suite for an hour and a half, and when he was through he gave him a hundred dollar bill, and he did not find out, till it was much too late, that he had been recognized by a reporter in the bar, by the name of Ozzie Dupont, who had taken photographs of them leaving the bar together and getting into one of the elevators, Roger's right hand resting on the boy's behind.

Had Dupont's editor not owed Roger Ambler a major favor, and had that editor not been aware that his own boss had been known to play tennis with Ambler when he came to New Orleans, the sky would certainly have fallen on Roger right there and then. As it was, having given the editor his personal guarantee that he would be well looked after for the rest of his natural life, and having been assured that Dupont would keep his mouth shut, Roger was able to fly back to New York unscathed. He had only averted disaster by the narrowest of margins, but he had, thank God, averted it, and he would never take such a risk again. This had been the first time, and it would be the last. He was going home to Jillian and little Roger, and more thankful for that than he had ever been for anything. He believed he had gotten away with it.

He was mistaken.

CHAPTER 23

Things between Laura and Tom just kept on getting better and better. They had lived together without the commitment of marriage, as Laura had insisted, for four months, and Laura had believed that nothing could ever be sweeter than the way it was for them at that time, and yet after they had tied the knot at Chelsea Register Office in May of 1990, their happiness had continued to strengthen. Tom was everything to Laura, lover, best friend, protector, and any lingering anxiety that she might, for the second time, have been seduced by wealth rather than by the man himself, had long since been laid to rest. Tom was a kind, gentle, loving and humorous husband. Tom was brilliant and capable of scathing criticism, but he disliked the idea of causing anyone unnecessary pain. Tom took care of things, took care of Laura and of Gus, but he never tried to take either of them over, respected their independence and their abilities. And when Tom and Laura made love to each other, he liked, more than anything, to be face-to-face with her, to watch her, to see her, to love her.

Having been two months pregnant at the time of their marriage, Laura gave birth to their first daughter, Helen, in December that year, and to their second, Alice, just over a year later on January 8, 1992. As Laura's days and nights became consumed by motherhood, Gus began increasingly to take over the running of Laura Andros Associates, and she thrived on it, giving up her market stalls and really stamping her unique personality on their business. The combination of traditional service and Gus's personal style had begun to pique the public's attention, and after Laura and Gus came up with a proposal to try to promote a catering training scheme via the Women in Prison organization, Thames News had broadcast a piece on them that had boosted business hugely. Gus coped magnificently with the upturn, leaving Laura almost entirely free to concentrate on the babies. Both raven-haired and pale-skinned, Helen had Tom's brown eyes, and was the most good-tempered of children, while Allie, whose eyes were as green as her mother's, was clearly destined to be more fiery than her sister. Both children were the apples of their father's eye, but in the months following Allie's birth, Laura began to alternate between bursts of euphoria and anxiety.

"I keep feeling that something must be lurking around the corner," she tried to explain to Gus early that May. "Something waiting to pounce—not literally, of course. Just the idea that something's going to spoil things."

"Postnatal depression?" Gus said.

"I don't think so."

They were in the garden, watching Helen toddle around on the lawn while Sam and Zoë snoozed under the red maple tree and baby Allie slept peacefully under an insect net in her pram.

"If my parents hadn't been killed in that plane crash," Laura mused, "this is probably the kind of life I'd have grown up with. Sometimes, I feel that maybe it makes it right, like a sort of circle."

"And other times you don't. I wonder why," Gus said, laconically.

"What do you mean?"

"Well, it's your old guilt rearing its daft head again, isn't it? Deep down you still think this is all better than you deserve—Tom and the babies, and being happy. Isn't that what you think?"

"Maybe."

"No maybe about it. Though I thought you'd got over it after you told Tom everything."

"So did I," Laura said, quietly. "I thought I'd resolved it all in one fell swoop—but I suppose you can't quite do that, can you?"

"I think you've got to," Gus said. "You've got to stop dwelling on what's dead and buried, otherwise you could damage all the wonderful things you've got now." She paused. "That's what I did, when you and Tom let me come and live with you."

"We didn't let you, we wanted you."

"I know you did. I could have got all stiff-necked and too proud to say yes, but I recognized that you and Tom—well, mainly Tom, really, because you were already family—"

"We're all family now."

"I'm trying to make a point. I'm trying to explain that I made a decision to live my life from that instant on, *really* live, I mean. No more looking back over my shoulder, no more blaming myself for what had happened to me—no more pretending I wasn't blaming myself."

"Do you think that's what I'm still doing?" Laura asked.

"I'm sure of it."

"Suppose it's time I stopped, too, then."

"Do you think you can?"

"You did."

Laura never tired of being with Tom, not for a second. She loved every long, graceful, loping ounce of him. The way his legs got in the way when he sat down on the sofa. The way he fell asleep while he was reading, his glasses slipping halfway down his nose. The way he had of untidying a room within moments of coming into it. The way he sang when he was happy, which was much of the time, great, deep-voiced bursts of Rodgers and Hammerstein. The way he woke her in the mornings, his mouth close to her ear, murmuring loving words. The way he looked when he lay naked on top of the bed, the flatness of his stomach, the leanness of him. His funny, downsloping eyebrows, and his lovely, quirky mouth. His expression when he held Allie, or gazed down at Helen when she was asleep, as if the intensity of his feelings for them filled him with awe.

Desire overwhelmed them both sometimes. There were days when it was hard, really hard, keeping their hands off each other, when Tom had to force himself to stay in an editorial meeting, or at the lunch table with Jon Ajax, the creator of the *Mutt* cartoons, or even in the newsroom, where, for the most part, he would happily have spent hours at a time. And if he could not bear it, if it was possible for him to tear himself away and to drive home to Laura, she was always ready for him, always longing for him as much as he was for her. It had been that way almost from the beginning, once she had got over how different sex with Tom was from sex with Ambler. They had made love in hotels and in Tom's office, in the Land Rover, in the garden, after dark, and in the riding stables in Surrey where they kept the horses that Tom had bought for them soon after their marriage. They had left restaurants abruptly, they had left piles of clothing scattered all over the house when no one else was around to see, and they had made love on the sofa, on the rug in the den—once even on the kitchen table, with Zoë looking bemused but benevolent, and Sam, according to Tom, taking notes.

In the spring of 1992, when Laura heard that Jillian Ambler had given Roger the son and heir he had always yearned for, she was relieved. The rivalry that apparently still existed in Roger's mind between himself and Tom was largely one-sided, since Tom had always accepted that while in the beginning, they had both had to compete for the same slice of cake—the slice that represented the floating, uncommitted readers in the country—after four years of survival for them both, they were by now in fair and square competition with *all* the weeklies, and the *Courier* was the least of the *Journal*'s troubles.

Britain was in the grip of recession, unemployment was rising, companies in every field were falling by the wayside and even major corporations were staggering, their work-forces ravaged by redundancies. In the ever-growing atmosphere of dirty tricks exposed, with Robert Maxwell's death and the subsequent scandal, with royal exposés stealing headlines from famines, wars and worldwide economic calamity, a weekly newspaper still guaranteeing *"Absolute honesty, or your money back"* on every front page was exactly what a substantial section of the news-reading public were crying out for. Without the help of pure sensationalism, however, the *Journal*'s circulation figures were still worryingly low, and continuing survival was the name of the Baileys' game, yet Laura was certain that Ambler still felt a real need to beat them into submission.

Perhaps now that Roger had his son, he might be able to feel that he had won his great victory, since Tom—who didn't give a hoot—had only produced girls. Laura didn't mind Roger feeling triumphant, so long as it didn't harm Tom. Her priorities were all straight and clear now. She had learned what was important in life, and what was not.

And then they began to hear the rumors.

CHAPTER 24

On the second of April 1993, a little less than a year after his scoop on Roger Ambler, the multimillionaire, had been buried by the editor of his New Orleans newspaper, Ozzie Dupont was fired. Having been caught for cheating on his expenses and for pilfering office equipment, he was told that he could count himself fortunate that the cops had not been called, but that he could whistle for any kind of a reference. Ozzie was mad at the editor, but not nearly so mad as he was at himself for getting caught. He was a gambler, and a lousy one at that, and this was no time to be losing his income. He needed money fast.

Having kept copies of his original story and photographs of Ambler, Ozzie had thought more than once about blackmail, but until now the practical difficulties of interstate extortion had daunted him, and besides, he had been too fond of his job to want to lose it, and too fond of his freedom to want to risk going to jail. Now, however, with all his debts, and with the kind of ruthless men to whom he owed that money, Ozzie no longer felt he had any choice. He wrote his two blackmail letters using newsprint from *Newsweek,* and he wore gloves while handling them, and he flew to Philadelphia to mail them, and then he took a bus to New York City and waited, in a seedy hotel near Times Square, for the appointed hour.

* * *

The first letter arrived at Trump Tower on April 20, one year to the day after Roger's greatest indiscretion. It was simple, and to the point.

> *You know what I got. $100,000 stops me going public about your golden boy.*

Roger called the New Orleans editor, who told him he'd just fired Ozzie Dupont, so there probably wasn't too much doubt who had sent the letter. Roger knew that there were no choices open to him. If he went to the police, they might get Dupont, but there was no question that the story would get out. If he handed over the cash, he knew the blackmailer might hold copies back, but still, what else could he do? He had no alternative but to pay.

The shakedown—Roger thought that was the word—was to take place in a bar near Penn Station, the kind of place with a back entrance and bathrooms you were loath to use in case you caught a disease or a knife in the back. He was afraid to go himself in case he was recognized by someone who might then prolong the whole sordid affair, so he decided to send John, his driver, in his place. John had been with Roger for twenty years, and he never asked questions. He could almost certainly be trusted to exchange one brown paper package for another without looking inside either, and without passing comment.

Anyway, Roger had to trust someone.

Ozzie had thought of a way of having his cake and eating it, too. He had the money stashed away, but he also still had the greatest freelance story of his career. History repeated itself, with one crucial difference. He tried to sell the story to the *New York Herald,* but the editor of that newspaper, though no friend of Roger's, was a great pal of Jillian Ambler's father, Senator Franklin Long. For the second time, Ozzie got paid, this time by the senator, in the amount of another hundred grand; but for the second time, Ozzie's great scoop was buried while the would-be journalist scampered back into comfortable obscurity, and Senator Long and his wife flew to New York to break the news to their daughter, and to whisk her and their little grandson back to the safety of their home in Virginia, just outside Washington, D.C.

"If you don't give Jillian every damn thing her father wants, this is going to be a circus," Brian Levy warned Roger darkly.

"What about my son?" Roger was ashen-faced. "I know I'll never get custody, but she won't be able to stop me seeing him, will she?"

"She may try." Levy shrugged. "It's too early for guessing games."

"Jillian's not the vindictive type."

"Maybe you never gave her cause before."

Because of Ambler's well-publicized ownership of his British newspaper, every tabloid in the country except his own reported the divorce, the *Journal* with more caution than anyone, since Tom was aware that if there was any paper Roger would be glad to slap a libel suit on it was his.

"They say she'll get at least thirty million dollars," Gus reported, waving the *Sun* at Laura over the breakfast table. "What I want to know is why you got nothing?"

"You know why." Laura watched Allie waving a toast soldier in the air and waited for it to fly, knowing that Zoë would catch it.

"Because you signed that stupid agreement, but I'll bet Ambler made Jillian sign one too."

Zoë caught the toast and Allie began to cry.

"Allie's naughty," Helen said.

"A little bit naughty," Laura agreed. "I'll make you another one, darling," she told her youngest, "but you mustn't play with food." Laura took another slice from the pile in the middle of the kitchen table and buttered it. "I didn't want anything more out of Roger, as you very well know." She shrugged. "Anyway, I expect he didn't get Jillian to sign anything that eighteen of her lawyers didn't agree with— she's the daughter of a senator, Gus, and probably very wealthy in her own right."

"Who's Jillian?" Helen wanted to know.

"A lady in America," Laura said.

"Mind you," Gus mused, "if you had got millions out of

Ambler, you wouldn't have had any problems with the bank, and Tom wouldn't have had to step in to help."

Laura leaned back, feeling relaxed. "And wouldn't you say we've got more than enough?"

"I'll bet he's in trouble," Gus said.

"I doubt it."

"He'll have to liquidate a lot of his assets to raise that kind of money."

"Get you." Laura grinned. "Why not just say he'll have to sell things?"

"Men like Ambler don't sell, they convert their assets into cash."

"Same thing."

"Allie's done a poo-poo," Helen said.

Allie began to cry.

Ozzie Dupont recognized a good thing when he saw it, and it seemed plain to him that this particular well was still some way from running dry. So what if he'd given the senator the negatives of his photographs—everyone knew you could have new negatives made from prints. Sitting back comfortably in his newly acquired apartment on New York's Christopher Street, Ozzie set about consolidating his story. It was easier than he'd dreamed. The maid who serviced Ambler's Trump Tower apartment had always disliked her employer, and for a thousand dollars she was only too happy to go snooping around for Ozzie, and righteously outraged when she found a folder of indecent pictures of small boys, together with a black lacquered box containing sex aids she described to Ozzie as the most *disgusting* things she'd ever laid eyes on.

Ozzie grew more enterprising. He talked to a number of people and learned a number of useful pieces of information, including the fact that Ambler's third wife, Laura, had left her husband, gone to England and ultimately married Ambler's greatest rival. Having completed his homework, Ozzie composed a new blackmail letter, telling Ambler that he could think of a number of editors who were not in his pocket, and one "Cowboy publisher in England" who would surely be disinclined to hush up the new information that

Ozzie intended giving him, which included evidence of Ambler's penchant for kiddie porn. One million dollars could shut down this story for keeps. It was entirely Ambler's decision.

Summer had hit London early, then sagged back into a typically English mishmash of lovely, balmy days when Laura and Gus were able to laze in the garden surrounded by paperwork, blooming roses, baby girls and dogs, and the other kind, when steely gray clouds hung everywhere and the endless teeming rain made even the inside of the house feel damp enough to switch on the central heating.

The anxieties that Laura had begun to feel shortly after Allie's birth had vanished, and she thought now that they might possibly have been caused by a kind of postnatal depression. Or maybe she had, at last, listened to Gus's wisdom, and turned her eyes clearly and decisively toward the future, to her new life with Tom and their daughters, to a life that she did, perhaps, deserve after all.

And then, on June 29, a Tuesday morning, when Tom and Gus were both working and Grazia had taken the children out to the park, the telephone rang, and Laura, in the bedroom reading *The Times,* answered it and heard Roger's voice asking her how she was.

"I'm very well." Her voice sounded high, almost tinny with shock.

"Aren't you going to ask me how I am?"

"Of course. How are you?"

"Troubled."

"Yes. I'm sorry," she said.

"Are you?"

"Why wouldn't I be?"

Laura held the receiver against her ear, and looked, as if for security, around the room, at the pale creamy magnolia walls, at the framed photographs of Helen and Allie that Tom had taken, at the round china bowl filled with roses from the garden.

"What do you want, Roger?"

"I have to see you."

"What for?" Her stomach clenched unpleasantly.

"On a matter of urgency." He paused. "I can't say more on the phone, Laura, but I can't stress enough how important it is, to you as well as me."

Laura took a moment. "You could come here this evening. I'm sure Tom will be glad to see you."

"My business is with you, Laura."

"Even so—"

"There's a place in Soho called Ed's Easy Diner. You could be there in an hour."

Anger flashed through her. "I'm busy."

"I thought Gus was running your company now."

"I don't think that's any of your business," Laura said coolly. "If you want to see me, you'll have to come to our house when Tom is here."

"You haven't understood me," Roger said, and his voice was calm. "You and I have some unfinished business to attend to. Business that will affect Tom and your daughters adversely if you don't come and see me in one hour, as I ask." He paused. "Twelve Moor Street. I'll be waiting."

Laura heard a click. She put down the receiver.

Outside, the sun was shining, but it seemed to her that the bedroom had grown darker. Silently, moving slowly and automatically, she began to get ready.

It was hard to imagine a restaurant less suited to Roger Ambler, a fifties-style American diner, complete with hot dogs, burgers and jukeboxes, and jammed with life, children in particular. They had not seen one another for nearly five and a half years. Laura looked at Roger, and thought he looked much the same, except that there was a pinched quality about his face that hadn't been there before, and the golden hair was well threaded with silver.

"You look beautiful," he said to her as she sat down, facing him. "Motherhood obviously agrees with you."

"Happiness agrees with me."

"What will you have?" Roger asked.

"I'm not hungry."

"You must have something. Have a hot dog."

"I'll have a Coke." She felt acutely nervous, but she

didn't want to give him the satisfaction of seeing that. "What is it you want, Roger?"

He ordered a plain burger with a salad for himself, and a beer. "I need your help," he said.

"How on earth could I help you?"

His eyes gave nothing away. "I believe the *Journal* is planning to publish an article about me. An exposé. I want to stop that happening."

A jukebox blared Jerry Lee Lewis. Laura knew now that he'd picked the diner for anonymity and the almost certain knowledge that they would not be overheard.

"How could I do that?"

"Any way you choose." Roger looked right at her. "Ask your husband not to print it—steal the file—burn down the *Journal* building." He shrugged. "I don't care how you do it, so long as it doesn't get printed and the material is destroyed."

Laura felt his tension across the table. "Assuming I could do such a thing, why would I want to?"

"To stop me destroying you, your husband, your children."

She felt ice-cold. "And how would you do that?"

"I should have thought that would be obvious to you."

"If you're talking about my past, Tom knows everything."

"Really."

"I told him before we were married. Long before." Laura saw that she had shaken him a little, that plainly he had not expected her to take the risk of telling Tom, any more than she had told him before their marriage. "So you see, there's no point in trying to threaten me."

Roger smiled. "Don't you know yet that there are at least two sides to every story, and a dozen or more different ways of telling them?" He paused as their drinks were delivered to the table. "It isn't Tom I plan to tell, it's the readers of the *Saturday Courier.* And it won't be your side of the story that gets told, it'll be my version." He sipped his beer. "And it won't just be your life that gets wrecked, Laura, it'll be your daughters' lives, too, not to mention your saintly husband's reputation."

Laura felt ill. She wanted to run out of the restaurant, to get out into the street, into the air. She sat very straight.

"How would your version differ from the truth?" she asked. "The facts are all documented. I told you, Tom knows everything there is to know."

"If Tom knew the things I could tell, he wouldn't have married you."

"Lies, you mean."

Roger shrugged. "The truth as I see it." He paused. "But you can stop me, as I told you."

"By stopping the *Journal* printing this so-called exposé about you."

"And making sure no one else gets to print it either."

"What makes you so sure Tom's planning to print anything about you? You must know he's hardly even touched the story about your divorce."

Roger's burger arrived. He didn't even glance at it. "There are stories even the Father Superior of journalism couldn't resist," he said. His lips still smiled slightly, but his eyes were cold. "Don't kid yourself, Laura. Tom would like to see me beaten every bit as much as I'd like to see it happen to him."

"You're wrong."

"I don't think so."

"You must be very scared," Laura said, quite softly, just clearly enough to be heard over "Jailhouse Rock," "to have to resort to this."

"I'm a practical man, you know that. I do what has to be done."

"Including trying to ruin the lives of innocent people."

"Innocent?"

"I wasn't referring to myself."

"Good." Roger paused. "Yes, I would do that, willingly. I will do it, unless you do as I ask."

"I don't see how I can."

"You'd better find a way, or it won't just be your marriage I finish."

"You couldn't finish our marriage, Roger."

"Maybe not. But I can certainly finish Tom."

Laura stared at him. "What has Tom ever done to you?"

Other than trying to fulfill his dream. Even you admitted he planned the *Journal* long before you thought of the *Courier*."

"You stop Tom printing the story about me, and I'll leave you alone, the pair of you, your kids, and Gus."

"Gus?" It was the first time he'd mentioned her name.

"Sure. Gus figures prominently in my version of the Laura Andros story. I'm sure you can imagine the kind of thing." Roger took his crocodile-skin wallet from the breast pocket of his suit, removed a twenty pound note and stood up. "You have two days to give me what I need."

Laura looked up at him. "Or you'll publish your lies about me."

"You know me. I fight dirty."

"But you'll be finished too."

"I may be in trouble," Roger said, "but I won't be finished."

Laura stayed where she was.

"Two days," he repeated.

"Go to hell," Laura said.

In the back of a black cab, Roger sat very still, staring into space, oblivious of the heavy traffic. The encounter hadn't gone as well as he'd anticipated. Laura had changed since they'd last seen one another, she was stronger, more confident, more mature. He had been so sure that she wouldn't have dared to tell Bailey about the schoolgirl killing—for all he knew, she hadn't told him, and what she had said just now had simply been bravado. If that was the case, then he had her over a barrel, though if the new Laura was capable of that kind of bluff, there was no way of knowing for certain which way she would blow. For herself, Roger thought she might have the strength to stomach even the most adverse publicity, but when it came down to protecting her husband and kids, he thought she might do almost anything to stop them being hurt. He hoped that was true—hell, he prayed it was true. Everything depended on it.

He thought about the latest letter from Dupont. The blackmailer had been enraged when Roger had told him he couldn't and wouldn't raise a million dollars in cash, and

Roger supposed that the little scumbag probably didn't believe him, didn't know anything about massive short-term debts or about bankers, made edgy by recession, refusing to roll over loans—Dupont probably figured he had a fortune in cash stashed away in some vault. Multimillionaire businessman, head of the Ambler Corporation, boss of thousands of men and women in America and Europe, and he couldn't raise one million stinking bucks without stirring up a hornet's nest. Rona might have helped him put it together, but that would have meant telling her and Nelson what the bastard had on him, and he couldn't face that.

There were a lot of things he couldn't face. A whole bunch of things that would happen if this story got out. Roger knew now that he was treading water, that all he could hope to buy was time, that it was only a matter of time until it did get out one way or another, even if Laura did manage to gag Bailey. The boy in New Orleans alone, he might have gotten away with, but packaged together with his small, insignificant collection of erotica, that spelled a full-blown scandal. That would lead to a major failure of confidence by shareholders and, more disastrously, by the banks, and if the money men really did pull the rug from under him, Christ alone knew what kind of investigations that might spark into his private life and business dealings.

He blamed Laura for it all, even now he blamed her for everything. All his wives had let him down, but her betrayal was the one that he could still taste most bitterly. He'd been the wrong husband for Suzy and Patricia, but Laura had been a nobody, a two-bit hustler too dishonest to admit what she was, too stupid to recognize what he had given her. If she had simply given him in return what he'd asked of her, none of this need ever have come about. Laura had brought him to this.

If she didn't get him what he wanted now, she would pay for it.

CHAPTER 25

The guilt was back. As dark and ugly and overwhelming as it had ever been. She had been wrong to believe that the past could be laid to rest. She had been wrong to marry Tom, wrong to have brought Helen and Allie into the world with her for a mother. She could accept punishment for herself—she had always known she had escaped too lightly. But not at the expense of Tom and their little girls.

For the first twenty-four hours of the two days Roger had granted her, Laura wandered around in a kind of daze. Externally, she functioned normally, went about her usual everyday business competently, spoke to people in a calm, natural manner. She played with Helen, changed Allie's nappies, cooked a couple of meals, watched Wimbledon tennis on television, made love to Tom, read Helen a story, checked Allie was sleeping soundly, went back to bed, even slept a little. Some moments seemed more real than others. An unsought embrace from Helen, those warm, rounded little arms clutching at her. A cuddle with Allie, after her bathtime, snug and fragrant with Johnson's, flesh of her flesh. Lovemaking with Tom, the moments just after orgasm when he was still inside her, and she wanted to keep him there, never let him go, never.

And then there was the confusion. What to do, how to do it, how to tell Tom that she had been right, after all, that he should never have married her, that her past was going to

ruin them, as she had told him it might. Confusion and
panic. *Ask him not to print it,* Roger had said. *Steal the file,
burn down the* Journal *building.* He knew, better than anyone, if anyone did, that the only way of stopping that article
being published was for Tom to pull it. So she had to talk to
Tom, she had to tell him that Roger Ambler was reduced to
blackmail, and knowing Tom as she did, that, more than
anything, would make him publish and be damned. And then
Roger would strike back, and Tom didn't deserve that, nor
little Helen, nor Allie, nor Gus. Only she deserved that.

At two o'clock on Wednesday afternoon, she went to the
Journal to tell him. She was glad it was going to happen in
the office, better than at home. Tom would know what to do,
she had come around to that. She ought to have told him instantly, she ought to have gone to the paper as soon as she
left the diner, and at least he would have had a little more
time to think or to act whichever way he decided. Another
mistake, another guilt.

"I should have told you right away."

"Of course you should."

The big picture windows in Tom's office were open as
they generally were in summer, because he liked fresh air
better than air-conditioning. The edges of the papers on his
desk, held down by bronze weights, ruffled in the breeze, the
leaves on the big rubber plants and ferns in tubs around
the room waved gently. They were sitting, side by side, on
the sofa.

"I'm sorry," Laura said.

"You were in shock."

"Yes." She couldn't read his eyes.

"And scared."

"I wanted to tell you. But I didn't want you to know. I
wanted it all to go on as it was, to be the same. Not to be
spoiled."

"It won't be spoiled." He was kind, even now.

"Yes," Laura said. "He'll spoil it."

"He can't change us, not you and me."

Laura swallowed hard, knowing this was no time to indulge in the comfort of tears. "Is he right? Do you have an exposé on him?"

Tom nodded, slowly. "In a sense."

"What does that mean?"

"It means I've been given information about him. The kind of stuff that would wreck his reputation if it got out."

"You didn't tell me."

"I thought it might distress you. It's personal, and it's dirty." Tom paused. "I guess you'd better see for yourself."

He stood up and went to his desk, unlocked a drawer, took out a large, buff-colored envelope and gave it to Laura. She opened it, and read, and looked. At the photographs, of Roger and the blond-haired boy, of other small boys, just children. And then, very quickly, she pushed the papers and pictures back into the envelope.

"You see why I didn't rush to show them to you," Tom said.

Laura nodded. "Poor Roger," she said, quietly. She was surprised to find that she pitied him.

"I agree." He took the envelope from her again, and locked it back into his desk drawer.

She looked at him. "This isn't the kind of thing you would print in the *Journal,* is it?"

"Of course not." He came and sat beside her again. "But whoever sent me this, won't leave it at that. If I don't publish it, someone else will, and as for destroying the material, you can be sure these aren't the only copies." He paused. "And it isn't all I have."

"What else?"

"The Ambler Corporation's got all kinds of problems. They own major properties all over the States leased to Supra Oil—a real triple A company, you know? Except that Supra's in big financial trouble, and in this market, Ambler won't find another mega-tenant."

"So he could lose the buildings?"

"Sure—at anything up to a hundred and fifty million bucks a throw." Tom shook his head. "Believe me, he's right to be terrified about this stuff hitting the streets."

Laura looked down at her hands, folded so calmly in her lap.

"What about his threat?"

"To write about you? It's illegal to publish someone's juvenile convictions. Though if he's desperate enough, that might not stop him."

"But he's threatening to write about *us*," Laura said. "What am I going to tell him?"

"Nothing. You tell him nothing."

"I could let him know the *Journal* isn't going to print."

"There's no way we'd publish the kiddie photos, Laura, but I can't say for sure on a Wednesday afternoon exactly what we are or what we're not to print about the Ambler Corporation's financial situation." Every trace of sympathy for his former friend had gone from Tom's expression. "Besides, I won't have Roger or anyone else believe I can be blackmailed into silence."

"So what do I say to him?" Laura felt vulnerable, even with Tom close to her. "He gave me two days. He'll want an answer tomorrow."

"Where's he staying?"

"He didn't say. I expect he'll call me."

"When he does, just tell him you have nothing to say."

"Roger won't accept that."

"Then tell him to go to hell."

Laura smiled slightly. "I already told him to do that."

"Better yet, put him on to me, and I'll tell him."

Laura stood up. She couldn't bear to look at Tom.

"Aren't you concerned, about what he might print?"

"If he sticks to the law and the truth, neither of us has anything to be ashamed of. If he doesn't, we'll sue him."

"As simple as that?" Laura said ironically.

Tom got up and came to her, took her left hand. "Not simple at all. He may do some damage, but we'll get through." He stroked her wedding band. "One thing does baffle me a little."

"What's that?"

"The Roger Ambler I used to know was a master of the big picture. He wouldn't be wasting precious time and energy fighting just one battle." Tom held onto Laura's hand. "For all of his real fear that we might print this smut, he must know that the *Journal*'s only the first in line—that what we drop, a whole string of papers will jump on the minute they're able."

"That's not so hard to understand," Laura said. "He hates me."

"I don't believe that."

"You should." She took her hand away and went over to the windows. "Remember when Rona came to see me, when Gus and I were trying to get the business off the ground? If I'd been in any doubt as to how bitter Roger was—about my leaving him, about my not wanting his money—about marrying me in the first place—Rona took care of that. I remember waiting for months after that, long after he tried to stop our business taking off, to see what else he would do to punish me. I suppose he was just biding his time."

"Even so, the Ambler I used to know ought to be tap-dancing around Switzerland or the Cayman Islands, or wherever else he can salt away some insurance against the worst."

One of the telephones on his desk started to ring. Tom answered it, spoke for a moment, put it down again, returned his attention to Laura, still standing by the windows.

"I wish you didn't look so troubled."

"I'm afraid," she said.

"Look at me, Laura."

She faced him.

"Tell me what you're afraid of."

"Of what he'll do to us." She shook her head. "I don't care what he writes about me, not for my own sake. But I'm sure he'll try to hurt you, and maybe even Helen and Allie, and that terrifies me. He even threatened Gus."

"They're still babies, darling. By the time they're at school, it'll all be long forgotten. And Gus can handle it."

"The legacy may not be forgotten," Laura said. "Not if he succeeds in damaging your reputation."

"He's tried to do that before, many times. He hasn't succeeded yet."

"He's never told the country the kind of woman you're married to before."

"I'm married to a remarkable woman," Tom said, gently.

"Who once served time for manslaughter."

"I thought we got over all that three years ago."

"I don't think we can ever get over that," Laura said.

Roger telephoned Laura at noon the next day.

"Have you decided?"

"There's nothing to decide," Laura said.

"Have you called your husband off?"

"I've spoken to Tom, yes."

"And?" Roger sounded curt.

"He doesn't respond well to threats."

"So he's going to publish?"

"I didn't say that." Laura gripped the phone so tightly that her knuckles blanched. She wanted to tell him that he was safe from the *Journal,* wanted to beg him not to hurt her family, but she knew that pleading with Roger was one thing that Tom might not easily forgive.

"Time to stop playing games, Laura. Is he, or isn't he?"

There was a fist inside her stomach, clenched and twisting.

"I can't discuss this with you, Roger." She paused. "I just want to tell you again that you're wrong about Tom. He's not interested in ruining you."

"Is that all you have to say?" Roger's voice was very cold.

"Yes."

"I think you may live to regret that."

The only mention of Ambler in the *Journal* that Saturday was in the business section and relating to his Supra Oil predicament.

Laura was the first into the hall to pick the *Courier* up off the mat. She saw her photograph on the right hand side of the front page, saw the words heralding a piece within:

SAINT TOM'S WIFE CONVICTED KILLER!

"Show me."

Tom's voice, behind her, made her jump. She held onto the paper, staring at the photograph. It was one that had been taken just after her wedding to Tom, outside Chelsea Register Office, and captioned accordingly. Her eyes burned, and her stomach churned with nausea.

"Let me see it." Gently, he pried it from her fingers. "Come on, love, come and sit down." He opened the door of the den.

"Helen wants breakfast," she said, numbly. "I have to see to Allie."

"Gus can do that," Tom said. "Give yourself a few moments."

"Have you seen it?"

"I'm not interested until you sit down. You're white as a sheet."

He sat her down on the sofa, sat beside her, both arms around her, feeling her trembling, trying to warm her, to comfort her. They were both wearing dressing gowns, their feet bare. They both felt cold.

"This doesn't matter, sweetheart," he said.

"You haven't even seen it yet." Laura's voice was muffled against his shoulder.

"I know what it says. I called a contact over at the *Courier* last night."

"You didn't say anything." Laura sounded accusing.

"I knew morning would come soon enough," Tom said. "I didn't see much point bringing it forward." He paused. "Whatever it says, it'll pass."

"Will it?" Laura took the newspaper, pulled away from him and thrust it in front of his face. "*Look* at it!"

"What's the bastard printed?" Gus stood in the doorway.

"Where are Helen and Allie?" Laura asked.

"In the kitchen. Helen's giving Allie her breakfast and being an angel, as usual."

Tom got up and showed Gus the front page.

"Swine," she said. "What's inside?"

"I haven't looked yet," Laura said.

"Why don't we just burn it?" Gus suggested.

"Let me have it." Laura held out her hand. "Please. It's about me, I think I'm entitled to know what it says." She stood up and took the paper away from Gus. Her hands shook as she turned the pages to find the piece inside.

"It's just a hook," Tom said. "He's telling his readers that a big juicy scandal involving the 'holier-than-thou proprietor of the *Journal*'—that's me—is about to be exposed in a *Courier* exclusive."

"It says," Laura went on, her voice very taut, "that Saint Tom's beautiful half-Greek wife is a convicted criminal who served several years as a teenager for the killing of a school friend." She looked up at them both. "And it says that there's much more to follow."

"That's all?" Gus asked.

"I'd say it was enough to be going on with, wouldn't you?" Laura sat down again, still very pale. "I wish to God now you'd printed what you have on him, Tom."

"You said yourself that's not the way the *Journal* operates, and certainly not before I have reliable confirmation of the whole story." Tom spoke much more calmly than he felt. "I talked to our lawyers last night—they're standing by for your instructions."

"To sue him, you mean?" Laura said.

"Or to take out an injunction, to stop him printing any more."

"What's the point? It's already there in black and white, isn't it. The damage is done."

"So what *are* you going to do?" Gus wanted to know.

Tom's face was grim. "I can't print what I have about Ambler, but I do know a number of people and agencies who ought to be in possession of all the facts."

"Who?" Gus asked.

He folded the newspaper neatly into two, and slid it into his dressing gown pocket. "I have some calls to make. Some people to wake up." He looked down at Laura. "Will you be all right, sweetheart?"

"I'll look after her," Gus said.

"I'm okay." Laura's voice was so quiet they could hardly hear her.

"You will be," Tom said. "We all will be. I guarantee it."

Roger, in Manhattan for a few days, knew that the worst was starting to happen. Supra Oil had gone under, the banks were threatening to foreclose, his Moody's debt rating had plummeted from an A plus to a B plus, and there were frantic messages on his desk from almost every director and financial controller in the Ambler Corporation. In the space of the last twenty-four hours, his offices in the city and in White Plains had been visited by state and federal investigators, all leaving their cards for his attention, discreet for the moment, but an inescapable sign of things to come. When he called Brian Levy to summon him to Trump Tower, and when the attorney politely but firmly told him that he would have to come to his office, Roger knew that he had already begun to lose control.

Levy had what he termed "disquieting" news for Roger. According to Jillian's attorney, certain photographs, indecent in nature, had come to light, and in view of this Jillian was seeking an injunction preventing Roger from seeing their son, even under supervision. And that was not all. The IRS had been tipped off about Roger's offshore accounts, and an investigation was already in progress.

"Do you know who tipped them off?" Roger was ashen-faced.

"How could I?"

"Jillian?"

"It's possible, I suppose. Not her usual style, though in these cases you never know." Levy paused. "What about Laura? Did she know about the accounts?"

Roger stared at the lawyer. "Not in any detail."

"But she knew something?"

"About their existence, in Geneva and Vaduz."

Levy shrugged. "Could be either of them—could be someone else altogether. Either way, it's a mess, I'm afraid."

Roger went to see Rona. Nelson was in Paris, and the twins were at school. They sat in her perfect sitting room, and he told her everything.

"I don't know what to say." Rona was very pale.

"Say what you feel."

She shook her head. "I don't think I even know what I feel."

"Do you hate me?"

"Of course not." Rona's eyes filled suddenly with tears. She could not remember when she had last wept. "I think you're a terrible fool, but I could never hate you." She shook her head, hardly able to take in the catalog of disasters. "I can't believe you've lost Supra Oil, on top of everything else."

Roger leaned back in the glazed chintz-covered armchair. His face was white and drawn and he was very weary, he could not remember ever feeling so weary and so hopeless. "It was nothing at all, you know. The thing in New Orleans. A tiny indiscretion. It meant nothing."

"But why couldn't you at least have been *careful*?"

"I thought I had been."

"But blackmail." Rona closed her eyes for an instant, suppressing a shudder. "Why didn't you tell me when it first happened, Roger? I thought you trusted me."

"I do trust you, Rona. I think you're the only person in the world I do still trust." He shook his head. "I couldn't bring myself to tell you. I was too ashamed."

"But we could have *done* something—something to get rid of that awful weasel of a reporter. Nelson would have helped—you know he can do almost anything that he really needs to."

"What would you have had Nelson do? Hire a hit man? That's not really our style, is it, sis?" His tone was ironic, but there was not a glimmer of humor left in his eyes, only defeat, only darkness.

Rona lifted her hands in a gesture of helplessness, then let them fall back into her lap. "It's that damned little bitch's fault, isn't it? It all started with Laura. If you'd only come to me then, at the very beginning, I'd have stopped you marrying her, and I'm sure none of this would ever have happened."

"Too late for that now," Roger said, softly.

"What are you going to do?"

"To be honest, I don't have the slightest idea."

"Can't we help? Is it too late to buy silence?"

"Much too late. Too many people."

Rona stood up, came to him and rested one hand on his shoulder. "I'll always stand by you. You know that, don't you?"

"I know, sis."

"I'm not sure what Nelson will feel—" She sounded very strained. "We have to think of the girls, of course—"

"Of course."

"But if there's anything you need—" She came to a stop.

Roger's smile was bleak. He reached up and took his sister's hand. It felt very cold. But not as icy as his own.

"Thank you," he said.

Knowing there was nothing left to be done, Laura filled his thoughts. Not as she had done in those early days after he'd first set eyes on her at the Ambler Agency in London. Now there was no desire left in him, no lust, either to have her, or to mold her into the perfect woman for his needs. The only desire he felt now was for revenge.

The articles in the *Courier* would hurt her badly, especially when the implications about Bailey began to bite, yet still he knew they would have each other. He had seen how much she loved him, how happy her second marriage had made her, her children. Even if his articles brought enough discredit on Bailey to finish the *Journal,* the cowboy and Laura would survive the crisis, would probably ride off into some romantic sunset together, their family intact, the Polish thief included. Besides, Bailey had more than enough ammunition to fight back, and as soon as he was able to substantiate Ozzie Dupont's story and whatever else the authorities decided to hit him with, the *Journal*'s disclosures about him would put his own attacks in the shade.

Rona was right. It was all down to Laura. He was finished, he had lost everything, and it had all begun with Laura.

He would have his revenge.

CHAPTER 26

As much as Laura loved the house when everyone was home, all the people she cared about most, she enjoyed the rare moments when she was alone there, too. It was a peaceful house, its atmosphere benevolent, its silences unthreatening. Or they had been until last week, when Roger had invaded her life again. Ever since that headline, she had been waiting for something else to happen. Tom's lawyers had urged her to take action against Roger, but Laura feared that would only magnify the publicity, and Tom could not disagree. He told her not to worry, reassured her repeatedly that they would handle any fallout from the *Courier* article, that all would be well again. Gus advised her to express her anger and then to try to put Ambler behind her once more. But Laura had a sense of foreboding that no amount of reassurance or common sense could shift. She knew there was more to come, that it was not, by any means, over.

When he telephoned again, early that Friday afternoon, she felt little shock. It was Tom's busiest day at the paper, Gus was out overseeing a job, and Grazia and the girls were playing upstairs.

"Aren't you satisfied yet?" she asked him. Tom had told her to let him know instantly if Roger got in touch, had told her not to talk to him.

"Hardly. Things aren't exactly going my way."

"And you feel that's my fault?" Laura was standing in the

kitchen, holding a cordless phone to her ear. It was a cool, wet afternoon, and the view out into the garden was bleak and unseasonable.

"I haven't called to talk about fault."

"Why have you then?" She felt strangely calm.

"I need to see you."

"You saw me last week. It did nothing for either of us."

"I really need to see you now, Laura."

"What for? More blackmail?"

"Call it that if you like."

"What else should I call it?"

"Compromise."

"What does that mean?" she asked. The kitchen door opened a little way, as Zoë nosed her way in from the hall, followed by Sam.

"It means that if you come and meet me again, I may pull Saturday's piece about Tom." He paused. "It's much worse than you imagine, Laura. I'm not claiming that it'll completely destroy him, but it'll certainly do him substantial damage."

"What do you want from me in return for dropping it?" she asked, wryly.

"Just come and meet me. Listen to me."

"I don't see any point," Laura said, though she knew already that she would go. She had known all week that, one way or another, she would see Roger again, that there was an inevitability about it.

"I'm pretty much washed up, you know," he said.

"I don't believe that."

"Yes, you do. Tom's told you what that little bastard sent him about me. He's probably shown it to you."

"He didn't publish it," Laura said.

"Not yet. But he will, when he's ready."

"If you believe that, why would you consider dropping your article about him?"

"Because I've come to the conclusion that I owe you."

She almost laughed. "Since when?"

"I've done some thinking in the last few days. Maybe it wasn't entirely fair of me to let you believe I didn't know about your past when I married you." Roger paused. "Please come."

Laura knew she should stop it right there, knew she should cut him off and call Tom.

"What if I don't?"

"Then you'll be putting your husband through a lot of unnecessary pain." He paused again. "I don't think you want to do that."

In the far corner of the kitchen, Sam and Zoë were playing with a red ball. From upstairs, she heard Helen and Allie laughing.

"Where are you?" Laura asked Roger.

"I've taken an apartment on Mount Street. Number 131, flat 4."

"I'd rather meet you in a public place."

"We can talk better in private." He waited a beat. "You're surely not afraid of me, Laura. I've never hurt you, have I?"

"Not in that way, no."

"Then you'll come."

She stared out of the window at the rain. "Yes."

"I knew you would."

The apartment was devoid of personality, one of those immaculately furnished service apartments that businesspeople on extended trips to London used if they wanted to pretend they had a home base. The furniture in the sitting room was mostly rosewood reproduction, and Laura could see through an open door into the kitchen, and that, too, looked pristine and cold. The windows were double glazed, but the noisy sounds of Mayfair traffic still penetrated the room, and the air within was warm and stuffy.

"I'm going to show you everything the *Courier* could publish if I gave Gordon Harrington the go-ahead," Roger said to Laura, as soon as she had sat down in one of the straight-backed leather armchairs.

"But you won't now, will you?" she said. "Now that I've come."

"We'll see."

Laura gave a small sigh, a little exhalation of breath, more weary than anything else. She sat very still, quite composed, waiting as he brought her a worn pigskin attaché case.

"Take a look." He sat down on the sofa, and crossed his legs.

She stared at the sheaf of photographs of herself and Tom, pictures taken when they had believed themselves private and alone and safe from prying eyes, most of them no more than snaps of lovers, strolling, holding hands, embracing. There was one photograph in which she and Tom were lying down in a stable, kissing, and though they were both fully dressed, Tom's left hand was between her thighs, and her hands were under the back of his shirt.

"You had us followed?" She was disbelieving.

"You know I did. How else would Rona have known where you were living when she came to see you?"

"But this was two years after that."

"I knew watching you would pay off someday." He gave a small smile. "You know how I like to plan."

"I don't see what use these are to you?" She shook her head in confusion. "They're not compromising—neither of us was married to anyone else."

"They're not dated," Roger said. "And I say that you were married at the time, to me. I say that Tom Bailey, the holier-than-anyone crusader, stole the wife of his former friend."

"But that isn't true."

"I say it is. I also say that he set up a ménage à trois with my wife—a teenage killer who failed to tell me that when she married me—and an habitual, man-hating thief."

"There's a law against publishing juvenile convictions," Laura said tautly. "I'm sure you know that."

"Do you imagine I care?" Roger dismissed, and went on. "I tell a fascinating tale of two young girls thrown together in the British juvenile penal system, and of the special bond that neither of the wealthy men that the killer married—for their money—could break."

The photographs slipped out of Laura's fingers and slid off her lap onto the carpet. The strange calmness, the numb sense of the inevitable that had pervaded her when Roger had telephoned, continued to dull her responses. She realized that she must have known, when she agreed to come, that he would not keep his word, that he wanted more from her than her visit to this flat.

"What do you want, Roger? I mean, what do you really want?"

"I'm not sure. I haven't quite decided yet."

"Yes, you have."

He shook his head, the silver threads in his golden hair glinting in the light from the overhead lamp. "No, really." He shrugged. "I guess I'm playing one of my games. I'm toying with you one last time." He still appeared quite calm; only his right index finger drumming lightly on the back of his left hand betrayed his underlying tension. "You were always so easy to play with, Laura, so easy to manipulate."

"Not always," Laura said. "I left you, didn't I?"

"If you hadn't, I expect I'd have thrown you out soon enough," Roger said, still easily. "I overestimated you when I met you. I thought the combination of killer instinct, hard times and strength might make you a formidable partner once I'd got you into shape. But you lacked the intelligence to see what I wanted for you, for us both."

"I don't think I ever knew what it was you really wanted from me. But we both know now, don't we?" Laura looked straight into his eyes. "A normal woman wasn't enough for you, couldn't excite you. You were turned on by what had happened to me."

"What you did, not what happened to you." Anger was there, at last, touching his eyes and his tone.

"I know what I did. I never needed you to tell me."

"That's always been your trouble, Laura. Guilt, instead of honesty. Such a pointless emotion. You'd have been so much better off facing up to what you were, what you still are."

"I know what I am." She started to get up.

"Sit down," he said. "Please."

"I'm not prepared to listen to any more of this, Roger," she said, but she stayed in the armchair. "Tell me what you want, why you asked me to come here, or I'm going home." She paused. "I know that you're in big trouble, we both know that. If you think there's something I can do to help you, just tell me what it is."

He stood up suddenly and walked out of the living room,

his shoes soundless on the wall-to-wall carpet. He was gone
for a few moments, and then he came back into the room.

"Give me your bag." Without waiting for her to move, he
bent down and picked it up.

"What are you doing?"

The bag was taupe leather, with a shoulder strap and zip
fastener. Roger held a key in his hand. "I just locked the
front door," he said. He opened the bag and dropped the key
inside, closed it again and set it down on the sofa.

"Why did you do that?" Some of Laura's calmness went
away, fear taking its place. She ought to have told Grazia
where she was going, she ought to have telephoned Tom.
She ought not to have come.

"Just part of the game," Roger said.

"I won't go to bed with you," she said, suddenly. "If
that's why you've brought me here—"

"I didn't bring you here. You came of your own accord.
And I have no desire to go to bed with you. You were a
lousy lover, the most disappointing of my life." He walked
over to the cocktail bar. "Would you like a drink?"

"No." She looked across at her bag, wondered if he would
stop her if she tried to leave now.

"Are you sure? I'm having a Scotch."

"I don't want anything."

He poured a good three fingers of whisky into a cut-glass
tumbler, added an ice cube and drank some of it immediately. Then he opened a drawer in the cabinet beside the bar
and took something out. He turned to face her. There was a
gun in his hand, a small, silver handgun.

Laura stood up.

"Sit down." His voice was calm. Laura remembered that
in the past, even when Roger had been at his angriest, he
had seldom shouted at her, had never struck her. Which
made this all the more alarming.

"I want to leave," she said, trying not to look at the gun.

"You can't."

"Why not?"

"We're not finished." He took another swallow of whisky.
The gun was in his left hand, held loosely. "Do you remember this?"

She looked at it. "Yes."

"It was yours."

"You gave it to me. I said I didn't want it."

"It's registered in your name. It even has your initials engraved on the handle, remember? Sit down, please."

She sat, looked away from the gun, up into his blue eyes. "You're not going to shoot me."

"Probably not," he said. "I haven't really decided anything yet. I may even have changed my mind about wanting to go to bed with you. You were dull, as a lover, but this might tip the balance, don't you think?"

The rest of the calm disintegrated. The room felt hotter. She felt stifled and ill. "You're not a rapist," she said.

"Probably not," he said again. He strolled back over to the sofa and sat down again, next to her bag. "I'll just finish my drink, and then we can decide."

"What do you *want*?" For the first time, panic colored Laura's voice. "Why don't you tell me? Is there something you want from Tom?" An image of her daughters came into her mind—she had to get home to them, she had to get out of this place *now*. "Tom will do anything you ask, anything to stop you hurting me."

"I'm not going to hurt you."

"Then put the gun away."

"I can't. That's part of the game, too." He drank the rest of the whisky, stood up again and went to pour himself more. He set the gun down on the bar for just a moment while he took the stopper out of the decanter and poured, and then he drank that too, and picked up the gun again.

"I'd like to stop this game now," Laura said.

"Why? Aren't you enjoying it?"

"No, I'm not."

"You'll like it better in a few moments."

"I'll like it when it's over," she said.

"It will be, soon enough."

He walked over to Laura's chair and stooped to pick up the photographs she'd dropped onto the floor. He slipped them back into the attaché case and handed it to her.

"You can have these, if you want."

"I'm sure there are copies."

"Of course. Gordon Harrington has his own set."

"Are you going to cancel the articles?" she asked.

"I won't be able to."

"You have control."

"Not after today," he said. "Though you may not need to worry too much about them. I think the *Courier* may have more dramatic news to print." He slipped the gun into his jacket pocket, turned around and sat down on the sofa. "Game over."

Laura didn't move.

"I'm sorry," he said. "I'm in a strange mood. My mind's been a little disturbed, I guess, but it was wrong of me to try to frighten you."

"Yes." The gun was out of sight, but she felt very sick.

"I'm finished, Laura. We both know that."

"I don't believe that."

"Sure you do." His voice was still quiet, but tauter. "In a few days, there'll be all kinds of people asking questions about all kinds of things. Have you ever noticed how one thing leads to another, Laura? It's like picking at a little scab and making it bleed, and if you're real unlucky, you end up with septicemia and you die."

"You're talking about the boy in New Orleans."

"And those other pictures. They weren't important, they were harmless enough, yet because of them I'll never be allowed to see my son again—"

Laura saw the pain in his eyes and knew that it was genuine. "You can fight that," she said.

"Fighting would just make it worse, you know that. And you know there's more—the financial problems."

"Supra Oil."

"Not to mention the IRS investigating me for tax fraud."

"I didn't know about that."

"Really?" His voice was harsh, ironic. "You have no idea, I suppose, who told them about my offshore bank accounts."

"Of course not—how could I?"

Roger's eyes were narrow. "You're telling me it wasn't you."

Laura stared. "How could you even imagine it was?"

He shook his head. "Oh, I've imagined a lot of things."

"I'm not interested in harming you, Roger," she said, "anymore than Tom is. I wish you'd believe that."

"Maybe I do, maybe not. Either way, it doesn't make a hell of a lot of difference to me now, does it?"

"You can't possibly blame me for any of the things that have happened to you." Laura grew angry, forgetting her fear. "I didn't tell you to take a boy to bed in New Orleans, or to collect pornographic pictures. It's hardly my fault, or Tom's, that Supra Oil has gone under, or that you chose to take money out of America."

"Okay, so I can't blame you."

"Yet you do."

"Yes, I did."

"And now?"

He gave a wan smile. "Now I just want you to do one last favor for me."

"What kind of favor?" She was wary.

"Stay with me, just a little while longer."

"What for?"

"Company."

She stared at him. "You just pulled a gun on me."

"You must have known I wouldn't use it. The gun was just a game." He looked away for a moment, and his voice was tight with emotion. "I've lost people I loved before, Laura, but now I stand to lose everything I've ever cared about. My son, my corporation, perhaps even my freedom."

For a moment, she thought he might be about to weep, and the wave of pity she experienced startled her. "It isn't like you to give up, Roger."

"Knowing when you're beaten's one of the most important parts of the game." His voice was dull. "Doesn't it satisfy you, Laura, just a little?"

"Of course not."

"Surely you think I deserve it?"

"That isn't the way I think, Roger."

"What about Tom?"

"It's not his way, either, you know that."

"No. I guess it isn't." He gave another of those wry smiles. "They won't stop now, you know, till they jail me or

ruin me, or both. I don't think I'll do real well in jail, do
you?"

She couldn't answer.

He stood up slowly. "You'd better go."

Laura rose, too, and looked into his face. There was a
glimmer of tears in his eyes. "I'm sorry, Roger," she said,
softly.

"Sorry enough for a good-bye hug?"

She stood very still for another moment, then took a step
toward him. She smelled the whisky on his breath, saw the
flush on his cheeks, realized how drunk he was. He put his
left arm around her, drew her close, quite gently, and Laura
shut her eyes, hating the feel of him but still pitying him.
Just a few moments more and she'd be out of there, out in
the cool, rainy London air, going home to Tom and their babies, and Roger would be all alone, with nothing.

"I am sorry," she said. "Truly."

She heard nothing, felt nothing, did not see him take the
gun from his pocket, yet suddenly it was there, small and
neat and silver, in his right hand. She gave a sharp gasp of
fear and tried to pull away, but his left arm gripped her so
tightly she couldn't move.

"Roger, for God's sake."

"Don't be afraid, Laura," he said, harshly. "It's me who's
going to die. You just have to watch me."

"No."

"Oh, yes," he said. He brought the gun up between them,
so that its snub nose pointed at his chest—

"No!" Laura grabbed the gun, and it was only a split second later that she understood that he'd let her take it, that
he'd *wanted* her to, and still his left arm pinned her to him,
wedging the gun between them. Only now it was in her
hand. Her heart pounded. She stared into his eyes.

"End of game," Roger said. "Thank you, Laura."

It happened so quickly, the swiftest, yet at the same time
the slowest moment of her life. Not another word, just his
hand over hers, forcing her middle finger onto the trigger.
She seemed to see everything in infinitesimal detail, every
vein on the back of his hand, the silvery sheen of the gun,
the pretty carving of her initials on the handle, appearing,

then disappearing again as their two hands struggled, as he forced her to squeeze the trigger. She felt it move under her finger, felt her legs shake so violently that she thought her bones rattled—and then the explosion flung her back, away from him, and Roger fell backward. His eyes stared at her, he staggered for a moment, and his arms went out as if reaching for something, and then he was down, on the floor, and she saw the blood, and smelled the smoke, and he was jerking on the carpet at her feet, and the gun was still in her hand.

She dropped it. It landed with a thud.

She stared down at Roger. The jerking stopped. Everything stopped. Her heart beat so hard and so high she thought she would choke on it. She heard her breath, gasping, sobbing. She fell on her knees beside him, felt her mind starting to spiral into blackness; she wanted to scream, to let herself go down into the darkness, but then another image of Helen and Allie and Tom came into her brain with such clarity that she knew she had to hold on.

Do something, she had to do something.

She stared at him. She thought he was dead, but she wasn't sure. The blood was flowing freely from the hole in his white shirt and trickling from the side of his mouth. *Stop the bleeding,* came into her mind. She tore at the buttons, felt his skin underneath, still warm, wanted to scream again, ripped the cotton, bunched it in her hand and pushed it hard against the wound.

Call an ambulance. There was a voice in her head, sufficiently detached to keep control, commanding her. She got up, ran to the desk near the window, picked up the telephone, pressed 999, told them to come, told them a man had been shot. And then she called Tom's direct line at the *Journal.* It seemed forever before he answered; she thought she would faint when she heard his voice.

"I need you," she said.

"Laura, what's happened? Are you sick? Are the girls—?"

"I've shot him. I've shot Roger." Her voice was hoarse. "He made me do it, but I shot him."

"Where are you? Laura, where *are* you?"

She told him, put down the receiver.

Keep him alive, the voice in her mind said.

She knelt down again, took Roger's wrist, felt for a pulse, found nothing. She looked down at him, and she knew precisely what he'd done to her, and she had never hated anyone so much in her life, not even Lucia Lindberg. And she bent her head down to his, and she tilted his chin the way they had taught her in the first aid classes she had taken after Helen's birth, and even though she hated him, and even though she knew that he was already dead, she began to breathe into his mouth.

CHAPTER 27

He was not dead. They took him away in an ambulance, and Laura remained, for a few minutes, in the flat, flanked by police officers. Tom came, white-faced and frightened for her, held her in his arms for a few moments until they made him stop, but Laura, numbed by shock, hardly responded, even to him.

They read her her rights and took her away from the flat, from Tom, and drove her to a police station at the back of Regent Street. Laura acquiesced to everything, answered questions, obeyed orders, felt little. They took away her clothes and gave her white overalls and plimsoll shoes to wear, and a police surgeon examined her, and Edward Truman, Tom's lawyer, came, and they interviewed her, took her statement and charged her with attempted murder and grievous bodily harm. And then they fingerprinted her and took her photograph, and she and Truman were left alone.

Laura had met him only twice before today. He was short and stocky, with sparse white hair and metal-framed spectacles.

"I'd like to go over it again. All right, Laura?"

"Yes."

"Did you shoot Roger Ambler?" Truman's voice was deep and calm, inspiring confidence.

"I suppose I did, in a way." She spoke softly. She felt very tired.

"Tell me again exactly what happened."

"Just what I said. He forced the gun into my hand. He made me pull the trigger."

"Why did he do that?"

"He wanted to kill himself. Only he wanted me to do it for him."

"Why?"

"Why did he want to die, you mean?"

"If you know the answer."

"He was in terrible trouble. He said he thought he was either going to end up in jail, or be ruined, or maybe both. Roger couldn't bear that."

"And why did he want you to do it?"

"Because he hated me. He blamed me."

Edward Truman looked at her intently. "Why did you go to the flat?"

"I shouldn't have gone."

"But why did you?"

"He phoned me. You already know about the piece in the *Courier* last week."

"Yes."

"He said there was more to come, and that it would hurt Tom badly. He said he would cancel the articles if I came to see him."

"You believed him?"

"Not really."

"So why did you go?"

"I didn't know what else to do."

"Maybe you went there to stop him," Truman said.

"Of course I wanted to stop him." Laura looked at him. "You mean did I go there to kill him?" She shook her head. "No, of course not. I didn't want Roger dead." She stopped. "Is he dead?"

"Not as far as I know."

"I thought he was. Even while I was breathing into him."

"You gave him mouth-to-mouth resuscitation?" the lawyer asked.

Laura nodded. "But it didn't seem to make any difference."

"Do you know how to give CPR?"

"I took some first aid classes after Helen was born—that's our oldest daughter."

"I know Helen. And Allie."

"Yes," Laura said. "Of course you do."

"Did anyone see you giving him CPR?" Truman asked.

"No. I had to open the door to let them in. Roger had locked the front door and put the key in my handbag."

"Why did he do that?"

"I don't know." She sighed, wearily. "He said it was part of the game. He kept calling it that, a game."

"It's a pity no one observed you trying to save his life," Truman said.

Laura thought. "There was some blood on my cheek, from his mouth. They seemed to think it was evidence."

"They might have thought you kissed him."

"Why would I do that?"

"You were married once. You were lovers."

"I'm married to Tom." Laura paused. "Do you believe me? That he made me do it?"

"I'd be happier if you stopped saying that, Laura. 'He made me do it' could mean all kinds of things. From what you say, Ambler actually pulled the trigger himself, forcing you to hold the gun."

"That's right. That's what happened."

"Then there's no need to keep saying that you did it. You didn't do anything, Laura."

"Didn't I?" she asked.

She kept wondering if she could have stopped it happening, if she could have fought harder to knock the gun away. She had felt so powerless, but she was no longer certain if it had been Roger's greater strength that had made her so helpless, or if it had perhaps been some inner wish to see him dead.

She slept for a while in her cell, and she dreamed of Lucia, in her shroud, walking toward her holding a silver gun in her hand, and then she was falling, falling off the edge of a steep hill, and there was a knife in her chest, and her doll's eyes were very blue and accusing, and then suddenly it wasn't Lucia falling, it was Roger, and he was speaking to Laura, telling her that it was all part of the game, just a game.

They brought her to the magistrate's court, and remanded her in custody without bail, for she had a previous conviction and they said that she was a potential danger to the public and, perhaps, to herself.

Roger Ambler was still alive.

When Gus heard that Laura had been sent to Holloway, she went to her bedroom and wept for more than an hour. Tom came in to try to comfort her, but she was inconsolable.

"She won't stand it, Tom."

"Laura's strong, Gus."

"Not strong enough. I've been there, I know."

"I know you have."

Gus sat up. "Where are the kids?"

"With Grazia. They're okay."

"What are we going to do, Tom?"

"We're going to get her out."

"But how?" Gus's eyes were desperate. "They don't believe a word she's saying—it looks so bad."

"We believe her, Edward Truman believes her. There's all the evidence in the world to prove that Ambler might have wanted to commit suicide." Tom paused, his eyes very dark. "And then there's Ambler himself."

"He's going to make it, isn't he?"

Tom nodded. "But he's still not talking."

"Even when he does, why should he back up Laura's story?"

"Maybe there's still a shred of decency in the man. There used to be."

"Not when I knew him," Gus said.

Rona came and sat by Roger's bed in the intensive care unit. He was hooked up to so many monitors, there were so many tubes, wires, small plastic bags hooked everywhere, dripping infusions into him, but he was breathing on his own now.

"She says you wanted to die, Roger. She says you made her do it. That isn't true, is it? You're stronger than that, better than that."

Rona's eyes were red from weeping, the suit she was wearing was crumpled and her hair and makeup were messed up, but she didn't care about any of those things, she only wanted her brother to wake up and talk to her and to tell her that the bitch had done this to him.

"Roger, darling, for the love of God, please come back and tell them all that she's lying. They've charged her, but I'm so afraid they might not find her guilty, and I couldn't bear that."

She talked to him all the time, when Nelson wasn't around. When her husband was with her, she just kept her eyes shut and held her brother's hand, and prayed for him to get better. She couldn't bear even Nelson to think that there was the tiniest question mark in her mind that it might have happened the way Laura claimed it did.

He'd been so depressed when he'd come to see her in New York, she'd never seen him so down, so unlike himself. But Roger was a winner, he would never have let them beat him, and sure, he might have been guilty of a few sexual peccadilloes, and of course the numbered accounts in Switzerland and Liechtenstein weren't strictly ethical, but everyone with any money to speak of had to take those kinds of measures, and it was her brother's advisers who deserved to be shot for not making sure the accounts were watertight. Of course Roger had been depressed, but he would never have considered suicide. Rona knew him better than that, she knew him better than anyone in the entire world. And she'd told him she'd always stand by him, no matter what.

She chose not to remember that she'd also said that she couldn't be certain about Nelson, and that they had their girls to consider. It went without saying that none of them would ever have let Roger down.

This was Laura's doing, no one else's.

Laura was afraid all the time. Coming into the prison had, in a way, been the worst of it. Made to wait in the reception office for hours, made to stand on a towel while the officers went through every item of her clothing, made to drop her robe and turn for them, naked, while they stared. Ordered to bathe, checked for lice and crabs, made to wait for hours in

a dressing gown for the doctor's examination. Being taken to
her wing, put into her cell. Waiting, always waiting, feeling
panics rise and fall, the panic of isolation and the panic of
confrontation, with officers, with inmates. Gus came into her
mind all the time, her stories of Holloway, starkly told, and
worse, those stories she had never told. Laura knew she was
lucky in her cellmate, an old woman named Susie in for
bashing up her husband with a Morphy Richards toaster.
Susie hated her husband, but she had a sense of humor and
she took to Laura right away, protecting her from the nasti-
est of the prison guards and the more dangerous women, but
still Laura waited for cruelty, stood rigidly in lines, for food,
for showers, kept her eyes averted but her chin up, the way
Gus the hard case had taught her eighteen years before.

Laura got through most days and nights by retreating into
herself. She remembered doing that at Kane House, after
they'd taken Gus away to borstal; it was her way of surviv-
ing. Susie helped a little, but there was nothing between
them, no real friendship, nothing to stop the terrors that suffocated her when the lights went out at night. She was luckier than Gus had been. No one had beaten her yet, nor tried
to rape her, and the women she came into contact with were
not, on the whole, unkind. But still, she was afraid all the
time.

She tried to think about Tom and the children as little as
possible. She was in a place where she knew evil prevailed
as often as good, where difficult prisoners could be strait-
jacketed, were often drugged until they could barely speak,
where despairing women tried to commit suicide, where the
strong overwhelmed the weak. It seemed wicked to bring
even a mental image of either Helen or Allie into such a
place. And when she thought about Tom and what she had
done to him, her guilt became unbearable.

Adam came to see her one day. He had flown to London as
soon as he and Fran had heard what had happened, frantic to
do what he could to set the record straight.

"I wanted to tell them what Ambler had done to me," he
told Laura, "but your Mr. Truman won't let me. He says it

would only strengthen the case for the prosecution—it would only prove you had more reason to want to kill him."

"He's right," Laura said.

"It's all so crazy, so monstrous, you being in this place."

Adam looked so fit and well, suntanned from the Long Island summer, and happy from his life with Fran and their children, and Laura felt terrible about dragging him all the way to England on a fool's errand, but he insisted that nothing could have kept him away, and that when this was all over, their two families would have to meet in Greece for a holiday, and Laura smiled with love and sent him on his way, and thought that she would never see him again.

Because she was a remand prisoner, Tom and Gus were allowed to visit her all the time. Laura knew what it cost Gus to come into the prison, saw the sick expression in her eyes, told her repeatedly that she didn't have to come, that she wouldn't feel she was being abandoned if she did not, but Gus wouldn't even discuss it.

"I'm the only one who knows," she said, more than once. "I'm the only one who can remind you that it doesn't have to finish you, that you can get it all back again."

"But I know that anyway," Laura told her. "You don't have to torture yourself to prove it."

"If I don't keep coming," Gus argued, "you'll forget. You'll get sucked in, and you'll crawl back into that hole inside your head, and you'll stay there."

"I won't forget," Laura said.

But Gus kept coming anyway.

Tom's visits were the worst of all. She loved her first glimpse of him, oh, how she loved that moment, but then there was the pain in his eyes, all for her, and the awful fear and longing, and the knowledge that she had done this to him, that she had been so terribly right when she'd told him not to marry her, drove her almost out of her mind with self-condemnation.

"Ambler's conscious," he told her. "They say he'll make a full recovery."

"Has he told anyone what happened?" she asked, though

she knew that he had not, for if Roger had told the truth, she would no longer be in prison.

"I don't think his doctors have allowed the police to interview him yet," Tom said, and Laura was sure he was lying, and Tom was aware of what she thought, but neither of them took it any further because neither could bear to.

"Helen drew you a picture." He gave it to her. "That's your red maple—" He pointed to a long brown blob. "And this is Allie—" A small pinkish blob. "And those two sausage-shaped things with tails are Zoë and Sam—"

"Of course." Laura was crying.

"And this is you and me." He looked stricken. "Sweetheart, please don't cry—we all love you so much, and you'll be home soon, where you belong."

"I know I will." She couldn't help crying, that was the awful part of his visits, that and the first hour after he'd gone, when the void seemed too agonizing to endure. "I'm sorry," she whispered.

"You have nothing to be sorry about," he told her, and he wanted to weep, too, and he knew that he would, when he left the prison and got into the car to drive home.

Laura wiped her eyes. "Promise me something."

"Anything."

"If they find me guilty, you'll get a divorce."

Tom looked stunned, as if she'd slapped him. "Don't ever say that again."

"It's the best thing—"

"It's not up for discussion." His eyes grew fierce, his mouth determined. "You will not be found guilty, and even if you were, I will never, ever give up on you, do you hear me?"

"You're a fool, Tom Bailey."

"I may have been born a fool," he said, "but falling in love with you was the wisest thing I ever did. And I don't ever want to have this conversation again, is that clear?"

"I don't deserve you."

"Enough."

"But it's the truth—"

"I said *enough*."

And after that, they just looked at each other, memorizing what they saw.

When Roger knew that he was going to survive, and that it was only a matter of days before his doctors would have to allow him to talk to the lineup of police officers and investigators waiting to interview him, he began to hide the medication the nurses brought him for pain and for sleep.

Rona came twice each day, and she was stoic now, and he thought he saw more of Mary Ambler, their mother, in her than he had ever seen before. Rona had taken a hard look at her priorities, and had found them lacking, and all she spoke about when she was with her brother now was his recovery, and the value of the life that they would all share, a value that had little—if not exactly nothing—to do with the millions of dollars they had both become used to.

Nelson came from time to time, duty visits, but Roger understood his brother-in-law and appreciated that he would do anything in his power for Rona and their girls. Brian Levy flew over from New York, to gently bring Roger up to date on his worsening situation. Hal Deacon visited, brought him grapes and his Wednesday agency reports. Jillian neither came, nor sent a letter or even a get-well card, and of little Roger, his own son, there was not a word.

He thought about Laura more often than he had expected to—though, of course, he had not anticipated having to think at all after their last meeting—and he found, to his surprise, that he felt increasingly uncomfortable with the knowledge that she was languishing in jail on his account. When he'd planned enmeshing her in his suicide, he'd felt no guilt, no qualms at all, only a pleasant glow of justification, but now the prospect of her receiving a potentially long prison sentence brought him no pleasure at all.

Maybe it was the drugs they were giving him—he did not, after all, stash away everything they handed him to swallow, and they were still feeding him all kinds of stuff through a drip and a damned tube in his nose—but he no longer seemed to hate Laura as much as he had done. He supposed, after all, that they were both victims in a sense. It was all one big accident waiting to happen. Some people escaped, others didn't. Roger Jefferson Ambler had been a winner for so long, a permanently ascending, world-class winner. Compared to the specter of becoming a loser, the prospect of dying held no terrors for him—he simply had no intention of waiting around to find out what true defeat felt like.

He trusted Rona and Nelson to keep things as quiet as they could, though in view of the fire he had personally lit in the pages of his newspaper, that might prove an impossible task. He contemplated writing a final piece for the *Courier*, but he suspected that Gordon Harrington might not even want to run it, so he'd save himself the effort. He was too weak to write much, anyway, and there wasn't even all that much left that he wanted to say.

He settled, in the end, for a few words of love for Rona and Nelson and his nieces, and another short note for his son, that he hoped against hope Jillian might relent enough to pass on, in time. And then there was one more line to write, in a handwriting grown so uncharacteristically weak and scrawly that he could hardly read it himself.

If at first you don't succeed . . .

He took the pills at night, after they'd switched out the lights in his room. He was no longer hooked up to the heart monitor, so with luck there'd be no warning for the nurses. He'd been especially cheery with them all that last evening, had told them all how much better he was feeling, had thanked them for their kindness to him. It pleased him to think that there'd at least be a few women out there who might feel warmly toward him, even if the warmth didn't last long once they learned what he'd done to Laura.

He wondered, as he drifted into sleep, how Laura would feel about him when they released her. His other wives would probably cheer him on down into hell, but knowing Laura as he did, he thought that, more than anything else, she would probably feel guilty.

CHAPTER 28

When Tom brought Laura home from the prison, the house was filled with flowers and the smells of cooking and the ecstatic howling of the dogs, and Helen, with Gus's help, had made a banner for the living room that read "*Welcome Home, Mummy.*" Laura held both her children close for a long time, her face bathed with tears, and Gus had prepared a dinner of all her favorite dishes, and that night, when they'd kissed their daughters good night together, Tom made love to Laura with the greatest tenderness, and they were both filled with gratitude.

As the days went on, Laura waited to feel normal again. She had expected to feel relief, even joy, at the great good fortune of her escape, at whatever emotion that had caused Roger, on his deathbed, to leave no room for doubt that the shooting, too, had been a suicide bid, compelling the Crown prosecution to withdraw. Laura went through the motions of celebration for Tom's sake, and for the little girls and Gus, but all she really felt, deep inside herself, was fear.

"Are you all right, love?" Tom asked her one night, cradling her head protectively in the crook of his arm.

"I'm fine," she told him, absently stroking the soft hair on his forearm.

"I know how much you've been through." He suppressed the urge to hold her even closer, to hug the sadness out of her. "It's only natural if you feel low, or strange, maybe—"

"I don't feel strange," Laura lied.

"You're sure? You'd tell me, wouldn't you, if you were unhappy?"

"Of course I would."

"Promise me."

"I promise."

The scandal surrounding Roger's suicide, and the financial chaos that ensued, threatened to endanger his whole empire. Rona fought valiantly and succeeded in steadying the old stalwarts, Ambler Shoes and Ambler Computers and the agencies, but the *Saturday Courier* had been a reflection of the man's ego, and consequently, in the aftermath, it reflected the irretrievable damage to his credibility.

"How would you feel about the possibility of a merger?" Tom asked Laura one evening in October, when she was in the bath, sponging soap over her arms and shoulders. "Between the *Courier* and the *Journal*."

"It wouldn't work, surely?" She was startled.

"As a matter of fact, I think it might."

"I didn't know it was even on the cards."

Tom turned away for a moment. In other circumstances, he knew he would have discussed the idea with Laura every step of the way, but she had still seemed so fragile that he had felt reluctant to broach the topic.

"It's a logical thought," he said, turning back. "We're both in big trouble for different reasons. A move like this might save two papers and two gifted workforces from going down."

"But you despise the *Courier*." She soaped her legs.

"Not at all." He paused. "It's hard to say this without taking potshots at a dead man, but with a less sensationalist mind at the top, it could be a damned fine paper. Gordon Harrington was Ambler's man, but he's put together a talented team—there are quite a few people over there I'd be proud to have work for me."

"And you'd still be editor?" Laura lay back to soak in what remained of the bubbles.

"That's the general idea."

"Sounds as if this has already been worked out."

"There have been a few meetings," Tom admitted. "I didn't talk to you about it before because I thought it might not come to anything—it still might not, of course. And because I thought it might be too painful." He paused again. "To be honest, I feel like a vulture. Roger would hate this more than anything."

"Yes, he would." Laura thought about it. "But you always said that the *Courier* was just another business to him, that he would never really care that much about the newspaper."

"Yet I think it did become more than that to him in the end."

They fell silent for a few moments. Laura was reluctant to get out of the bath. She felt safe in the warm, scented water.

"What would the new paper be called?" she asked.

Tom shook his head. "Too soon to think about that. Conceivably the *New Courier,* incorporating the *Journal.* More likely than the other way around—the *Courier* has more readers, it would make sense." He took one of the big white towels from the heated rail. "Come on, let me dry you."

She stayed where she was. "What about your guarantee?"

He smiled. "I'd fight for it, but I might have to let that go. I'd have to compromise on a lot of things, sweetheart—it wouldn't be my dream child anymore, not my perfect baby, anyway, but I think it might be worth it."

"And we could stay here," Laura said. "We wouldn't have to uproot."

"Does that make you happy?" Tom said.

"I think I'd be happy anywhere with you and the girls," she said, and climbed out of the bath.

Laura had never really lied to Tom in the past. The occasional, commonplace fib, generally told to save unnecessary anxiety or simply time—"*I'm fine,*" when you were feeling lousy—"*I don't mind,*" when you really minded quite a good deal—but nothing major, until now.

She told Tom and Gus she was happy because she knew she ought to feel that way. Things were good, things were wonderful, they were all healthy, there was a good chance that the *New Courier* might become a reality, with Tom becoming a greater force in the newspaper world; the gossip was dying down, and no one believed anymore that she had tried to kill Roger Ambler.

That was the worst of it. She didn't understand the way she felt. She didn't know why she woke up in the small hours, her heart pounding so hard that she thought she might be dying. Nor why she found herself rooted to the spot while walking down a street, nor why in the middle of shopping in Harrods or a supermarket—perhaps even in the few minutes it took for a sales assistant to wrap her purchase—she would suddenly experience an overwhelming need to escape from the crowds of people—all of them normal and able to cope—and to get home as fast as possible, so that she could breathe full breaths, so that she could steady her trembling, so that she could hide.

The fear grew worse. It started out senseless, a nameless panic that she put down to anxiety following the trauma she had been through, but gradually Laura began to understand what she was so afraid of, and fear developed into full-blown terror.

She was afraid of what was inside her. Of what had really caused her to kill Lucia Lindberg, of what had really allowed her to let Roger squeeze the trigger of that lethal little gun. It was not enough to accept that she had been scared of Lucia, or that Lucia had somehow run into that knife, just as it was not acceptable that Roger had forced her to hold that gun to his chest. She had held that knife, she had held the gun. And what terrified her now, more than anything in her life ever had, was that she might, someday, do such a thing again. Those things had happened *to* her, that was what Gus, and later Tom, had always tried to convince her of, but who could guarantee that moments like that would never happen to her again? Who could guarantee that she would keep control?

Her fears became more focused. She began to dislike the knives in her kitchen drawers. She tried not to touch them unnecessarily, even tried not to look at them, fought to hide the fact from Tom and Gus and Grazia. She began to feel apprehension of anything that might be used as a weapon, even the most innocent things; an old baseball bat at the back of one of Tom's wardrobes, the fire irons by the fireplaces in the den and sitting room. And more disturbing than anything, she began to fear her own hands, when she bathed Allie, her beautiful little daughter whom she loved with every fiber of her being, or when she drew up Helen's covers in her bed and kissed her good night. She knew, she knew, she *knew,* that she would never, ever hurt a hair on Allie's beloved head or on Helen's, yet a small and terrible voice in her mind returned over and over again to haunt her and to taunt her. *But are you sure, Laura? Can you really be sure?*

Gus went to the *Journal* to see Tom.

"I'm worried about Laura," she told him. "She isn't herself. She's here, and she's doing all the things she normally does, and she says all the right things, and yet sometimes I feel that she isn't really here at all."

"I feel the same way," Tom said. "I've tried to talk to her about it, but I know I have to keep it gentle, and there's that look in her eyes, as if she's scared of something."

"It's that bloody guilt of hers again," Gus said, "I'm sure of it. Only it's worse than ever—almost as if she feels she doesn't have the right to be happy, to have the things she has, or the people she loves."

"I've been hoping you might get through to her. You know a little of what she's been through."

"I've been inside," Gus said, "but I've never been in Laura's head."

"I thought at first she was suffering the way you did, after you—" He stopped.

"After I was raped." She shook her head. "It's not the same, Tom. I mean I know I went through that crazy time when I wondered if maybe I was to blame, somehow, for that, and for what happened in prison, but that was just some kind of stage I think I had to go through."

"And you don't think this is just a stage with Laura?" Tom had only kept himself going for the past few weeks with the hope that Laura's remoteness was a passing phase.

"No, I don't." Gus's eyes were bleak. "I think that guilt has become a part of her. I think it's taking over, that's what I'm afraid of."

"She won't see a doctor, she won't talk about it."

"I can relate to that," Gus admitted. "It's one thing seeing that someone you love needs help, it's another thing accepting that it's you who needs it."

"So what do we do?"

"Just go on, I suppose. Just be there for her, as much as possible, as much as she'll let us."

"She's different with the girls, too," Tom said unhappily. "They've both noticed it, though they don't understand what's different. She doesn't spend the time alone with them that she used to, she keeps going off to be by herself."

"What about that doctor, the one who came to see me that time?"

"Christine Morfield." Tom shrugged helplessly. "I talked to her last week, and I mentioned her to Laura, but she doesn't want to know, and Christine says she can't do anything unless Laura's willing to see her—"

"Or she cracks up like I did."

"Exactly."

The dogs sensed Laura's despair. Often, when she was alone and when the dark feelings began to swamp her, they came to find her, and then Sam would sit beside her and lean his full weight against her legs, and Zoë would put her head in her lap and gaze up into her face with her beautiful eyes, and then Laura would start to cry, and she felt a little lighter after that, a little better, for a while at least, for letting it out. But it never lasted for long. She tried to occupy herself more, told herself it was time she took more of an active interest in the business again, but Gus ran it so tightly, so easily, that there was little to engage or stretch Laura. She saw her daughters' eager, needy expressions and Tom's growing misery and Gus's anxiety, but she didn't know how to make them feel better, and their concern only added to her burden and her culpability, and so, as with the knives, she tried not to look at them more than she needed to.

Her dreams alternated between black nightmares, in which Lucia and Roger invariably figured, with newer torments added, her babies covered in blood, or her own hands, scarlet and unwashable—and sweeter dreams in which all her fears were gone, and she and Tom were happier than they had ever been; and sometimes she even dreamed of her grandfather, and he was so gentle, so loving and warm, and she felt protected and cared for, and in their way, those dreams were even crueler because the dread, on waking, was still there, clutching her, gripping at her heart and her mind every morning, every day, every night.

Laura began to long for sleep. Dreamless, endless, unwaking sleep. It was the only way out of the pain, out of the fear. If she stayed as she was, the moment might come when she lost control, and she could not risk that. She remembered how good it had felt to be alive: as a child on Aegina with Theo and Adam, as a young adult in Finborough Road with Gus, in France in those first, heady days, when she had believed that what Roger offered her, above all, was freedom. With Tom, in their bed, so close, so loving and passionate; with Tom in the labor ward when she had Helen and Allie; her first sight of her daughters' faces, the inexpressible, searing love.

All gone now. All that was left now was this endless horror, this unendurable specter of insanity. And the knowledge, suddenly certain and unshakable, that they would all be better off without her.

She left no notes, for she had no words to make it better for any of them. She knew how wrong it was, knew that of everything she had ever been guilty of, this was perhaps the worst, but she knew, too, that she had no choice.

She took a taxi to Paddington Station and stood in the crowd watching the indicator board for the first train that would take her to Westbury. She bought a sandwich and a cup of coffee, but she neither ate nor drank anything. She was oblivious of the people around her, felt no more surges of panic; her heart beat steadily, her breathing was even.

The taxi driver who picked her up at Westbury and dropped her as close as possible to the White Horse warned her that, being November, it would soon be dark, and that these hills were not a suitable place for a young lady on her own to be wandering at night.

"I won't be staying long," she assured him.

"I could wait for you then."

"It's not necessary, thank you. I'll walk back down."

"I don't mind waiting," he said.

"No, really," she said. "But thank you."

Laura walked slowly through the long grass. The ground was uneven. Twice she stumbled, but kept her footing. It was a murky afternoon, drizzly and cold, but she scarcely noticed.

She came to the top of Westbury Hill. Far below in the valley, the tall white chimney of the cement works still funneled smoke up into the sky. Laura turned her head to the right and saw the White Horse, saw its remembered, elegant head and long, slender legs. Three men stood in a huddle near the top of the escarpment, and it looked to Laura as if they might have been working on the horse, perhaps rescouring the chalk. She stood, for a moment, watching them. She had not expected anyone else to be there so late in the day. And then the men began to walk away, to a van that Laura had not previously noticed, parked on the flat ground a few hundred yards back from the hill. She heard the doors bang shut, heard the engine starting, saw the van move away and disappear, leaving her alone.

She edged closer to the top of the escarpment, tilted her face toward the horse, and closed her eyes, remembering. The image was still so clear, as if it were happening again. They were all there, surrounding her. Priscilla and Abigail, Gerry and Freddy. And Lucia. And Gerry was holding her again, gripping her tightly. And the knife was in her hand. And Lucia was coming at her.

Laura opened her eyes. She felt weak and dizzy. There was a bench just a few feet away, but she did not go to it, just sank down where she was, onto the hard, sodden ground.

The cold November wind howled, and the rain intensified.

When Grazia told Gus that she had not seen Laura since breakfast, and that she had gone out without a word of explanation, had simply hugged the little ones and left, Gus grew afraid.

"I think you should come home," she told Tom on the telephone.

"You've no idea at all where she might be?" he asked, his voice tense.

"Not a single one." She hesitated. "I know there's probably nothing to worry about—she could be anywhere—"

"But you're scared."

"I'm terrified."

"I'm on my way."

They were so helpless, it was maddening. There was no point in searching for her, but they went out looking, anyway, driving around, walking the embankment with a flashlight, Tom hanging onto his mobile phone in case Grazia called with good news, staring at every figure they passed, but they both knew that it was hopeless.

"She could be lying somewhere," Tom said through gritted teeth as he drove.

"She isn't."

"But she could be hurt—"

"We'd know about that. She took a handbag, she'll have identification."

"Where the hell *is* she?" Tom's fingers gripped the wheel tightly, his eyes wild with fear, looking around all the time. "We should never have left her alone."

"It's my fault. I had an appointment, but I could have—"

"I didn't mean that, Gus. You're not her guardian, and Laura hates to be crowded anyway."

"She never used to feel crowded," Gus said.

"I should have insisted she see a doctor, I should have made her talk to Christine Morfield, I should have done *something.*"

"She'll be all right, Tom." Gus's eyes burned from searching.

"She has to be."

The telephone rang at seventeen minutes past eleven. Tom and Gus were in the den, Gus sitting on the edge of one of the armchairs, Tom pacing. All the curtains in the house, except for the nursery, were open, all the lights switched on, as if they half believed Laura might be out there, watching, needing some extra signal of assurance.

Tom snatched up the receiver.

"Laura?"

For a moment, he heard nothing.

"Laura, is that you?"

"Yes," she said, very softly.

The relief was overwhelming. "Sweetheart, where are you? We've been going out of our minds." Across the room, Gus was up on her feet, hot spots of excitement on her pale cheeks.

"I'm all right," Laura said. "Will you come, Tom?"

"You bet I will—just tell me where you are."

"I want you to come alone."

"Of course—whatever you say."

"Only I need to talk to you, explain things."

"Please, just tell me where you are, Laura."

"I'm at the Westbury Hotel."

"In Wiltshire?" He saw his own confusion mirrored in Gus's eyes.

"Yes." She sounded terribly tired. "Don't worry about me, Tom. Just come."

"I'm on my way."

Part of the hotel dated back to the sixteenth century, but Laura's bedroom was modern and pleasantly decorated. She was sitting on the end of the bed when Tom came in, her back straight, her eyes closed. She opened them when she heard his voice. He came to her swiftly, and she stood and let him hold her tightly, though she did not embrace him in return, simply stood very still, leaning against him a little. It was quite dark in the room, just a single lamp over a bedside table switched on.

Tom drew back to look at her. "Tell me what happened." He saw that she was utterly exhausted, guessed that she had walked a long way and had probably eaten little, if anything.

"I went to the White Horse."

"The place where Lucia died."

"Yes."

"Come and sit down," he said, gently. He took her hand

and led her to the chair near the window. She sat, and he got down on the floor beside her, needing to be as near to her as possible.

"I went there because I thought I wanted to die, too," Laura said.

Everything inside Tom seemed, momentarily, to stop. He didn't speak.

"I've been having a bad time," she went on, still so softly that he might not have heard, had he not been so close. "I've been having these fears."

"What kind of fears?"

"I've been afraid of most things," she said. "But mostly, I've been afraid of myself." She paused. "It's the hardest thing of all, you know, to stop trusting yourself."

"Tell me," Tom said. "Can you tell me?"

"Not easily, not now, anyway." She licked her dry lips. "I'm not coming home with you."

"Then I'll stay."

"That isn't what I mean."

"What do you mean?" There was a new dread in him.

"It isn't safe—at least, I don't feel safe."

"How don't you?" He was bewildered, but trying not to show it. "Can you try to explain?"

"I need to see a doctor," Laura said. "I know you've wanted me to, but I was afraid of that, too, of admitting what I was feeling."

"I can call Christine in the morning—or now, if you want me to."

"It doesn't matter."

Tom looked up into her face, trying to read her, but she was unfathomable. "When you say you don't feel safe, what do you mean?"

She was a long time answering. She felt heavy, it seemed a great effort to speak at all, yet she knew it was mostly shame that made it so hard.

"I took a life," she said, at last. "I know—I *know* it happened a long time ago. But then I caused another death, even though I didn't mean to."

"You didn't cause Roger's death. He killed himself."

"Please," she said, "just listen. It isn't easy to explain."

"I'm sorry."

"I've become afraid," she went on, "that I might hurt someone else." She licked her lips again. "That I might hurt our children."

"You'd never hurt Helen or Allie," Tom said quickly, almost harshly.

"No, I know I wouldn't—and yet lately I've felt that I couldn't really know that, not for certain."

The words were out, and that in itself was a kind of release, and now the tears came, flooding her eyes, and her voice sounded strangled, yet it became easier to speak.

"I started thinking that way a few weeks ago—just a momentary flash, nothing tangible—more of an idea, or a feeling, not even quite that. I'd been feeling so *guilty,* you see, about Roger, and everything else came back—it hadn't been that way for years, but suddenly it was so much worse than it had ever been, as if I'd never really allowed myself to feel it all before—"

She stood up, went over to the bed, opened her bag and fumbled in it.

"What is it, sweetheart?" Tom got up, too.

"I need a handkerchief." Her face was wet with tears, and her nose was running.

"Here, take mine."

She mopped at her eyes, blew her nose. She sat down on the bed.

"I started being afraid of knives."

"That's understandable, isn't it?"

"No," she said, fiercely, still crying. "It isn't normal."

"After what happened to you all those years ago, I'm surprised you haven't always felt that way." Tom fought to keep his tone calm.

"That's just the point—I never felt that way before. Suddenly, everything looks like a weapon to me—it's crazy—" She raised her eyes to him, imploring. "I think I'm going mad, Tom. I'm losing my mind. That's why I can't go home."

"But isn't home the best place you could be?"

"No." She shook her head. "Not now."

"Because you're afraid you might hurt the girls?" he asked, steadily.

"Yes," she whispered.

He came and sat next to her, on the bed. "Okay if I put my arm around you?"

"Oh, yes. Please."

He held her gently, felt a shudder of relief go through her. "We're going to take care of this, Laura. You know that, don't you?"

"I hope so." She was still whispering, as though normal speech was no longer possible.

"I'm going to call Gus, to tell her that we're not coming back. And then I'm going to call Christine Morfield, and we'll arrange what's best—"

"I think I should go to a hospital."

"If that's what you want."

"I feel as though I need to talk now, to a doctor, maybe a psychiatrist." She leaned against him again. "I think it may be okay if I start talking about it, letting it out. Maybe if I'd done that a long time ago—"

"That doesn't matter now."

They sat in silence for a while, just as they were.

"I have to ask you something," Tom said, at last.

"Yes."

"You said, before, that you went to the White Horse because you thought you wanted to die."

"Yes." The shame was still as acute as it had been.

"What happened, to change your mind?"

Laura turned her head a little way to look at him, saw the fear in his eyes and looked away again. "I'm not sure, really. I went there because it seemed like the only way to stop it— the only way to get away from the thoughts—from myself. I wanted to go to sleep and never wake up."

"But you came away."

"Because when I was up there—I was sitting up there in the dark, in the rain, right on the edge, looking at the horse, at where Lucia fell." She hesitated. "I don't remember everything exactly—I don't think I was really myself. I remember I started thinking about going to hell—which is strange, in a way, because I've never believed in hell." She paused again. "I just know that I suddenly realized that maybe there might be another way, after all—that all I'd been wanting to do until then was run away. Trying to escape from myself. Facing up to the way I felt hadn't seemed possible, somehow. I was too much of a coward, and I felt so *ashamed.*"

"You have nothing to be ashamed of," Tom said.

"But I was. I still am. I couldn't bear you to know the things I was feeling—I didn't want anyone ever to know." She stood up, suddenly, restlessly. "But then when I was sitting up there, I suddenly saw how unfair I was being, to you, and to the children, and to Gus—"

"And to yourself."

"I thought, suddenly—what if someone could help me with this? I'd be giving up everything I cared about, everyone I loved, for no reason—it would be such a waste. And it would be the most terrible, the most wicked thing I'd ever done."

"Thank God," Tom said, quietly, still sitting on the bed.

She looked back down at him again. "You didn't know, did you?"

He shook his head. "I knew you were troubled, of course, but I didn't have the slightest idea what you were really going through."

"You musn't blame yourself for that," Laura said.

"Of course I blame myself," Tom said, bitterly. "I've been so involved with the merger, with the damned paper. I was so grateful just to have you back, so happy that my little world was intact again—"

"You tried to help me. You wanted me to see someone."

"And you said no, and I just went along with it, because it was easier."

"We can't see into other people's minds, Tom, however much we care."

"I guess we can't."

Christine Morfield recommended Laura to a small private nursing home in Hertfordshire, not far from the stables where she and Tom had first gone horseback riding in England. It neither looked nor felt nor smelled like a nursing home, it was a charming red-brick house with rose trellises around the front door and ivy on both sides. Being November, the garden was not at its best, though good long walks, well-wrapped against all weathers, were encouraged; but there were two sitting rooms downstairs with fireplaces and oak beams, and most of the communal therapy sessions were held in one of these rooms, whose atmosphere was conducive to intimacy without intimidation.

For the first four days, Laura slept almost continuously, partly with the help of medication, partly because she was more exhausted than she had realized. And after that, she began to talk, as she knew she was now ready to, and though it was sometimes acutely painful, and seldom, if ever, easy, the wall between herself and the rest of the world had already been smashed, and she knew enough to be sure that she would never allow the lines of communication that linked her with those she loved, to be severed again.

"I feel as if my brain's full of tunnels," she told Tom, at the end of the first week. "They're so long, and so dark, and yet sometimes things—old, old memories and feelings— seem to come straight up to the surface for me to take a look at them. And yet I know there's still so much locked up deep inside, things I need to deal with, want to deal with."

"How far back are you trying to go?" Tom was curious.

"Oh, it isn't back to childhood and beyond, not that sort of thing at all. No one's trying to suggest there's anything deep-rooted in me that made these things happen to me— even I don't feel that." Laura paused, trying to explain. "It's more sharply focused on all that I've buried and suppressed over the years, the way I felt at Osborne, my isolation there—"

"And Lucia."

"More than anything."

The first thing that Christine Morfield and her colleagues wanted to tackle was Laura's fear that she had been losing her mind, losing control. She was not mad, they reassured her. She had turned understandable, rational anxieties into irrational fears. There were no grounds for fearing that she might injure anyone. She harbored no deep hatred, she wished no one harm, she was an innately gentle person. They impressed upon her that the worry of the weeks before Roger's suicide, and the shock of the shooting itself, had rekindled all kinds of long-suppressed traumas. They taught her relaxation techniques with which she could help herself at any time. She asked one of the psychologists with whom she had daily sessions in a pleasant, bright room with pale blue walls and cream-colored furniture, how she could stop her bad thoughts creeping back, and the psychologist told her that once a thought had manifested itself, it was pointless trying to pretend it had never existed, but it was possible to try to deal with it logically. Millions of thoughts passed through every person's mind each day, without being dwelt upon. It was harder, of course, when the thoughts were unpleasant, but Laura could learn to put those away, too, partly by confrontation, partly by learning to relax and, sometimes, simply by trying to follow an irrational thought with a rational one.

It was a long and at times, Laura found to her surprise, a fascinating process. She had never talked about herself so much in her life. Talk and rest, the acknowledgment of emotions, positive and negative. More talk and more rest.

Tom and Gus and the children all came to visit her, sometimes staying for just a little while, at other times for hours on end. Gus was a wonderful visitor, so straightforward, so unafraid of asking what she wanted to know, so able to accept the answers Laura still felt unready to give. It was hardest when Helen and Allie came; those were the only times when Laura felt she was in a hospital environment, because of the awkwardness, the loss of intimacy, the impossibility of behaving naturally with the children. It was a little hard, sometimes, with Tom, too, because of the intensity of his love for her, and because she knew how much he missed having her at home with him. That knowledge was an additional pressure, though it was a burden that she welcomed at the same time, for Laura had begun to feel that she was no longer the isolated, strange, unhappy woman she had been. That she could, after all, trust herself. That the only dangers had been in her mind.

* * *

At last, she felt that she was ready to go home. She would see the psychologist in her Harley Street office once a week for as long as they both saw fit, but she accepted that she was ready to leave the nursing home. She wanted to leave. She had been away from Tom, from their children, for too long, though she was grateful for every day that had strengthened her. She had taken care of old business now, had cleansed herself as much as she ever would be able to. It didn't mean that she would not, or should not, think of the traumas again—she would, she had to. But it did mean that she could put them into their proper perspective, and that she could move on.

It was shaky at first. Helen and Allie, so accustomed to having only Gus and Grazia looking after them while Tom was working, acted up, and on several occasions, Laura caught herself feeling guilty again.

"Stop it," Gus would say, if she was in the room.

"Stop what?"

"You know."

And Laura would smile, and the guilt would be gone.

She grew stronger, things became better, easier. Life at home fell back into place, grew normal and natural again, then, with the early spring of 1994, began to blossom and thrive. The *New Courier* became a fact, met with critical approval, attracted a host of new readers. Gus, aware that Laura was strong enough, signed a lease on an apartment just around the corner in Oakley Street. They received a takeover bid for Laura Andros Associates and turned it down. Laura became pregnant again. Tom was more content than he had ever hoped to be.

"We should take a vacation," he said, in April.

"Can you spare the time?" Laura asked, without irony, although in almost four years of marriage they had never taken more than a few days away at any time. The newspapers had absorbed Tom so utterly, and Laura, having traveled so extensively with Roger, had taken pleasure in the security of her new home base. So long as she had her family and Gus close at hand, Laura didn't think she cared if she never traveled again.

And then Tom suggested they all go together to Greece, and no idea had ever seemed more perfect. They planned to go in May, before the heat grew too wearing for the children, and Tom told Laura that he had mapped out a voyage of discovery and that he had chartered a sailboat to take them from island to island, and for a moment she remembered the *Laura*, and it was the most romantic of memories without any bad associations at all, and she found that she was able to enjoy it, and even talk about it, briefly, to Tom, without guilt.

They flew to Athens, landed at Hellenikon, as Laura had done only twice before in her life, the first time when Theo Andros brought her to his home, the second when she had her brief reunion with Adam, cut short, she was certain now, by Roger, manipulating even then.

"Are we staying in the city?" she asked Tom on the plane, for he had kept the plans a secret from her, telling her only to pack for a month, with a few clothes for city living, but mostly for ease.

"We're going to pick up the boat."

"Gus, do you know where we're going?"

"Every last detail, but I'm not telling you, so forget it."

"Helen, do you know?"

"Yes, Mummy, but Daddy says I'm not allowed to tell you."

"Allie, what about you, my darling?"

"Don't you try wheedling it out of our daughters." Tom grinned.

"I give up," she said, and leaning back, Laura closed her eyes.

She knew that they would be going to Aegina at some point, whether at the beginning or as a climax to the vacation she couldn't guess, but she knew Tom well enough to know that he would have made some sort of arrangement for her sake. Perhaps he might even have talked to the present owners of Chryssos to see if they could visit. She hoped so, for she was ready for that too now, though she would try not to show disappointment if they weren't able to go inside.

She did not have long to wait. They picked up the boat in the harbor at Piraeus and set sail in the afternoon sunshine. She hadn't known that Tom was a fine sailor—it hadn't occurred to her that a newspaperman born and raised near Chicago would like boats, but then again, she realized that there must still be many things about her husband that she didn't know.

"Where are we going?" she asked Gus.

"You can have my name, rank and serial number," Gus offered.

"She knows where we're going," Tom said.

"Do I?" Laura was innocent.

"You know me, I know you."

"I love you, Tom Bailey," she said.

"Not as much as I love you."

"I wouldn't bet on it."

He guided the boat into Souvala, and they piled into a motor launch that was ready and waiting for them, and Laura was silent now, filled with tension and a strange kind of longing that she didn't entirely recognize. She knew the way so well, knew the coastline, the little beaches, and up on a rocky hill, the pine forest, less sparse than she remembered.

"The house is just behind those trees," she said, very softly.

No one said anything. They glided smoothly toward the small private beach, and Laura saw from a distance that there were people standing on the sand, and as they drew closer she saw that they were Adam and Fran, and two little boys.

"Oh, Tom," she said, and then was silent again.

They took off their shoes, rolled up their trousers and hitched up their skirts to wade from the boat, and they all got far wetter than they'd intended, but no one minded, and after that it was squeals of joy and incredulity and wonder and gratitude.

"Are they going to let us into the house?" Laura asked, eager now, no longer needing to conceal her longing. "I knew it, I *knew* you'd try to do this, but I didn't want to think about it in case you couldn't manage it."

"I couldn't," Tom said.

"Oh." For a moment, her smile faltered, but then she forced herself to mask her feelings. "It doesn't matter, Tom, truly it doesn't. At least we're close, we can look from the outside. Don't they mind us tramping about their beach?"

"They probably would have," Tom said. "But the new owners don't give a damn."

No one else spoke. Gus watched Laura's face intently and Adam and Fran held hands, their two sons looking with some suspicion at Helen and Allie, who were already down on their knees playing with sand.

"Who are the new owners?" Laura asked, very quietly.

Tom shrugged. "Some American newspaperman and his wife."

"They say she was raised here," Gus said.

"Maybe I know her," Adam said.

"Shut up, Adam," Fran said.

Laura was staring up at Tom. "I don't believe this is happening."

"It is."

"You've bought Chryssos?"

"*We've* bought it. It's in a bit of a mess, but I didn't think you'd mind."

"You were right."

"Want to take a look?"

She nodded, unable to speak.

"Will you folks excuse us?"

"Go for it," Fran said.

Laura looked at Adam. "Can you believe it?"

"I can now," he said. "I'm very happy for you, *moraki mou.*"

"For us," she said.

It was all so much as she had remembered it. The white stone walls, the ocher roof just beginning to glow red-gold as the sun started to set. The cool, shabby marble floors, the big stone fireplaces, the heavy wooden shutters—and outside, the wildflowers and the dark greenness of the pine trees and the sounds of birds and crickets. And Laura knew now what that curious longing she had felt on the motor launch had been for. It had been for roots, for belonging, for the giving back of her stolen childhood.

Gus found her about an hour later, on the beach, sitting on

one of the rocks where she'd sat as a child when she'd
needed to be alone to think things through. She sat hugging
her knees, her face pointed out to sea, her hair blowing in
the breeze.

"You've been crying," Gus said.

Laura nodded.

"Because you're happy."

"Mostly." Laura didn't look at Gus. "You think I deserve
this, don't you? And Tom."

"I know you do."

"I'm beginning to believe it." A gull swooped low overhead, its mew haunting in the dark blue evening hush. "I'm
starting to put it all together, instead of struggling to keep it
separate, trying to forget the bad bits, pretend they never
happened."

"We never forget." Gus leaned back against Laura's rock
and kicked her sandals off, digging her bare toes into the
cool, damp sand. "I'm happy, too, now, but I haven't forgotten Pavel, or borstal, or those two men. I still can't talk
about them, though—I'm not as brave as you."

"You're much braver than I am," Laura said.

Gus shook her head. "I haven't really faced up to things
the way you have. I don't suppose I ever will. But that's just
me, the way I am. I know my life isn't exactly normal—no
men, no sex, no kids."

"It's your life, Gus. It doesn't have to be the same as anyone else's."

They heard footsteps on the path above them, and Tom
and Adam appeared, carrying two boxes.

"We thought we could barbecue out here, if you like."
Tom dumped his box on the sand. "It's not too cool, is it?"

"It's gorgeous," Gus said, and went to see what the men
had brought.

"Any room for me on your rock?" Tom asked.

"My rock is your rock," Laura said.

They put their arms around each other and leaned their
heads together.

"You okay?" he asked.

"Much better than okay," she said.

"Still feel like home?"

"Like I was never away."

"You and Gus and the girls could stay a little longer, if you wanted, when I have to go back."

"I don't want to be anywhere without you," Laura said.

"I guess that means you're happy." Tom kissed her hair.

"They haven't invented the word for what I feel," she said.

She felt not a trace of guilt.